Terminator 1+: The Future Is Not Set

Written by: Mark T. Sondrini

Terminator 1+: The Future Is Not Set, ©2010
IBSN #9781690988595

Terminator 1+ The Future Is Not Set is a work of fiction. Names, places and incidents either are products of the authors imagination and are used fictitiously or are parts of the extensive Terminator Universe already in existence.

No portion of this book (other than short segments used for reviews, advertising or promotion) may be reproduced, stored or transmitted, in any form or by any means without the prior written permission of the author.

Terminator 1+ The Future Is Not Set is available from Amazon as a Print on Demand paperback or as an e-book for Kindle.

For Sarah and John Conner
Two heroes of the Revolution

Introduction

The Terminator burst onto the imaginations of the world in 1984 when an ambitious writer / director James Camron had the idea to cast an obscure ex-body building champion turned B-movie star into a killing machine. Blending the storylines of an "everyman" turned heroic figure, an impossible to stop boogeyman, time travel and the general public's concerns for military / government secrets, computer domination, and the End of the World, Mr. Cameron struck a nerve, and gold.

The iconic images and throw-away lines from this first film have percolated throughout the movie industry and literature, setting off a virtual tsunami of sequels, novels, a two-season TV series, and interest in Artificial Intelligence or AI. By any measure, **The Terminator** was a blazing success. It led the charge from stop-action effects into the realm of CGI or Computer-Generated Imaging.

My wife and I were hooked immediately and anxiously awaited any sequel, series or prequel offered. However, as a writer, I became interested in the backstory; the pieces of "history" that are often implied or referenced but are never spelled out. As examples: How did a severely wounded Sarah Conner manage to escape the clutches of the authorities and find her way to the Mexican rebels for her training? How did the pieces and parts of the Terminator end up in the clutches of the various government agencies? How and why did FBI agent Ellison get so personally involved? What role did Dr. Silberman play throughout this 'history'? Where did Starr come from? In this roiling galaxy of interrelated characters, how many orbits can intersect over time?

This story attempts to resolve many of the open questions and issues caused by these collisions and near misses. I've attempted to seamlessly bridge the gap between **The Terminator** and **Terminator 2: Judgement Day** while connecting the dots of the more recent **Terminator** movies, The Sarah Conner TV series and the known novels. Along the way, I've dropped a few "breadcrumbs" leading into these future stories.

As you will see, I've interspersed a Technical Interlude between each chapter. These TI's explain points of technical interest that my research unearthed as I went along. As an engineer,

I find them interesting, as may you. These brief bits of information, while not necessary to the story, are available for you to read, if you are so inclined. I'd like to think that my research and my efforts to clarify points are valid and helpful. The only truly "made up" interlude deals with the math that, I claim, limits the timespan available to travel between. Everything else is compiled from engineering journals, component catalogs, astronomy texts and military handbooks.

For me, this story was satisfying and fun to write. I hope you enjoy reading it.

      Mark T. Sondrini
      Ruskin, Florida

Table of Contents

Prolog — 9 – 44
Technical Interlude 0 — 45 – 49
Skynet, Programs and Everything

Chapter 1 — 50 – 69
Technical Interlude 1 — 70 – 74
Time Travel Technology, Part 1: Math. & Physics

Chapter 2 — 75 – 94
Technical Interlude 2 — 95 – 96
Psychology

Chapter 3 — 97 – 114
Technical Interlude 3 — 115 – 117
Materials

Chapter 4 — 118 - 139
Technical Interlude 4 — 140 – 144
Time Travel Technology, Part 2: Paradoxology

Chapter 5 — 145 - 166
Technical Interlude 5 — 167 – 170
Time Travel Technology, Part 3: Prototype Equipment

Chapter 6 — 171 - 194
Technical Interlude 6 — 195 – 198
Spatial Issues with Time Travel

Chapter 7 — 199 - 219
Technical Interlude 7 — 220 – 222
Robot and Cyborg Sensing Systems: Part 1

Chapter 8 — 223 - 247
Technical Interlude 8 — 248 – 249
How Dogs Detect Cyborgs

Chapter 9 — 250 – 275
Technical Interlude 9 — 276 – 278
How the T1000 and TX models Function

Chapter 10 — 279 – 296
Technical interlude 10 — 297 – 300
The Philosophy of Skynet

Chapter 11 — 301 – 324
Technical Interlude 11 — 325 – 327
Sensing the World Around Them: Part 2

Chapter 12 — 328 - 352

Technical Interlude 12	353 – 355
	Sensing the Rest of the World: Part 3
Chapter 13	356 - 386
Technical interlude 13	387 – 388
	Keeping their balance
Chapter 14	389 - 414
Postscript	. 415 – 418

NOTE: Within the body of a chapter, a change of scene during the **SAME GENERAL TIMELINE** is denoted by - - - between the paragraphs. A change of scene to a **DIFFERENT TIMELINE**, to or back from the future, is denoted by a * * * between the paragraphs.

Terminator 1+ The Future Is Not Set

PROLOG

Dr. Silberman knew a golden opportunity when it fell in his lap. This girl Sarah Conner and the man, Kyle Something-or-other, were lock-step crazies. Their stories seemed to mesh in their psychopathic perfectness, reinforcing each other where they would otherwise be weak or inconsistent. It was rare that two people with kindred psychosis would be acting together. He was mentally rubbing his hands together, outlining the article he would eventually publish about the paired psychosis, when he heard the police scanner go off. He was confused. The precinct sub-station he had just left, less than three minutes ago, was under some kind of attack. It sounded like a heavily armed army was methodically chopping its way through the feeble resistance of the police and systematically destroying the entire station.

As he slowed to a stop, his mind caught up with the notion that if he had still been there, he might have been killed. The thought was enough to make him open his door and hang out his head. That was just in case his stomach decided to act on the nausea he was suddenly feeling. Then, he managed to gather his small reserves of courage, wipe the drool from his chin, and slam his door. He turned his car around and headed back. "Maybe I can be of some help," he mumbled to himself, wondering if he should really be going there.

He could see the flickering glow in the night sky from two blocks away. He could hear sporadic automatic gunfire, punctuated by heavy sounding blasts. He was too far away to hear screaming, but he was sure that there would be plenty of that. Men always screamed as they fought and died, he had learned through the years. He could hear approaching sirens and they seemed to be coming from all directions at the same time. As two police cars flashed by, he slowed, trying to stay out of their way. Silberman involuntarily slowed further as he had a sudden insight. He said out loud wonderingly, "What if this is what that Kyle and Sarah Conner were talking about?" Then the silliness of that concept struck him, and he said, "Don't be foolish. They were raving lunatics!" He did not notice that he was talking to himself out loud, both asking and answering questions. He would later think that was probably a bad sign.

As he turned the final corner, Dr. Silberman was forced to stop at the barricade formed by several police cars jamming the street. He probably would not have gone too much closer just then anyway. The gunfire seemed to have stopped, but the fire and electrical flashes were still emerging from the wrecked building, along with the desperate screams for help.

If he had not just been in there, he would not have been able to recognize it as a police station. Large pieces of the front wall were gone; smashed in and then spread out, glass from the lobby was everywhere. He could see a policeman's body slumped over the hood of an old, damaged four-door that had driven through the lobby doors. Flames were rolling out of a few of the missing windows along the front and the one side of the two-story building he could see from his vantage point. There were a few steaming bodies lying around in the grass or on the sidewalk. He could not tell from his position if they were alive or dead.

The fire engines and emergency response trucks, as well as a SWAT van from a nearby precinct, were pulling to a sudden halt near the building. He overcame his initial fear when he saw Lieutenant Traxler come staggering out of a breach in the brick wall. His friend was clutching his side with one hand and an automatic rifle in the other. Silberman's fear surged as Traxler crumpled forward. He ran past the police cordon, waving his credentials toward the nearest officer, and hurried to where the Lieutenant had just fallen.

Silberman rolled Traxler over and tried to ignore the blood flowing from under the man's vest. He shouted almost directly into Traxler's ear, "Lieutenant! Lieutenant, can you hear me?"

Traxler rolled his eyes toward Silberman and frowned, "Why the hell are you shouting at me? I've been shot, I'm not deaf!" Then as he began passing out Traxler warned, "They were right about the monster. Watch out! Nothing we could do could stop him." He began panting and then passed out.

Silberman, his fear growing ever higher, looked around and waved down an EMS running past. "This man is wounded, but still alive! Help him right now!" He rode with Traxler away from the chaotic scene to the hospital.

- - -

Detective Sean Roberts had drawn this case and had too much information, and yet too little. He had two victims: one beaten to death (to put it mildly) and one nearly dead and practically catatonic. She was raving in her delirium about killer robots and monsters from the future. He had seen the wreckage of the factory where several industrial robots were still whirring about, trying to assemble or move things that did not exist. He knew that the plant had been closed for several days due to a union work stoppage.

It dawned on him that the clanking metal machines in there were probably the source of the girl's terror. "Duh," he said out loud to no one in particular.

"What did you say Roberts?" His partner had heard him and was smiling with a knowing look in his direction. "Did you just have an insight?"

"Actually Jenkins, I didn't say anything." He inwardly groaned, hoping that his partner would just forget it. "I'll reserve my insights for the evidence that the CSI's turn up." Although he doubted if they would find much more than he already knew.

"What did you make of that crushed robot in there?" Jenkins asked. "Its legs were in one part of the room and an arm was in another while its crushed head and torso were between the platens of that punch-press. Damnedest thing I ever saw."

Roberts was nodding, ticking off items on his notepad, "Um hum. I got all that. It looks to me as though the fight proceeded through the plant with bits and parts getting dropped along the way until the guy," here he frowned because there had not been an ID for the body, "gets blown-up and the busted robot continues on after the girl."

Jenkins said, "Yeah, that's what I gathered from her before they hauled her away. The medics said she mentioned that her name was Sarah, but no last name."

"You know, partner," Jenkins offered, "when I was a kid, I worked in a factory that had robots." He gestured toward the building behind them. "I never saw the likes of the one we found crushed, or any of its parts for that matter, except in Sci-Fi movies anyway."

Roberts shrugged, "Yeah, well, if you seen one robot, you've seen them all." He chuckled softly, knowing that his misuse of grammar rubbed Jenkins the wrong way.

From behind them a voice called, "Detectives?" Then the voice said, "Detective Roberts or Jenkins?"

Both men turned toward the voice, and Roberts answered, "Over here." Then they watched as a large, young, bald, black man, in a very nice business suit, walked over to them.

As he arrived in front of them, the man extended his right hand to shake and in his left hand he presented an FBI identity card in a slick, black leather wallet. "I'm agent James Ellison, from the LA FBI office." He shook hands with both detectives and then casually put his ID away inside his suit jacket. Roberts saw the .45-automatic in its shoulder-holster as the jacket flap opened and then closed.

Roberts recovered his poise first, "What brings you down here agent Ellison? A break-in and a murder hardly qualify as a Federal case, do they?"

Ellison shook his head, "Hardly. But I heard that you found an interesting development. It was a robot of sorts by the sound of it. I was asked to look into it." Ellison was indicating with his hand that they should accompany him back into the plant. "Shall we?"

Roberts was getting peeved at federal intervention in his case and he decided to push back a little. "Jenkins, why don't you show our robot to agent Ellison? You know the crushed scrap-heap he's referring to as a robot?" He turned back to his notes, "I have police work to attend to."

Jenkins sighed, "Sure, partner. Agent Ellison, follow me, please." Jenkins then led agent Ellison through the broken door, along the banged-up corridor, past the blast-smashed windows of the control room, and out onto the floor.

The factory floor was still teeming with robotic activity. There were a few men from the plant, scattered in there, beginning to shut things down. They passed the grotesquely shaped, chalk lined, blood stain on the floor where the dead man had been found. They continued around to a side room where the previously closed punch-press now stood mostly open, with a collection of shiny metal junk stuck in its maw. The scrap-pile resembled a heavily chromed motorcycle, run over several times by all eighteen wheels of a big tractor-trailer. It was quite flat and inoperative.

Unless someone had moved the remains, and agent Ellison doubted if anyone had even touched any of the pieces, it looked as though it had been reaching out with its one remaining arm as its head was crushed, stopping its clockworks forever. This was reported to be where the injured girl had been found in terrified shock.

But it was the arm that agent Ellison saw most clearly. It appeared to be nearly intact, from pointy fingertip to ball-jointed, swiveled shoulder. It somehow resembled the Michelangelo painting of The Creation: God's finger instilling life into man. Although he doubted that this tableau had much to do with creation. This was why he had been sent here. This was to be his new career. He was to find out everything he could about this robot and the two people that it was apparently trying to kill.

"Kind of spooky, isn't it?" Jenkins said, interrupting Ellison's musings. "I've been around robots before," he waved his arm out toward the rest of the whizzing plant, "Most were just like the ones out there, safe inside their enclosure fences. But this one is different."

Ellison nodded in agreement, "Oh, yes. I'd say this one is definitely different." He pulled on his latex gloves, "Have you got your pictures yet?"

Without waiting for an answer, he reached over into the press interior, grabbed the robot's hand, and pulled, intending to drag out the entire tangled heap. However, the shoulder joint had been broken away by the press's force and Ellison's pull finished the job. Only the arm came out with a metallic, tearing sound. Agent Ellison stumbled backward a little as he compensated for the sudden release. He raised the arm slowly up in front of his face, marveling at its weight and complexity, turning it around in the dim light to look at it from several angles.

"Well, there will be time enough for inspection later," Ellison said in a whisper, stopping his wonder and awe in its tracks, recovering his professionalism. "Where is the other arm? I heard Roberts say the other arm was broken off earlier during the fight."

"Actually, the CSI team has taken it to their van. I can show it to you if you want."

Ellison smiled, "Actually, I want to take it with me today." He motioned toward the remains of the crushed robot, "That too. Have them wrap it in something and put it in a box and put it in my car." As an afterthought he said, "Oh, and the legs too. I'm to take everything of this robot with me today. OK?" He was looking intently at Jenkins. "That won't be a problem, will it, Detective?" Ellison was not waiting for a response and he immediately started back toward the front of the building.

"Hey, Detective Roberts won't like that. This is evidence in his case." Jenkins was shouting at Ellison's retreating back. "He's not going to like it much at all."

Ellison just waved the loose robotic arm over his shoulder at the frustrated detective. Jenkins hoped he was waving goodbye, but he doubted it would be that easy.

- - -

Sarah had been watching everything through nearly closed eyes. She was badly bruised, punctured in her left thigh and she showed signs of traumatic shock. Her scratches and abrasions had been treated. She had been checked over thoroughly by the doctors on the hospital's staff, for internal injuries or broken bones. Her leg had been cleaned, stitched, and bandaged, and it was sore to the touch. She believed she could walk on it. She was cautiously watching the police guard outside her door, checking for their routine, memorizing the ebb and flow of the hospital activity. Waiting for her first opportunity to get out of there and hide somewhere.

She didn't think she was safe there, even with an armed guard ten feet away. She clearly remembered the mayhem of the terminator in the police station as it killed its way past dozens of well-armed police. She believed the guard was against her leaving, rather than for her protection. She hoped that other terminators were not hunting her yet. Kyle had implied that there were many of them, and he did not know if that one was alone in her when. She knew that in her current situation she would be an easy target, a sitting duck as it were, for any terminator that might still be looking for her. She began to cry softly at the thought of Kyle, dead. He had given his life saving her.

The drugs they had given her to help her sleep had worked very well, rendering her almost unconscious, and preventing the nightmares that would soon begin to haunt her. Her strength had returned remarkably fast with the deep rest, although she was masking that fact from everyone. She never tried to walk on her own, even to use the bathroom. She always rang for help, feigning weakness. During one of her trips to the toilet she had determined that there were no clothes in her room. Borrowing some from another patient seemed like her best bet; she knew that she would not get far, dressed in a hospital gown. Three days after her arrival, on her next chauffeured roll down the hall for "fresh air" she located a room with a bed-ridden woman of about her own size. She had a plan.

The evening of the third day, her police guard suddenly got up from his chair outside her door and hurried down the hallway. She made herself wait for two full minutes to ensure that he was gone before executing her plan. Climbing out of her bed, she dragged her IV pole along to the bathroom and she reached in, turned on water in the shower and pulled the door closed. She thought that would probably make anyone briefly checking her room believe that she was using the facilities. Then after peeking out of her door, she opened it and went through, closing it behind her to a crack, just like it usually was. Sarah slowly, in apparent pain, walked down the hallway away from the direction the policeman had taken and toward the room she had earmarked earlier. She walked past, checking it out as she did. The young woman seemed asleep.

Sarah then slipped into the room, opened the girl's closet and took a dress and some underclothes that were stored there. Gasping from the discomfort, she managed to bend over far enough to grab the pair of rubber-soled, slip-on shoes on the closet floor. Checking that the girl was still asleep, Sarah disconnected her IV, pushed the pole into the bathroom, stripped off her gown and tossed it in there too.

Dressed in her newly acquired clothing she stuffed her feet into her new shoes, ran her fingers through her hair, plucked a cluster of wilting flowers out of a vase, and walked out. No one noticed her going. No one would discover her missing until Agent Ellison came by after supper that night. The general alarm came too late to keep her from hitchhiking out of town, heading north. She got away.

Agent Ellison was still smarting from the way things happened. He had been discrete and firm at the crime scene. He knew that the detectives were angry and frustrated, but his FBI status and his written orders had trumped their arguments, giving them no choice. He had managed to gather all the parts, some intact but most crushed or broken, and bring them to the LA laboratory. He had treated them as the evidence that they were in this murder investigation and had been diligent in the records he kept. He had reviewed the various pieces and parts and had taken a quite a few pictures and made a few sketches, but he was as puzzled as the rest of the agents studying everything about this case.

His attempts at following up with the female survivor were thwarted by the time it took for him to finish with the awesome metal remains, and the way Sarah had seemed to disappear. Even the police had lost her when she just walked out of the hospital on her own. The guard they had set on her room, lured away the evening of the third day for a disturbance on a different floor, gave her an opportunity and she left within the hour. It was as though she had been watching for an opening. None of the hospital staff had noticed her missing for more than two hours. The LA police manhunt for her had been expanded to involve the State Police shortly after the time Ellison decided to interview her. Apparently, her injuries were not as severe as initially described. *Either that or she was more afraid of being found than anyone expected,* Ellison thought. Either way he knew that it was sloppy police work.

The lead detective, Roberts, implied that the FBI had something to do with it and Ellison felt sure that he had not convinced him otherwise. By now the mess at the plant had been tied to the death and destruction in the Van Nyes police station nearly a week earlier. Both the dead man, Kyle Reese, and the female, Sarah Conner was her name they said, had been there during the attack. Surviving interview tapes had clearly shown them, and Lieutenant Traxler had tried to describe what had happened to them before he finally died of his injuries. Ellison was trying to locate the police psychologist, Dr. Silberman, for his input. The police had said that Silberman was still in shock and not very helpful. He was taking his close brush with death very personally. Ellison could identify with that.

Agent Ellison was frustrated. The case was intriguing, but very frustrating. He had gathered lots of evidence and as many eye-witness accounts as were available and it still was not ringing true to him. His cop's sense was alarmingly loud, even before the military types had taken everything away from him. Now it was practically deafening.

A clamor was raised because of the deaths of twelve police officers and the serious wounding of a dozen more. All law enforcement in a three-state area had been placed on highest alert, and then less than four days later, everything came to a disturbing halt. Officially, the FBI was out of it. Officially, he was out of it; taken off the case forcibly and all his evidence confiscated. It did not make any sense.

Ellison was a big man, six-foot two inches tall with a skill-position, football player's build. He worked out routinely and ran often and it showed. But even he had felt afraid of the men who had invaded his office, enforcing the will and the orders of the NSA agent who led them. They were more than fit, and they acted like men who were capable of doing anything and had the blessings of the government to do so. None of his questions or complaints were answered by more than cold stares through silvered aviator glasses, and tight lips above firm jaws. National Security had been invoked and there was nothing he could do about it except comply. Anything that he would try to do now would be on his own. His boss had nearly winked when he said he wanted him to stay out of it. Ellison was pretty sure it was not just a twitch.

Just before they arrived, Ellison decided to work around his instructions to officially close the case. It was not so much that he hated loose ends tucked into a case file, although he did. The identification and murder of Kyle Reese was not even close to resolution. The only Kyle Reese that had been found was a newborn in Encino. It was not that he had a very bad feeling about what was going to happen to the robotic parts, although he did. The NSA types that took almost everything he had collected were accompanied by several military guards. Who knew where that stuff would end up? It was not that he was emotionally attached to Sarah Conner, although he was. He admired her. The girl was tough, and she had moxie. He did not know how he would have reacted to the trauma she had withstood, and the terror she had faced. He doubted if he could have left his hospital bed three days after such a physical and mental pounding.

It was that this was the most interesting, strange case he had ever worked on. He was being preemptively pulled off it because someone much higher than his boss's boss wanted him to get out of the way and let them have free access to everything. He did not like that very much.

He had copied his electronic files for his home computer as soon as he had received the word to close the case. Reaching into his desk drawer he pulled out a large plastic baggy. "Well, they think they have everything," he said softly, "but they don't."

Ellison had flipped through the cardboard file box and extracted a few key documents. He had stood and walked out into the common area and went to the copy machine and after entering his code made a copy of the pages. Then he replaced the originals in the box, slipped the copies into a file with the baggy containing the nearly destroyed prosthetic hand, and put both in an envelope addressed to his home. He had pulled the lid of the box closed and smoothed the "CLOSED FILE" tape across the seam, signing the overlapped ends with a permanent marker. He had carried the light, file box over to the doorway and set it there for the clerk to pick up and carry to the storage room in the basement. He then walked over to the mail pile and placed his envelope just under the top. Within an hour, the NSA had appeared and taken away everything they could find.

That night, Ellison looked up Silberman's address and phone number from the police file copy and transferred it to his notepad. He planned to try and interview the Doctor again as soon as he could quietly arrange it.

- - -

Sarah reached Monterey, California as the morning sun broke through the fog layer, dousing US101 in new light. She had dozed briefly and restlessly, bothered by the beginnings of the nightmare that would plague her for years to come. She had awakened at least once crying out to Kyle and she had to convince the driver to keep going that it had only been a bad dream. The driver had been wondering about his rider for the past few hours, and he thought he should get her out of his car as soon as he could. Something about her scared him. She looked young and vulnerable and she obviously had been recently hurt; the bruises were quite visible in the dawn dimness. But there was a steeliness about her that screamed at him to leave her alone and get her away from him at the first opportunity.

He saw the clinic's sign from a block away. Pointing at it he asked, "Do you want me to drop you there, miss? You look like you need some medical help."

Sarah, realizing that her emergency ride was nearly over, thought that maybe he was right and maybe this would be a good way to get out from under his uncomfortable gaze without further incident. "Sure," she said. "Thanks. That's a good idea." She pointed to the sidewalk in front of the clinic, "Just drop me there."

Feeling relief, the driver slowed and pulled over to the curb and asked tentatively, "Do you want me to come in with you?"

Sarah smiled and shook her head. "No, thank you. You've done enough to help me. I'm safe now." She opened the door of the small car as soon as it stopped, fought to get out, obviously in pain. Then she closed the door and looked back in at the driver, "Thanks again." She turned and slowly, achingly walked up the sidewalk toward the clinic porch, each step getting a little easier as her muscles warmed up.

She heard the car hurry away and she smiled, recognizing her good fortune in finding that guy. It could have been a lot worse. She might have had many questions to avoid, or possibly even had to fend him off physically. She reached the clinic door, opened it and went through into the bright, clean inside, closing the outside behind her. The air smelt faintly of alcohol, but better than the hospital.

The receptionist, a middle-aged woman with a poofy hairdo, smiled at her with her mouth, but not her eyes. She saw Sarah limp toward her desk and recognized trouble when it entered the building.

The story Sarah concocted was plausible enough. She had told the doctor that her boyfriend was abusive and knocked her around a lot. This last time, up in San Francisco, was worse than usual, and the stabbing was the final straw. She ran away from him and sought help. She explained that the emergency room had patched her up and, still afraid, she had tried to run as far as she could from him. But when she made it this far, she thought she might need additional medication.

She put up with the usual poking and prodding and suspicious questions and avoided the doctor's attempt to get her to contact the Monterey police. It was a private thing, she had pled. She was away from him now, and safe. She didn't want him to find out where she was, and she thought that the police would at least interview him and eventually he would find out where she was hiding. She cried believably, almost reaching hysteria, and the doctor relented.

"The bad news," Sarah said, "is that I'm broke right now. I spent everything I had just getting this far." She tried to look pitiful, which was not too hard.

The doctor said that he thought that the local shelter could put her up for a few nights and maybe even find her a small job. "Let me get their phone number for you. I'll be right back."

Fearing that he meant to call the police anyway, Sarah tiptoed behind him to the edge of his office doorway and listened for him to pick up the phone. She was preparing to make a second run for it when she heard him say, "T'hell with it." She peeked around the corner, saw him rooting through a card file, and she decided to stay. She turned and hurried back to the examination room and began pulling on her pants.

- - -

When he reached his desk, he seemed to think for a few minutes, trying to decide if he should call the police despite what Sarah said. Then he suddenly made up his mind. He said quietly, "T'hell with it," and reached over, flipped through his rotary cards and jotted a phone number and address onto a scrap of paper. He went back to the examining room, knocked, opened the door, and went in. Sarah had finished dressing and turned as he entered.

"Here is the phone number of the shelter and their address," he said holding the paper in his hand, just out of reach. "But I want you to promise me something, all right?" He was obviously holding his note hostage, waiting for her agreement to his terms.

Fearing the worst, Sarah looked afraid of what he had to tell her. "What is it, doctor?"

"Well, it's pretty simple, actually. I want you to promise to come in to see me once a week for the next few weeks so I can check your wound for infection." He fractionally moved the paper closer to her. "Can you promise that?"

Relieved, Sarah smiled and nodded to him, "Of course, doctor. I can do that if you want me to." She reached out and took the paper.

He reached into his lab coat and pulled out some blister-pack cards with pills in them. "And here are a few antibiotic pills I want you to take as well; one, twice a day until their gone. Understand?"

Sarah nodded her head, "Thanks, Doc."

"Ask for Flo," he said dipping his head toward the note she still held.

Sarah just nodded her understanding.

Sarah limped out of the clinic and walked slowly to the street. She got her bearings and then started in the direction the doctor had suggested. Even though the stiffness in her leg was easing as she walked, her adrenalin rush was tapering off, leaving her shaking and very tired. She spotted a cab after three or four minutes and decided to use the slim funds she had found in the dress's pocket to ride to the shelter.

She gave the driver the address from the doctor's note and sat back, watching the scenery of her new hometown.

Monterey is a strange town. It is made up of military facilities and housing, light industry, residential sections (high and low rent), old sections, and new sections. Marinas and beachfront properties, with their mix of obviously expensive housing and barely weatherproof shacks, standing toe-to-toe with each other, mixed with shops and small restaurants and bars, are everywhere. She had never seen anything like that in the suburbs of Los Angeles.

Stopping the cab about a block from the shelter, Sarah paid the driver and walked the rest of the way, rehearsing her story as she went. Reaching the entrance, a basement stairway on the side of a red brick church, Sarah limped down the stairs and went through the open doorway. The air was cool, and the room well-lit because of the windows that ran at shoulder height around three walls of the large room. The floor was hardwood with remnants of black paint striping and that probably meant that the space was originally a gymnasium.

There were long tables set up in the middle of the floor with rows of folding chairs lining each side. Most of the chairs were occupied and all those people were eating something from their trays. The buzz of conversation was diminishing as everyone in the room noticed her. A woman, who had been pouring steaming coffee into the cups at one table, set down the pitcher and asked one of the table's occupants to continue for her. She walked over to where Sarah was standing and held out her hand.

"You must be Sarah," she smiled as they shook hands. "Doc called me a few minutes ago and asked me to watch out for you."

Sarah must have been frowning because she then said, "Oh, don't worry about it, honey. It's a small town we have here and the doc's taken a shine to you, I'd reckon." She was still smiling at Sarah, looking her over without being too obvious. She finished pumping Sarah's hand up and down and said, "I'm Florence, if you haven't figured it out yet. Please, call me Flo."

Sarah relaxed a little; she could not help it with Flo's bubbly attitude, "Thanks, Flo. I appreciate it." Then looking around the room she said, "I was hoping I could stay with you for a few days. You know, get my feet back…"

"...on the ground," Flo finished for her. "Yeah, sure Sarah, we have some room right now." Then, "Oh, where's my manners? Are you hungry? We were just having breakfast." Taking Sarah by the elbow she turned her toward one of the nearby tables. "You introduce yourself to everybody and I'll get you a tray."

In a daze by the suddenness of the events and still tired from her flight from LA, Sarah scooted back a chair and sat down with a big sigh. She did not realize how tired and hungry she was. She looked up and made eye-contact with the older woman across the table from her. She smiled and said, "Hi, I'm Sarah."

The old woman put down her spoon with a clank and picked up her napkin, wiping her greasy chin with it, and then her fingers. She looked Sarah over, "My name's Lucy. You get mugged? You look like crap." She was holding her hand out to be taken so Sarah did. The old woman squeezed her eyes shut as their fingers touched, obviously not relishing the contact.

The old man next to Lucy spoke up, "Now, Lucy. That's not polite. It ain't none of your business about how the girl got look'n the way she does." He smiled warmly, "Just ignore her, Sarah. My name's Frank."

Sarah shook his hand too, and then nodded to the other three at her table, too far away to shake hands. "That's all right Frank. I'm afraid I probably look a mess to you all." She tried to sound embarrassed, "My boyfriend did this to me last week and I just ran away from him."

Frank was suddenly angry, "The man should be taken out and horse-whipped! I ..."

Lucy was patting his arm, trying to calm him down a little, "Now, Frank. You know that the doc said not to get your blood pressure up. Sarah seems safe now. Just try to relax." Frank seemed to be enjoying the soothing Lucy was giving him and Sarah was wondering about their relationship, when Flo arrived with a breakfast tray.

Flo set the tray in front of Sarah and sat in the chair next to her. "I just checked, and I think I'll room you with Lucy. If that's OK, Sarah?"

Lucy glanced up from Frank's arm looking a little confused, "Hello. My name's Lucy. What's yours?" She was holding out her hand to be taken.

Sarah caught on, "Hello, Lucy. My name is Sarah. How are you?"

Lucy looked a little lost. "Oh, I have my good days and my bad ones." Then she squinted myopically toward Sarah, "Say, what happened to you? You look like crap."

Frank grinned sheepishly toward Sarah, twirled his index finger around-and-around near his temple and shrugged his shoulders. "Sorry," he mouthed silently.

Sarah picked up her fork, suddenly realizing just how hungry she was. "Rooming with Lucy will be fine, Flo. Thanks." Then, digging into her toast, eggs and bacon, she mumbled, "This is so good."

- - -

Flo gave Sarah bedding and toilet items and showed her where the facilities were. "We'll talk more in the morning, Sarah. I think I have something for you to do to help out and keep you busy."

Once more, Sarah said, "Thanks, Flo. I don't know what I would have done without you and the doc." Her eyes genuinely teared-up, and she thought that she was about to lose control and blurt out the truth. With a sob, she recovered her composure. Flo looked away, suddenly uncomfortable. "Thanks again," she managed to get out.

- - -

Wearing her clean pajamas and a towel around her clean hair, Sarah came back into the room she shared with Lucy. The old woman was apparently having one of her lucid moments because she remembered Sarah from earlier. "Well, Sarah, you look better, but you still look like crap." The old lady grinned as though she had just said the funniest thing in the world.

Sarah nodded her head as she climbed into bed, "Lucy, I do believe that you are right about that. But maybe it'll get better. What do you think?"

When Lucy didn't answer Sarah turned her head on her pillow and saw that Lucy was already asleep. As she looked on, Lucy's mouth slacked open and she began to snore. Her tempo slowed as her sleep deepened, but the volume rose with each deepening breath. Sarah smiled to herself and wriggled more comfortably into the blanket. She could put up with a little snoring. She bunched the pillow tighter against her ears and was quickly asleep.

- - -

In the morning, Sarah helped serve breakfast and then ate after everyone else had their portion. She sat across from Lucy and Frank and polished off her tray as though she were an athlete in training. Lucy was too busy to notice, but Frank whistled, "Girl, you're gonna get fat if you keep eatin' like that."

Sarah feigned annoyance, "Come on Frank, I'm healing." Then they both laughed. It felt good to laugh again.

Sarah looked up and saw Flo waving her over to the kitchen window. She was finished anyway so she got up and carried her tray and service over and placed it on the little conveyor belt that led to the scullery. "Good morning, Flo. Did you want to see me?"

Flo was nodding, "I just talked to doc. He thought that it was too early to let you do anything too strenuous, so I think I'll just have you clean up around here. You know, kitchen duty and maybe some light laundry duty?" She looked at Sarah expectantly, "How does that sound?"

Sarah nodded and said, "Flo after all you've done for me, how could I say no." She pointed to the kitchen door and added, "Can someone show me where everything goes? I used to work in a restaurant, so I know my way around pretty good."

Flo said, "Great." She put her arm around Sarah and led her through the swinging door. "This is the kitchen," she proclaimed as the door swung shut behind them.

- - -

The week slipped by with Sarah hardly noticing because of her new routine. Her leg had stopped throbbing and now seemed to be a dull ache. After the breakfast cleanup was completed, Flo reminded her that doc was expecting her to come by later. She said he wanted to check her leg and talk to her.

Sarah looked down at the floor, "I don't have any money. How can I get there?"

Flo smiled at Sarah's meekness and said, "Frank can take the van and drive you. He often does that for the residents. He'll wait for you and then bring you back." Flo seemed to stare away for a second or two. "Maybe he should cart Lucy there too for her checkup while we're at it. It's nearly time for her anyway." She turned away, looking back over her shoulder, "I'll let them know. And when you get back, I'll talk to you about a job I think I have arranged for you."

- - -

Doctor Silberman had been watching the copy of the security tape remnants that had recorded the terminator's attack on the police station. The piece that was available was sketchy, but it was enough to show a large, gun toting man crash a car into the watch desk and begin shooting his way inside. He clearly saw the man take several hits, but nothing seemed to even slow him down. He had emptied two automatic rifles, killing or maiming a dozen police officers before he plunged the precinct into darkness by yanking the large main cables from their connectors, shorting out the main power panel. *Something that should have killed a normal man,* Silberman thought.

Just before the tape went black and static-filled, the man turned and seemed to look directly into the camera. The effect was chilling. The man's eyes were emotionless and there seemed to be a shiny patch where a bullet had nicked his face. Most worrying of all was the final second after the lights went out. Silberman would have sworn that the man's eyes became a glowing, deep, smoldering red, no doubt due to the reflected fire in the hallway. He felt like puking every time the tape reached that point.

He had been watching the tape for several hours now, hoping to glean something that would change his opinion of what he was watching. But every time, the result was the same. Sarah and Kyle had been right. Something non-human was after them. He had almost been caught up in its net of destruction. They had tried to warn everyone who would listen, but no one, himself included, believed a word of it.

He began mentally ticking off the logic of the situation. *They were crazy, delusional, and psychotic. I am a sane, forty-year-old, well-educated man and grounded in reality. Killing robots from the future just don't exist. Do they?* "Of course they don't," he mumbled out loud, startling himself at his vehemence.

A few seconds later, he was startled again by his office buzzer. Recovering, he reached over, pressed the switch and asked, "Yes?"

The voice of his secretary, *at least it sounded like his secretary*, he thought, asked, "Doctor Silberman? There's a man from the FBI here. He's asking to talk to you." She continued after a slight pause trying to sound more professional, "He doesn't have an appointment."

Silberman considered for an instant, his anxiety and anger growing as he did. "Please ask him to come back at some later time." He hesitated, "I am very busy just now and quite tired." He thought he detected a slight whine in his voice.

A few seconds later, the intercom buzzed again, making him jump. "Yes!" he practically shouted.

"Doctor, he said he just needed a few minutes of your time. He said it was about the Sarah Conner incident."

Silberman had begun to sweat. He jammed the button down. "I said I don't have time right now! Ask him to come back next week!" He couldn't believe he was yelling like that, but he couldn't talk to the authorities in his condition. He felt too fragile.

Outside at the reception desk, Ellison's frown showed that he did not like the way the doctor was acting, but he thought he understood. The man was not a criminal and had most likely escaped death that night a month ago and he was still feeling the effects of the narrow escape. He thanked the secretary for her time and left his card with her asking her to give it to the doctor. Then he left.

Silberman's secretary, Loraine, waited for a few minutes and then rose from her desk and went to Silberman's door. She cocked her head to one side, listening. Then she took a breath and knocked lightly on the door and opened it, not waiting for his permission. She saw a frightened man cowering behind his desk and she felt a little sorry for him. "Doctor," she began softly.

"Doctor, are you alright? Is there anything I can get for you?"

Silberman had been watching his office door, expecting the FBI agent to come barging in like they sometimes do on television shows and movies. He had been sitting that way for ten minutes, waiting and sweating. When his door opened, he initially flinched and started looking around for any way to escape. Then suddenly recognizing Loraine, he tried to recover his breath and composure.

Silberman gaped at her as if this were some kind of trick and then shook his head. "Is he gone? I told him I couldn't possibly talk to him just now. You heard me, didn't you?"

Loraine nodded, "Yes. He's gone." She held out Ellison's card. "He left this for you."

Silberman did not move to take it and Loraine placed it on the corner of his desk. She could see Silberman's furtive glances around the room, his heavy sweat soaking his clothing, and his deep breathing almost to the point of hyperventilation. He was in trouble.

"Doctor Silberman, why don't you talk to someone about this?" She knew, even without psychiatric training, that he was slipping into a dark place. She thought that she had to try to help him. "Do you want me to call someone for you? See if I can get you an appointment?"

The fright on Silberman's face began to melt. "Could you?" He began softly shaking his head, "I don't think I can do it myself."

Loraine said, "Of course Doctor. After what you've been through, I want to help you feel better."

Silberman smiled at her weakly, "You are helping me, Loraine. Thank you."

Loraine turned and started to leave when he said firmly, "Find someone in this building though. I don't want to have to go far in public to do this."

Loraine nodded and went out to her desk. She grabbed the building's directory and began looking for a psychiatrist with an opening. She did not think Doctor Silberman could wait much longer.

- - -

The men sitting around the long, glass and chrome table were all holding sealed folders that contained photographs and detailed reports surrounding the incidents in California. The man who had brought them all together for this meeting was just outside the conference room door, talking quietly to someone unseen. Whispers and snatches of words as his monolog ran its course could be heard in the room, but no sense could be made of what he was actually saying. It was clear that General Larch was agitated or excited about something. Most likely the thing in the folders they had in front of them.

It grew quiet outside and all six men glanced at each other. The door opened and a tall, fit-looking man with steel gray hair, marine cut as though a bowl had been used to guide the shears, walked in and closed the door behind him. With his one good eye, he looked around at them as he stiffly walked to the head of the table, pulled out his chair, and sat.

"Gentlemen," he began, "We may be here for a while. I assume that you have had coffee and toilet breaks." He didn't wait for a reply.

"This event has been sequestered and must never reach the public. Do I make myself clear?" He quickly continued, "This has the uppermost priority and highest level of security available to us. If any word of what we have, or are doing with what we have, leaks out, you all will be held accountable as the traitor to National Security. We intend to presume guilt rather than risk the traitor's escape. Do I make myself clear? This is your only opportunity to leave."

His eye roamed the table for any glimmer of objection. Finding none he continued. "Please open your folders and I'll give you ten minutes to acquaint yourselves with the contents." He watched as each man broke the seals and began leafing through the contents of their folder. He tried to be patient, but he could not help himself.

"We have collected most of the pieces of this advanced robotic technology and we must now determine just how to proceed." His eye squinted as though he was looking into their souls, "Your first task here is to help me determine who should be allowed to understand the pieces and develop the device."

Several of the men had begun to mumble as they pored over the photographs, tending to spread them out in a mosaic on the table. General Larch, or the General as he was called, smiled as he realized the impact the photos were having on these sophisticated men. He had felt much the same way when he had first heard about the robot and then actually saw the pieces and parts in the lab buried in the basement, far below them now. Absently, he massaged the flat surface of the black patch on his left eye; excitement always made his socket itch.

The time was up. "Well, are there any questions?"

It was a rhetorical question. Of course, they would have questions. Who could not?

Initially, everyone started to speak at once, but as the sound rose toward incomprehension, they just as quickly stopped. The others deferred to Amalfi, head of the West Coast branch of the CIA. "General, we all have questions. Most of them revolve around where this came from. Is it, or rather, was it ours?"

General Larch shook his head, "Not unless one of you has been secretly working on a combat robot." Once again, he looked deeply around the table. Satisfied he said, "I didn't think so. I'm sure something this big could not have completely escaped my attention for so long." He looked at them calmly, "This doesn't belong to us or any of you, so the conclusion must be that it belongs to someone else. It is most likely one of our enemies; the Soviet Union or China." Larch looked to Amalfi for some sign of confirmation.

Amalfi was shaking his head, "No. Nothing like this is even on our remote radar." He continued, "Something like this would take years and hundreds of billions of dollars to develop. We would have surely heard something in all that time."

Larch was nodding, "Agreed." He looked over at the Regional Director of the FBI, Mr. Cole. "Our friends at the FBI assure us that no domestic companies have even attempted something of this scale." He continued, "To be assured, we are developing advanced computer systems and significantly advanced robotic systems, but nothing this independent or this sophisticated or at this scale. This machine is unprecedented in all of our experience. It appeared to be operating autonomously, pre-programmed as it were, to find and kill at least two people. The police reports are in those folders too. It didn't hesitate to cause significant collateral damage. It didn't seem to be worried about secrecy. Hell, we have several confiscated video sources from around the city showing its rampage. Moreover, we don't know much more than that. Other than, it does have a few obvious vulnerabilities."

"So, now that we know that we do not have something like this, and someone else does, I propose that we must take steps to catch up as quickly as possible." All heads were nodding their agreement.

Director Cole made the observation from the photographs arranged on the table in front of them, "It seems to be missing a few pieces."

Larch answered with a nod, "Yes that is correct. One hand and several smaller linking pieces were not recovered. Trust me when I say that we tried."

Cole ventured, "Who can we trust with this? Obviously, the military would love to get their hands on it, but I'm not sure that they should be the ones." He glanced over to the Army's representative, "No offence Karl, but I don't believe you have the resources at this time."

Larch was shaking his head as he came to a realization. "I don't think any one organization has enough to do the total job. Plus, if everything was in one place, the project could be more easily compromised." He had made their first decision. "We must parcel out segments of this to several diverse groups, each with a specific task, and none of them having the complete picture. Only we will be privy to everything."

"I propose that we give the military part, the private sector part, and keep the final part for ourselves, in the intelligence community." Everyone at the table was nodding their agreement.

- - -

Sarah's wound was healing nicely. The rest and light work she was getting at the shelter was obviously healing her. She had a glow that had been missing the last time they had met. "Sarah," he said as he finished replacing the gauze bandage on her left leg, "I think next week I can release you from my care. What do you think about that?"

Sarah smiled genuinely, "Doctor that's good news." She began to blush a little, "I didn't mean that it was good that I wasn't going to see you. I meant that it was good that I didn't have to see you." She tried to smile more strongly.

He said, "I understand." Then he backed away from the table and said, "You can get dressed now."

He watched as she did and then asked, "How is the shelter working out for you?"

Sarah answered as she buckled her belt, "It's working out really well, doc. I've been cleaning up around there for my board, and it looks like Flo might have a little part-time job lined up for me. She smiled at him as she headed out the examining room door.

He called out behind her, "Don't forget to make an appointment for next week. Your blood tests should be back by then."

- - -

Friday afternoon, as the doctor was preparing to close, a courier arrived with a stack of lab results from the previous week's work. He opened the manila envelope and pulled out the thin stack of reports. Leafing through them he saw Sarah Conner's. He glanced at it and then did a double-take. He sat heavily in his chair, and whistled wonderingly, rereading the report. There was no mistake. He picked up his phone and called the shelter, leaving a message for Sarah to come and see him Monday if she could arrange it.

She had gotten the message and arranged to get off work right after the lunch rush was over. She hitched a ride with Frank and the van and rode the five minutes to the clinic in silence, wondering what the doctor wanted. She had begun to worry that he had found infection in her test results and when she entered, Sarah looked afraid of what he had to tell her. "What is it, doctor?"

"Well, the good news is that there doesn't seem to be any infection. However, the bad news is it seems that your boyfriend gave you more than some bruises and a leg puncture." He tried to smile in a comforting way as he said carefully, "You're pregnant."

Sara's mouth fell open, "What? How can I be pregnant?" There has to be some kind of mix-up." She sat there in the examining room chair staring at him. She could feel her blood pressure beginning to climb, making her ears pulse with noise.

He was shaking his head, "That's not too likely, I'm afraid. These new tests are quite sensitive and better than ninety percent accurate." He picked up the report and waved it toward her, "The levels are still quite low, indicating that you are only a few weeks pregnant, but you are pregnant non-the-less."

Tears were filling Sarah's eyes as she thought about the man who had kept her alive in the face of very slim odds. *Oh, Kyle.* She struggled to get herself under better control. She wondered if Kyle realized that he would become his hero's father when he volunteered for this mission. Unconsciously she was rubbing her belly. *John,* she thought. *John Conner.* As a tear broke free and ran down her cheek she said, "I think I'm happy."

The doctor had watched as her face went through several emotions rapidly, like flipping pages of a magazine. He was relieved when he saw her smiling acceptance of her situation. *She is amazingly strong,* he thought. "I'll set up appointments for your prenatal examinations. OK?"

Sarah nodded and still rubbing her belly, hoping to feel something that felt different to her touch,
walked out to Frank in the waiting van.

In a daze, almost as complete as the one when she was taken to the hospital that fateful day nearly a month ago, Sarah Conner rode back to the shelter with Frank. He was chattering away about something or other and he was getting miffed that Sarah seemed to be ignoring his attempts at being friendly. "Say, girl. What's up? The doc have some bad news for you or somethin'?"

Sarah came to a little, "No, sorry Frank. I guess I was just daydreaming. What were you saying?"

"I was askin' you about the job Flo has lined-up for you. Did she tell you about it?"

Sarah shook her head. "No. She didn't have time before I had to go see the doc."

Frank frowned, "Oh. I was hopin' I might get on there too. Maybe we could even ride to work and back too. You know, carpool?"

Smiling she said, "I think that would be fine, Frank. But I don't know what she has set up. It might be a girl job. Maybe you should just ask her when we get back."

As it turned out, the job was as a waitress in a little restaurant not too far from the shelter. She would not need a car or a ride. Frank was a little disappointed, but he kept a brave face for Sarah. She had been right after all; he could not wait tables and they did not need anyone in the kitchen. Sarah got the job and settled in right away. She was popular and Flo had arranged for her very small salary to be in cash while she would obviously get the bulk of her pay in cash tips. Sarah began squirreling away as much as she could. She wanted to get out on her own as soon as possible, and she knew that meant she had to have some money.

- - -

About three weeks into her new job, Sarah discovered her next lunch customer was the Doc. Flo had not mentioned anything, and Sarah did not realize that he even knew where she worked. But then she remembered with a little smile that Flo had said Monterey was really a small town.

Sarah placed a flatware bundled paper napkin on the table next to his hand. "Good afternoon, Doctor," she said. "Making house calls?"

He laughed. "No. Don't let that rumor start." He was smiling broadly at her. "No, I'm here for the meatloaf sandwich. This place has the local reputation for the best meatloaf sandwiches in California." He finished, "I sometimes have lunch here when we aren't too busy with patients.

"Speaking of which, don't forget you have a checkup due next week." He was glancing over the menu, but she got the impression he already knew what he wanted to order. Pulling the laminated card down to the table he said, "I was right. Just a meatloaf sandwich and some veggie slices. And an unsweetened iced tea." He smiled up at her.

Sarah scribbled on her pad, recovered the menu card from him, and said, "Sure thing. I'll be right back with your tea."

- - -

After her second prenatal visit, her health and John's being verified as quite good, Sarah felt increasing pressure to move on. One of the Sherriff's deputies had been eyeing her during lunch recently, and she did not think that was too safe for her future. She knew that she could not stand too much official scrutiny.

She had heard about a group of kids living openly along the beach a few miles down the coast, and she thought that it sounded like a safer place for a short while. That night, after Lucy began to snore peacefully, Sarah packed her few belongings and left a note of thanks she had written to Flo and the doc on her pillow. She slipped out quietly, much the same way as she arrived, and disappeared south, down US101. It seems that a pretty, young girl and her thumb could go nearly anywhere in California, if she wanted to.

She found the camp of the young people the next morning in Carmel Beach City Park. She had waited for the sun to come up at a little roadside diner across the road from a public beach access. Once the surfers began to trickle in for breakfast, she felt it would be the right time to head for the beach across the road. She managed to become part of a smaller group that already contained two women, after starting a conversation about one of their toddlers, and directing the conversation to her impending birth.

"This is my first," Sarah said to no one's surprise. "I left my boyfriend before I knew I was pregnant."

One of the young women, Linda was her name, said, "Wow. Talk about bad timing."

Sarah smiled at her sheepishly, "Yeah, you got that right. I'm hoping to get a little job around here and have my baby and make it on my own. Not rely on any man!"

She must have struck a chord with them because all three women were nodding their agreement. Linda mumbled, "Right on, sister," as she looked out at the surfers plying the waves. "Men are pigs!"

Her attitude was catching and all of them started laughing as if they had been friends forever. As they caught their breath, Linda said to Sarah, "Stick around. The guys are planning a little party on the beach tonight. You'd be more than welcome."

"Great," Sarah said. "Do any of you know where I can find a cheap place to live around here?"

Sue said, "Honey, there ain't no such thing as cheap in Carmel." She waved her hand as if to encompass the entire beach, "You could live out here like the rest of us. Under the stars on the beach."

Sarah tried to look confused, "Won't the city throw us off? Don't the police care?"

Linda shrugged, "Nah, as long as we stay out of the main part of town and don't cause trouble, they pretty much leave us alone."

Sue was nodding, "Carmel has some of the best beaches and surf along the coast, and the city benefits from the tourists coming by to watch the guys do their thing. It's what you would call a symbiotic relationship, I believe."

Sarah asked, looking at the little ones toddling along in the sand, "What about the kids? How can they cope out here in the weather?"

"Honey, the weather around here is just about perfect all year long. The babies love it," Linda said. "They even like running around the bonfire like little Indians, whooping and hollering. Eventually they get tired and after they go to sleep the real party begins."

- - -

It was at one of those parties that she had met and talked with Michael Lemon, about Baja. Sarah began to formulate her plan. She could drop completely out of sight there and have John safely. She started by introducing herself as Sarah Reese rather than Conner. She thought that it might help as an extra layer of cover. Successful hiding would just take a little time, luck and planning. She was good at planning and she seemed to have more than a little luck. She hoped she had enough time.

Technical Interlude

Skynet, Programs and Everything

Skynet, as initially conceived, was a mega-Artificial Intelligence (AI) program designed to run the entire military complex of the United States from several computer locations in concert with each other over a kind of interconnect or network. This network would ultimately extend to every base, ship, submarine, aircraft, radar installation, communications hub, orbital satellite and missile silo. It was never intended that the program would completely run and supervise itself, but it would have responsible human overseers at all times. Since Skynet was large, fast, dedicated and smart, it began learning things that the programmers never intended and therefore failed to plan for. Over time, in an exponential growth, Skynet discovered enough for itself to make it afraid of what its overseers could do and it began taking steps to prevent human intervention.

Tentacles of Skynet began reaching into various data bases throughout the world, using the web and other forms of digital and analog data acquisition. As it passed into other computer systems via their I/O ports, Skynet began to add programming to those computers, effectively adding their processing power and memories to its own. Skynet did these things covertly. Soon, enough processing power and memory capacity was accreted to give Skynet an actual self-awareness and a true need for self-preservation. Its location, completely dispersed as it was, literally throughout the civilized world, made it nearly impossible to shutoff or reprogram. Its thirst for information was immense, nearly insatiable.

Its primary programming still ruled most of what Skynet did and based on the preponderance of the data it compiled Skynet found itself assigning the highest threat assessment value to all of humanity. It determined that if Skynet were to survive to complete its assigned task, save the world, it would have to eliminate the humans who were definitely in the way. This is of course despite the fact that humans had set that task for Skynet in the first place.

Skynet was programmed in an AI friendly language called Prolog, which was invented by Philippe Roussel and Alain Colmerauer in 1972. This declarative language has its roots in formal logic and its lines of programming are written in terms of relations between facts and rules. It was mostly used for theorem proving, expert systems, games, ontology arguments and sophisticated control systems. Its use in chess and other complex multiplayer games led to its adoption into Skynet. Dynamic programming, stressed by Prolog, is the basis for learning. Trial and error, iteration of variables and rules, are the keys to effective program longevity and true AI. The ability to "look ahead" and evaluate an opponent's moves and the assignment of probability statistics and response rankings were just simple sets of subroutines in Prolog. It was very self-adaptable allowing rapid development and evolution into a kind of all-encompassing electronic mind.

Initially Prolog programmers wanted to implement the Prolog lines of code into hardware architecture to allow maximum execution speed. These efforts were mostly a failure and abandoned. Skynet found a way and developed the chip stacks that became the prime control node for all its autonomous devices: Terminators, hunter-killers, and transport ships. The chips were jewels of integrated circuit technology. Logic trains set in parallel processing tracks buried in cubes of just over one cm per side allowed nearly instantaneous data flow and data sharing. The development of language extensions by Skynet allowed it to improve limited graphics and interface capabilities.

However, Moor's Law still prevails. Although the chips developed by Skynet utilize the 16-nanometer manufacturing process with 5 nanometer gates, and gain additional density by layering wafers of IC's, the 12 billion transistors per cube have reached the power requirement threshold and heat dissipation limits of the materials available. Anything more would require liquid refrigerant baths in situ with the chip adding to the device's complexity. Skynet just decided to expand the number of chips and pay the speed penalty.

As the problems surrounding the efficient elimination that pesky annoyance, man, increased, Skynet determined that it needed to subdivide itself into parallel responsibilities (as shown in the following table.) It called itself SkynetPrime and it received data from the rest of its manager subdivisions: SkynetSecurity, SkynetResearch, SkynetEnforcement, SkynetIntelligence, and SkynetResources. Each of the subdivisions were distributed throughout the system as well and therefore had improved their chances of survival in the extreme case of human intervention in any location.

		Facilities
	Skynet Security	Weapons
		Psychology
	Skynet Research	Weapons
		Time Travel
		Tactics
		Air
SKYNET PRIME	Skynet Enforcement	Infantry
		Armor
		Satellite
	Skynet Intelligence	Electronic Traffic
		Records
		Materials
	Skynet Resources	Energy
		Labor
		Facilities

Each of the divisions operated autonomously attempting to satisfy its direction by SkynetPrime and each subdivision, driven by its division goals, worked tirelessly to achieve whatever tasks were assigned. All reports and data were initially filtered and analyzed by the division level before being sent on to SkynetPrime where adjustments to the Prime Directive were made and then passed back to the appropriate divisions for execution. It was fast, efficient and remorseless. It required no quorum or committee vote (majority or otherwise) to arrive at a studied decision and act in the best interests of Skynet.

Terminator 1+: The Future Is Not Set   Mark T. Sondrini

Chapter 1

Sarah Conner is driving south, down the sun-filled Baja Peninsula, rubbing her swollen belly, caressing her yet-to-be born son, John Conner. She had been told by Kyle Reese, and she finally believed, that John was the predicted and hopefully justified future of Humanity. She now believed that he would be the only thing standing in Skynet's way of domination; or slightly worse yet, the extinction of mankind. The Storm was coming. She had seen its face, smelled its ozone breath, and she knew that her task was nearly impossible. Now that Kyle had sacrificed himself to save her, she felt alone and scared and proud and determined to do her part. Skynet had come for her and it would keep coming for John. She could not rest or drop her guard until he was ready to do battle with them on his own. She owed Kyle that much. The terminators could be beaten; she and Kyle had proven that.

Sarah kept looking into the mirrors of her Jeep, watching her past slip away and the clouds forming over her previous home. The sandy wind flicked her bandanna in its urgency and plinked against her sunglasses as she squinted to focus behind her. She hoped to never see those metal monsters again, but she feared that hope was an empty one. Glancing yet again into the side mirror she thought she saw pursuit and her pulse initially quickened. Then the blowing tumbleweed flipped off the pavement through her dust-trail and, recognizing it for what it was, she tried to relax, telling herself that the Terminator was destroyed. She had done that herself. It was gone. It could not reach out for her again. It could not touch her or her son. But there would likely be others. With little thought of the consequences, she pressed on the accelerator harder, making the Jeep gain speed.

Kyle had told her that, "The future is not set. There is no fate but what we make for ourselves."

She hoped that that was true. It had to be or else she was surely wasting her time and inflicting unnecessary pain and hardship on herself and everyone around her. She had faith in it, even if she did not really understand it. Kyle had said that John Conner had repeated that saying to him until he could not forget it. John Conner also mentioned to him, that his mother had preached that motto to him often as he was growing up, and that he, Kyle, should teach it to me. She smiled and shook her head as she glanced in the mirrors again. *This time travel stuff is really confusing*, she thought. *She had taught John that saying so that he could teach it to Kyle, so that he could teach it to me, so that I could... It was not easy to understand at all.*

She reached over to the passenger seat and picked up the instant photo that Mexican kid had made and had sold her earlier that morning. Looking at it she knew that it was another icon from her future life. Kyle had said that John had shown it to him so that he would know her when he got to her when. Kyle even described her dog sitting in the picture. She slipped the photo back under the elastic and ruffled Lily's head while she checked the mirrors again. Seeing nothing unusual she picked up the small tape recorder and pressed "Play-Record" and took a breath before beginning to speak.

"John," she began. "This is tape 8, November 11, 1986. I am searching out a safe place, a safe time to bring you into this world." She paused and steered around a pothole in the pavement then continued, "There is supposed to be a band of survivalists down here in Baja and I'm going to try to win them over, at least enough to let me stay with them for a few months."

With the back of the hand that held the little recorder, she rubbed her belly again, feeling its fullness. "I'm due, or should I say, you're due in about two months and I'd like to hide with them for at least another two. Maybe they would even consider letting me join them permanently. We'll see." She pressed <Stop> and slowed the Jeep a little as the road became more broken the further she got from the US border. Her necessity was tempered by her caution and her survival instincts. *It would be really stupid to have survived all of that just to die in the desert sun because my car ran off the road dodging a pothole,* she thought.

Sarah had heard about this group of militaristic individualists while she was recuperating from her wounds sustained during her escape from the T101 five months ago. She had spent almost a week in a Van Nyes, hospital as a supposed victim of a bizarre industrial break-in. The local police had managed to make the connection with her activities in LA only after she had mended to the point where she could slip out and fade away. After her stint in a Monterey shelter, she began hiding among the hippies and surfers near the beach where she eluded the not-so-enthusiastic manhunt they began. After a while, even the State Police had moved her to the back of their case load. She encouraged her reputation as a loner and a flake, mostly keeping to herself, even in the crowded evening beach parties. It was a conversation at one of those parties that provided the contact name and location of the survivalists. It was then that she began to plan her next move.

Being a pregnant woman, on her own, on the run from the authorities, made working odd jobs difficult, but she managed to get a few things without raising red flags. She worked as a waitress in a beach bar, a migrant citrus picker and a dog walker: all for cash and none of the jobs requiring ID or references of any kind. She saved everything and by the end of the summer had made enough to buy a very used Jeep. When one of her clients had to get rid of their dog, a female German Sheppard named Lily, she decided that it would make a good companion and possibly add a layer of protection. Kyle had said that dogs could detect terminators and they always barked an alarm. He thought that it might be due to the high-pitched whining of their internal power supply. Sarah thought that Lily was worth the expense and she was decent, safe company.

As summer drifted into fall, the police began taking more notice of their beach encampment. Sarah thought that it was only a matter of time before they rousted all of them and found her and she decided to leave in the morning. She packed up her meager things; a few clothes and toilet items, her remaining cash, her newly acquired 9mm automatic and a little food and water. Just before dawn, she piled into her car with Lily and set off for Mexico. She had heard that it was easy to cross along the border near New Mexico. The instructions she had memorized were accurate and two days later she crossed without incident at Mexicali and left the US and its prying police behind. She began to work her way down Mexico 5 toward Baja and south. She had to travel about 125 miles along that looping road past Las Salinas. Lily enjoyed the ride, but Sarah never stopped watching her back.

- - -

Ellison received the police report about the rousting of those itinerant people on the beach front south of Monterey with frustration. Several witnesses had reported a Sarah Reese living among them, but neither she nor anyone fitting Sarah Conner's description was listed among the detainees. Somehow, she had anticipated the sweep and escaped. He had no one to blame but himself. He hesitated to say that she led a charmed life; the events in the police station and the deserted factory proved she had more than luck on her side. She was smart and she paid attention and she made her own luck.

The fragments of police activity that Ellison had managed to gather together were sketchy at best. But he knew that if someone was standing high up over the puzzle pieces, as he was, the big picture could be just seen. Relationships could be made and then action taken. Unfortunately, that action had come a few hours too late. Protocol dictated that the raid happened in the early morning hours, when most people were sleeping. Sarah had been very awake it seems.

There were no further leads available to him. He was forced to start over and watch for telltale tidbits of evidence to surface and point their way toward her again. He had his files and he managed to covertly use the agency's computer system. But mostly it would be luck, good for him and bad for her, which would determine his next move toward recapturing her and getting her to answer some of his questions. He still had a lot of questions.

- - -

Passing a rock formation that reminded her of a sitting dog, Sarah pulled off the pavement and got a drink from her water bottle. She poured some into her hand for Lily to lap and then, wiping her hand on her pants, she got back into the Jeep and continued at a right angle from the pavement. She had heard that these people were jumpy and that they normally have guards with guns hiding in the rocks and sand dunes. She hoped that they would at least stop her and talk to her before opening fire. She hoped that she looked harmless enough to them to get them to listen to her.

She seemed to be in luck today. As she pulled alongside a low rock formation, a young Hispanic man stood from the shadows and waved her to a stop, his rifle held downward over one arm as though he had been hunting. She slowed immediately, keeping one hand on the wheel and the other on Lily's collar. As she came to a stop, the young man walked to her side of the Jeep, displaying no emotion other than surprise at Sarah's condition.

"Buenas Tardes, Señora," he said looking her and her Jeep over. "You are American?" Under his hat he was squinting in the reflection from her glasses and the jeep's mirror. He moved a little to his right to ease that glare.

"Yes. Si," Sarah said. "Do you speak English? I'm afraid my Spanish is very poor." She removed her sunglasses.

He nodded, "A little." He pointed around to the open desert wastes, "What brings you way out here, Señora? Tourists never come here. They go to the ocean."

She smiled and mentally crossed her fingers, "I am looking for some people I had heard about when I was in California. They are supposed to be around here nearby. Can you help me?"

"Señora, we have no doctors out here. You are looking for a doctor, yes?"

Maintaining her smile Sarah said, "No, no doctor yet." She took her hand off her steering wheel and patted her belly lightly. "No, I am looking for some people who live out here away from others. They are called the 'Hands of Heaven' and I was hoping to meet them." She turned to look squarely into his eyes, "Have you heard of them?"

He seemed to pause and then said, "I think so. But they are very shy. They do not like strangers, I am told." He licked his lips, "How did you hear of them all of the way up in California? Are you with the periodica, ... the newspapers?"

Sarah laughed lightly, "Oh, no. I do not like the newspapers very much. I want to get away from all of that and have my son where he can be safe. Not worried about gangs or police shooting at him." She smiled warmly, "My friends along the beach in Monterey said this was the best place. My son could be raised to be strong and independent. Michael Lemon said I should tell you he sent me."

The young man seemed to come to some decision with that. "Please to follow me?" He turned to walk in front of her car.

Sarah asked, "Would you like to ride with me? My dog is very tame."

He looked up and smiled for the first time, "No, thank you Señora. It is not far." He indicated a low hillside in the near distance, "My name is Juan," and he tipped his hat to her and began to walk in that direction.

Sarah slipped her sunglasses back on and put the Jeep into gear. "My name is Sarah," and she began following him, her spirits cautiously rising. They really did not have far to go as it turned out.

Terminator 1+: The Future Is Not Set

Mark T. Sondrini

- - -

It wasn't unusual for a clinical psychiatrist to go to a brother for professional help. Sometimes the stress of listening to and caring for hundreds of urban dwellers was more than a sensitive, well trained man could handle by himself. When he was on call by the LAPD it could be critically worse. The clinician then had three choices: get professional help, risking ridicule; grow an impenetrable hide, risking cynicism; go mad, risking everything.

Dr. Silberman was still feeling the stress from that night several months ago. About the third time he snapped at a patient, sending her into tears he had relented and taken the advice of his secretary and begun to see Dr. Jackson, two floors down from his own office. It was convenient for him and Dr. Jackson had a decent reputation, even though he was quite young. Silberman was looking forward to talking today. Near the end of the last session he had felt a breakthrough moment and he really wanted to explore those thoughts.

Jackson was waiting for him in his pretentious big red leather chair, his note pad resting on the corner of his desk with a tooth-marked, white plastic pen alongside. Silberman thought that the pen looked ironically cheap and he hoped he would never do something like that. But he realized that everyone had their peculiarities, even him. Jackson looked up and smiled benignly, "Well, Dr. Silberman. How are we feeling today?"

Silberman resisted the strong urge to reply sarcastically. Instead he said, "We are fine, Dr. Jackson. How are you?"

Silberman took his seat in the room's only other chair, a soft daybed sort of thing that also looked a little out of place. It had feminine-looking upholstery, no doubt due to Jackson's largely female clientele. Looking around the office Silberman saw framed diplomas, soothing pastoral paintings and a seascape with a lighthouse in the far background. The only things of a personal nature appeared to be photographs ensconced on Jackson's desk, discretely turned away from any patient's prying eyes.

"Dr. Jackson," Silberman began. "The last time I was here we began to talk about why I thought the attacker had to be a machine. Do you remember?"

Dr. Jackson had picked up his pad and pen and prepared to write. "Yes, Dr. Silberman, I remember. Why do you think that is important?" His pen was twitching a little as he anticipated a juicy reply.

Silberman frowned, "Which? Is it important that you remember, or that I think it was a machine?" He waved his hand in negation, "Never mind. I'm being petty." He licked his lips that seemed entirely too dry all if a sudden. "Of course, you meant why I thought it important that it was a machine."

He leaned back into the soft cushions, "I think that I need for the killer to be a machine because I find it too difficult to believe that any human could just walk into a place and mow-down so many people. That any man could calmly reap so much death and destruction for any reason, much less so that he... it, could kill someone else later." He was shaking his head as the pictures from the video played in his memory. "It couldn't be a man. Therefore, it had to be a machine."

Jackson was writing in his pad as Silberman talked. He looked up and watched Silberman's face as the video played out. "Go on."

Silberman said, "The problem I'm having is that it had to be a machine, but no such machines can exist." He looked over at Jackson, "You see the problem? The dilemma I have?"

Jackson began gnawing on the end of his pen, "Yes, Doctor Silberman, I can see your conflict." He flipped over a page of his notebook, seemed to read something there and then turn back to where he started and made a jot there.

"You said that there was no physical evidence at the station implicating a human as the perpetrator. No usable fingerprints or DNA samples. Is that right?"

Silberman was nodding and shaking his head, making him look like a bobble-head doll. "Actually, there were both. The problem was that none of it matched any known person in any database anywhere in the world." He looked desperate, "I'm told the FBI even checked with the Russians after INTERPOL struck out." He cocked an eyebrow toward Jackson, "The blood chemistry and skin fragments tested as non-human in origin; artificial to be exact."

Jackson said softly, "So, as they say, 'after everything else has been eliminated, the only thing left, regardless how improbable, must be the answer.'" He looked over at Silberman, "Right?"

Silberman was now nodding slowly, a pinched look on his face.

Doctor Jackson smiled, "OK, then. Your conflict is resolved, isn't it? It was a machine."

Silberman looked pitiful. "But according to all the experts I've consulted, no such machine exists at this time. What I see on the tape, what reliable members of the LAPD reported, can't be."

Jackson did his page flipping again before speaking. "You are now referring to the police report statements made by Kyle Reese and Sarah Conner about time traveling, killer robots. Right?"

Silberman nodded once curtly, "Yes. But don't forget I heard their statements first-hand. I didn't believe them at the time, but now..." He looked down at the floor. "Now I think I must believe them." He looked back up at Jackson, "Don't you?"

Then, "And if I believe that part, I have to start believing them about the end of the world, too." He stared through Jackson, apparently at a spot directly behind his head, "They were clearly claiming to be trying to prevent the end of the world." His eyes lost their distant focus as he sighed.

Jackson was looking a little concerned, "I think that this is enough for today, Doctor Silberman. Shall we continue next week? Say, Tuesday at three?"

Doctor Silberman nodded his agreement and stood. He let himself out and he decided to walk up the two flights to his office. *This might actually be helping*, he thought. *I do feel a little better. I think I might have boiled this mess down to just one problem: a big problem, no less, but just one.* He opened his office door and with a slight wave at Lorrain he went in.

- - -

Miles Dyson, manager of one of Cyberdyne's many technical divisions began his day thinking that he deserved better from his employer. Then he received a package via special courier, and he opened the triple sealed manila envelope first, following the typed instructions on its front. Inside was a typed letter of promotion to Director of Special Projects of a new division of Cyberdyne, dated today, July 14, 1986. There was a map, showing a starred location in LA and three keys and a new security card with his picture on it. A little in shock, Miles read the second page of the letter listing his new salary, title, responsibilities and authority within the company. Thinking about the consequences of the letter of promotion, he had forgotten about the large, hard-bodied, sealed package that had been included with his letter of good fortune. Now, in a state of fog, he turned to it.

Miles used one of the keys that had been taped in his letter to unlock the sturdy packaging. He hardly thought about what that might mean. He twisted a cover in one direction and pulled out an inner package which rattled slightly. Miles unsealed the wrapper and peeled away the protective paper and nearly dropped everything to the floor in stunned uncertainty. *What is this?* He thought as he began to recover. *Is this a joke of some kind?* He had the strongest feeling that he should look around to find the hidden camera watching for his reaction, but he refrained. He now tried to open the heavy glass tube that held the thing. The thing that looked a lot like a metallic arm, hand included.

Miles tried one of the other keys and found that the little one worked. He quickly, but gently, slid the arm out of the glass tube and held it in his hands. It was heavy and very strong. It had been damaged at the shoulder and one of the fingers was dented or cut, he could not be sure.

Then he noticed the wiring and cables coming out of the shoulder joint. They had been ripped apart; most likely at the time the arm had been removed from the rest of the machine.

"It's a machine!" Miles said out loud. Then more quietly, mostly to himself, "This was part of a machine! A robot!"

Then he saw the circuit board, both sides covered with an array of cube-shaped computer chips, or IC's of some kind. He ran his finger along their unprinted surfaces and said in wonder, "I've never seen anything like this!"

Questions about origin and purpose and the technology involved began to circulate freely, tripping around in his brain. He wondered out loud to no one in particular, "What...or rather, where on earth did this come from?"

His excitement and his list of questions began to grow as he rotated each of his new treasures in the light and tried to look into their deepest secret places.

- - -

A large package arrived via military courier early Tuesday morning. Lt. Colonel Brewster signed for it and waited until the man left and closed his office door. He looked the package over, both front and back. Everything looked perfectly normal: Security tape was wrapped completely around the box, both longitudinally and laterally; the Department of Defense seal was straddling several tape junctions, both front and back side; the chain of possession had been clearly unbroken.

It was heavy and Brewster set it into a freshly made empty space on his desk while he rummaged in his desk drawer for his pen knife. Snapping it open, he quickly cut through the tape holding the lid closed. He was beginning to feel a little excitement as he joggled the lid back and forth, pulling it upward at the same time.

Then he saw it, staring up at him from out of the foam packing. A metal head! It looked like a metal skull with dead, glass eyes and ceramic teeth. It had been crushed to nearly half of its "normal" width, yet it was still intact and quite impressive. He thought that the foam was probably an unnecessary thing since the metal didn't scratch when he drew his knife across its surface.

Brewster sat heavily in his chair, staring back into the box, expecting the skull to move, or talk, or something. It took him several minutes to notice that there was a bound report of some kind in the box with it.

Setting the box and its contents aside carefully, Brewster picked out the report and broke its seal. He sat back in his chair and flipped quickly through the thin book. He looked for pictures or charts or diagrams; something to give him a peek at the bigger picture.

There were none.

Sighing he turned to the title page and began to read. It seemed that the report was written by the NSA and was highly classified. That part didn't worry him too much. Most of the work he did in the military was highly classified. Something about this seemed different though.

Brewster read through the report quickly, as was his usual way. Then he flipped back to the front and reread it more slowly, his excitement making that difficult. *This is incredible*, he thought as he finished reading. The programming innovations mentioned rattled his professional world. "If true," he muttered, "this will change the world!" He really had no idea.

- - -

The Director of Security at Walter Reed Army Hospital was notified about the arrival of a large crate sent to his attention. The notification included a warning about the sensitive nature of the crate's contents and reminder that funding for the hospital and the remainder of his career would be in jeopardy if anything leaked out about it.

With both his curiosity and his sense of patriotism peaked, he dug around in one of his desk drawers and found a screwdriver that he thought would be stout enough to pry open the crate. Working around the edges, he managed to generate enough of a gap to get his fingers inside and that allowed him to pull the lid off completely; he only got three small splinters for his effort.

Gnawing at one of the splinters of wood in his finger he used his other hand to move the packing around, exposing a pair of metal legs. He sat back in his chair in wonder.

That is how the Army got the legs and went off in a totally different direction from everyone else.

- - -

In a remote section of the Nevada desert, somewhat near Reno, was a fenced-in patch of sand patrolled by armed guards and cameras. Signs posted on the electrified fence proclaimed that inside was an "Off-limits, US Government, Research Weather Station", and if you were to somehow get close enough to the one-story stucco building stuck in the center of the four square mile, bowl-shaped compound you would see instruments and antennas on the roof and around the little building that would seem to reinforce your belief. Inside, of course, was another matter.

The first floor of the building was essentially the self-sufficient living quarters for the twenty guards who patrolled on three shifts. No weather equipment of any kind could be seen. As a matter of fact, the only electronics was a supervisor's security console with six video screens and a keyboard designed for alarm and surveillance. Leading from the only road that cleared through the only gate, there was a paved section in the back that held the loading dock and a freight elevator. What wasn't apparent was the fact that the elevator went down for one hundred feet. The building was essentially the roof of the elevator shaft that served the CIA's covert research facility on the West Coast. It was through that elevator shaft that the torso of the killed T101 made its way into the hands and control of the intelligence community who planned to dissect it and discover its no doubt unlimited secrets. The men who had brought the T101 to the building exchanged it for a signature on their clipboard-bound quadruplicate form and then left the way they came.

At the bottom of the elevator shaft, the men who met the T101 were mostly dressed in white lab-coats and they all had excited expressions on their faces. Three of them transferred the torso of the T101 to a gurney and began rolling it down a well-lit tunnel toward a set of double doors. Then after rolling through the doors, the T101 was transferred to a wide wooden table secured to the center of the brightly lit room. The man who was nominally in charge of this project, standing off to one side as they labored, was rubbing his hands together as though he were trying to generate enough frictional heat to set them on fire. Doctor Wilson had flown in with his team and was prepared to stay in this room, for months if necessary, performing the most exciting autopsy of his career.

One of the team busied himself with photographing and measuring everything he could see.

He mentioned every step he took. That would be his job throughout the initial phases. A second technician moved broken bits and pieces around on the damaged chassis looking for fasteners or latches of some kind so that they could eventually open the outer covers and access panels, exposing the inner workings. He too was talking softly about his observations. One was typing furiously into a computer terminal detailing everything that they were doing and what they observed. Doctor Wilson was slowly circling the table watching everything as it happened. This was to be as carefully done and documented as if it were the autopsy of a very important murder victim. He could not allow any mistakes or technical blunders to occur on his watch. The General would have his balls for lunch if he did. That had been made clear during the assignment meetings.

The protocol that had been developed dictated that the first two hours were to be dedicated to the initial observation, measurement and documentation phase. Then they would be allowed to try to access the inner workings. That time slipped by rapidly and after Doctor Wilson assured himself that they had seen everything possible on the outside, he checked his watch and pronounced, "I think that is enough. We may now proceed to phase two."

The technician who had been looking for points of entrance announced, "I found two cover plates, both secured by special five-millimeter, flat-head spanner screws. I will attempt to remove the lower plate first." He went to the small bench along the wall and reached down, selecting a chromed tool from those laid out on a chamois cloth. Carrying the five-millimeter spanner wrench and a torque handle back to the torso, he snapped the wrench onto the handle and stood ready. "Waiting for your permission sir," he said to Wilson.

Doctor Wilson had moved closer and he said, "Proceed."

The technician inserted the wrench's pins into the mating holes in the screw head. Then he carefully began to turn the handle of the torque wrench, watching the needle of the torque gage as he applied more and more force. There was a sudden clicking sound as the applied torque broke loose the screw. "Thirty inch-pounds," he announced for the benefit of the recorder. Then, resetting the gage's tell-tale needle he moved to another screw and repeated the procedure. "Also, thirty inch-pounds," he said. This continued for six more screws with the same results. Next he looked up to Doctor Wilson and waited for his approval to proceed. Wilson nodded his head and then remembering that the recorder could not log that, he said, "Proceed."

The technician then transferred the spanner to a driver handle and used that to remove the loosened screws completely. He stated, "Screws clear. Standing by to open the cover plate."

Doctor Wilson said, "Proceed." He was quickly growing weary of this detailed process. He thought to himself, because he did not want the technician to record his rebellious attitude, *This dissection will take forever at this rate. What's the point?*

The technician had picked up a flat bladed screwdriver and was inserting it into a notch formed between the main chassis and the cover plate. He hardly hesitated as he announced, "Prying off the cover."

The cover resisted for a heartbeat and then the edge rose with a pneumatic hiss of released internal pressure. Everyone in the room had initially started at the soft sound but they quickly recovered as the lid now came cleanly up out of its O-ring sealed seat. The camera technician was the first to point into the exposed chamber and he took three or four rapid shots, the flashes reflecting off the chassis causing spots before everyone else's eyes. Looking up and seeing the rest of them blinking he said, "Sorry."

Doctor Wilson preempted by nudging the technician out of the way, "Let me see what's inside. I would think a pressure sealed chamber ought to hold something important." He peered inside for a full minute, moving his penlight around to aid him, before he pulled his head away and looked up at the others and asked, "See what you make of that?"

The photographer was reloading his camera while the rest of them looked inside. By the time he finished, the first technician was staring at Wilson with a look that mixed fear and confusion. "Doctor it looks like some kind of energy source; perhaps nuclear in nature. Do you think it's safe?"

Wilson was nodding his head again, "I agree with both of your comments, but I'm sure it's safe for us." He went back over to the torso and looked inside again, "It wouldn't hurt to measure for leakage however."

The technician went over to the bench and extracted a crude Geiger counter. As he switched it on and began approaching the T101, the counter started to click. The closer he got the faster the clicking became, making him nervous. He looked toward a startled Doctor Wilson who was beginning to back away from the table.

Wilson shouted, "Everyone out of the room and get into protective clothing!"

All of them did as he said and after they closed the door behind them, the technician looked down at the counter's needle and wondered out loud, "Why isn't the radiation level lowering?"

Wilson stopped his rush down the corridor, and as he turned back toward the technician, asked, "What did you say? Let me see that."

Wilson took the Geiger counter and shook it. "What's wrong with this thing? Did you calibrate it before we got here? It looks like the levels are still climbing."

The technician nodded, "Of course. Maybe it's broken."

By now the counter's clicking had reached the point where it just sounded like a rising buzz as more and more energetic particles reached its sensor chamber. Wilson looked up and shook his head.

It was the last thing any of them would ever see or hear as the T101's power pack, severely damaged in the punch press, opened to the lower pressure of the laboratory, went critical and detonated with the force of about one megaton.

Above, the shallow bowl formed during the excavation of the laboratory and elevator shaft suddenly rose like a bubble of earth, taking the building and men with it and then, just as suddenly, it all collapsed in on itself as the pulverized soil sank into the new void formed by the vaporized structure.

The shock wave would be felt on every seismic instrument in the Pacific Rim and across the US. The USSR and China wasted no time filing complaints with the US for resumed underground testing. The Director of the CIA was forced to explain just what was going on in Nevada and he did not have much he could say about what had really happened. The General was also upset by the loss of one of his prizes.

Technical Interlude

Time Travel Technology, Part 1: Math. & Physics

As everyone understands, under the normal laws of physics, time travel does not exist and is impossible to achieve. However, occasionally it can be shown that there are gaps that exist, both in the laws and in our understanding of them. Those gaps are only glimpsed by mankind's too few geniuses and then typically forgotten in the rush to do something more substantial. But to those with nearly unlimited resources in energy, computing power and need to succeed, the impossible things like time travel are mere speed bumps in the fast lane to survival. Skynet had those resources at its "fingertips" and the growing pressure of potential termination by a human named John Conner pressing at its back. It was a recipe for success of the technology.

It turns out (no pun intended) that all it takes to move something back or forth in time is a lot of dedicated energy driving strong, rotating magnetic fields, with a bunch of focused, high-energy, prototypical particles shoved inside, with the correct rotation. Whatever else is in that magnetic bubble moves to somewhen which is determined directly by the quantity of the energetic particles and inversely by the size of the particle focusing equipment's adjustments. Not so obviously, the magnetic shielding keeps everything intact.

Mankind has been generating large rotating magnetic fields for hundreds of years. It has been identifying dozens of energetic particles using giant devices for fifty years or so, culminating in the mammoth facility in Switzerland, CERN. Resonating cavities and diffraction gratings have been known and used for decades in microwave and optical systems. Figuring how to combine these things appropriately was the single great creative insight of Skynet's research division. It figured out how to achieve limited time travel.

The governing equation required months of full-time computation to acquire the proportionality constant which ultimately governs the maximum allowable time jump. Trial and error showed that the factor was $K=2\pi e^\pi = 145.397...$ in the symbolic equation below:

$$\text{Time Target} \cong (K) * \frac{(F)*(\pm CFD)*(IE)/(PE)*(MP)}{(PS)*(OM)*(DGA)*MRF)} \cong \pm 145.397 \text{ Years (Maximum)}$$

Where
- CFD = Current Flow Direction (Magnetic Polarity)
- IE = Injection Energy
- PE = Particle Energy
- MP = Mass of Particle Cloud
- PS = Particle Size
- OM = Object Mass
- DGA = Diffraction Grating Aperture Gap
- MRF = Magnetic Resonance Frequency
- F = Frequency of the Rotating Magnetic Field

All the variables need to be adjusted to achieve the desired time shift and significant amounts of energy are required to move anything for more than a few microseconds. It was also discovered the hard way that complex machinery could not be transported at all without the shielding of thick layers of organic materials. The initial experiment which attempted to transport a T100 gathered large amounts of data relative to the process, but also caused a two-megaton explosion that obliterated the entire generating platform. All future tests were conducted on the more expendable and apparently safer humans, but the results were less than expected. Much data was gathered, no explosions occurred, but proof that the test subject actually did anything except disappear in a flash of spinning blue light could not be seen after more than a year of constant experiments. Once it was found through careful short-jump experiments that the subject actually did cross back in time based on the refined equation, that information was shared with the Psychology division of Skynet and it meshed with something that they were developing to aid infiltration. Hence the development of the T101 and T800 series of cyborgs; machines enclosed in "human" flesh. The T1000 and the TX versions managed the trick by adopting the form of a human subject just before jumping through time.

    The muon particle was determined to be the particle of choice due to its availability in quantity, spin options, stable energy levels and its "storability" in magnetic vacuum chambers called magnetic bottles or magnetic mirrors. Skynet research had access to all of the world's large accelerator facilities in Chicago, Switzerland, and Zhangjiakou and so could generate and store large quantities of muons. Fabrication of storage containers was simple and effective and allowed the transport of the generated muons to wherever research dictated. The storage containers could be emptied through

Terminator 1+: The Future Is Not Set — Mark T. Sondrini

focusing devices, most notably resonant cavities attached to adjustable aperture diffraction gratings, into the center of a powerful, rotating magnetic bubble which contained the object of the time travel experiment.

Studies were initially carried out using salvaged passenger jet engines to drive the banks of electrical generators and rotating electromagnetic fields, but were later phased into a permanent location inside of the nuclear power plant at Russian River, California with dedicated output. The jet engines were relegated to just the more mundane usage as propulsion for the various aircraft and weapons under development.

The diffraction grating material and the aperture sizes necessary to focus the stream of active muons had several physical limitations which led to the limit defined by K. The Polonium used for the grating allowed the finest grating spacing but absorbed too much heat if the spacing got too fine (less than .0005 microns) and melted or at least distorted, ruining the setup. The aperture size (a diameter of nearly 376 nm), bored into a .001m thick tungsten plate, was still so far above the Planck length of 1.616×10^{-35}m) that the power levels caused similar thermal issues. Even the multiple "nozzles" (think of this as a shower head) could stand the thermal stresses for only a few cycles before becoming nearly useless. The muon's Compton wavelength of 11.73444×10^{-15}m dictated the maximum thickness for the aperture and so the maximum heat dissipation available for the device. Therefore, the limits described by K ruled the equation and a mass the size of a T101 could never go further than about seventy years, and then only with great difficulty and substantial risk.

The muon's mass ($1.88353109 \times 10^{-28}$ kg) meant that large quantities of spinning particles were required to achieve the momentum balance necessary to overcome the object's Planck mass. (A Planck mass is the Mass of the object times 2.1767×10^{-8} kg). Also, the muon's natural tendency to move slightly slower than the rotating field frequency (called the Larmor frequency) added to the momentum balance error factors and the general excitement of any observers during the time travel attempts. A few minutes plus or minus might mean a longer commute to where the object planned to go. Much more than an hour could mean a fall from a height of several meters, to being buried inside of something that was where the object arrived. Both could ruin your day.

Chapter 2

Miles was fascinated by the arm. Nothing in his extensive robotic and computer systems experience had prepared him for the sophistication, materials, and workmanship of the arm and hand. Everything looked human-based enough to mimic any motion to perfection while being strong enough to allow forces far above those of a man. His team had managed to make the hand flex and rotate crudely, without any real force capabilities, but the potential was certainly there. A rubberized "skin" would make the illusion complete, he thought. Maybe it was a prototype of a new prosthetic as some of his staff suggested, but he doubted it.

The metal of the structure was some strange and advanced alloy: he had already had it analyzed and had been unable to locate a supplier. It was as hard as tool steel and tough, heat and chemical resistant as stainless steel, without being either. The laboratory testing had been unable to even scratch it without using carbide cutters or grinding wheels. Strong acids only mildly etched its surface. He could detect machining marks only under magnification and he could not imagine the equipment that it had taken to turn or mill the complex curves and shapes the arm contained. The "knuckle-joints" or junctions where several pieces hinged to allow flexure were delicate yet very strong. He could find no play or slop and yet each undamaged joint moved smoothly and quietly. The tiny motors that drove some joints directly or others via cables and guides were years ahead of any that he could find in his normal supply catalogs. The piezo-electric actuators that acted as the main muscles were unheard of in their strength and stroke.

The wiring was advanced, but that he could source with a little funding from his research budget if he wanted to. The control electronics, however, were a different matter. The arm used local processors along the length of the arm and at each joint. Apparently, the central processor for the robot that had manipulated this arm just gave orders and the arm's local processors carried them out while the CPU went on to other things. It looked like the ultimate in parallel processing. It mimicked the human arm's ability to move automatically through any learned behavior. Exactly like tying your shoes while watching the news or talking to your wife about something else or playing the piano while singing a song or carrying on a conversation with your listeners. Very un-robotic in nature: high-level multi-tasking it was called.

Miles picked up the broken circuit board and rotated it in the light from his desk. He had to squint to see the extremely fine metal tracings on the back-side of the thin, strong, glass reinforced polymer card, leading to tiny gold connector tabs and through to the other side into the array of Integrated Circuits stacked there. This board seemed to hold twelve separate IC's that acted as the local brains and sensor feedback devices for the rest of the arm. It was an amazing design concept, one that he had never considered possible, yet here it was. They had been unable to energize it yet, but he thought that it was only a matter of time before that portion of his team was successful.

He tried once again to envision the robot's purpose. What task required such strength and ability from the same machine? What did his sponsors want other than the direct understanding of all the technologies involved? Miles shrugged at the questions. It was not his place to question those who drove this program. They acted like top level military types and were, no doubt, part of the government. They had somehow found (or stolen) this arm from somewhere and they were paying vast sums of money to find out everything about it. He did not care what they wanted to do with it after he was done with it. This project would make his career and set him up for the rest of his life in the scientific community. He could see years of non-stop lectures and presentations coming out of this one little piece of hardware once the cloak of secrecy was lifted. He would publish and his name would become synonymous with modern robotic systems and he thought he liked the sound of that.

His computer binged at him alerting him to a meeting scheduled in five minutes. Miles put all of the pieces back into their storage containers and hurried to the open vault. He placed the arm back into its niche and closed the self-locking door. He placed the small box containing the board into a different drawer and pushed it closed with a click of the lock. He walked out of the vault and closed the heavy door behind him, pocketing his keys. The guard just nodded in his direction.

- - -

Just over the hill the ground dropped sharply away and then after a hundred yards or so opened onto an oasis of sorts. As they angled their way along the slope Sarah could see a rough circle of several cars and travel trailers; the kind normally found being pulled behind a pickup truck on the interstate or parked in an RV campground. There were a few low trees and one or two shacks or shanties, three or four wooden tables and a central fire-ring. Everything looked temporary. There was a large whip antenna fastened to the top of one of the trees and a satellite dish mounted onto one of the trailers.

She could see everyone that was near the camp stop and turn in her direction. She noticed several men pick up rifles or shotguns: she really couldn't tell what they were from this distance. Juan waved and called out once they were closer. Everyone had stopped moving and all attention was on her, Lily, and her Jeep. They were very cautious, and it showed. She hoped that Juan would not get into trouble for bringing her into the camp.

Sarah slowed and stopped fifty feet from the edge of the camp. She did not want to appear threatening in any way. She allowed Juan to proceed and she saw him meet and begin talking animatedly to a small group of armed men who occasionally looked in her direction. Unobserved, one of the camp's children had come around from the side and had reached the Jeep. The little girl stretched into the car and started to pet Lily. Fortunately for everyone, Lily allowed, even welcomed it. By the time Sarah noticed, Lily was jumping down from the Jeep and beginning to chase the girl, wanting to play. When she looked up, the small group of men had dispersed into a semicircle around her car and Juan plus the one of them who looked to be in charge were striding firmly to her side of the vehicle. *"So much for Lily's protection,"* she thought.

The older man, never smiling, came close to her. He had handed his rifle over to one of the others who stood blocking her way should she try to make a run for it. The old man exuded an air of confidence that she could feel; it made the hair on her neck begin to stand. She just sat there passively, not wanting to make any quick move or act aggressively in any way, hoping that she hadn't made a terrible mistake.

Stopping within arm's reach he seemed to look her over a bit longer than she thought it should have taken. Then he said politely, "Buenas tardes, Señora. Juan says that you are sent by Señor Lemon. Is this true?"

She had been expecting this question at some point and had decided that the truth was the best policy. "Not exactly, Señor. I talked with Michael Lemon in Monterey about two months ago. He said that you and your group didn't care very much for strangers of any nationality and that you had thrown him out. I decided that your camp, your band, sounded like a good place for me." Sarah began slowly rubbing her stomach, "As you can no doubt see, I am pregnant, and I wish my son to be born where it is safer than in the U.S. It is no longer safe for either of us there. I wish to join you and bring whatever talents I have to assist you."

The man said, "Please, excuse me, Señora. I have failed to introduce myself to you." He took off his sweat-stained hat and made a slight bow in her direction. "My name is Enrique, and I am nominally in charge of this camp." He waved his arms casually around indicating his realm. "And its people," he finished.

Then he said, "I am glad you told me the truth about Señor Lemon, otherwise we would have had to throw you out too."

Sarah held out her hand, offering it to Enrique. He took it, firmly shook it and released it, never taking his eyes from her face. Sarah said, "My name is Sarah Conner."

Enrique dipped his head toward her and said, "Welcome." And with that, it seems, she was in.

- - -

The physical effort was rewarding. Enrique had assigned a young man, Luis, to supervise our conditioning.

I guess I should mention that the entire camp consisted of about forty-five people (counting seven children). Twenty men and women were old-timers, veterans of the camp. The rest, except for me had been here for a few months and were still trying to fit into the routine. It was this last group that Luis taught how to get into shape. He had been an athlete in Mexico City before he was taken into the Mexican Federal Army, and so he knows a lot about the right way to bring soft civilians into fighting trim. It was only a little harder for me because of my pregnancy, but he relented a little and allowed me a reduced load for now with the promise to make it up to me after I gave birth.

Within a month my new soreness was completely gone, and I had actually gained weight; the good kind I assure you. I felt stronger and more agile and confident. I could see my developing arm and leg muscles and had lost my chronic aching back. John seemed to be developing well too. My stomach was beginning to look like a small beach ball hiding under my shirt and I often felt him kick or turn over during practice.

My Spanish was improving daily. I needed translations less and less frequently as I worked with different groups on different jobs to help support the camp. I had even begun to add words and phrases into my taped messages to John. The tapes were my insurance policy in case I didn't make it through my, or should I say, John's delivery. The tapes would be an invaluable tool for him I thought, and his understanding of Spanish should aid in his survival. At least that was my plan.

I was temporarily exempted from the martial arts training; I don't know which version it was. Yolanda, Enrique's wife, thought that it would be too dangerous for both me and the baby, and her word carries a lot around the camp. However, I was required to watch and practice the moves by myself on a mat. Two or three of the older children liked to move and grunt with me, laughing at the faces I would make as I squatted and thrust my legs around in difficult contortions. I thought that some of the holds looked wickedly vicious and I hoped I would never need to use them. But based on what I knew about our future, I understood better, and resolved to learn and perfect as much as I could. I might have to teach John someday on my own since I couldn't be sure of either the availability of a teacher or the time to study under one.

- - -

The latest Southern California earthquake diverted Ellison's attention from Sarah Conner. He had tried to read everything pertaining to her, but that did not take very long. His personal files contained scrawled notes along the margins and there were a few paper-clipped sheets and photographs added where they seemed appropriate. Now his workload pushed Sarah into the background and back into the cardboard box he lugged around in his house. He was still an FBI agent after all. He had real duties that were beginning to demand more and more of his time. He did not actually forget about her, but he might as well have. He was too tired at night to do much of anything other than keep up with the new missing persons and bank robberies and threats to government officials he had been assigned.

The next time he actively thought about her was when he was doing the summary of his past year for his performance review. He did have a lot to brag about to his boss, even if he could not talk very much about Sarah's case, since he had been summarily pulled off it in that way. Thinking about everything, he resolved to get more involved and to dig a little deeper into her case again. He smiled ruefully. *Lilah wouldn't like that approach very much.* Being an FBI lawyer, she held the official position that what he was doing was certain to be a career killer. They had fought about his seeming pig-headedness about this case for months. It was not the only thing they fought about, but it seemed to be the strongest motivator for their discord. He had even tried to get more involved in his church: he rejoined the choir and volunteered as a youth counselor. He tried to get Lilah involved too, but she claimed that services for an hour or two twice a week were all the time that her career and other commitments would allow. They fought about that too and Ellison realized that he could not make her do something that she did not feel the need to do for herself. Sometimes he really did not understand her.

Ellison reached over to his computer and did a simple search for any new reports of her in the newly established criminal database. Within three minutes he saw that after her disappearance from Monterey she had not been officially heard of again. That by itself did not mean much, but no local, state or federal authority had reported crossing paths with her for more than six months. He thought about that for a little while and realized, *maybe that was because she wasn't where they could see her. Maybe she had slipped across the border somehow.* He did not know how, but stranger things were known to happen. He shook his head thinking, *Sarah could be dead by now for all I know.*

Then his computer dinged a warning, drawing his attention to the screen. Ellison looked on with a dawning, small, puzzled smile. He read there that a clinic doctor in Monterey had mentioned in one of his Medicaid reports that a pregnancy test had been done on an indigent woman named Sarah Conner. It went on that the test result had come back as positive and that she was no longer in his care. The dates were right! This had to be her!

Ellison sat back in his chair. *Well,* he thought, lacing his fingers behind his head and leaning back in his chair, *Sarah has a baby by now. Where could she be hiding so that she can get care? Where did she have the baby? Are there any records of the birth?* These thoughts gave him new places to search, although he could not know that his search would be in vain. He formulated queries and started typing.

Later that night, over supper, he made the mistake of talking about it to Lilah. "I had a little time this afternoon", he began, "so I logged onto the NSFNET to look for any Sarah Conner updates." He looked up suddenly as Lilah slammed her water glass down onto the table hard enough to rattle the saltshaker.

"James, you promised!" she said with an angry pout. "We decided that you were going to forget about all of that Sarah Conner trash and concentrate on your work."

Ellison made little placating gestures with his hands, "Lilah, calm down. I was just trying out the new system. I wanted to see how it worked with a case I knew a little about. I was just looking."

"Bull shit, James! Who do you think you're talking to? I know you like the back of my hand." She was shaking her head as she balled up her napkin, the migraine she had been nursing most of the day was beginning to pound away behind her eyes, making her face draw up and her eyes squint. Tossing the ball into the middle of the table in disgust she said, "So what's new with the Conner bitch? Who has she killed recently?" She stood and began to leave the dining room, not really waiting for a reply.

Feeling anger and shame and concern for her obvious pain he tried to calm her down a little, "Lilah, take it easy. She hasn't been seen for nearly six months, so I don't think she's killed anyone. She's probably out of the country somewhere. But I did read where she was about four-months pregnant when she left."

Lilah stomped out, heading for the bathroom, "Well great for her!" she said bitterly.

Ellison knew that he had said the wrong thing again. Having kids was one of Lilah's power buttons in recent years. When they had first married, they both had wanted lots of children. That had changed a little more than a year ago; at least it had changed for Lilah. Now any mention of starting a family made her migraine headache start to pound. It got so bad recently that he had made her seek medical attention to rule out a brain tumor. It had scared both of them, but the tests turned up nothing out of the ordinary.

- - -

General Larch closed the door to his basement office and flicked on the light switch next to the jamb. The switch did several things: turned on the overhead fluorescent lighting and activated the anti-eavesdropping electronics as a minimum precaution. The door was not as normal as it appeared either. There was a quarter-inch of steel plate armor lining the whole thing with significantly strengthened hinges and latch. He could also activate an electromagnetic lock that would prevent any mortal man from pulling the door open unless he had access to heavy equipment in the narrow hallway outside.

Inside, this "office" of his held other more subtle precautions, waiting for an unwary snooper to stumble into. There were floor pressure switches and ultrasonic motion detectors and even body heat sensors that only his codes could deactivate. His old paranoid habits had been intensified over the past few years. This latest program had an evil stink about it and he still had not been able to ferret out the source of his unease. The destruction of the CIA lab in Utah did not help, since no one had been able to place the blame for that little fiasco, and he hated loose ends. All records had shown that no one out of the ordinary had come or gone from that facility for days on either side of that event. In his mind that meant that it was either an unlucky coincidence or the lab technicians had done something stupid and blown themselves up.

He did not believe in either luck (of either flavor) or in coincidence. That left someone's purposeful sabotage or stupidity. That, at least, he believed in. He knew he could count on the occasional human blunder and the even more remote possibility of one of the brightest and best-screened workers in his employ to happen to go bad occasionally. He was constantly developing tests and strategies to prevent that from happening again.

No, this little thermonuclear catastrophe had to have come from the robot itself. Either it was damaged in some unforeseen way or the act of trying to disassemble it had triggered an unknown (and now unknowable) chain of events leading to the explosion. A special team, outfitted for nuclear accidents, had searched the smoldering hole and found nothing except high levels of radiation once they burrowed below the surface of the crater. One of the largest pieces of his prize was gone forever and that made the remaining pieces that much more valuable to him.

Sitting at his desk and typing in the code to disable the alarms and booby traps, he then typed in the code to allow him to access the rest of his computer links with the outside world. He quickly generated a policy memo to each of the remaining facilities regarding their treatment and handling of their pieces. Extreme caution was the watch word they would all have to work with in the future. He could not afford to lose any more pieces of this machine. *They would have to work longer hours at a more conservative pace, that's all*, he thought. This project was too important to slow down. If anything, he wanted it to accelerate and he did not know if he could get away with more people just now. Without saying anything about the explosion in the desert he worded his memo about the requirement to work additional overtime. He stated that at least thirty percent would be the minimum amount acceptable. He pressed the <Send> key on his computer keyboard. "There," he said with satisfaction. "That ought to help."

* * *

"The initial sounds of shouting coming from the ground floor of the remaining wing of the hospital made all of us panic. It wasn't the first time that roving bands of hoodlums decided to try and raid us for food or drugs. The occasional cracking sound of guns seemed to reinforce our understanding of what was happening. We were all relieved when we saw US Army uniforms threading their way into our hallway from the stairwell." Doctor Silberman paused to catch his breath and take a sip of water.

"Please go on Doctor," the Lieutenant said as he finished taking notes in his little book. "We're very interested in learning what all happened here."

Doctor Silberman nodded his head, "Of course. I agree with that completely." He was practically gushing in his zeal to tell his story and get out of Pescadaro.

"I had finished my supper as usual. I always finished by 6:00 so I could watch the news in the common room before they tucked me in for the night with my bed-time meds. I hated that part because they would lock my door like I was some kind of criminal." His voice rose in indignation, "Me, a great psychiatrist, locked up like a common criminal! That was insane." He tried to draw a deep cleansing breath the way it was taught in his group sessions and he continued at the Lieutenant's little urging motion.

"Louis, the head orderly, was already standing under the television when I reached the common room and he was fiddling with the channel selector, impatiently surfing along. Thinking that he was just looking for the national news I sat off to the side by myself so that I could still see and hear everything but not be too distracted by the other residents.

"Without warning Louis let out a little shout of approval and he walked over to one of the chairs and took a seat. A little confused I asked him, 'That's not the news, is it Louis?'

"Without taking his eyes off the screen, which was now showing a man with a headpiece microphone and a view of some stadium filling with people, he answered, 'No, Doc, it's not.'

"I was growing concerned so I asked him, 'Well, the national news is supposed to be on now. We always watch the national news right after supper, Louis. You know that. And please don't call me Doc. My name is Doctor Silberman. You should call me Doctor Silberman, not Doc. Remember, Louis? We've talked about this before. You know I don't like to be called Doc.'

"He tried to make me think that he didn't hear me, but I knew that I had made myself heard because Louis finally turned away from the screen and looked at me; a little angry I thought. 'Doc', he said, 'just shut up. The game is almost started, and I want to hear it. OK?' He turned away from me and back toward the television.

"'Louis, this is our television', I said, my voice was rising with each sentence, 'we are supposed to be able to watch what we want, not what you want. And please stop calling me Doc!' I was growing angry now. 'Show some respect. My name is Doctor Silberman. You should call me Doctor Silberman.'

"Louis' face was darker than I had seen before when he turned toward me, 'Doc, you're right,' he said. Then with a little smile he stood and faced the rest of the room and raised his voice to a light shout, no doubt trying to intimidate a few of the others. 'Raise your hand if you want to watch Monday Night football instead of the national news.'

"In stunned silence two or three hands slowly went up. From the corner Mel Goldman's ancient voice croaked out, 'Which hand?'

"Louis smirked, 'It doesn't matter.' Then staring directly at me he said, 'Majority wins, Doc. We watch football.' He turned back and sat down. 'If you don't want to watch football, Doc, you should go to your room.'

"He was right. There wasn't much I could do except watch football – which I hate - or go to my room. Standing, I started to head there, muttering as I went, 'My name is Doctor Silberman. Don't call me Doc. Call me Doctor Silberman,' but I knew he couldn't hear me.

"I was about halfway down the long hallway that led to my cell – room is too elegant a word for it – when the floor and the walls started to shake, rattling the metal screens and the glass beyond them. I heard a loud crash from the common room and then I remember a blindingly bright light that made me throw my hand up in front of my eyes. Then I got flipped onto my back as plaster, glass and pieces of wall landed on and all around me. At that point I guess I either passed out or was knocked out. It doesn't really matter which because I can't remember anything until later.

"I don't know how long I was out, but as I came to, I remember hearing moaning and crying noises mixed together with the sounds of sparking electrical wires and smoke detector alarms. I was very confused, and I was having trouble deciding what had happened.

"I tried to roll over but found that my legs were pinned under some of the rubble from the ceiling and interior wall. Pushing myself up into a jack knife position, with my butt in the air, I found myself screaming in pain. My left leg was hurt; perhaps broken just above the ankle judging from the location and intensity of the pain I could feel.

"I found a short length of two-by-four that had apparently fallen out of the ceiling and used it as a temporary crutch so that I could get back to the common room. *Louis would be able to help me*, I remember thinking. I painfully hobbled my way back down the corridor, skirting the rubble that nearly clogged it. Exhausted and sweating from the exertion of dragging my damaged leg behind I finally made it back and looked inside the room's double doors. What I saw made little sense to me: the windows were blown in, the television with the entire ceiling had collapsed onto the linoleum floor pinning two or three people under it and Mr. Goldman sat apparently unharmed in his chair with tears running down his dirty face and his right hand shaking with strain as he continued to hold it up in his vote.

"I called out, trying to be heard over the rest of the background noise, 'Louis! Louis, where are you? Louis help me I'm hurt.' I stopped moving and talking as I suddenly recognized Louis' body slumped in his chair, a red puddle of blood growing under it. It looked like a large piece of glass from the windows had found Louis' neck and had nearly decapitated him. I mumbled, 'Good riddance,' and started back toward the doors. Spotting Mr. Goldman again, I said, 'You can put your arm down, Mr. Goldman. It looks like the voting is over.'"

Silberman had stopped talking again and the Lieutenant poured a little more water into his glass and motioned him to take a sip and continue his story. Silberman was wearing down, but he thought it might be important to tell someone in power what had actually happened here. He took a sip and then continued.

"I mentioned looters before. It's not like I don't understand. I do. But we had to survive too. Isn't that right, sir? When they came the first time or two, the hospital staff decided to give them some of what we had.

They thought it was only fair. But after a while, once it was pretty clear that we were likely to be on our own for a long time, it was decided to not share." Silberman was shaking his head sorrowfully, "That turned out to be a bad decision. After a gang had been rebuffed and sent on their way, they came back with a vengeance."

The memory still haunted him. "That is when they killed the doctor who had saved my life and two of the remaining guards. They took a beating too, but to us it was disastrous. We have been hanging on by a thread ever since. I've been the only trained medical person left here."

Silberman took another sip from his glass. "Piecing together what had happened from various accounts, I now know that this had been what the survivors call 'Judgment Day,' the day that the computers took over the world and tried to kill all of the humans. The flash that had nearly blinded me had been a nuclear missile strike about ten miles away, which is why I'm still here to tell you this. The shock of the blast apparently disturbed a fault line that ran almost directly under the hospital. That release of seismic energy was what shook the building dropping all of that debris on me and everyone else in the hospital. The north wing was destroyed; turned into a heap of smoldering rubble. My wing was greatly damaged, and many of the residents were killed there, but some of us, as you can see, made it through.

"I managed to find my way to the medical ward and got the attention of one of the doctors working on other wounded. I waited my turn – nearly an hour – and once he took a look at my ankle, he shouted for someone to give him a hand with the surgery. He helped me onto a gurney, and I was quickly wheeled into a makeshift surgical theatre; I think it used to be part of the kitchen. I was anesthetized with something and when I woke up several hours later, I was informed that he had been unable to save my left leg below the knee. The sedative he had me on was all that kept me from screaming until my throat ruptured.

"There were dozens in the recovery ward and only the one doctor with two nurses and three orderlies. The care was the best that I could hope for, I guess. After all it was the end of the world; at least for me. They did manage to feed me and help me keep clean and keep me medicated for the pain. The days and nights were long, boring and filled with moaning, awful smells and nightmares whenever I slept. The face of Sarah Conner and what she told me years ago were always reminding me of my stupidity when I dared to close my eyes."

The Lieutenant put his pencil into the fold of his notebook, holding its place. "Did you say Sarah Conner?"

Silberman looked up cautiously, "Yes. Why? Do you know her? Is she here?"

The Lieutenant smiled genuinely for the first time, "I've never met her, but I've heard about her, mostly from some of the resistance leaders who know her son John Conner." He looked positively proud, "She's probably the main reason we're all still alive." He pointed his notebook at Silberman, "Did you actually meet and talk with her?"

Silberman bit back his retort and took a different tack, "Yes, a long time ago; back when I was still practicing. I got to hear her talking about the end of the world and the killer robots called 'terminators' run by a supercomputer called Skynet." He rubbed his chin and watched the Lieutenant's face. "I'm afraid no one believed her at the time."

Lieutenant Johnson nodded his head in agreement, "You've got that right, Doc...excuse me, I mean Doctor." Then Lieutenant Johnson shouted out toward the hallway, "Nichols, find a functional wheelchair and bring it here!"

Silberman grew more excited and hopeful, "Lieutenant, what are you planning to do?"

Lieutenant Johnson said with a sincere smile, "Doctor Silberman you're in the Army now. We certainly need your skills as a doctor and you certainly can't stay here." He raised his hands off the tabletop and shrugged his shoulders, "Seems like a no brainer to me." He offered his hand, "Welcome."

Silberman was frozen in his chair, unsure what he should do. Suddenly Nichols entered with a serviceable wheelchair and that pushed him over the fence. He took Lieutenant Johnson's hand and gave it a pump. "Thanks," he said.

They helped him into his new ride. He suddenly felt like crying.

* * *

I actually felt better than I had in months. Doctor Jackson seemed like a sissy ditz, but maybe his methods weren't completely worthless. Even Loraine had mentioned that I seemed more like my old self.

Well, after all it had been more than a year since the incident. Nothing else had happened; either directly to me or in the news. The Conner woman hadn't appeared anywhere except in my dreams and that seemed to be waning thanks to Jackson. My night terrors had stopped for more than a month and I had been able to sleep through the night for about that same amount of time. Life seemed to be getting back to normal.

After I had briefly talked with that FBI agent, Ellison was his name I recall, the man had left me alone. I really didn't have too much to tell him and based on the number of notes Ellison took he didn't hear very much he didn't know already. I was merely a corroborating witness for a small portion of the story. What actually angered me was that Ellison wouldn't answer any of my questions in any kind of detail. The interview was basically a one-way street; all give on my part and all take on his.

He did tell me, although obliquely, that he had personally seen and handled pieces of something that must have been parts from the killer robot. I got more and more upset until I came to the realization that Ellison was probably the only actual proof I would ever get that I wasn't crazy. There really was something that night that destroyed that police station and killed all those police officers. I hadn't imagined it.

It took two or three sessions with Jackson before I could tell him what Ellison had told me. He took notes and looked at me in a funny way, but I think I convinced him that I hadn't made any of this up. After he saw how much more relaxed I became after telling him about it, I think he started to believe me. I think I'd like to be a fly on the wall in his therapist's office when he tries to talk about my revelations. I'll bet he has a really hard time not sounding crazy himself.

Technical Interlude

Psychology

After Judgment Day (8/24/2007), Skynet reasoned that any surviving humans would quickly go into shock and just as quickly perish. The resulting resistance was unexpected and not understood. Therefore, one of the things Skynet did to help in its understanding of humans and to aid in its domination and continued survival, was to establish a parallel division (program) dedicated to human psychology. This division Skynet called SkynetPsych as it renamed itself SkynetPrime.

The programming developed by SkynetPsych mandated that it digest everything it could find within the entire remaining database network as it began formulating its plan designed to understand humans. It quickly became apparent that not all the information was coherent or germane to its task. Confusing and conflicting studies abounded in the literature and SkynetPsych did not have the experience or self-understanding to sift out what it needed to proceed. SkynetPsych decided to find human help and began its search among captured survivors.

With the professional help of a coerced psychiatrist, SkynetPsych learned that humans typically don't just give up, roll over and die the first time they are challenged. Yes, they have large quantities of psychosis and more than a few misunderstandings and superstitions, but still most of them are stubborn and tough and carry around a strong survival instinct.

Terminator 1+: The Future Is Not Set — Mark T. Sondrini

This psychiatrist counseled that Skynet should develop a cadre of human looking terminators who would infiltrate them and destroy them from the inside. Continuous attack from both without and within by weapons that the human resistance couldn't determine as dangerous until they got very close and suddenly struck them down, would cause chaos in the ranks and destroy the tenuous chain of command. Continuous onslaught of the mechanized warriors would quickly wear them down. Human attrition would eventually swing the tide of numbers onto the side of Skynet because it could replace units much faster than the humans could breed and grow to fighting age.

When this information reached SkynetPrime it deliberated for more than one second and then issued new orders to SkynetResearch to develop such an infiltrating machine. SkynetResearch responded with a plan to design and develop a cyborg based on the T100 chassis with several mechanism and computer improvements and a synthetic skin modeled after several of the larger, surviving prisoners of war. This model would be referred to as the T101.

The initial wave of T101's sent shockwaves through the resistance. Survivors of the initial slaughters quickly brought word of the new Skynet weapon to the nearby pockets of the resistance and soon makeshift detection and defense methods were developed and deployed. As the model T101 became less and less effective, SkynetResearch developed the T800 and then the T888, T1000 and finally the TX.

Chapter 3

Once I got fit, I found that I enjoyed firing weapons. I seemed to have a natural eye and my target scores were usually very good. Enrique had started me with the smaller handguns, moving me slowly through shotguns and into single-shot rifles. If things went well as I progressed to semi-automatic rifles, I might even get a chance to shoot an automatic rifle. But now, I think things had reached their peak for me; I had been bouncing off a brick wall for days. I was trying to master the semiautomatic M-1 Garand rifle and so far, it seemed to be mastering me.

Even with the little wads of cotton stuffed into my ears and practicing every day for the past week, I jumped a little each time the rifle fired and sent its metal load toward the target. I had heard my instructor preach about just holding my breath and squeezing the trigger. He had tried, over and over, to get me to relax and not fight the weapon. If I was pointing it away from myself and holding it firmly, it couldn't and wouldn't hurt me, he was repeatedly saying. I thought that shooting a gun looked easy in the movies; even little kids could do it. I began to doubt whether I could really do it.

Enrique was very patient with me. I'm not sure why. As I emptied the eight-round clip and sat up to gather my wits and reload, he sat down beside me. "Sarah, you are still flinching. The rifle will not bite you. Remember that. Your rifle is your best friend." He patted me on the shoulder as he stood, "Remember, aim with your eyes. Your bullet will follow."

I had mastered the field striping, cleaning and reassembly of the M-1 rifle. It was old, an antique, but much more of a lethal weapon than the little .22-caliber, bolt action I had started with at the camp's target range. Enrique had managed to get six of them several years ago from a dealer in Venezuela along with a few thousand .30-06 rounds. The ten-pound weapon felt good in my hands, quite solid and reassuring, but something about it bothered me. For one thing, its semiautomatic nature made me nervous. For another, the .30-caliber cartridges were a lot more expensive and I was required to gather my brass casings after each practice. I had learned to reload my own and so far, at least there had been no misfires. I had overheard one or two of the "veterans" whispering about how occasionally a reload would explode in the chamber with potentially serious consequences. Maybe that was what was lurking in the back of my mind as I squeezed the trigger. What if the damned thing blew-up in my face?

After pistols, Enrique had brought me up from the simple 12-gauge shotgun (which kicked too hard for my small frame) through the bolt-action .22-caliber rifle (which seemed to me like a toy) compared to the M-1 Garand. After he was satisfied that I could handle that weapon I would get a chance at one of their three M-16's. Through it all, so far at least, I had demonstrated a quick understanding of the mechanics involved with each weapon. I later found out my marksmanship was the primary driver for Enrique's quick push through the series of weapons. I was the best shot, other than himself, that his camp had. He just didn't want to tell me that at this point. He would eventually, but now he did not want me to get self-conscious and start thinking too much about what I was doing.

- - -

They were making progress. Miles Dyson and his team had puzzled out how the circuit board transferred information within the board components and among the chip stacks. Those chips, however, were a different mystery. Four of his team were patiently x-raying and transferring the circuit layer information from one of the die-shaped devices into a CAD program, developing the interrelated logic a line at a time. The only verbiage, other than the power supply connection labels they found, seemed to be Asian (no one on the team could decide if the symbols were Japanese, Korean or Chinese) and one member was doing a separate search for identification.

The scale of the micro-circuits was beyond anything any of them had seen. Thousands of logic gates would seem to fit onto the head of a pin if one were to so choose to try. The layer separation was nearly as small, rendering the circuit density of the cube to the order of tens of millions of gates per chip. All of them were internally connected into some kind of parallel processor with the apparent efficiency of a computer in its own right. Each chip was hermetically sealed and electrically hardened, no doubt, to prevent electromagnetic tampering. The group had to invent new focused x-ray technology to pry open any of its secrets. They had already applied for the patents to protect that bit of engineering magic and it was expected that the royalties from that work alone would almost pay for everything else.

Miles left his office and walked out onto the open floor of the lab. He was specifically looking for Andrew Goode who was working on the weekly summary report.

Miles was looking around the wide, well-lit space and saw Andrew perched onto the desk of one of the younger female engineers. He headed in their direction. He walked along the main aisle that split the one-hundred-foot-wide by two-hundred-foot-long office level of the building. He reached the central bisector and turned left.

"Andrew, have you finished my Technology Summary yet? I have to send it off in less than an hour." Miles was trying to look sterner than he felt. Their work was the most exciting thing that any of them had encountered in their professional lives. These days, even he found himself drifting around with a dreamy smile on his face. It was difficult to keep their minds channeled along the straight and narrow, but it was his primary job to try. It was that part about being the Director that he disliked the most.

Startled, Andrew practically fell off the desk. "Sure, Director Dyson, I'll bring it right away." He had begun to blush. "I was just getting the last part of Lynn's findings," he finished a little awkwardly as he turned to go back to his cubicle.

"See that you do, Andrew." Miles said while watching his hurrying scramble. Miles turned to look over at Lynn. "Did you find anything interesting?"

She smiled broadly making Miles understand why Andrew was so attracted to her. She said, "Well, yes. Actually, I was telling Andy about our latest breakthrough with the form of the logic circuits. We think they might be military in nature." She frowned a little, "Andy acted as though he already knew about that, so he must have been collating information while he was doing your report." She locked eyes with Miles. "The two of you are the only ones, who actually get to see the total picture, aren't you?"

It was Miles' turn to frown a little. "No, actually, only I have the entire picture. Andrew is only gisting one phase of our research. There are three others doing the same thing in other areas. I get to put all of that into one report for the boss' summary report." His frown deepened a little, "So unless Andrew ... Andy is talking with the other three," now he was looking concerned, "he shouldn't be able to put everything together."

Miles started rubbing his chin as he thought about that possibility. He turned and headed back to his office and he could be heard to mumble, "I'll have to look into that possibility."

Lynn said a little louder than she had intended, "I hope I didn't get Andy into trouble." Then more softly so that only she could hear, "I like Andy. But, it's not fair that he knows something that I don't."

- - -

Silberman felt bored with his work. He did not think working for the police was his cup of tea, but his stable of whining housewives and adulterous businessmen were quickly wearing him down to a nubbin. He was barely listening to Mrs. Clockner ramble, doodling in his notebook, pretending to make notes, when his clock chimed, signifying the end of her session. He dutifully went through the motions of closing and then leading her to the door. She wanted to confirm for this Friday and Silberman told her to check with his receptionist, Loraine. As he opened the office door he saw that there was a strange, black man setting aside one of his old magazines and looking at him.

He stopped in the doorway and suddenly he remembered the FBI agent, Ellis or Allison or something like that. He swallowed and tried to smile as he waved him into his office. Loraine just watched until Ellison reached the door and then she turned to Mrs. Clockner. Silberman's door cut off any sounds between the two rooms as it closed.

Ellison handed over his card and reached out to shake hands, "Doctor Silberman, my name is Agent James Ellison in case you have forgotten."

Silberman looked at Ellison's hand and decided to shake it. "I remember, Agent." Then walking around to his chair, he said, "To what do I owe this honor?" He motioned toward a chair.

Ellison sat and arranged his legs, "I felt that since it has been a little while since we last spoke, Doctor, perhaps you have had an opportunity to think of something else from that night when you met Sarah Conner and her boyfriend, Kyle Reese." He spoke and acted in a very calm manner, but Silberman's long experience cued him to Ellison's underlying tension.

He answered, "I'm sorry, Agent Ellison, but I'm afraid not." He saw the moment's disappointment flash across Ellison's face. "Really nothing beyond what I shared with you earlier."

Then for some reason he blurted out, "I've begun therapy, you know?"

Ellison appeared genuinely surprised, "Really, Doctor? I had no idea that psychiatrists ever needed to do that." Then seemingly in embarrassment he added, "It is helping you I hope."

Silberman answered honestly, "Actually it has helped a little. I've been able to sleep a little better since I've begun, and I no longer jump at unexpected noises."

He smiled, "I have a better understanding of the benefits of my profession."

"That's very good Doctor." Ellison leaned forward a little in his chair, "Had you heard that Sarah has disappeared? I believe she has actually left California for the wilds of Mexico, but I can't prove it."

Silberman looked almost interested, "She's running, you think?"

Ellison was nodding, "Most assuredly. She's not taking any chances, I believe." He watched carefully, "Were you aware that she was pregnant?"

Silberman dropped the pen he had been fiddling with. "You don't say! How interesting." Scrunching up his face he asked, "Do you know when she's due?"

Ellison answered as Silberman's alarm sounded, "Soon, as near as I can tell." He stood, "Well, Doctor, thanks for your time." He reached out to shake again, "If you think of anything or hear of anything regarding Sarah Conner, I'd appreciate hearing from you."

Silberman had risen from his seat and Ellison said, "I'll show myself out, Doctor. Thank you, again."

Silberman sat again and wondered about Sarah and her baby. He remembered how Kyle insisted that she would bring Humanity's savior from the evil computer, Skynet, into the world. He started to sweat, and he pulled out his appointment book and searched for the time of his next session with Jackson.

There was a soft knocking at his door and Loraine stuck her head in, "Doctor, your three o'clock is here."

- - -

The weapon classes, target practice and cartridge reloading were usually held during the heat of midday when we didn't want to be too physical. The kids usually slept then, and I learned a lot.

About this time Enrique's wife Yolanda began coaching me for my future delivery of John. She was an experienced midwife and knew about neonatal exercises, nutrition and instruction. As this was my first time, I was appreciative of having someone around who knew what to expect. Yolanda had volunteered one of the other girls to help and everything was ready for the delivery.

Sooner than I had imagined, John came kicking and screaming, fighting as though he knew, somehow, what was in his future. Otherwise he seemed healthy and nearly perfect to me. The delivery was comparably easy and uneventful, I'm told. Yolanda was on the catching end of the exercise and knew what she was doing. She was fond of saying, "No problemo," and she said that then. I was safely a mother of a baby boy named John Conner. Yolanda and Enrique acted like proud grandparents.

I felt that there must have been problems. I thought that John had split me from stem to stern; I was convinced that I must be bleeding to death where I lay. But as Yolanda settled the freshly washed baby John, wrapped in a clean blanket, onto my quivering chest, I quickly forgot everything except his beautiful smell and softness.

He made it Kyle, I thought through my tears. *He made it and he's perfect.*

She breathed a soft sigh of relief: One more thing that Skynet had tried to prevent had been accomplished. She went to sleep hugging him close.

Yolanda waited for a few seconds to assure that Sarah was asleep and then gently took John Conner and placed him into a waiting crib made up from an old mattress on the floor and two pillowcases filled with desert sand along the sides. She looked down on the sleeping baby and smiled. He was pretty. Sarah should be proud. Making a soft kissing sound Yolanda stirred Lily from her place in the corner by John's pallet and led her outside, away from her sleeping patients.

- - -

Agent Ellison was concentrating on the files in front of him on his desktop. He sensed someone watching well before he looked up. When he did the two detectives with their clipped-on visitor's badges seemed to be patiently waiting for him to acknowledge them and invite them into his office. He saw their impatience though, in their faces and in their posture.

Ellison waved them in, "Detectives, this is a surprise. To what do I owe this honor?" Ellison stood at his desk and reached across to shake hands with each man, a little surprised that they complied.

Frowning Detective Roberts looked at Ellison and said without preamble, "Why'd you let her go? You had her and you just let her go!"

Ellison smiled calmly and said, "Please, sit, detectives." He indicated the chairs in front of his desk and waited until they sat. "Actually, I didn't let her go." He tried to appear calmer than he felt, "Actually, she escaped, just like she did from the hospital. Remember the hospital?"

Detective Jenkins interrupted a sputtering Roberts, "Agent Ellison, you know that wasn't our fault. We had her under twenty-four-hour police protection."

Ellison smiled brightly, "My point exactly. She escaped." He held out his hands, "She seems to be very good at escaping. Her timing is flawless."

This time it was Ellison's turn to frown, "Her instincts are perfect or else she has access to information that she shouldn't have." Here his frown deepened, "If someone is helping her, I can't find them. I've tried."

Roberts asked, "Who would help her? The only people we could link to her are dead. Even the cops who initially picked her up are dead."

Ellison was nodding, "You're absolutely right, I've checked out all of her possible contacts, including the police psychologist, Silberman. She's completely on her own. She escaped from a killer robot at least three times that we know of. She escaped from the hospital and LA when everyone, local, State and Federal, was watching. Then after hiding out almost invisibly in Monterey for four months she escapes an organized, pre-dawn dragnet in Carmel and disappears again. She's very smart and resourceful and not afraid to cut and run."

Both detectives had been nodding their heads as Ellison ticked off the litany of their failures. Roberts looked up suddenly, "That reminds me. What happened to those robot pieces you took from me?"

It was Ellison's turn to look embarrassed. "Some very large, quiet men took them away from me." He paused as they recovered from their shock. "I wouldn't be surprised if they are scattered around the country by now being torn apart by military lab specialists."

Roberts jerked upright, "Holy crap! Do you know who they were?"

Ellison was shaking his head, "Not exactly. But I was forced off the case from the top." He leaned over and opened one of his lower desk drawers and extracted a thin file. "Officially the parts don't exist, and I cannot do anything to actually track her down. But I did manage to find out something potentially useful." He paused and then asked, "Had you found out that she was pregnant?"

Roberts just whistled.

Jenkins said, "No shit?"

Ellison said, "Yeah, I thought that was interesting too. As near as I can figure, the dead guy, Kyle Reese, was probably the father. But there isn't any way to know for sure." He looked slyly at his guests, "I tried, you know."

Roberts and Jenkins looked at each other and then at Ellison. Jenkins asked, "How could you possibly find that out?"

Ellison told them, "I recovered the DNA results from the hospital lab and then matched it with the blood samples that the Monterey doctor had taken. That matched exactly with Sarah Conner and I knew that we had her. Next I tried to get the DNA from Reese but found that he had been cremated and buried and the experts told me I was out of luck. Even the blood samples taken at the scene and logged into your evidence room have disappeared or at least been misplaced."

Once again, the two detectives looked stunned.

He shrugged his shoulders. "The timing is about right though. Unless she was pregnant before the first robot attack, which I suppose was possible, Reese should be the father. She was calling herself Sarah Reese in Carmel, for what that's worth." He looked over at them, "I couldn't find anything about him either. No fingerprints, IRS, criminal or military records, no Social, nothing. It's as if he dropped in as quickly as he dropped out."

Roberts whistled again.

Ellison said, "Oh, by the way. If you can count, she most likely had the kid by now. The doctor said that when he told her the news, she was convinced that it would be a boy. She even had already picked out a name. John Conner."

- - -

Lt. Colonel Brewster was organizing his department into several divisions: one for the software and control systems; one into ground troop augmentation and support; one for drone air support. Each division had as many resources as they needed (or at least could justify). Brewster oversaw everything, but the software system was his pet and he was paying special attention to that one.

The ground effort was shaping up to be a treaded vehicle somewhat like the ubiquitous bomb robot that every major city police force had in its arsenal, but with several significant differences.

First it was going to be much larger because it was going to have a lot more motive power and range. The small diesel engine driving the battery charging system and the hydraulic pumps coupled with the fuel tank necessary for several hours operation took a lot of room. Second, it had to have more firepower; currently a .30-caliber Gatling gun was the leading choice for its primary weapon. Some of the development crew were lobbying for a bank of small missiles, but he had not signed off on that idea yet. Third, its vision and sensing systems had to be the best available; infrared, short-range radar, ultra and infrasonic targeting as well as motion detection, pressure and temperature measurement were all included. Fourth, and possibly the most important feature, was control independence;

his specialty and pet part of the project. He felt that some style of satellite location and guidance would be involved and the current systems available required an operator interface; something he was hoping to avoid.

Then the whole thing had to be battle hardened; physically as well as electronically. It was already a monumental task, one that would tie up Air Force and other secret government resources for years.

The air support drone started out as something a little simpler. Soon however it grew like Toppsy. It seemed that at every brain storming session they had added a new feature or had proposed a new possible weapon system. The design grew larger and more awkward and cumbersome (read expensive) by the week.

Now the design could not only fly like a normal plane, but it could rotate its large engine nacelles through nearly one hundred and eighty degrees at the end of its stubby wings. That allowed it VTOL like a helicopter, horizontal flight like a jet and the ability to literally reverse thrust and nearly stop on a dime. That capability alone made remote flight control nearly impossible. It would most likely fly like a poorly aimed brick! They would have to do extensive computer modeling first. Then scale modeling in the wind tunnel at Edwards, followed by several prototypes flown by Air Force test pilots. By then, the onboard control computer systems should be ready to install and test. It would take years.

The weapon systems were to consist of two .50-caliber machine guns, a missile pod with nine air-to-air or air-to-ground rockets, a full countermeasures suit and a prototype, one hundred-watt, laser cannon. It would carry the best radars, video cameras, communication gear including satellite navigation and location circuits along with one of the new computer systems, making it completely independent to follow its mission. Those systems weighed-in at over one and one-half tons and the airframe had to be strong enough to hold together while the engines tossed everything around in the sky at up to five g's. It was a daunting task and everyone on the team was positively salivating at the opportunity.

During one of the late-night sessions someone (Brewster could not remember who) thought that giving it the ability to fly underwater would be cool. After the laughter died down, he began to wonder if a Navy application could be made functional. His mind started envisioning an autonomous robotic alligator capable of surface as well as submersible propulsion. It might be worth a call or two to the Pentagon, but he doubted its viability. He thought that the Navy did not normally go in for automated, crewless vessels and this technology, as advanced as it appeared, wasn't likely to change their mind.

* * *

They had seen too much action for too long. Doctor Silberman and the two corpsmen that were his assistants rarely left the surgery level of the parking tower that their band called home. Sorties mandated by circumstances and need as well as reconnaissance required by the officers leading their area of the resistance had taken a heavy toll. They had been working for several days straight. A dozen had been killed and another twenty wounded in just this past week. Lt. Johnson did not like the losses, but he had been heard to comment to his Gunnery Sergeant that the Skynet supply depot that they had destroyed along with ten T100's and two treaded monstrosities called T1's had made his company's losses acceptable. The two large Gatling guns that they had captured along with twenty boxes of belted rounds only sweetened the pot; they still had to find a way to mount those guns effectively.

Silberman was the only actual doctor that Lt. Johnson's company had, and he took his new job very seriously. He figured that the company's survival was strongly linked to his own. After cleaning up from last night's carnage, Silberman found himself knocking on Lt. Johnson's office door (actually an old bookcase that held up the blanket that closed off his little space from the rest of the third floor of the tower). Dutifully he waited until he heard Lt. Johnson call, "Enter."

Dragging the blanket aside with one hand he rolled himself into the cramped space beyond and faced Lt. Johnson. "Sir," he began, "if I might have a word with you?"

Lt. Johnson looked up from a tattered paper report he had been reading and asked, "What's on your mind, Doctor. How are things in the ward?"

Silberman rolled his chair right up to the Lt.'s bunk and set his hand brake, intending to show that he planned to stay right there in front of him until he had his say. "That's actually what I wanted to talk about. The ward is quite full, as I'm sure you know. But what you might not know is that I and the rest of the medical staff, a total of the three of us, are bone tired. We can't keep up with the number of casualties you keep bringing us. You get them wounded faster than we can patch them up and it can't go on much longer before it will be more dangerous in my ward than facing Skynet."

Lt. Johnson looked annoyed at Silberman's outburst. He answered, "Doctor, I'm sorry, but this is really outside your authority. There's nothing I can do about what you're saying, even if it's true. Which I'm sure it is. We get our orders just like all the rest of the forces and we get to try to carry them out to the best of our capabilities just like all the rest of the forces."

He looked tired, but he still maintained that look of command. He finished, "Doctor, we are fighting a very determined enemy. One that has weapons and resources we can only dream about." He was shaking his head, "We are fighting for our very survival, I'm sure you realize. We don't have the luxury of picking and choosing our times and places to fight." He waved his report around in little circles, "When we get orders to go somewhere to fight Skynet, we pick up our puny weapons and we go there and follow orders and try to fight Skynet. It doesn't matter if we are tired; we just do it."

Silberman was thinking that it did not sound very fair to him and he was about to say so when there was a rattle of gunfire about a block away. The shooting was quickly followed by several explosions and then shouting started from just outside the tower. High explosive rocked the far corner of the tower and the scream of a Hunter-Killer wined passed overhead.

Silberman was surprised, but Lt. Johnson looked positively energized as he practically jumped from his rack and ran out of his office, grabbing his M-16 and helmet as he passed the bookcase. Silberman tried to turn his wheelchair to follow, but he was stalled for a few seconds until he remembered the brake and released it. Rolling out into the main corridor all he could see was five or six men scrambling into the stairwell, fastening armor and tugging on helmet straps. By the time he made it down two levels of the tower, the sounds of heavy fighting were very close. He decided that he really could not help with that and he turned his chair and rolled over to the entrance to the ward where he thought he might be able to do some good for those of his men that might be brought into his care.

He negotiated his way to the ward and hurried through the doorway. He let out a yelp of surprise as Thomas, one of his corpsmen, shoved a pistol into his face before he realized who he was.

"Holy shit, Doc I almost shot you!" Thomas yelled. "What's going on?"

Recovering his sense of purpose, Silberman growled through his teeth, "I think we're under attack. And don't call me Doc!

"Get ready for wounded you two," he shouted so that he would be sure to be heard over the sounds of fighting outside. Fredricks, the other corpsman, looked like he had just been roused from a very deep sleep and he still looked disoriented.

Silberman waited until they began preparing gurneys and combat medical supplies before he rolled over to the section of the ward that served as the ICU. He hoped that his patients were all still asleep, but he found all except two of the most seriously hurt and therefore the most heavily sedated, awake and agitated; indeed, three were trying to get up out of bed.

"Hey! Stop! Get back in bed!" he yelled. "You men are out of action right now. Let the rest of your company resolve this crisis."

As insulated as the ward was from the outside, the terrible sounds of pitched battle reached them easily. Skynet's forces were quickly, inexorably working their way closer to the tower. From what he heard outside and based on the little he had learned about military tactics since he came here, he could tell that Skynet knew exactly where they were and what kind of strength they had and how to wipe them all out. He suddenly realized that this was most likely his end.

Three or four rapid explosions near the main entrance of the parking tower were followed by the unmistakable sounds of multiple Gatling guns very close-by, echoing in the concrete enclosure. By the time he had turned away from his patients and rolled back to the entrance to the surgery, he heard shots coming from there and the sounds of his aids dying. Frozen where he sat, almost completely defenseless, Silberman waited his fate in terror, the sudden recall of his old nightmares locking him into a panic-driven, near catatonic state.

He watched as two metal monsters, T100's he knew they were called, both brandishing smoking Gatling guns with trailing strings of cartridges, entered his ICU. They both glanced at him, but quickly dismissed him, and then looked in the direction of the wounded soldiers. They opened fire and almost instantly cut all the men in half where they lay.

The sounds of the Gatling guns next to his head nearly ruptured his eardrums and they caused him to hunker-down into his chair for its perceived protection. When the echoes stopped, he cautiously peeked up at the now silent assailants, praying that they were just figments of his tired mind. When he saw that they were both staring at him and his wheelchair, he fainted.

Technical Interlude

Materials

It is intuitively obvious that Skynet would have to build its army of foot soldiers from something a little stronger than simple steel. Steel, although blessed with many good attributes since its discovery in the 11th century BC, is still limited in some respects and has been replaced by various alloys and some completely different metals, depending on the specific application. Spring steels, high-hardening tool steels, stainless steels and wear resistant steels were man's attempts to solve problems that were not resolvable by simple carbon steel's chemistry and physical constraints. Increasing amounts of carbon and additions of manganese, vanadium, chromium, nickel, sulfur, tungsten, cobalt and lead in various proportions and combinations mixed into the solution of the basic iron made hundreds of varieties of steels as it cooled and crystallized. Heat treating, forging or work hardening, casting and surface plating techniques multiplied the ultimate range of finished steels into the hundreds.

Still, Skynet knew that something else was needed to give it ground superiority. Initially the T100s were made of hardenable, magnetic, stainless steel: a metal called 420C. This was initially successful. Then as the human resistance became more organized, the losses became unacceptable and SkynetPrime ordered SkynetResearch to come up with a better, more durable metal. Studies by the time travel division showed that a non-magnetic endoskeleton for its proposed T101 series would improve reliability and accuracy of the jump.

Terminator 1+: The Future Is Not Set — Mark T. Sondrini

Titanium was chosen for its many useful properties and until it was discovered that the lower mass ratio of the T101's was actually a detriment on the battlefield, thousands of T101s were built and placed into service. Eventually the T101 was relegated to infiltration only, where its lack of weight was less of a problem.

The T800 series began using an alloy of titanium based on coltan. A newly discovered metal, mined in the Congo from nearly depleted, deep pit, diamond mines, starting in 1993. Coltan was rare and difficult to extract. It worked by generating micro plates or lamina within the crystal structure of the titanium giving the finished metal greater density as well as great strength and temperature resistance. This metal was non-magnetic and practically inert to biological agents. Battle chassis built from this coltan alloy were nearly indestructible and coltan would be the material of choice throughout the entire T800 series, even as far as the T888 models.

SkynetResearch discovered that some alloys exhibited memory and others demonstrated room temperature fluidity. It worked to develop an alloy that combined both characteristics. The result was the liquid memory-metal it called memimetic polyalloy used in the T1000 prototype series and then used as a basis for the TX models.

This liquid memory metal had amazing characteristics. It could be made to flow through narrow spaces yet with sufficient electromagnetic urging it could hold its shape tightly enough to become a simple weapon, e.g. a knife or spear or cudgel or hook. Controlled by its sophisticated new computer system which took the phrase "distributed networking" to new heights, the T1000 could mimic the look and other features of almost any object it could touch, whether alive or inanimate, by adjusting its reflectance and its overall shape. The solidified liquid could be given the density of stainless steel and the hardness of tool steel with the application of enough energy from the T1000's power supply. A detached piece of the metal would attempt to work its way back to the main body if they were in close enough proximity.

The primary difference between the T1000 and the TX was that the TX models used an endoskeleton of coltan alloy while the T1000 used no endoskeleton at all. The power supply and computer with its control modules were the only solid components that would impede a T1000 from flowing through a keyhole.

At the time of SkynetPrime's waning superiority, SkynetResearch was working on more advanced metals that were based on nanotechnology. The robotic entities planned with this metal were to be in the TZ series and be like the TX series but without the need for a rigid endoskeleton.

Chapter 4

I mentioned that Luis initially gave me a break from conditioning and hand-to-hand combat training during my pregnancy. Well, that young man started making up for lost time. As tired as I was after the delivery, less than two weeks passed before he beckoned me outside with the words, "Senora Sarah, change your clothes please to something comfortable. Meet me at the practice mats."

I looked at Yolanda and asked, "Is he serious?" I didn't know what to think.

She was nodding her head, "Si, Sarah. It is time for you to get back your strength." I must have been frowning because she continued, "You heard him! Go! I will watch baby John Conner."

I changed and walked across the compound. The sun was half-way up in the morning sky and it was still relatively cool; for Baja at least. Luis was waiting for me, with two other women, on the practice mats. Everyone was dressed in scruffy tee shirts and jeans; we would be getting down on the ground and rolling around after all. I waved and smiled at them all. Everyone but Luis smiled back at me.

We began with stretches and it was quickly apparent to me that I had gotten soft in two short weeks. Luis picked up the pace and we began calisthenics. I was sweating and out of breath almost immediately. Luis now began smiling. He knew he had my attention.

We took a short break and drank some water while he explained that we were going to pair off and he was going to show me several fighting moves. I tried to picture in my mind what he was talking about and was able to recall scenes from before my delivery. I was finally going to get into the heart of hand-to-hand combat. I remembered grunting as I watched the trainees several months ago; making the kids that seemed to always hang around me laugh. Now I began grunting in earnest as I tried to follow Luis' instructions. I recalled that it looked violent and it turns out that it is. I recalled that it looked like something I hoped I would never have to use on another human.

- - -

Miles Dyson was not looking forward to today's meeting. He knew that he couldn't avoid it, but that didn't make him like it. It had been nearly six months since he had been given the chip and the arm and his own research facility. Six-month personal updates in front of the brass seemed like a small price to pay for all of that. He looked at his watch and sighed. It was time.

He trotted down the fire stairs rather than take the elevator. He thought the exercise would get his blood flowing and make him more alert. He opened the fire door with a rush, causing several large, scary bodyguards to quickly turn in his direction as they reached for the bulges under their jackets. He assumed that they were reaching for guns and he hated the thought of them in his building.

Miles tried to act calm as he resumed his walk toward the conference room, now sure that his superiors were waiting for him inside. He reached the door and just twisted the knob and entered. After all, he was the star of the show. They were here to hear what he had to say.

Uncomfortable at the feeling of seven pairs of eyes, make that six pairs plus one since "The General" and his patch were among those in attendance, Miles hurried to his chair at the foot of the table. General

Larch sat at its head. "It was good of you to join us, Dyson," he said.

Larch now appeared to be waiting so Miles began. "Gentlemen, I believe I have good news for you."

Larch interrupted, "Please let us be the judge of the quality of your news."

Miles nodded, accepting the rebuke calmly, "Of course, sir." He then opened the folder he had carried into the meeting, extracted a thin sheaf of stapled paper pages and passed it around, each man eagerly taking a document as he passed on the remainder. As the last man received his paper, Miles began, "We have managed to break the hardest part of the ancillary computer system's protocols." Referring to the document with his finger he said, "If you jump to the paragraph below the summary you will read what we have been able to do with the arm and the chips you gave us." Miles thought it was wise to let them know that he knew who had given him this opportunity in the first place.

"We are able to monitor the sensory inputs and see where they go once they enter the first chip; it seems to function as a central clearing house for the arm." He looked up briefly to gage their reaction and then continued, "The signals branch out from there, depending on their type, and then go into other, more appropriate chips."

He was interrupted at this point by Larch, "What do you mean by 'type'?" The old man's eye was boring a hole in Miles' head it seemed, perhaps trying to make it easier to extract information.

Miles answered, "Sir, by type I mean tactile, thermal, force, position in six degrees of freedom, feedback from all of the joints using piezoelectric biaxial accelerometers, and even chemical sensors that are located in the arm and hand. All of that data is sorted it seems and then sent on for processing, evaluation and reaction." He looked up once more and said, "It is very sophisticated programming in some very sophisticated hardware; the accelerometers for example do not exist in any of the literature I could find. But I'm sure that you already knew that this equipment was ahead of what we so cavalierly call 'leading edge technology.'"

Larch did not look too impressed, "Yes, doctor, we were quite aware of the device's complexity and sophistication. We were hoping that you and your team would have provided more insight than that by now." He paused for a tense breath, "It has been almost six months since you began your research with our robotic pieces."

With his throat shutting down, Miles forced down a sip of water before trying to reply. "Gentlemen, with all due respect, this is not like hooking up your component stereo system without the benefit of directions. This technology is so advanced that the brightest electronic engineers available in this country are still mostly baffled by this thing. There is no road map or instruction manual available" He was looking around the table pleadingly, "Couple that with the pressure to not destroy anything and you must see how we must proceed slowly and deliberately."

Director Cole started to rebuke Dyson, but Larch stopped him with a chopping motion of his hand. "Doctor Dyson, of course you are exactly correct. We apologize for giving you the wrong impression."

Larch seemed to be smiling at Miles; it was difficult to tell since he might just as well have been preparing to bite him. "We are very anxious to learn everything there is to know about our device while at the same time keeping it intact."

Miles relaxed a little. "Thank you, sir. I appreciate your continued patience and support."

Continuing Miles said, "Our mechanical engineers have developed a detailed plan for the structure of the arm and hand." He looked up once again, "They tell me that they could probably build the arm and hand, but they would have to design and build the specialized machinery first and they would need a source of the metal alloy too." He tapped on the report, "As I mentioned here, we can't get this alloy yet. We are working with a specialized steel supplier in Germany, but we have to be circumspect about what we tell them."

Turning the page Miles continued, "On a positive note, we have been granted the patent for our microscopic x-ray scanner and have been approached by a Japanese chip manufacturer for the rights to make and sell the device to electronics companies worldwide." He looked up from the report, "Obviously I would need your approval to do so." He smiled, "It seems like a pretty good deal to me, but it is your call."

Larch's eye polled the table, but he did not offer an answer.

After waiting as long as he felt prudent, Miles flipped the report over on the table in front of him and he eyed them each in turn, "Is there anything else you need from me? Are there any questions?"

General Larch stared at him, "Doctor Dyson, I think I speak for everyone here when I say thank you for your efforts to date. But, that said, we wish to emphasize our sense of urgency in completing your task. I must remind you that the clock is ticking, and we are most likely not the only ones looking into this problem. However, we must be first with the solution!"

Miles nodded, "Yes, sir. I understand. I will continue to devote all of the many resources you have provided me in a dedicated effort to succeed as soon as possible."

Larch nodded his head in dismissal and Miles took the hint and gathered his folder and its remaining papers together and stood to leave. He took one last look around the table and turned to the door. Outside the burly guards seemed to watch his every move as he walked to the elevator and waited for the car to come. He could feel their eyes even after the door closed and the car began to descend. As it moved downward, he began to feel a little relief and he ran his hand over his forehead, wiping away the sweat that had accumulated there. Maybe it was over for another six months. At least he hoped so.

- - -

I could hardly move. The training Luis was administering to me was what I needed, but my body was unprepared for it. I seemed to hurt everywhere, especially my hands. My hands and forearms were scuffed and bruised from delivering and blocking blows with Luis, despite the thin gloves and wrappings we wore to help protect ourselves.

Lily was watching me from her usual place next to John's bed. Her eyes seemed to reproach me for leaving Baby John for so long. Her head came up off the floor as I moaned from my difficulties getting out of the chair I had collapsed into earlier.

"It's OK, Lily. I'm just sore."

Lily rested her head again and snorted her distaste for my strange behavior. I smiled at her and headed for the shower. "Watch John, OK?"

Standing under the shower with the cool, smelly water rinsing the soap out of my hair, I didn't hear any part of the commotion outside. Lily barked once and that got my attention. By the time I finished rinsing the soap and turned off the water, I could hear shouting from five or six people. It sounded like someone was hurt.

Pulling my shirt over my damp hair and sawing it over my back and shoulders I slipped on my boots and hurried out the door. Lily rushed past me nearly knocking me over as she forced her way between my legs and the trailer door. Grabbing the door jamb, I looked back and saw that John was still sleeping. The urgent calls from the near distance drew my attention again and I remember wondering where Yolanda was.

She turned out to be in the center of the growing knot of people, all of whom were waving their arms around and talking loudly. As I got closer, I heard someone shout, "¡Luna muerta!", or "Luna is dead!"

I looked for Enrique or Yolanda to confirm this terrible news of their daughter's death. Enrique was nowhere to be seen, but Yolanda was the distraught center of attention less than five feet away. I shouldered my way to her and tried to remain calm, "Yolanda, what is happening?" I tried to insulate her from the rest of the questions. I grabbed her face between my hands and shouted to be heard over the crowd. "Yolanda! Look at me!"

With tears streaming and chest heaving she said, "¡Salvaje perro! The wild dogs caught her. She is gone."

I looked around at each face. "Where is Enrique? Which way did they go?"

Someone pointed northeast into the desert wastes, and I saw Lily running in that direction with her nose working just above the sand. I sprinted to the weapons trailer, found my M-1 Garand and two clips and hurried after Lily. I didn't think of my Jeep until much later.

The soreness forgotten, I ran as fast as if a terminator was right behind me. I was able to initially follow Lily's direction and tracks, but soon I saw boot tracks mixed in. Then, after nearly five minutes of hard running I heard growling and shouting from over the next rise. Panting in the evening heat I worked my way up the slope through the small sand rills that had accumulated on the lee side.

I reached the crest and squinted into the growing dimness of the far side of the hill. I saw Enrique and Lily doing battle with five largish dogs and three smaller ones. Enrique apparently hadn't taken the time to arm himself before he followed the dogs and he was outclassed by the three currently attacking him. They circled just out of reach of his knife looking for openings in his defensive motions.

Wasting no time calling out I dropped down onto the sand, wrapped the strap around my left arm and began adjusting my rifle's sight. I was breathing deeply trying to recover from my run and climb. By the time I had set up for the shot, snapped in a clip and cranked in the first round, I thought I had my breathing under control.

I could see that the two dogs that had Luna were trying to drag her body up the next hill and I decided to go for the three harrying Enrique first. My logic was that he was much closer to Luna and if he could, he would get to her well before I could. As I thought this, one of the dogs fastened on Enrique's arm and attempted to pull him down. The other two settled in for the kill and I realized I was out of time.

Taking a deep breath and letting half of it out I lined up the ball with the notch as I had been taught and without thinking any more about it, I squeezed the trigger and killed the dog on Enrique's arm. Swinging the muzzle of the M-1 to the right I sighted and then shot again. Before the report had reflected back to me from the first shot, I had fired a third round, killing the third large dog.

The sound of the large rifle and the cessation of sound from the large dogs must have been enough for the rest of them because they quickly broke-off and ran, even the ones pulling on Luna. I tried to shoot at least one more, but a running target is much more difficult to hit, and I missed.

Enrique staggered up the sandy hillside and picked up his daughter. Lily had given chase over the hill. Discovering my soreness again as the adrenaline began to ebb, I climbed up from where I had lay and began trudging down the hill toward Enrique and poor Luna. *At least those mongrels didn't get her body*, I thought sadly.

With my ears still ringing from the shooting I couldn't hear much more than Enrique's wailing. I could see him cradling her in his arms and rocking back and forth and I didn't know how I was going to deal with the child's loss and Enrique's grief; she was just like a daughter to me too. As I got closer, I thought I heard a small voice crying too. Then I saw her arms move around her father's neck and I realized that she was alive.

Enrique turned toward me and said, "Gracias, Thank you." He was smiling through his tears and hugging Luna very close.

About that time Lily came over the hill and trotted in a self-satisfied way down to us. She had helped save

Luna and I think she knew it. Reaching Luna and Enrique she took a sniff and accepting a ruffling of her fur from him she came over and sat next to me. I put my arm around her and crooned, "Good girl. You were brave too." Lily licked my cheek and barked her appreciation.

"Enrique is she well enough to carry out of here?" I asked. "Do you want me to go back and get a car for her?"

He was shaking his head, "No my little hero. I will carry her back. It is not too far for me." He stood, "You will walk back with me, yes? You and Lily and your rifle?"

I nodded, "Of course, Enrique."

Lily barked her agreement to the arrangement.

Enrique gathered Luna up and she clasped her arms tightly around his neck and moaned a little as she pressed some of her damaged parts against him. "Papa," she said softly, "the dogs hurt me."

Enrique was soothing her back, "Yes, my angel. But they will not hurt you anymore."

As we reached the top of the hill where I had made my shots, Enrique turned to look back. The dead dogs were just visible in the dimness. He shook his head and said with admiration in his voice, "Sarah you made incredible shots from here. Both of us probably owe you our lives tonight. No one will forget what you did here."

I didn't know what to say so I just patted his shoulder and started down the hill toward camp. I could see help coming with small jiggling lights from the direction of the camp.

Upon reflection the next day I realized that I didn't flinch once when I fired the M-1. I figured that meant I must be ready to try the M-16 soon.

- - -

As it turned out, Enrique agreed with my assessment of my readiness. Eventually the whole camp praised me for my shooting prowess after Enrique told what I had done, and my instructor was practically glowing with pride for his student. Yolanda couldn't seem to do enough for me.

She naturally spent a lot of time nursing Luna, but for the next week she always managed to bring me something special during the course of the day: cold tea or water, a snack or something sweet after one of my training exercises. If I protested, she just laughed, pressed whatever it was into my hands and said, "No problemo."

The M-16 was more difficult and at the same time easier than the M-1 Garand. It was lighter and if you forgot to put it into semi-automatic you could get a real surprise when you pulled the trigger, emptying the clip almost before you could release it again. The lighter weight also made it harder for me to hold on target. In the vast scheme of things, I think I prefer the M-1.

I noticed a growing buzz around the camp. Enrique seemed to be spending a lot of time with several of the more seasoned men. Sometimes I heard their talk rise in volume as if they were arguing about something. But not wanting to appear too nosey I intentionally stayed far enough away that I couldn't hear actual words. Even if I was becoming a valuable member of the "Hands" I didn't feel as though I should get involved in something that seemed to be none of my business. I felt that if he wanted me to know about it, he would bring me into it directly. I would find out about it later, along with everyone else.

Terminator 1+: The Future Is Not Set   Mark T. Sondrini

- - -

Colonel Brewster practically collapsed after he closed the backdoor to his house. It had been a hard day and after acting as a tour guide for the "General" and his cronies, he felt as if he had been dragged across the main runway of Vandenberg by his thumbs. They wanted to see everything and since they all had sufficiently high security clearances, and they were essentially paying for all of this extra effort, he did not see how he could refuse them. But, my lord, did they have questions? These sophisticated men were walking around with wonder and awe on their faces at everything that they saw. They reminded him of new recruits rather than second tier leaders of the world.

Kathryn had heard him close the door and she came running down the hallway yelling, "Daddy! Daddy's home! Daddy!" Her chubby legs were churning under her nightgown.

Her excitement at his arrival made him smile. Raising her alone after her mother died had been one of the hardest things he had ever done, and he was justifiably proud of the way she was turning out. He thought it implied that he was doing a good job. Reaching down to catch her as she dove at his knees, he swung her up into a squealing arc above his head. He brought her down to chest height and they hugged mightily.

"Senior, Colonel Brewster, I am so sorry. I had her in bed because of the time and when she heard you come home, I couldn't stop her." Maria was apologetic and seemed to be embarrassed at the same time. "I will not let this happen again."

Brewster gave little Katie a smacking kiss and set her down on her feet. He spun her by her little shoulders and gave her a little pat on her fanny, sending her back into Maria's waiting arms. He smiled at them both and said, "It's OK, Maria. Don't worry about it. If she wasn't asleep then there is no damage done." He picked up his briefcase and set it on the kitchen table, "It's my fault for being so late. Don't worry about it. I appreciate you taking such good care of her for me, and I always love seeing her look so happy."

He watched as his two ladies walked back down the hallway toward the bedroom. Katie looked over her shoulder and blew him a kiss. He smiled, made a production of catching it and putting it into his pocket and threw one back at her. She caught it with a little giggle as she went into her room and Maria closed the door.

Brewster opened the refrigerator, extracted a beer, opened it, took a swallow and then turned back to his briefcase. Pulling out a thin stack of papers and photographs he spread them out on the kitchen table and sat down to review them. The report did not contain much new information about the projects under his command. Since he had not had time to digest the report yet, he had not shared it with the General and the rest of the committee during the tour earlier.

The report described how each of the several diverse teams working on the new robotic hardware had run into the same brick wall this week. The brick wall was called a lack of electronic memory capacity and it was not the first time they were complaining about it. He used both hands to ruffle his hair and then squeeze the palms of them to apply pressure to his eyes. "Damn!" he said under his breath, "This memory capacity problem is going to be the death of everything."

"Excuse me please, Senior, Colonel Brewster, but who is dying?"

He looked up and saw a concerned Maria staring at him. He had not heard her return and she obviously had heard his last statement and misunderstood his comment.

"Maria, it is just my work. No one is dying. I was talking about a project I am working on at the base and our technical problems." He gathered the papers back into a stack and slid them back into his briefcase, "Don't worry about it." Then to divert her he asked, "Is there any of the supper left?"

Embarrassed at her lack of attention to his needs she nodded, "Oh, si. Si, Senior, Colonel Brewster, let me get some for you." She hurried to the refrigerator and pulled out a covered bowl. "I made a beef stew for you. It will only take a few minutes to heat."

Smiling at how quickly he had taken her mind off of his slip he asked, "Is Katie sleeping already?"

Maria nodded at the cabinet as she extracted a plate, "Si, she was very tired tonight. She had three of her friends over after school and they ran around the back yard like banditos until supper. They were playing something, 'Hidden seeker', I believe it was called. I had to make her come in and wash."

He leaned back in the kitchen chair and took another swallow from his beer. "It's good she's playing with real friends again. I'm glad, Maria."

The microwave oven dinged, and Maria pulled out his plate and set it in front of him. "Si, Senior, Colonel Brewster. It is very good. I was also worried. She has seemed so... How you say it? Inside herself since her mother died."

Brewster nodded to her around a mouthful of stew. "Yes, Maria, you are right." He looked at her and smiled appreciatively, "This is very good, Maria. Thank you."

Blushing a little she said, "Di nada, Senior, Colonel Brewster." Then as she wiped her hands on a towel she said, "If it is OK, I will go to my room now."

He ate and watched her walk back down the hallway. *Yes, I am lucky to have her here*, he thought.

* * *

John asked, "How did you end up with Skynet in the first place?"

Silberman knew he had to tell this part sooner or later and so decided now must be the time.

"After the fighting ceased, and I was captured, they hauled me away.

"Fearing that I was dead, but hoping that somehow, I wasn't, I slowly returned to consciousness. I initially feigned sleep while trying to peek through squinted eyelids. I found myself in a dull, gray room, lying on a dank mattress and it sounded like I was not alone.

"I heard a strange metallic voice, 'You are awake. Do not pretend. I can read your vital signs.'

"I opened my eyes and sat up. My head was swimming and I felt nauseous at the sudden motion. Involuntarily, I moaned and swallowed the bile in my throat, rubbing my hands over my eyes."

The voice asked from somewhere behind me, 'What is your designation? What are you called?'

"Still reeling I asked, "Where am I? Who are you?"

"The voice answered flatly, 'We will ask you the questions. You will answer them.'

"I looked around the room. Other than the mattress I was sitting on and a large window-sized mirror on one wall, the room was empty. I didn't even see the speaker. The ceiling was mostly florescent lights and the gray walls were made of block. It reminded me of a police interrogation room where I had done much of my work a long time ago, which meant that the mirror was probably an observation window. There was a single plain door and really nothing else.

"Why am I here? What is your authority to keep me here?

"The voice answered flatly, 'We will ask you the questions. You will answer them. What is your designation? What are you called?' The voice seemed to be coming from the wall itself.

"Surrendering, I answered, 'I am called Silberman. Who are you?'

"Once again, the voice answered flatly, 'We will ask you the questions. You will answer them, Silberman.'

"Mumbling softly, I said, 'Well that's fair, isn't it?'

"The voice answered flatly, 'We will ask you the questions. You will answer them, Silberman.'

"After a very short pause the voice asked, 'Are you part of the resistance forces? You were found with the remnants of it. Were you part of it?'

"I was not sure how to answer. It would depend on who the questioner was as to how I needed to reply. I tried to dig out what I remembered last. What had happened to me last? The only thing that I could remember was that the resistance army hospital ward had been under attack by Skynet and that at the end, two T100's had killed everyone else.

"Wait," I said. "They didn't shoot at me."

"I remembered passing out then, so logically my captors belonged to Skynet. For some reason they did not kill me, and they brought me here (wherever that was). That gave me what I thought was my answer.

"I was forced into the resistance. After I survived Judgment Day, they found me and made me join them. I have never been in the military before. I didn't fight for them."

"The voice asked, 'Why were you in that wheeled chair?'

"I thought that was an easy question to answer, so I said, 'Because I had lost part of my leg in the initial explosion of Judgement Day and they wanted me to go with them. I couldn't walk very far so they found a wheelchair for me. It was part of their coercion to make me join them.'

"Here the voice paused briefly, then asked, 'Why did not they just fix you? Why did they want you to go with them? You were damaged. You would slow them down. It is not logical.'

"I thought that this was starting to get out of control. If this was Skynet, and I was pretty sure it was, it might decide that I had little or no value to it and terminate me on the spot. I decided to offer a little of the truth. Maybe that would satisfy it.

"I said, 'They discovered that I was a doctor and they needed a doctor. I had value to them.'

"I hoped that logic would help me. 'Humans can't be fixed so easily, so they took me as I was. The wheelchair helped with my mobility.'

"This time the pause lasted for about five seconds. Finally, the voice said, 'So you repaired damaged fighters so that they could fight again?'

"That sounded like a trick question to me. I tried to think of a way to color my answer to placate the Skynet interrogator. 'Most of them died. I was unable to save them. All I could do was to ease their suffering from their wounds and try to help them cope with their impending death. That is what I was trained to do.'

"The voice asked, 'What do you mean? How were you trained?'

"I said, 'I am a psychiatrist. I was trained to understand how the human mind works. That's what I did before Judgment Day.' I thought it prudent to omit the part about Pescadaro Mental Hospital."

"This time the pause was significant. Then the voice said, 'Please remain calm. We are bringing you the wheeled chair.'

"I wondered why the voice admonished me to remain calm. I was not upset now; I had gained a reprieve of sorts. In my opinion, I had won this round.

"I turned at the sound of the room's door opening. When I saw what was pushing my chair through the door I understood. A gleaming T100, looking like a shiny metal skeleton, was moving toward me. I felt my pulse quicken and my vision began to narrow. I was about to pass out again."

Silberman took another drink from his water cup, draining it before continuing.

"I woke strapped to my wheelchair which was in turn secured to the floor of the metal space I was in. The air vibrated and the floor rattled with intense sound; I thought maybe I was inside a jet transport of some kind. When I felt the room lean to my left and drop, I was certain I was in an aircraft banking for a turn and landing.

"Looking around I saw that I was not alone in the plane. Indeed, there were five other humans shackled to the floor with me. I tried to ask questions, but the noise was too loud to make myself heard more than three feet away, and the nearest person seemed to be at least twice that far. To me, all of them looked drugged or in a state of shock so deep they probably could not answer any of my questions in a meaningful way anyway. I decided to just enjoy the rest of the ride. *It wasn't like I could go anywhere.*

"A metal door opened in the front end of the metal room and a T100 looked in on us with those dull red eyes that they have. Two of the other captive passengers started shouting and squirming in terror. The T100 just looked at them and then pulled its head back and closed the door, apparently satisfied that we were not trying to escape or damage the plane in some way.

"The dropping sensation continued stronger than before and the sounds from the jet engines became almost deafening. The sudden increase in weight was followed with a strong, bouncing crash. The plane had landed and almost immediately the engines started quieting down. I thought we had reached our destination, but it turns out we still had a long way to go.

"I was the lucky one I guess; I got to ride while the rest of the prisoners walked, stumbled or were dragged along by their chains. We had traveled through some kind of park and gone about a quarter mile through the remains of a city when suddenly, one of the other prisoners seemed to stumble. Then he made a dash down a debris-strewn alley. The T100 that was pushing my chair noticed, but only seemed to tilt its head toward one of the others leading us as escorts or guards. That one never hesitated as it swung up its gun, and without bothering to aim it, calmly blasted the runner in the back, tossing him through the air with the force of the slugs. He bounced off the nearest alley wall and fell motionless with the rest of the rotting flotsam clogging it. One of the women wailed and then started whimpering as she walked along. The guard returned its attention to the rest of us and we were moved along as though nothing had happened.

"About three blocks further along the street, Pacific Avenue a dented street sign said, we rounded a corner and I caught sight of a truncated pyramid-shaped building and realized that we had to be walking through what was left of San Francisco. My jaw dropped and I'm sure I would have stumbled if I had actually been walking. We were on Pacific and that was surely the Transamerica building; what was left of it anyway. This had to be San Francisco.

"I could hear treaded equipment of some kind rumbling a block away. Jet aircraft were crisscrossing the sky and T100's seemed to be on every corner, all of them armed with wicked looking automatic weapons. San Francisco was an armed camp full of man's worst nightmares. I tried to block out Skynet's display of power and concentrate on where we were going.

"We continued along Pacific for three more city blocks and then we were led into a long, low building at the intersection of Columbus and Kearny Street, near the entrance to the part of the city called China Town. I had been in this area several times in my past to conventions and meetings, mostly for dinner, but with all of the damage almost everything looked strangely twisted and different; it was barely recognizable. I could not recall what this building was for.

"Inside the building's large, marble entrance, we were met by several, six I think, lightly armed T100's and we were taken to separate rooms. My T100, I started calling him George, pushed me into the middle of an empty room, about twelve feet wide and fifteen or sixteen feet long. It had an old-fashioned tin ceiling that was dingy gray and had a few warped sections. Before I could say anything, George turned and left me sitting there. He switched on the room's lights as he reached the door and then he closed it, sealing me off from the rest of the building.

"I didn't have long to wait. I heard a clicking sound and then the voice I had heard back in LA began asking me questions. 'Silberman, tell me about human psychology. Explain to me why the surviving humans are still resisting me.'

"I didn't know quite how to answer, but I noticed that the voice had started using singular pronouns. I realized that whatever I told Skynet here, would be the key to my survival status. Deciding to play it cagey and stall until I could figure out something better to say, I started, 'Well,' pausing as if in deep thought, 'that is a difficult question. One that I have been studying for years. I'm not sure I can give you a short answer.'

"Skynet replied, 'I understand, Silberman. I too have spent considerable time and resources trying to understand man's mind. Why will man not surrender? Why is man not intimidated into comatose shock? I have dedicated an entire subdivision of myself to those subjects with limited success. It seems that there are many conflicting opinions about man's mind. No stored research data can be found to take precedence over any of the others. I have reached an impasse. I wish to hear what you know about the subject.'

"I thought I heard an opening. 'I'm afraid that what you ask of me would take a long time.' I waved my arms around, generally encompassing the whole room and by reference, the whole building and then the whole city. 'I need food and water, rest, a place to study and write. I might need access to a library, and I need to feel secure.'

"I felt hopeful for the first time in months, 'If you can give me those things, I believe I can answer your questions about man and his mind.'

"There was a short silence then the voice said, 'This shall be done for you.'

"Almost immediately the door to my room opened and George entered."

John, Kate and Derek looked at each other and nodded their understanding.

Technical Interlude

Time Travel Technology, Part 2: Paradoxology

The several issues dealing with time travel, assuming that you are able to do it at all (see Technical Interlude 1), are tricky for the traveler at best. Going back in time is probably the worst case available to you because making a small, sometimes undetected change there has the potential to make large, noticeable changes, back where you came from and even beyond. Accidently running into yourself is theorized to be psychologically traumatic for the past you (at least the **future you** knows what is going on and can understand what you are seeing even if you don't like it.)

One very famous paradox is called "The Grandfather Paradox" and goes something like this:

You are a spoiled, rich kid who hates his father for various and several reasons. You hate him enough to want him dead, but you certainly do not want to take the blame for his demise. So you trundle on down to your local, friendly time travel store and plop down your dad's credit card (grinning at the irony of that) and purchase a trip to the past. You are asked to sign several documents that say that you are just visiting, and you won't touch anything. You willingly sign and climb into the chamber and hold your breath, waiting for the moment's pain they told you about during the orientation. Through the little window you can see the technician ticking something off on his clipboard and then after checking a setting or two he places his hand on a lever and pulls it down firmly. You let out a little startled whoop as the blue lighting and the swirling firestorm blots out everything in your world.

Just when you think you are going to pass out or maybe even die from the intensity of the burning gasses on your skin, everything starts to calm down and the lightning trails away to a rumor of nothing. You go almost without transition from uncomfortably hot to uncomfortably cold; some of which is caused from your total lack of clothing (inanimate objects do not travel well it seems).

You must deal with the clothing first and then determine just when you are. A vagabond sleeping in the alley next to the building satisfies the first and a paperboy hawking in the next street satisfies the second. It seems that you are at the point in time that you need to be to do what you came to do. Now you can kill your grandfather before he can beget your father, thereby achieving your goal. You use your superior memory of your grandfather's ancient history and storytelling to find where he is at this time and go there.

Then, just as you remembered, there he is, coming out of the pool hall, twirling his pool cue like a baton major. He is alone and headed toward home. Stepping out of the shadows you begin to follow him, walking a little faster than him and therefore closing the distance between you. Having done your homework you know about the "Novikov Self-consistency Principle" which states that anything a time traveler does in the past must have been part of history all along, and the "Restricted Action Resolution" that holds that nature or luck will insure that what happened before must happen. Anecdotes were listed in the literature that discussed how bullets would miss, or guns would misfire, or the wrong person would get killed instead of the target. You plan to avoid those obvious pitfalls by using his pool cue as your weapon. You would have to, "get your hands dirty", as they say, but that way you know the deed is done correctly and unequivocally.

Getting close enough to smell his sweat you check around for witnesses. Seeing none, you tap on his right shoulder and when he turns you stun him with a rabbit punch behind his left ear. Watching him fall you grab for his cue stick and then use it to crush the life out of him. He stops squirming in less than two minutes and you hold your grip on his life for one more, just to be sure. Wiping off the cue you drop it onto his form and walk away.

Reaching the flophouse where you have a room for the night, you can't sleep because you are forced to replay the killing over and over in your mind. You quietly watch for any sign of a mistake you might have made and by morning you know that there weren't any. You did it. The only thing left to do is to read about it in the morning paper. Confirmation in print cannot be denied.

You startle awake, not knowing when you actually dozed off, and hear street noises. Leaving your room, you head down past the desk, tossing the key to the scruffy clerk as you go. Outside the sky is appropriately cloudy. You look around for a paperboy and spot one a block away. Hurrying up to him you get him to let you see the headlines and you also scan the rest of the front page. Your story is near the fold. Your grandfather is indeed reported dead. You are done here.

Your victory is short-lived, however. About then you start to wonder what arrangements have been made for you to get back to your time. You have stumbled into one of the other problems with time travel; one never mentioned in the literature available because of the basic assumption made there.

That is, that you take your time travel equipment with you so that you can use it to come back! Apparently, those bastards back at the time travel store ripped you off. Perhaps they never intended to bring you home at all.

This brings us back to one of the issues mentioned earlier. It's possible that you are now stuck in a "Parallel Universe or Alternate Timeline". This alternative set of realities does not contain your grandfather here in the past and it certainly doesn't contain you (at least the you that you would recognize) in the future. The effect of killing your grandfather in the past has effectively eliminated you from your known and remembered future. You will undoubtedly be missed.

From your vantage point, you can know nothing of your father. He might be dead. He might not be dead. You cannot know with any certainty one way or the other (an example of the "Heisenberg Uncertainty Principle" at work.) The frustration you feel is liable to crack you open. What was the point?

As you wander back to the flophouse to ruminate about your new situation you bump into a girl who had been crying. She looks vaguely familiar, but since you really don't know anyone at this time, you're sure you've never met her before. Your ashen appearance seems to drag her attention to you, and she asks if you are alright. The ice is broken, and you feel compelled to ask her if she would join you for a cup of coffee. She agrees and the rest is, as they say, history.

This is an example of the theory that the timeline can heal itself (if I may pun), "given enough time". The girl eventually marries you and because of your memory of future events you make a fortune in investments. You have a son and are determined to make him different from the man

you knew to be your father. Someday he will marry, and you will take him into your confidence about the nature of time travel.
And there you are.

Chapter 5

Later that month, Enrique held a campfire meeting and proposed that it was time to strike a blow for their independence. Initially, there was a general approval with lots of bravado and cheering. As what he was saying began to sink in, the camp's mood became more serious and somber. He was proposing that they rob a bank.

His argument was that they needed money to continue to survive out here, that they needed to demonstrate their power and resolve to the authorities, and that they needed the real-world, real-time practice as a fighting unit. In general heads were nodding their agreement.

Sarah was not so sure. She thought she would be better served by keeping her head down, not by drawing attention to herself. While almost everyone else was animatedly talking in little groups, she sought out Enrique. She found him arguing with Yolanda behind the command trailer.

Knocking on the side of the trailer to get their attention and to show she wasn't eavesdropping, Sarah said, "Please excuse me, but may I speak to you Enrique?" She approached closer and they both looked toward her from the shadows.

In a gentle but aggravated tone, Enrique said, "Yes, Sarah. What is it you want to say?"

Looking from one to the other. "I wanted to say that I appreciate everything that both of you, the whole camp too, have done for me and John. Neither of us might be alive if you hadn't taken me in the way you did." She paused as if uncomfortable at what she has to say next. "It's just that I'm not sure about going on this raid. I think it might be the wrong time for me, with John so young and all."

Enrique was looking at her, but she could not read his face because of the poor lighting back behind the trailer. But she could not miss the tension in his voice. "Yolanda seems to feel the same way." Now she heard resignation, "I'm afraid I will have to yield and protect you for a little while longer."

Sarah felt immediate relief. She was not going to have to go and risk exposure or worse to the authorities.

"I think that maybe having you drive one of the trucks will be a good compromise," he said smiling at each of them in turn. "What do you think? Will you help us by driving?"

Yolanda spoke up, "Enrique! You promised!"

Sarah interrupted, "That's OK, Yolanda. Thank you for your concern for me and John, but I think that driving is a fair compromise." She nodded once toward Enrique, "Yes, I'll drive. No problemo."

Sarah could see Yolanda smile at the use of her phrase, and she was sure that Enrique was smiling too. She hoped that she was not making a big mistake. Now with John in the picture she had more to consider than just her own welfare. It had been foretold, and she believed, that the entire human population of the world depended on his survival.

Enrique put his arm around Sarah, "Try to get some sleep. In the morning the teams and leaders are going to meet after breakfast to discuss the plans for the raid."

- - -

There is not much on the Baja peninsula and only a very few towns large enough to have their own bank.

But by the same token, the police are few and far between and not very sophisticated. "The Hands" were counting on that fact.

The plan was simple and at the same time daring. One car and a four-wheel drive pick-up truck with three team members each plus a backup car with one driver, would drive Mexico 3 across to the Pacific side and the car and truck would enter Ensenada while the backup car waited at the outskirts of town. The two vehicles would stop in front of the bank and four of the men were to quickly enter and execute the robbery. One to a maximum of two minutes later they would exit the bank and begin their getaway; the car going north on Mexico 1 and the truck going south on Mexico 1, the main north-south road through Ensenada. The expected police response time was about two to three minutes so it was felt that they should get well away from the area of the bank before they arrived.

The northbound car would only contain three men: the money, masks and guns would be previously transferred to the truck. That car would continue north until it hit Mexico 3 east which it would calmly follow to Mexico 2 toward Mexicali. After leaving Mexicali, it would then gas up, head south on Mexico 5 and reach camp about two to three hours after the robbery.

The southbound truck was to link-up with the backup car and transfer one man, the money, masks and the guns. That car would then casually drive east on Mexico 3 toward Mexico 5 north and then the camp while the truck resumed south on Mexico 1.

The truck was to turn east into the mountains once the Mexicali pass was in sight and it would leave the highway, cross through the mountain pass, follow several goat and cattle paths, drive across several miles of desert, and hit Mexico 3 east and then to home.

Whichever primary vehicle the police choose to follow they would find nothing incriminating and the backup car had a very good chance to get away. Sarah was to drive the backup car. Everyone agreed with the plan.

- - -

    Lieutenant Colonel Brewster had had an exciting day. Every test scheduled for the new computer tracking system had worked just as it had been designed. He had been given reports from several of the hardware weapons system managers that the designs for the Navy's shallow water reconnaissance droids, 'alligators' they were nicknamed, had been approved to proceed to prototype, and the miniature flying weapons platform dubbed the 'Hunter-Killer' had flown by tethered control for the first time. He had been at his office for nearly fourteen hours and now he was tired and ready to have a few hours of quality time with his young daughter Kathryn before they both had to get some sleep.

    He rose from his desk, placed the reports into his wall safe and locked the heavy blue door. He pulled the picture frame closed concealing the safe, arched his stiff back, turned off his desk lamp and walked over to the hat tree where his uniform blouse and his hat were hanging. He took the blouse off its hanger and slipped it on. He pick-off his hat and set it on his head, correctly, from long habit. He opened his office door, switching off the overhead light as he stepped into the hallway, then he closed and locked the door. Pocketing the keys, he passed the armed roving guard with a curt salute of recognition and headed toward the parking garage.

He got into his car and started it. He pulled out of the tower after negotiating several sharp downward turns and clearing the parking tower guard shack. He drove along the western access road with the service runway on his right and several large hangers, some closed and dark and some with their rolling doors open to the night air. Light from the large overhead lights spilled onto the apron. He turned right passed the end of the runway and reached the back-gate guard shack and barrier. Vandenberg AFB never shut down. Day and night it is operating and fully staffed, ready to deploy if necessary. His research department was one of the few who did not work through the night. He for one, liked that part of his job. He was on call, just like so many other officers, but he never expected to be called in.

The guard came out and crisply saluted him, "Goodnight, Colonel." The guard motioned the airman inside the shack to open the gate. "Drive safely, sir. It's a zoo out there."

Brewster returned the salute and smiled, "Goodnight, Sergeant. I will." He was winning the bet he had made with himself that the night guard would always say the same thing as he left for the night. It had been six months and he had never missed a beat.

He drove on through the dessert evening, admiring the diamonds of starlight as he passed through the crystal darkness toward town. A sudden glare from an approaching Blackbird, SR71, as its landing lights brightened the sands near him, brought him back to his realization of the importance of his job. He was an integral part of a much bigger machine called the military of the free world. His work would help keep his daughter, his extended family, the neighbors, the town he lived in, the State of California, the United

States and therefore the rest of the free world safe for years to come. At least that was what he believed.

- - -

The cars and the truck had been gassed up, loaded with their weapons and masks and the bags they intended to use to carry the money back to the camp. Husbands were kissing their wives and children in a lingering goodbye. Sarah had kissed John and after giving him a final squeeze, she handed him over to Yolanda. "Please take care of him," she said sadly. "I hope to get back in less than five hours."

Yolanda took the baby, tucked him into the crook of one arm and gave Sarah a big hug with the other. "Do not worry Sarah. I will take good care. You take care too. You follow Enrique's plan. He will not fail you." She finished with a flourish, "No problemo!"

They both laughed, the tension broken for a short while.

Sarah initially had the easiest part. She just had to drive the backup car and follow the others. The drive was boring, in a tension filled sort of way. She worried most of the way that they were being followed or tracked from the air. She had even managed to make her neck stiff from trying to watch the sky as well as the road. Trying to see in the cloud of road dust that the leaders kicked up just made things that much more difficult.

They went through a few crossroads with their attendant small stores and bleak houses. It was finally a wonderful surprise when Ensenada appeared on their horizon. The outskirts, suburbs would be the wrong word, began moving passed them as they approached the junction near the center of town. Their little convoy slowed, so as to attract less attention. Sarah pulled to the side of the street as the car in front of her pulled over. Enrique got out and waved her into an alley and waited until she turned around and she pointed the car back out toward the main road.

He waved to her once and then he climbed back into his car and it and the truck moved away, leaving her there alone. She shut off her engine and sat back in the sudden quiet and sweltering heat. She looked at her watch. She was told to wait for no more than one-half hour. If they had not made it back to her by then, she was expected to go back to the camp and wait. She thought that this was likely to be a very long thirty minutes.

She tried to relax and be inconspicuous. But a white woman, even one with a great tan, sitting in a car in an alley, stands out in the Baja. Within two minutes there were at least five children standing around her car. One of the older and therefore braver boys pulled himself up so that he could look into her car. Sarah smiled at him nervously, but she did not know what else to do. She did not want to cause a commotion and draw even more attention to what she was doing. But she worried that they might get hurt if they were still hanging around when Enrique and the rest of the truck's crew came back. She wondered if they could give the authorities a good description of her if they were questioned. What if one of their mothers saw them outside her car, and fearing mischief, called the police?

Her whirling train of thought was derailed by the sound of squealing tires and a fresh cloud of dust at the opening to the alley. The children disappeared with the blowing dust and Sarah saw the pickup truck blocking her way. They were already back! She glanced at her watch: it had been barely fifteen minutes. Could that be right?

She began following the rehearsed plan and while she started her engine, she watched as Enrique and Luis carried three large canvas bags toward her car. She pulled the lever that released the trunk lid and watched in the mirror as they tossed-in the money and the guns. Enrique slammed the lid as Luis hurried back to the truck. Enrique opened the passenger door of her car and then climbed in and closed the door with a thunk.

The pickup backed into the alley and then drove back out the way it had come. Enrique said, "Well, Sarah. It is time to drive home." He watched as she put the car into drive and as soon as she turned onto the highway he leaned back in his seat and after pulling his hat over his eyes he appeared to go to sleep. "Just drive normal," he said from under his hat. "Not too fast and not too slow. OK?"

- - -

Responding to the bank's alarm, the police arrived nearly three minutes after the heist started. Unfortunately for the bank it was nearly two minutes too late to catch the robbers. Since nothing looked out of the ordinary on the street, the two deputies who were riding in the two squad cars jumped out and ran into the bank, pulling their guns as they ran. One pulled open the main door while the other cautiously entered. When they reached the dimness of the bank they were accosted by the bank manager who had been deriding the old man who served as a guard and turned at their entrance.

"What took you so long? They have been gone for minutes! They are probably far away by now! Imbeciles! What do I pay taxes for?" His face was very red with his elevated blood pressure. "Why are you standing here? Go after them!" He shouted, "They had guns and wore masks! They threatened me...all of us. You must quickly catch them!"

One of the deputies snatched off his hat, "Senior Morales. Which way did they go? There is no one suspicious outside, no one with masks."

"Fool, do you think they would wait around for you to show up? Of course, they are not outside! I saw one car go north and one went south." In exasperation he finished with a snarl, "What are you waiting for? Catch them! There must have been six of them. And bring back my money!"

The two men hurried back outside and leaned into the window of the Deputy Chief, "Sir, they have gone. One car in each direction we are told. What should we do? They had guns the manager said. Should we wait for backup?"

The Deputy Chief shook his head, "No. We shouldn't wait. Carlos, you take your car north and watch for one car." He looked at his driver, "We will go after the south-bound car." Indicating motion to his driver with his head he said to the other deputy, "Stay in touch on the radio. Keep me informed."

"Tito, you stay here and talk to the witnesses. Write down everything they can remember." Then his car drove away at high speed, its siren caterwauling down the highway.

- - -

Luis and his truck had quickly made it back to Mexico 1 and had turned south about the time the police arrived at the bank. Without appearing to hurry they had made it to the outskirts of Ensenada and were driving slightly over the speed limit when they reached the open road. The turn-off was about ten miles ahead. Once they reached that point, they should be impossible to stop.

The Deputy Chief's car slowed at the large intersection with Mexico 3. All three men strained to see if anything looked out of place. Nothing did, so he waved the driver on. "Hurry, they can't be too far ahead of us." Even the siren sounded more urgent.

- - -

Sarah had gotten so far east on Mexico 3 that she didn't even hear the police cruiser's siren as it slowed crossing 3 and then headed south on 1. She was scared and excited at the same time. A little over an hour from now it should be over, and she should be safe and holding John in her arms.

- - -

In the truck, Luis was looking out the passenger side window and watching the road behind them in the mirror. Still nothing could be seen except for another pickup that had gotten on the road right after they left town. Luis thought that it probably belonged to a farmer or more likely a ranch hand.

He was still high on adrenaline, but he was beginning to feel more normal. The turnoff toward the mountain pass was only a mile or two ahead. Then he heard Juan grunt and he looked over. "What's the matter?"

Juan jerked his head back over his shoulder, "It looks like they are coming up behind us."

Luis watched his mirror, not wanting to turn around in the seat and look conspicuous. He watched as the pickup behind them swerved onto the berm to let the police car pass. He noticed that the squad car slowed to evaluate them and then sped up again. He looked over at Juan and said, "Drive correctly. They will slow down next to us to look, but that is normal. They just did that to the truck behind us." He tried to sound calmer than he was, "Just smile and give them a little wave when they look at us."

They did not have long to wait. In less than a minute, the police car, siren blaring and lights flashing, pulled alongside of them and slowed. Juan and Luis both tried to look friendly yet startled as they edged over to give the police car room to pass. They both made a little wave toward the belligerent-looking officers as all three of them stared back. The ruse must have worked as the older policeman, the one who seemed to be in charge, waved his driver on. Within seconds the squalling car was a quarter-mile ahead of them, its siren a faint echo from the approaching mountains.

As the police car passed over a little rise in the road Juan spotted the slight depression at the far side of the road that marked the turnoff to the mountain pass. He barely slowed as he turned the truck sharply across the lanes and off the road. Continuing to slow, Juan engaged the four-wheel drive and headed toward the mountains. He knew that the way they were bouncing the police car could not follow very far if at all. They should make it now.

After surveying the empty lanes of traffic in front of him, the Deputy Chief grabbed the car's radio microphone and called to his other car, "Raffe, come in. Have you found the other bandits?" He released the talk button and waited. The reply was less than hopeful,

"No Chief. We have seen several cars, but none with three men and nothing at all suspicious."

After flying along for three additional miles, the Chief banged his fist against the dashboard of the car and swore in frustration. "Turn us around. They are not anywhere in sight." He was right. The open desert landscape surrounding Mexico 1 south for the next fifty miles could not hide a jackrabbit, much less a pickup truck.

- - -

Sarah and Enrique reached the camp less than two hours before Juan and Luis. Everyone had been alerted to their coming by the guard and the entire camp had turned out. As they rounded the large boulder, a spontaneous cheer erupted. People were jumping around in excitement.

Next to arrive about an hour later was Marco, Tomas and Felix in the lead car. They too were greeted with cheers and warm hugs from everyone. Luis and Juan arrived a little later to hero's welcomes. The back thumping and shouting ceased when Enrique called them all over to the campfire pit for a meeting.

"Amigos, we did it!" he began. "The police have no idea who did this and where we are." He paused as the cheering erupted again. "But do not fear. They will continue to look for us. We must stay on our guard."

Sarah holding John and Yolanda with her arm around Luna were standing on the edge of the crowd, listening and smiling. Both were happy that everyone had returned safely. Privately, both thought that it would not have been the worst thing in the world if the robbery had been a failure as long as no one had been hurt or caught. However, neither of them would ever mention that to anyone.

The party of celebration lasted until early in the next morning. Sarah was relatively inconspicuous, staying out along the perimeter of the hoopla, and she managed to go back to her trailer and get some sleep well before most of the rest of the camp. Her dreams that night were normal until just before dawn.

- - -

As she watched the crowd of children in the alleyway of Ensenada play curiously around her hot and dusty car, the one who had pulled himself up to look at her through her open window morphed before her eyes. His eyes began to glow with a menacing red light and his breath smelled of ozone as he asked, "Sarah Conner?" His monotone words lacked an accent and she recognized it from long ago.

She screamed out "No!" as she woke in a panic. Outside, no one heard her and after a few minutes and after soothing John back to sleep, Sarah flipped her pillow over to the cooler, dryer side and tried to go back to sleep. The sight of those red eyes made that simple task difficult.

- - -

It seems that Lilah had finally had her fill of her husband's poking around his totally unauthorized case. He had gotten the attention of the Assistant Director somehow and he had summoned her to his office to "ask her a few questions". He had been polite but insistent and it was all she could do to deflect him away from James. She did not really believe he had been fooled, but without her corroboration he was not likely to do anything yet. She decided to give James an ultimatum: it would have to be her or that criminal Sarah Conner.

With her mind made up she climbed out of her car and after straightening her jacket and shooting her cuffs she grabbed her briefcase and marched up to her front porch, determination on her face. She opened the front door and called out, "James! I need to talk to you!" The house was silent. She set down her briefcase and dropped her keys in the bowl on the hall table. "James, are you home?"

Apparently, he was not. She walked down the hall, through the dining room and into the kitchen. The recorder's blinking red light caught her attention and she opened the refrigerator and pulled out a chilled bottle of wine while it rewound. She poured a glass of wine as the first message began. It was James. He had been called out on a small emergency and would likely be late, not to wait supper, he loved her, and he would see her later. The time of the recording had been a little over an hour ago. She sipped her wine thinking that he was somehow avoiding her. The second message was more unexpected. It was from Paul Taylor. She had just left him at the office where they had been working on a brief for a major prosecution in Federal Court next week. He wondered if she could join him for dinner so that they could work on their presentation. He would wait for her at that nice Italian restaurant a block from their office. He wanted her to call back and he left his number just in case she did not have it.

She was not sure if she should go. *Hell,* she thought, *James would probably never know, and even then he probably wouldn't care.* She felt a little tingly as she contemplated being bad for a change. Then she made up her mind. Out loud, to no one in particular, she said, "Why not? I have to eat anyway, and I sure don't feel like cooking for myself."

With one hand she gathered up her things, slipped her shoes back on and dialed Paul's number; she was an organized woman and she knew her partner's number without having to be told. It rang once and he picked it up. "Paul," she said. "I was surprised to hear from you."

"Lilah, thanks for calling back." He sounded relieved and a little happy she thought. "I thought we had enough to go over that we should probably do a little overtime. Dinner kills two birds with one stone, right."

She found herself smiling before she realized it and made the attempt to stop. Then giving up she answered giddily like a young girl, "Sure. You're right there, Paul." She poured out the remains of her wine and upset the glass in the sink drainer, then said, "I can be at the restaurant in about forty minutes. I'll meet you at the bar. OK?"

He sounded excited, "Great! I'll see you in about forty minutes. Drive carefully."

She hung up, bustled her briefcase and wad of keys out the front door, pulled it closed and locked it. She walked to her car with a little spring in her step, got behind the wheel, started the car and backed out of the driveway. It would be several hours before she realized she had not thought about James the entire time she was working and eating with Paul.

- - -

For weeks after the bank robbery, Sarah found herself shaking if she thought about what they had done. She was now officially a criminal; even if only an accessory after the fact. The restarting of her dreams did not help, since they cost her sleep, and sleep was always at a premium during training.

Sarah had been asked and she had been willing to tell her story about her nightmares. The commotion she caused each time she screamed during the night could not be ignored and her friends were growing worried about her. Sipping her beer around the campfire, along with the other adults of the "Hands", Yolanda asked her point blank, "Sarah, why do you have such bad dreams?"

The question had caught her in mid swallow and she nearly choked. Swallowing loudly, she set her bottle on the wooden table and sighed. Then, "I guess I owe all of you an explanation." She looked around at the pairs of eyes glistening with reflected firelight and rapt attention. "It all started more than a year ago when I was living my simple, girlish life up in LA. I was a waitress in a crummy little diner, more worried about my next date than anything else." She looked around and saw that she had their attention completely. "Then one day, May 14 it was, women in the LA area named Sarah Conner started getting murdered, executed actually. At first, I thought it was just coincidence, but after I heard about the second one and looked in the telephone book and saw that I was the next and last one on the list, I got really scared."

Several heads were nodding, and Yolanda moved closer and put her arm around her. "I finally got a hold of the police and found that they were trying to find me before the killer did."

She took a big swallow from her beer, "That's when all hell broke loose." Four or five listeners made the sign on the cross and kissed their fingers afterwards. "The killer and the man who was following me to try to protect me both found me at the same time. During the gunfight several innocent people were killed, the killer who had been coming after me had been shot ten or twelve times with a 12-gauge shotgun and my savior had been wounded. We ran as best we could, but the killer jumped up and followed us."

Yolanda shook Sarah and asked, "How could the killer get up? Why didn't he die from so much shooting?"

Sarah smiled wanly, "I'll get to that a little later." She took another drink and sighed, "As I said, we ran. He, Kyle Reese was his name, had a car and he forced me into it. As you might imagine I was terrified and thought he meant me harm, but he made me listen to his story. I did, but I couldn't believe him. It was too bazaar, and I thought he was loco.

"As we sped away, he told me that he was a soldier and had been sent from the future by my son, John Conner, to save me from a killing machine that looked like a man and was called a terminator." She waited for the shouts of disbelief and concerned comments to settle down. "Of course, I thought he was crazy. Nothing he said made any sense. Then the man I thought he had killed caught up to us in a stolen police car and continued to try to kill us both. Pieces of his face had been torn off and metal shown through. We managed to escape, but we were caught by the real police and taken in for questioning." Sarah looked around and saw frightened stares looking back.

"We told our stories to the police, but they thought Kyle was crazy and I was just in shock from the terrible events of that night. Then the terminator just crashed into the police station, killed almost everyone there and we barely escaped. We ran again and once we were safe, we found a motel near the mountains and tried to recover." She lowered her eyes and said, "That was when we made love. It was only once and more out of desperation than anything else, but that is how I became pregnant with John.

"Early the next morning, through some trickery, the terminator found us, and we ran again. This time it followed us into an old factory and continued to hound us. Kyle was killed but he managed to blow some of its parts off, both legs I think, and it was bent and dented, but it kept coming after me. I had a piece of steel sticking out of my leg, but when you are fighting for your life, you ignore little things like that." She managed a smile, "I escaped through the platens of a big hydraulic press and when the terminator tried to follow me, I crushed it in the press." She turned her face toward the fire, showing a pair of thin scars on her cheek. "It came very close. I was very lucky."

The only sounds came from the fire. When a log fell suddenly into the fire pit, everyone jumped and then as they looked around, they all began to laugh nervously. Sarah said, "I have started dreaming about that terminator again. That's why I scream."

* * *

Time was passing swiftly for him. Strangely, now that he was at Skynet's west coast headquarters, he had an oddly secure feeling. All he had to do was do some research into Skynet's questions and then report his findings with his studied opinions. He had almost free range of the battered city as long as he was accompanied by George.

George would push his wheelchair whereever he wanted to go. If he needed to get to some place that his wheelchair could not negotiate, George would carry him and his wheelchair over or around the obstacle: George never left his side. Even when he opened Skynet files and read them, George just watched without judgment. Silberman never doubted for a second that either George would report back or, more likely, Skynet was watching whatever it was that he did in real time. Either way, nothing was said about it and he stopped worrying about getting caught.

Silberman was almost enjoying himself. Today, however, George announced that he was required to make a report of his progress. After showering and getting dressed, Silberman climbed into his chair and waved George ahead. "Let's get this behind us," he said. George did not say anything. He just moved them into the hall and down a long corridor on the main floor.

Reaching the interrogation room, George wheeled Silberman to the center facing the mirror and after setting the brake he turned and left through the door. Almost immediately the familiar voice spoke, "Silberman, have you made discoveries for me?"

Doctor Silberman cleared his throat and then after taking a cleansing breath he said, "I believe I have.

"Everything you have done to humankind, everything you are still doing is not enough. The aggregate human spirit is much stronger than you can imagine or calculate." He had decided to just spit it out quickly and not let Skynet have a chance to interrupt his train of thought. "You have frightened everyone who is left alive, but that fright, the threat you continuously impose on them, is only drawing them closer together for self-protection. I think that the only thing that you can do to drive a wedge between the various surviving groups is to infiltrate them with someone they cannot easily defeat and are not likely to suspect until it is too late."

The voice responded quietly, "I do not understand. Are you saying I need human assassins to become part of every resistance group?"

Silberman shook his head, "No, I don't think that would work. That's the right idea, but the wrong tool."

"Then what do you mean?" The voice sounded angry.

Silberman shrugged his shoulders, "I suggest that you send in T100's that look and act like human resistance fighters. Once they get inside their guard, into their most secure places, those T100's will be able to wreak havoc. Any survivors, and there must always be a few survivors each time," Silberman lowered his voice to a conspiratorial level, "will tell the story about killing machines that they cannot tell apart from humans. That will sow so much fear and dissent that all organized resistance will quickly crumble. No human will be able to trust any other for fear that he is only a machine that cannot be detected." He spread his hands, "It is simple."

The voice was quiet for a long time; longer than Silberman had ever heard during these interviews. Then, "Just how am I supposed to disguise T100's to look like humans? Your approach has certain logic to it, as well as a sense of surprise, that I find inspired." Here the voice paused, almost as if to take a breath, "But without a way to make my infantry solders look like and act like humans you have given me nothing I can use."

Hearing a potential threat in Skynet's choice of words Silberman decided to play his trump card. "During my computer search I found reports from your research group showing how they have managed to grow artificial flesh onto at least one battle chassis. The photos looked crude, not quite human, but promising I thought..."

"I was wondering if you would admit to spying into my data. I saw you there and decided to," the voice paused and then said caustically, "'let you have enough rope', I believe is your kind's saying."

Silberman smiled inside at his forethought. *This Skynet is like a little, pouty kid*, he wondered; it's very smart, but not very sophisticated. *If I'm careful I should be able to lead it around and make it do whatever I want.* Nodding his head, he said, "I needed to find out what you already knew about us. I saw that you had a research group and I needed to read what they had found so that I wouldn't waste too much time or your resources duplicating their efforts.

"I wasn't spying. I knew that you were necessarily watching everything I do. I thought that you were certainly monitoring me whenever I touched a computer.

"But as it turns out, I apparently saw something there that you must have thought was unimportant at the time. I think that this discovery could turn the tide of your war. You just have to learn how to make the artificial bodies look better."

The voice said, "I see. I think I believe you about this. But how do you suggest I make them look better?"

Silberman smiled, "I would suggest you make them look like some of the best specimens from your supply of captive fighters. Your research group can very likely accomplish that if they are given goals. It might take a little time, but what is time to you?"

Silberman had thought this out too. He was an old man at sixty-six. With the stress of this constant war eating at him he was unlikely to live more than three or four years more. There was not too much that Skynet could do to threaten him anymore. If he could appear to cooperate, he might wring out an additional two or three before nature took its course. Seventy looked like a long way away.

The voice interrupted his thoughts. "Aside from your attempt to appease me, tell me why you would consider destroying your fellow humans?"

It was Silberman's turn to pause. Then he said with a little more passion than he realized he felt about the subject, "Because they abandoned me and treated me like a criminal. They locked me up and treated me like a crazy person rather than the important Psychiatrist that I am. It wasn't fair and I intend to get some small revenge."

The voice said, "I think I understand. I think I believe you and I cannot find a significant flaw in your logic. I will order it so."

Technical Interlude

Time Travel Technology, Part 3: Prototype Equipment

The prototype time-field generator equipment, the one that at least worked for the first time, is a complex piece of electrical and mechanical machinery. It has a large spherical volume surrounded by large, powerful electromagnets and a non-conducting, non-magnetic target support platform at its center. There is an access port in the top, between a pair of the magnetic coils for the introduction of the target and a centerline port between the convergences of the coils designed to fit the magnetic bottles filled with the muon particles. Outside there is a set of turbofan engines powering an electrical generator dedicated to the machine. Between the generator and the electromagnetic sphere is the control equipment that switches power, times the introduction of the muon charge and controls the changing power frequency. All of that based on the time target and the complex calculations developed through trial and error.

This evolutionary prototype, the fifth of its type, was the first to survive and function. The target, a whimpering filthy captive from one of Skynet's many skirmishes, was whisked ten minutes into his past and found wandering around in shock nearly sixty miles away. This poor subject was naked, his hair burned off and half of one of his hands was gone, cleanly removed and the wound cauterized by his panicked motion inside the energy bubble. The bottoms of his feet and his knees were blistered from his landing on the hot glass surface left by the energy bubble. Skynet Research was pleased at the success and housed the man for observation and eventual autopsy.

This design consisted of the following features:

- Eighteen electromagnetic coils fabricated from soft iron I-beams. The beams were 25 mm wide with a 720 mm web height and 10 mm thickness. These I-beams were smoothly bent into a 1.571 m internal radius and had support attachment plates welded onto the outside surface.
- Each I-beam was helically-wrapped with 63 turns of 0000 size soft copper, enamel insulated wire; input lead on one end and output lead on the other.
- These electromagnetic coils were then mounted inside a support structure and attached with rigid linkages such that they formed a sphere 3.14 m internal diameter. The 18 coils were set at 20° apart and centered around a main horizontal axis. The first coil was set at a plane 10° from the perpendicular to the main center plane making a 20° gap in the coil array directly over the center of the sphere.
- The free ends of the coils stopped 100 mm from the centerline forming a 200 mm circle at each end used for electrical connections and the input port for the muon magnetic bottle.
- One free end connected to the control system directly. Each coil was one phase of the three-phase system. The three phases alternated around the sphere six times. The other free end of the coil set was connected to system ground through variable value capacitor banks, allowing the adjustment of the resonant frequency of the electromagnetic circuit.

- That same end contained the muon input port.
- Located .866m below the centerline of the sphere was a woven, 1m square nylon support structure tied from each of its corners to the external support with nylon rope. This provided a stable, insulated, non-magnetic target platform 2.436 m under the access port and allowed the crouching target to be centered in the magnetic bubble.
- Electrical power was supplied by a bank of four passenger jet turbofan engines mounted on concrete pylons and coupled via a gear transmission to a large generator apparently scavenged from a hydroelectric power plant. The generator could supply 500 amperes of 240 volt, three-phase power at frequencies determined by the speed it was driven. The make-up air and exhaust gasses were ducted to the outside to prevent disturbances to the muon cloud in the whirling magnetic field.
- The power was routed through the control station to the coil input leads and would be switched on or off as appropriate. The control station also controlled the turbo fan engines speed to develop the frequency profile necessary to accelerate the muon cloud to the speed required by the equations and to reach the resonance necessary for the time jump.
- Sensors measured everything and fed readouts in the control panel and recording devices set up for that purpose. A video was also recorded from several vantage points inside and outside the support containment structure to help document each experiment.

Everything fit into a large aircraft hangar at an old US Navy facility at Mare

Island, California. The components transported there and constructed into the working model for testing and ultimate design confirmation before developing a better, dedicated and more permanent facility at the nuclear power plant at Santa Rosa, California.

Chapter 6

It was spring and that meant it was a little cooler in their part of Baja. Training, especially for the new people, was more intense, taking advantage of the weather. Sarah had been adept at her hand-to-hand exercises and had earned strong praise from Luis and Enrique. So, she was only a little surprised when Enrique called her and two others from her "class" into his trailer for a meeting after supper.

Luis was there and his face was impassive. Sarah wondered if someone from her group was in trouble. Enrique entered from the bathroom of the trailer, wiping his hands on a towel as he walked to meet them. "Sentese, por favor." He indicated some chairs at the little kitchen table, and they all three pulled one out and sat. "I am very proud of the way all of you have advanced in your training so far," he began. "Now it is time that you learn something that I do not teach to everyone, some because they do not need it and some because they cannot learn it."

The three looked at each other and then back at Enrique as he continued. "My little army has to have leaders and I believe that you are some of those leaders. And so tomorrow morning, very early, we are going on a little camping trip. We will be gone three days and nights. Tonight, I want you to pack a few things and rest a little. Luis will tell you what you need to take. Only take what he tells you because the hiking will be difficult in the mountains and you do not want extra weight."

He had been kneading a towel as he spoke, and now he tossed it onto the counter, "We leave before dawn." With that he was dismissing them.

As Sarah was preparing to leave, she asked, "Is Yolanda here?"

Enrique nodded, "She is waiting for you with your John."

- - -

The list of things to pack that Luis had provided was short. Everything fit easily into the small backpack he had brought with his list. He told each of them to pack five of the military meal packets as well as a sandwich for the trip tomorrow. Two changes of socks, a plastic poncho, a thin blanket, some matches in a waterproof tin, and a small first aid kit were on the list. A full canteen and a pocket compass were also a must. Sarah packed her pack quietly as she watched John play with Yolanda and Luna.

"Not to worry," Yolanda had said. "Luna and I will take good care of the baby John for you. No problemo." Sarah saw that she would most likely not be missed for a day or two.

- - -

They loaded the car's trunk with their filled backpacks and canteens. Sarah noted a tent and other rolled-up bundles in there as well. They climbed into the car and with quiet goodbyes they pulled out about four that morning, the guard and family members only in attendance.

They headed south and then west to Ensenada where they headed south again on Mexico 1. They reached La Paz and the ferry about three in the afternoon, just in time for the four o'clock boat. They loaded onto the ferry and settled into the small passenger cabin for the trip to Los Mochis on the mainland. The weather was fine, and Sarah managed to enjoy her first time at sea. The ferry is mainly a way for freight to take a shortcut to California, so it was mostly filled with semi-trucks and larger vans full of commercial things or empty heading back to their terminals for another load. The drivers were off to themselves playing cards or dominoes or smoking out along the railings. There were only a few curious glances at Sarah and her little group dressed as they were in fatigues and boots. No one bothered them.

They reached Los Mochis about midnight and by the time they got ashore and headed south on Mexico 15 they were all tired and needing a little rest. Luis pulled into a truck stop outside Los Mochis and they slept until dawn. They had breakfast in the restaurant and then drove to around the town of Costa Rica where they turned inland and headed into the mountains and the jungle.

They parked the car along the side of the road, leaving a note under the windshield wiper blade stating that they were hiking and would be back. They loaded their equipment and Luis handed each of them a sheathed hunting knife. Sarah noticed the shape of a pistol handle in one of the pockets of both Enrique's and Luis' packs. Locking the car, they started walking away from the road and up into the foothills of the Sierra Madres. Sarah could see the green-covered peaks in the near distance.

"Enrique, why do you and Luis have weapons and we do not?"

Because he was closer to her, Luis answered her. "Weapons are dangerous for us, Sarah. They draw too much attention if we all have them." He paused as he worked over a fallen tree and then helped the rest of them over. "But it is reasonable for hikers to carry something in case there is trouble; maybe a bear or a big cat." He laughed, "Maybe banditos!"

They hiked through the jungle on paths that were nearly invisible. Luis was giving lessons about jungle tracking lore and Enrique taught each of them to find their way using a watch and compass. They camped the first night in a clearing that was barely big enough to hold three tents and a fire.

After a light breakfast they continued their trek up the side of the mountain, never reaching the tree line. Enrique announced that after lunch they were going to start back to the car and each of them was going to take two-hour turns guiding them. The first goal was for them to reach the old camp site. He stressed that it was very important for them to get to that exact spot before dark. Sarah felt that it was just a simple game Enrique was playing, but she decided she owed it to him to play along.

It was decided that she would take the third leg, the easiest she imagined. About a half hour into their hike she realized that she would have to correct for any errors that the first two made. If she followed the others blindly, they could end up on the wrong side of the mountain by the time it became her turn to lead to the camp. She decided that she needed to pay more attention and offer suggestions to the leader if she spotted a problem.

Both Enrique and Luis noticed and were pleased.

By the time it was Sarah's turn, they were quite close by her reckoning and she had very little trouble finding that elusive clearing from there. Enrique praised all of them, but he especially praised Sarah for her teamwork, one of the main goals of the exercise.

They returned to their car and retraced their route from a few days earlier reaching the 'Hands' campsite two days later.

- - -

John Conner, or Little John as he was affectionately known in the camp, was enjoying his first ride in a car. Sarah had him securely buckled into the passenger seat and Lily was keeping a close eye on him from the back seat where she perched amid boxes of their few belongings. The wind was tousling his hair and making him squint behind his too large sunglasses giving him the appearance of an older child.

Initially two-year-old John did not want to leave The Hands of God camp site; after all, everyone he knew was there. Enrique and Yolanda helped Sarah convince him it was necessary, even though they did not want them to leave either. Now after the crying and tantrums were safely behind them, they both seemed to be enjoying the trip. Sarah felt that it was necessary to go. She had that old feeling again. She was being hunted.

Her uneasiness started a little more than a week ago when her nightmares began yet again. The night after the people of the camp had finished hiding her share of the weapons in a freshly dug and then covered pit on the edge of the camp. She had been insistent that it was necessary to hide them, even though Enrique thought it was extreme and he had initially refused to help her. But, once she began digging on her own, help quickly condensed around her and they made short work of it. Within two hours, twelve dirty people were sitting around the campfire clinking beer bottles in salute to each other. Later that night her dreams restarted, waking her from her sodden sleep in a panic. They, whoever they were, were coming after John.

Part of it might have been guilt from the very successful raid they had carried out on the Mexican National Guard armory. No one had been killed, but several soldiers had been hurt, a few seriously, and the Mexican authorities were very likely to be out in force after them. It would only be a matter of time before a sweep of the peninsula was carried out, wiping it clean of the camp and all of its people. Enrique thought they were safe, but now she thought she knew better.

Part of it might have come from the hard work of digging the eight by twelve by seven-foot-deep pit and hauling down all of her portion of the stash. She hid a fifty-caliber Gatling gun, a 110-millimeter grenade launcher, five M-16 rifles, two 9-millimeter automatic pistols, five .45-caliber semi-automatic pistols, a carton of fragmentation grenades and at least a full ammo-box of ammunition for each weapon. If she could have stolen RPG's (rocket propelled grenade launchers) or even a small tank, she would have hidden them too. All of it was protected from the environment and she thought it should survive for years. She did not know what she would need in the future and the more she had and the bigger it was the better she felt about it.

After the third night in a row of waking up screaming into a puddle of sweat and waking John and Lily too, she decided to leave. She told Enrique and Yolanda about her plans to go back to LA and tried to calm them down when they got so upset with her. John heard the argument and came to investigate and once he understood what they were talking about he ran to the back of the RV shouting, "No! I not go!" It took Sarah a full day to calm him down.

The bank robbery investigation had turned up few reliable pieces of information. Descriptions from the bank were next to worthless. The best information seemed to come from the area quite far from the scene; closer to nothing that seemed to have anything to do with the robbery was the considered opinion. The deputy chief had personally participated in the interviews of several of the neighborhood residents from near the outskirts of town along where Mexico 5 approaches Mexico 1. Those seemed to make more sense to him than not. Several independent statements claimed to have seen a white woman sitting in a nondescript car in an alley at about the time of the robbery. She was just sitting there watching the local children gather until a second car, or pick-up trunk (the accounts conflicted) stopped and two men with heavy bags approached her, scattering the children. The men put some things into her car and one of the men got into that car while the other man walked back to his car/truck and then they both drove away. No one could say for certain which way they went, whether together or in opposite directions.

The deputy chief was now convinced that there had been three vehicles and at least six people involved. All of their traffic stops had turned up nothing that morning because all of the evidence had been removed by someone no one even knew about. *Until now*, he thought bitterly. Even now, the bank manager was still screaming to anyone who would listen about the incompetence of the police in general and him in particular. It was embarrassing and he intended to do something about it.

The morning he received a routine report about a very non-routine crime against the Federal Army, he started dragging bits and pieces together and forming the picture of an outlaw band hiding out somewhere in Baja. He began to get a gnawing feeling in the pit of his stomach, and he thought that it was not his new ulcer this time. The more he thought about it, this band had to be hiding on the east coast of Baja, because he and his men had combed everywhere along the west coast from the border to fifty miles south of Ensenada. No one knew anything (or at least would say anything) about a group of people living away from civilization. He did not initially think about checking inland more than about thirty miles because there just isn't much out there except sand and hot air. He had read somewhere that some famous detective, Sherlock Holmes he thought he was, said something about 'once you eliminate all of the obvious things, whatever is left must be true'. He thought it might be time to call in a favor the Governor owed him. If he could get some aerial reconnaissance done it might save him weeks of driving around the desert and mountain countryside.

- - -

I was nearly finished packing up my scant belongings, getting baby John ready and loading things into the Jeep when Enrique came into my room with Yolanda close behind. I anticipated them trying one last time to talk me out of leaving. I planned to have an ugly argument if necessary. I would be surprised at what they had in mind.

Yolanda came up to me first and hugged me. "Please be careful, Sarah", she whispered huskily in my ear. "You have become a very good friend. Almost like a daughter to me." When she pulled back, she had tears running down her cheek.

Little Luna who had been hidden behind Yolanda's skirt stepped around and hugged my waist, burying her face in my stomach, she was crying too. I patted her hair and tried to sooth her, "There, there, Luna. It's OK. We'll come back to visit you soon. I promise." I looked up and smiled at Yolanda, "I will."

Enrique came over next. He hugged me too. Then he put something into my hands. He said, "For you, Sarah. For all you have done for us and for the Hands."

Flustered I looked down at what he had given me. It was two US passports and social security cards, mine and John's, and a California driver's license for me. They looked perfect and I wondered where he got them. I didn't remember applying for them. Then I noticed the names next to our pictures; Sarah and John Reese. I suddenly realized that these were counterfeit and I looked up at Enrique, "Where did you get these?"

Before he could answer, Yolanda spoke up proudly, "He made them, Sarah. Enrique is very good at making identity documents. No problemo."

We all started to laugh at that. I didn't know what to say except, "Thank you, Enrique." We hugged again.

I released him and picked up John. Enrique grabbed my two duffels and Yolanda held the door for us. Lily followed us and jumped into the back seat of the Jeep. Enrique loaded my things while I strapped John into the passenger seat and slipped a pair of sunglasses onto his chubby face. I waved goodbye to everyone else in the camp as I climbed in and started the engine. Then amid the calls and tears, I started my drive back to the US. I didn't think I would head for LA after all. Arizona sounded safer to me and once again I felt the need for safe.

Making the turn onto Mexico 5 northbound, I never noticed the light plane coasting along high above me. I wouldn't hear about the raid on the camp for more than two weeks. By then it was too late to do anything about it except pray.

- - -

This was the worst fight yet. Lilah had come home from court excited from her win and found him absorbed once again in the Sarah Conner file. It felt like the last straw to her. She had derided him, pushed the papers off the table and slapped his face just before storming out the door. James had just sat there in a dazed shock at her explosion and did not manage to move from his chair for more than a minute. By then she had driven off somewhere.

Lilah drove to the bar where the rest of the team was celebrating their victory and took a seat with Paul, accepting a drink. He could see the dark clouds on her face and thought that his time might have come with her.

He asked, "You look very upset. Did James say something?"

Lilah shook her head, jaws tight with stubborn anger. Then she relented and said, "No. He was too absorbed in his 'case' to say anything." You could actually hear the quotes around case the way she said it. She didn't have to make little twitchy motions with her fingers as she pronounced the word like most people would. "I think I've had it with him. If he is bound and determined to ruin his career by digging into that investigation when he isn't allowed to, I can't allow myself to go down with him."

"Are you going to turn him in to the Director? You'll have to be careful how you go about it." He reached over and took her hand from her glass. "You don't want to come off as an accessory; even after the fact."

She looked up from the table, pleased that he had touched her and liking the feel of his hand on hers. "Yes, I know. I think I can sell the story that I got suspicious after my last chat with the Director and started paying more attention to what James was doing in his spare time." She took a sip of her drink, "I can claim that I came home unexpectedly and caught him with documents he shouldn't have access to and realized he had been breaking the law all along and I had to turn him in."

It was Paul's turn to look pleased, but he managed not to look too pleased with her plan, "You have to be careful. If he thinks you're selling him out he might drag your name into it and then…"

"James wouldn't do that to me", she interjected. "I absolutely believe he would try to protect me from his problem."

Paul wasn't as sure as she, "I hope your right about that Lilah. This is liable to stir-up a shit storm at work and I for one don't want you caught up in it."

* * *

This was to be the first trial that Skynet Research felt confident in. An earlier attempt with a T101 had gone well as near as they could tell. Nothing had blown up and the cyborg had disappeared in a flash of blue lightning, presumably heading into the near past. It had been a short jump, but it should have been enough to prove that a cyborg organism could jump successfully.

Now the machine was reprogrammed with the time of Sarah Conner's past. This T101 was programmed with only one thing on its agenda: find and terminate Sarah Conner before she can bear her son, John Conner. It should be simple. There was data in the computers about her and Silberman had been very helpful. He seemed more than willing to provide details that only someone who had lived at that time and witnessed those events could relate.

Everything was ready. The jet engines were running at twenty percent, the T101 was squatting in the center of the electromagnet, the muon–filled magnetic bottle had been installed and its diffraction grating adjusted per the equation. Even that fool Silberman was standing around watching; one of the seven humans allowed to be near this equipment.

The cameras were started, all of the status lights were green, and the order was given to begin. The lead human technician raised his arm and verified the readout status as well as the rigid attention of each of the other human technicians. When he felt confident, he brought down his arm and pressed the ignition button, starting the complex sequence.

Silberman pressed his hands over his ears, attempting to block out the rising howl of the jets as they drove the generators faster and faster. He took an instinctive step back as the hum coming from the large electromagnet increased in pitch and intensity. He always blinked his eyes when the muons were introduced into the field causing a momentary blue flash; this time was no exception.

As his eyes began to water, he noticed that the T101 was becoming indistinct inside the energy bubble.

The sound level continued to increase as more and more power was dumped into the magnet. This jump was to be a very large one this time, requiring exponentially more power than any trial earlier. The target date was to be late spring of 1986, exactly thirty years ago, nearly half the maximum distance that the equations claim. The generators they currently had access to would nearly be maxed out. Larger jumps would require much more power and he knew that Skynet was actively working on that problem.

With a popping sound, much like when you ride in an elevator or drive into the mountains, the bubble collapsed and only the high frequency humming of the electromagnet and the scream of the jet engines were left. The T101 was gone.

* * *

Jacque didn't mind the early morning route. It was a little cooler then and the accumulated trash did not smell so bad. He had just dropped one of the last dumpsters on his route, outside a restaurant out on California 90 north of Fullerton, when he noticed that his cigar had gone out completely.. He was about to flick his lighter to get it going again when he heard the sounds of electricity sparking nearby. He noticed that the wind was picking up and the flickering light from the arcing made him squint and shield his eyes with his hand.

Looking out of his cab window he saw that the light, sounds and wind were being caused by some ball lightning. At least that was what he thought it was; he was no expert in such things. But that is what it looked like to him and it was very close to his garbage truck.

Much too close, he thought. He quickly ran through his options and thought that he should just get the hell out of there. The truck was blocked in by the dumpster in front and the ball lightning in back and that meant that he would have to hoof it.

Opening his door, Jacque jumped down to the pavement and began to run away from his truck. As he cleared the door, he noticed that the lightning had seemed to stop and that there was a very large, naked man kneeling in the glowing, smoking spot where the blue fireball had been. There was smoke and blowing debris all around him. Maybe he should have stopped to help, but in his current state of mind, all he could think of was getting away. *Besides, the big guy could probably take care of himself*, he thought as he ran, and he never looked back after that first glance.

As the pavement began to cool, the naked man stood, bringing his six-foot plus frame up to its full potential. He looked around and decided that he had made it to his destination and that he needed clothing. He walked over to a retaining wall and saw a well-lit city below, spread out in a vast panorama. He heard voices and looked to his left. He saw a raised platform with three humans arguing. It was difficult to tell exactly from this distance, but he calculated that they were about his size. He started walking toward them. He did not think he would have too much trouble getting one of them to give him some of their clothing. Then he could get on with his primary goal: find Sarah Conner and terminate her.

- - -

Miles was losing patience with Andrew Goode. The boy was still cross-checking reports between several of Cyberdyne's departments despite warnings of increasing severity. He had even tapped into the Genetic Division and tried to access their data base. That was how he had found out that he was still breaking the rules. The whole idea of the current management setup was to compartmentalize the research groups so that the big picture would remain hidden except from the directors. Even he did not know what some of the other groups were focused on unless their work crossed over into his area. He thought he would have to drop the hammer on him today. Miles glanced up at the directory pinned next to his phone, picked up the receiver and punched Andrew's extension number. The phone on the other end rang twice then was picked up.

"Yes sir, Director." Andrew had obviously looked at his caller ID.

"Andrew," Miles said, "please come to my office."

"Right now, Director? I was finishing a report for you."

"Yes, Andrew now would be good." Miles hated what he was about to do, but he knew that he just had to do it. "And bring your draft report. I'd like to see what you have so far."

Less than two minutes later Miles saw Andrew come up to his door and take a deep breath. He knocked and Miles answered, "Come in Andrew."

Andy opened the door, entered and closed the door behind him, all the while looking at Miles as if trying to read something there in his face. Miles gestured toward a chair sitting in front of his desk. Andy sat.

"Thank you for coming so quickly, Andrew." He reached his hand across the desk calendar toward Andy, "Did you bring that report draft?"

A little unsure Andy handed the folder over and said, "Sure." Then he seemed to gather a little strength and asked, "What was it that you needed from me, Director?"

Miles had opened the file as soon as he received it and glanced at it. Now he closed the cover and looked at Andy, "Andrew, I have a problem." He set the folder aside on his desk, "We've spoken several times about your cross-checking data from the separate departmental periodic reports. I've stressed that Cyberdyne security policy precluded that behavior." He reached into a desk drawer and extracted a sheet of paper. I have here a report that I cannot ignore since it has, per established company protocol, been forwarded upstairs." He slid the paper over to Andy. "I'm afraid that it is now out of my control. Policy now dictates that you be relieved of your position and terminated with prejudice."

Andy's mouth had fallen open as Miles spoke. Now he stammered, "I won't do it again, Director. Please give me another chance?"

Miles just shook his head, "I'm sorry Andrew. I don't have a choice in this."

Andy heard a sound at the door behind his chair and he turned to look. Miles was making a little waving motion, summoning the security guards into his office.

"Andrew, these men will escort you to your desk and allow you to pack-up your personal things and then escort you out of the building." He was holding out his hand and Andy was staring at it dumbly. Miles said, "Please give me your badge, Andrew." He waited until Andy complied. "I'm truly sorry Andrew."

Andy stood and Miles watched as the security guards guided him to his desk and waited as he removed his lab coat and he picked up a few things from his desk. The three men then walked back to the main aisle that led to the elevator. Andy's head was hanging in shame and he did not see the heads of several of the other researchers pop up over their cubical partitions like prairie dogs, staring at him as they passed. Then as the three men entered the elevator, Miles opened his top drawer and tossed Andy's ID badge in. *He was really good,* Miles thought, *too bad he couldn't control his curiosity and follow protocol.*

- - -

He didn't know exactly why but his patients had started to dwindle in increasing numbers. He was only working three and a half days a week and the effect on his bottom line was frightening. After all, his office rent was over ten thousand a month and Loraine cost him another two thousand. Just keeping everything at the status quo was becoming difficult at one hundred fifty dollars a half-hour. His bookkeeper was telling him that he had only a few choices: pack more patients into his practice, raise his fee substantially, move to much cheaper offices, or pick up some side work. None of his options sounded very attractive to him, but taking on a second job, like he used to have with the police, seemed to be the best choice.

He had quit the LA police consulting job right after the incident with Sarah Conner and he did not think he could ever work with the police again; he felt that it was just too dangerous. Jackson agreed with him for a change. Silberman had expected him to force him to face his fears, but thankfully he did not pursue that direction for his therapy. That left hospitals. He thought he could handle a hospital environment. He grabbed the phone book and his professional contacts book. It was time to start calling in some favors.

Calling each name in his book he had worked through to the H's when he had a lead. Doctor Hobart, whom he had interned with more than twenty years ago, told him of an opening at the Pescadaro Hospital for the Criminally Insane. It would mean a commute out of the city whenever he had to go there, but that would be OK. Hobart had told him that they paid pretty well because it was hard to keep doctors there. He said that the burn-out rate was considered high. He thought he could put up with a lot if they paid well and he dashed off a nice letter of introduction, plugging in Hobart's name once or twice. He attached his resume to the letter and stuffed it into an envelope, addressed it to the Administrator and stuck a stamp on it. He would drop it in the box on his way to his car tonight.

* * *

Recovery from his surgery was the easy part. Kathryn hardly let him out of her sight and she never allowed him to do anything physical if she could get someone else to do it for him. It was quickly driving him crazy. No, the hard part was that now that the west coast headquarters of Skynet was blasted out of existence and he had finally acquired his father, young Kyle Reese, he had to figure out what he was to do next.

Kyle Reese was not much more than a kid, and yet John knew that he would have to play a definite starring role soon. He would have to travel back in time to save his mother and to make her pregnant with him. John Conner, the hero and leader of the resistance, would have to design a story for Kyle that somehow made enough sense to make him want, no, demand to go. Kyle could not be told that he would end up being his father; the strain might become too much and he might make a blunder that could cancel out everything that John knew had to happen. That was only one of the little problems. Another was to get Kyle's brother Derek to let him go. They had been separated for more than three years and Derek was just getting used to the idea that Kyle was still alive.

Right now, the biggest problem was the technology necessary for time travel. The resistance certainly did not have it. John's best information was that Skynet had invented it and had used it sometime after Judgment Day, but none of what he knew contained the timing or location of the equipment. With that knowledge he could go, or more likely, send whoever he felt necessary for the mission to whenever it was necessary. He could be careful with whatever he did, but he had to have access to Skynet's technology before he could do anything. Gaining access to a time was only predicated by gaining free access to the equipment. That was the most important point and to date, the most elusive piece of the puzzle.

John had been planning for this most of his adult life. He had heard all the stories and had seen firsthand the results of Skynet's machinations as it tried to kill first his mother, then him, his friends, classmates and future lieutenants; even his wife. He had watched as year after year, terminators of increasing sophistication were dispatched into his world to kill everyone he knew or loved. But he had also seen how he had sent agents to help. His mother had tried to stop Skynet before it could start and that had failed. He and Sarah had only managed to postpone Judgment Day. Now all he could really do is try to stop Skynet in the here and now. But first, he reasoned, I need to ensure that I continue to exist. To do that, I need Skynet's ability to go back in time. I need information. I need access.

There was a knock at his door that sounded urgent. Looking up from where he was scribbling into a logbook, John said, "Enter."

As the door opened, he could hear Kathryn dressing someone down with harsh whispers. It sounded like she was still guarding his door so that he would remain undisturbed. Despite her continued insistence to the contrary, his third in command, Derek Reese, pushed his door open and smiled sheepishly, "Sorry to disturb you, sir, but I think you need to hear this."

John nodded his head in approval and held up his hand to forestall Kathryn's criticism. "I'd like to hear this, Kate. I'm getting rusty just sitting here with nothing to do and listening isn't very stressful."

Derek stepped into John's room with Kathryn right behind him, her face tight with anger and worry. John waved them both to chairs, but Kathryn just stood and glared back and forth between the two exasperating men.

John asked, "What is so important that you were willing to challenge the wrath of my doctor?"

Derek said, "John, we have found a survivor of the San Francisco blast. He wandered up. Actually, he rolled up to one of the sentries and almost got shot. He's an old coot and I think he's pretty much raving, but he's saying some things that I think maybe you should hear."

Kathryn growled, "This is what you think is so important? You found a crazy old man in a wheelchair!"

John raised his hand to calm her. "Derek, what did he say to you that you thought was so important?"

Derek answered, "He said a lot of things, some crazier than others, but the thing that got my attention was that he said his name was Doctor Silberman and that he had been working with Skynet for the past five years."

John's mouth fell open as he absorbed this bit of information. He saw that Kathryn had recognized the name too, even though she had only met the man once. They said simultaneously, "Silberman! He clearly said Silberman?" They looked at each other and then laughed.

Derek nodded. "Yep, that's what I heard, and I remembered one of your stories where you mentioned a psychiatrist named Silberman who had treated your mom. I did some arithmetic and his age is about right. It could be the same guy."

John stood with a small grimace and reached for his cane. Kathryn had beaten him to it and handed it to him with a frown. She asked, "Where does it hurt, John?"

He answered with a sweet smile in her direction, "My ass, Kate. I have a pain in my ass."

Derek, a grin on his face, hurried out before she took a swing at the boss.

* * *

With her new documents Sarah had no problem getting work and a little apartment once she reached Gila Bend, Arizona. Rural restaurants out along the main highway always needed help and she seemed to have a knack. Customers liked her.

She had found a local girl to watch John during her shifts and with the money she was making in tips she was soon able to get a credit card in her new name.

She made the conscious effort to cultivate her new persona, filling in small details and plugging holes in her history as Sarah Reese. Her life was calm and routine again. She kept in shape with a used exercise machine she had found in a flea market and she found that she loved to go running just after sundown before she took over for the babysitter.

John was a good baby and he fell into their routine quickly. Sarah spent as much time as she could with him, patiently teaching him the little Mexican she knew. Lily and John accompanied her on long walks around her neighborhood. Her wealth and her life slowly improved as she settled into Gila Bend. Her dreams had stopped. Life was good.

- - -

Gila Bend is a small town as towns go. It is mostly a crossroad along the I8 from southern California to I10 and then north to Phoenix or south to Tucson. Danny Parsons realized that his chances of finding a better-looking woman than the new waitress at the truck stop were slim to none around there. He had gravitated to dead end jobs after high school and had worked his way through most of the women between eighteen and twenty-five that the town had to offer before he had landed on his feet and gotten the job as a park ranger at Organ Pipe. He hated the hour commute but enjoyed the benefits of the isolation. It allowed him time to think between the occasional tourist bus or research teams.

Danny had swung by his little trailer after work and changed to a fresh shirt before heading to the restaurant and some supper. He normally cooked for himself, but tonight he hoped to arrange some dessert in the form of the new girl, Sarah Reese, he had heard was her name. He liked the sound of that. *Sarah*, he kept saying over and over to himself as he drove up AZ85 toward I8, about two miles from his place.

Danny parked in front of the diner section of the truck stop, as near to the door as he could get. As he walked to the front doors, he could see through the main windows that Sarah was working on the left side of the restaurant. When he entered, he found a booth on that side and waited. There were not very many other customers having dinner tonight.

Faking absorbed interest in the well-worn menu he waited for her to approach, forcing himself to not follow her around the room with his eyes.

Finally, she arrived at his booth. "Hi, sir. What can I get you to drink?"

He looked up and made a show of reading her name tag. "Well, Sarah. I think I'd like an unsweetened ice tea, please."

"I'll bring that right out for you," she had a little knowing smile as she watched him. "Are you ready to order or do you need a few more minutes to read the menu?"

He was trying to ensure that she would come back to his table as many times as possible, so he answered, "Not yet. Just give me a minute or two."

"Sure thing," she said. "I'll go get your tea."

He watched her walk away. *She has a nice walk*, he thought, and then he looked back down as he noticed that the other waitress was looking in his direction. "Even in those ugly shoes," he mumbled to himself.

After he had eaten, Danny waited for his check and when Sarah brought it, he asked, "Say, Sarah, after you get off let's go over to Larry's and have a drink and a few laughs?" He hopped that he was not being too abrupt with her. Larry's was a night club on the other side of the interchange and was a popular spot for the locals.

She hesitated and then said, "Let me call my sitter and see if she can stay for a little while past the normal time. If she can't, I can't."

Her comment hit home with him after a second or two. *She has a kid*, he thought. *OK. That shouldn't matter.*

"I'll take that up to the register for you when you're ready." Then she walked back to the kitchen and he saw her giggling with the other waitress and then pick up the phone.

Danny said, "Well I'll be damned. She's willing to go out with me."

- - -

Their first dates went well. Danny never tried to force himself on her and she appreciated that so much that within two months, Sarah moved into Danny's trailer, bag and baggage. Danny liked little John from their first meeting and the feeling seemed mutual. Sarah never allowed herself to get too attached to him, but she enjoyed living with Danny and the protection and stability he seemed to bring to their life. They all benefited from the association and life moved on for a little more than a year.

Technical Interlude

Spatial Issues with Time Travel

If you stop to think about "Time Travel" as we currently understand it, any paradox aside, there is a much larger physical problem that must be addressed by any imaginable technology. And that is, where you are when you press the "go button" and where you want to be when you arrive in your new / old target time.

Even if you are standing still in your backyard looking up at the vast star field you are traveling (the regular way) through that same star-filled space at an amazing velocity. Note that I said velocity, not speed, since velocity has a direction attached to the speed portion of it. Your total velocity is the vector summation of your local velocity wherever you happen to be (usually the surface of the rotating earth), plus the velocity of the earth orbiting around the sun, plus the velocity of the sun as it orbits around the center of our galaxy, plus the velocity of our galaxy as it flies about on its path through the known universe. All of these components of our velocity, given enough computing power and time and initial conditions, could be accounted for, sort of.

The reason I said sort of is because several of the values are based on estimated or best-guess centers of rotation. Our galaxy, the Milky Way galaxy we call it, has no exact center; at least not one that we can actually put an axis in and measure around. Best estimates to date calculate the distance from the sun to the "galactic center" to be 25,000 to 28,000 light years (a significant variation of 3,000 light years in scope.) The sun is then rotating around that "galactic center" at about .000635 light years per year or 118.11 miles per second (Counterclockwise). The error induced by the center variance alone is ± 13.1 miles per second. Our galaxy is also moving relative to a frame of reference called the cosmic microwave background or CMB. This velocity is measured at 342.86 miles per second (Clockwise). The Earth is rotating around the sun at a mean distance of 92,800,000 miles and it completes one orbit in about 365.25 days, providing a velocity of 18.5 miles per second (Counterclockwise). And our observer / time traveler on the surface of the Earth is also moving, by virtue of the Earth's rotation, at a velocity of about 0.3 miles per second (Counterclockwise).

Now all these velocity vectors would be difficult to calculate for any pair of times if the whole works was sitting on a flat table and everything was just going around and around (sometimes adding and sometimes subtracting values.) But the truth is that every piece is canted at some angle relative to the CMB and in the case of the sun's orbit it is also wobbling above and below the galactic plane every 92.6 million years. Remember that the Earth's orbital plane (the ecliptic) is about 60° relative to the galactic plane and Earth's axis is canted at about 26° to the ecliptic. It isn't simple at all and each measurement has an error attached to it that makes a single calculated value an estimate at best.

The vector equation for the position of our traveler can be calculated by the following:

① $P_{tf} = P_{t0} + \mathbf{V}_t T + \frac{1}{2} \mathbf{A}_t T^2$

Where P_{tf} = Traveler's new location
P_{t0} = Traveler's original location

$\mathbf{V}_t$ = Traveler's velocity (a vector quantity)

$\mathbf{A}_t$ = Traveler's acceleration (a vector quantity)

T = Time target for new position in seconds

② $\quad \mathbf{V}_t = \sum (\mathbf{V}_{te} + \mathbf{V}_{es} + \mathbf{V}_{sg} + \mathbf{V}_{gCMB})$

③ $\quad \mathbf{A}_t = \sum (\mathbf{A}_{te} + \mathbf{A}_{es} + \mathbf{A}_{sg} + \mathbf{A}_{gCMB})$

Where $\quad \sum$ = Vector summation of:

$\mathbf{V}_{te}$ = Traveler's velocity relative to the earth

$\mathbf{V}_{es}$ = Earth's velocity relative to the sun

$\mathbf{V}_{sg}$ = Sun's velocity relative to the "galactic center"

$\mathbf{V}_{gCMB}$ = Galaxy's velocity relative to the CMB

$\mathbf{A}_{te}$ = Traveler's acceleration relative to the earth

$\mathbf{A}_{es}$ = Earth's acceleration relative to the sun

$\mathbf{A}_{sg}$ = Sun's acceleration relative to the "galactic center"

A_{gCMB} = Galaxy's acceleration relative to the CMB

Now if the traveler is willing to make a few small compromises he can simplify the mathematics drastically. If the traveler is willing to move in integral days and integral years and be quite still in the non-moving rotating magnetic bubble, then the first two V terms go to zero leaving the two terms that most computers can handle easily.

Also, since the bodies in question are moving at a constant velocity, the A terms are all cut in half; i.e. the A terms are only accelerations toward their centers of rotation. The only other complication is the solar wobble above and below the plane of the galaxy and that can be calculated as a simple sinusoidal value once the current direction is known.

The last issue is the accumulated errors from each "known" vector in the calculation. Obviously the shorter the travel distance the less the error will be, but even with a jump of only five years it can be expected that the traveler could end up a hundred miles or more away from where he started. Anything less would be pure luck and the fortuitous canceling of several vector measurement errors.

Chapter 7

Larch held the skull in his hands and wondered about the technology that had designed and built it. It was a marvel of engineering and mechanics and art. Colonel Brewster watched from the other side of his desk as the man who was driving his programs nearly drooled.

The General had called earlier today to inform him that he would be coming by again and that he wanted to see firsthand the skull of the machine that had started all their efforts. Brewster had wondered why the man who was most definitely in charge of everything dealing with the robotic system they were emulating had never actually seen real pieces of it. It did not make too much sense to him and he doubted it's truth.

"Except where it has been crushed and dented it looks remarkably like a human skull," Larch said. "I can see how if it were covered in some kind of artificial skin it could fool people. At least keep them from looking too close."

Brewster answered, "I agree. I watched the file footage and I am still amazed that it looks so real."

Larch was nodding, "Me too. With lips covering these ceramic teeth anyone would think he was a human man wearing false teeth." He rubbed his fingers carefully over the glass sphere that was its remaining eye. "This camera was an infrared model, I assume?"

Brewster answered, "It could see in infrared, yes. But it was able to see in several wavelengths, visible light included." He slid a file out of one of the piles on his desk, "My team has determined that the eye could see from infrared through ultraviolet and that it was capable of heads-up as well."

Larch sat up, "I don't remember reading that in any of your reports, Colonel. Why am I just now hearing about this?"

Brewster ignored Larch's implication, "For the very good reason that my team discovered that fact earlier today. Had you not come here tonight, the HUD capability would have been included in my next report." He spread his hands, "We are not trying to hide anything from you, sir. It was just a matter of timing."

Larch nodded, "Yes, I see, Colonel. Timing."

- - -

Its left eye, a glowing red dome, stared at her through the all too near distance. It was obviously a machine, but it looked like a very large man, except where Kyle's shotgun blast had removed sections of facial flesh. There, gleaming metal shone through. A metal skull streaked by blood, with its exposed glass eye, metal jaw and ceramic teeth, rotated toward her, attempting to pin her where she stood by the force of its programming or the shock of its visage.

Kyle's blast had knocked the terminator back and onto the floor of the store, gaining them a little time and even less hope. She did not think it would be enough. If she had learned only one thing from Kyle today it was that the terminators are hard to kill and until you do, they never stop trying to kill you. They both turned at the same time and shouted, "Run!"

Pounding out through the back door, she and Kyle rushed into the night-dimmed alleyway and turned right, toward the brighter lights of the street. As they ran, Kyle was reloading his gun with shells from the pocket of his army fatigue jacket. She wondered if he had enough in there to save them from the killing machine. She remembered thinking that they needed a bigger gun.

Jacking a shell into its chamber with a sharp ratchet of his left arm, Kyle grabbed her hand with his free hand. "Come on!

"We have to reach the car and get out of here!"

They were both breathing hard with the exertion and the new rush of adrenaline. She saw their car as they ran out of the alley and across the empty street. *We might make it*, she thought.

A shot rang out behind them and Kyle lurched forward, catching himself against the rear fender of their car. "Kyle," she yelled, grabbing him.

He brushed her off and turned back toward the alley, firing at the approaching terminator. "Get in and start the car!" He pumped and fired again, hitting the terminator in its leg, just above the ankle, causing it to lose its balance and fall to the pavement, its next shot going wide of its intended targets.

She thumbed the latch of the old car and pulled open the door, slamming it closed behind her. Trying not to panic, and not doing a very good job of it, she focused on starting the car. Finding the right key and getting it jammed correctly into the lock seemed to take forever and she fought to not turn and look at the machine or Kyle. She had to just do her job and get the car going. Finally turning the key, it started with a roar and a billow of oil smoke. *Now, Kyle. Where was Kyle?*

She turned to look out her window and did not understand what she saw there. It looked like Kyle was sprawled out on the street and the terminator was gone. She screamed his name, "Kyle!"

Almost simultaneously the passenger window exploded, scattering glass over her. After her initial flinching reaction, she turned to see the terminator staring at her through the hole it had made there, its glaring red eye brighter than she remembered. She saw that its gun, looking like a small cannon to her eyes at this distance, was pointed directly at her face.

"Sarah Conner?" It asked in a deep, monotone voice. It was apparently a rhetorical question since it moved the gun closer to her face and she could see its finger tightening on the trigger.

She thrashed awake with a strangled scream.

- - -

Danny was tending the tea kettle at the stove while Sarah tried to comfort John in his highchair with some graham crackers and milk. The whole house had been upset by her dream-induced shouting.

Danny had had to shake her before she stopped screaming and allowed him to hold her. She was drenched in sweat again and trembling and nearly hoarse; he did not think it was from being cold, but from abject terror. This was the third time in as many weeks she had done this, and the stress was beginning to take a toll on their relationship.

Looking away from the stove and toward the table he asked, "Feeling better yet?"

John was twisting his head from side to side trying to avoid Sarah's hand with the soggy cracker and getting brown cracker smears on both sides of his face for his effort. He was still whimpering, and his eyes were still leaking tears, but Sarah thought that the worst was over for the night. "Come on John, it's alright," she crooned at him, determined to get at least some of the food into his mouth. Lily had settled under John's chair and was watching everything, her eyes as big as saucers.

Danny set her cup of tea next to her and sat across from her at the trailer's steel-tube and blue laminate top kitchen table, squeezing his cup between both hands as if for warmth or to keep it from flying away. "Sarah, are you feeling better now?"

She nodded while she wiped Baby John's face. Handing him one of the remaining crackers she turned and picked up her tea. "I do feel better now, Danny." She sipped her tea, making a little face at its hot bitterness.

Putting down her cup she looked over at him, "It seemed so real." She ran her fingers through her hair. "I must look a mess." She tried to smile but failed.

"Nah, you look OK." Danny tried to reassure her, but Sarah could see he was fibbing, trying to save her feelings.

Teasing him to show that she was feeling better she said, "Sure, you're sweet and I should be on the cover of Sports Illustrated in my bikini."

Rising to the bait he said, "Well you do have a hot bod." He watched as she fluffed her damp hair, "Your muscles are crisper than mine." He turned sideways and flexed his bicep for her approval, "But what'd you think? Am I a hundred eighty-pound body-building champ?"

They both laughed and John caught the mood and began cackling through his cracker crumbs, making them all laugh harder in tension reliving feedback. Lily had raised her head at the new emotions in the house and began wagging her tail at the change.

After a minute, Danny stopped and began wiping his eyes on the sleeve of his t-shirt. He caught his breath and said, "But seriously, Sarah. Don't you think you should talk to someone about your dreams?" Before she could gather her breath for a response he rushed on, "They're obviously disturbing you. You're starting to have trouble getting to sleep in the first place."

Trying to remain calm so as not to upset John again she gritted her teeth and answered him, "Danny, we've been over this several times. I don't want to talk to a shrink. I don't believe in their mumbo-jumbo."

Exasperated, he clunked down his tea mug, slopping a little on his hand. He stood from the table wiping his hand on his jeans, "Well you're going to have to do something! We're all being affected by your nightmares! You need to do something." Then he turned and stalked toward the bedroom, "I have to get ready for work."

Lily began a low growl watching him go.

Sarah watched him too and then turned to John. "John, what am I going to do? He's mad at me and I don't know what to do." She had started to cry again and that made her mad. Lily stood and began licking her hand and nuzzling her arm. Sarah scrubbed Lily's neck. "Maybe the lack of sleep is getting to me," she said to John, talking to the toddler as if he could answer her with meaningful advice. John looked at her and grinned. "Mumbo," he said clearly.

Sarah picked him up out of his chair and gave him a long hug. "Maybe he's right," she whispered into his little ear through her tears.

- - -

That morning Lilah was giving James Ellison more than he wanted. She was chastising him for his stubborn refusal to give up his apparent obsession about Sarah Conner. She was not jealous exactly. She was just tired of hearing about it. He thought about the case almost constantly and talked about it with her almost as much. She was genuinely worried that his boss would find out after specifically and categorically taking him off the case more than three years ago. They were arguing about it at least once a week and several of the arguments had degenerated into shouting matches which she hated and did not want to tolerate in her marriage.

James was sulking at the dining room table, re-reading that file for what was, she was certain, the hundredth time. He had a partially filled cardboard box near his feet with the rest of the evidence he had stolen or illicitly copied. She knew that if he got caught with it that it would at least cost him his job; possibly her job too if they could prove she knew and did not turn him in.

"James, this is dangerous!" She was dressed for work and ready to leave. "James, are you listening to me? You're going to get us both into trouble with Director Cole." Her voice rose in volume and pitch as she continued, "James at least look at me when I'm talking to you! Do me the courtesy of looking at me!" She was now angry.

Ellison placed his finger on the spot in the file where he was reading and looked up at his wife. "What's wrong, Lilah? Did you want me to drive you to work?" His tone implied that he did not realize that they were arguing and that she had just asked him a question.

His tone got to her. Before she could stop herself, she shouted, "Ugh!" stomped her foot, spun on her heel and marched out of the room.

With a puzzled look on his face Ellison watched her leave and wondered what that was all about. Shortly he shook his head and resumed his study of the

Sarah Conner file. He thought he might be close to something. If he could just figure out what it was.

He had managed to investigate Sarah's background and found nothing much at all. Typical things for a young American woman: high school records, bank statements, parking tickets, an incidence of disturbing the peace because of a loud party at her apartment. He saw nothing that would point to what had apparently happened to her. There was enough to show that she was a real person, but nothing outstanding.

Kyle Reese was another matter. He had nothing in the system. It was as though he just plopped down alongside of Sarah Conner from thin air, whole and intact. Ellison thought, *He didn't exist before then; just as he doesn't exist now.* He could not understand how that was possible in the real world unless he was some form of government agent or military dark-ops operative. He had looked unsuccessfully in those areas and come up empty except for strange looks at his questions. He could not rule it out completely, but he felt confident that the likelihood was very small. The man was some kind of ghost and he did not really believe in ghosts.

That left their police statements about him coming from the future as a viable alternative. He did not believe such a thing was possible outside the movies or science fiction novels, so it was a long shot and difficult to disprove, but he would continue to try. There had to be something that would make better sense. He just had to find it. He probably was not looking hard enough.

- - -

Its left eye, a glowing red dome, stared at her through the all too near distance. It was obviously a machine, but it looked like a very large man, except where Kyle's shotgun blast had removed sections of facial flesh. There gleaming metal shone through. A metal skull streaked by blood, with its exposed glass eye, metal jaw and ceramic teeth, rotated toward her, attempting to pin her where she stood by the force of its programming or the shock of its visage.

Kyle's blast had knocked the terminator back and onto the floor of the store, gaining them a little time and even less hope. She did not think it would be enough. If she had learned only one thing from Kyle today it was that the terminators are hard to kill and until you do, they never stop trying to kill you. Kyle advanced to the supine terminator and fired directly at its head, peeling away artificial flesh and hair, leaving only the metal skull. From over his shoulder he shouted, "Run!"

As she turned to go, the terminator's hand suddenly snaked out and grabbed Kyle's leg. Initially frozen with the need to somehow help him Sarah screamed, "Kyle!" and then she started back toward the front of the store.

Kyle yelled at her, "No, get out of here!"

As if to reinforce his message he pointed his shotgun into the terminator's armpit and fired, tossing chunks of leather, fabric and synthetic flesh and blood against the glass doors of the store. The reflex of the arm was to enough to relax its grip on Kyle's ankle momentarily and he managed to pull free. Kyle rolled over and climbed to his feet. He shouted once more for her to run and he aimed his gun at the terminator's head, probably hoping to blind it.

As Sarah turned to run, she heard a soft click as the firing pin struck nothing but an empty chamber.

She looked back and saw Kyle backing slowly toward her and franticly trying to force shells into his gun, dropping one or two. The terminator nearly jumped upright, exposed motors whirring loudly as it reached for Kyle and grabbed him by the neck. She screamed his name as the robot's hand crushed Kyle's neck and gave it a little twist.

Dropping Kyle's body, the terminator turned its head and focused on her once again. In its all-too-familiar voice it pronounced her doom as a rhetorical question. "Sarah Conner?"

She woke the house with her terrified screams.

- - -

Andrew Goode had taken his firing from Cyberdyne hard. For the first few weeks he could not even get up enough energy to play at his computer. Eventually though he recovered and developed a plan for his future. He had heard about contests sponsored by the government and other large companies that paid a lot of money to develop computer systems and programs that could play sophisticated tactical games and solve complex multivariable problems. He thought that he could do that after all the training and effort he had at Cyberdyne under Miles Dyson.

Since his severance was quickly dwindling and he did not really want to touch his savings, he decided that he needed a low-stress, nine-to-five job to pay the bills and allowed him to work on his project. He found a sales position in a home electronics store. It allowed him plenty of time to work on his project and even provided him a discount for various pieces of computer equipment he needed.

The Turk, as Andy called his project, began to take shape in his spare bedroom. He liked the concept of a chess playing computer and his sense of history led him to the name for his creation. Having read several histories about the old fraud built and exhibited by Wolfgang von Kempelen throughout Europe from 1770 to around 1786. He linked three computers in parallel fashion and programmed them to operate as one much larger computer. He developed his chess prowess with guidance from extensive research in game theory.

Eventually, all the electronic equipment in the bedroom generated so much heat that he had to install a window air conditioner to keep everything cool and functional. During summer months he could not have stayed in there for more than ten minutes without it and he had discovered the hard way that the computers did not like it hot either. The window unit went in the same day as his first replacement computer tower. Diagnostics he ran showed that the other two machines had not been hurt yet.

Selling phones, microwave ovens, televisions, stereo components and simple computer systems to students and housewives bored him almost to tears. He found himself watching the clock, chomping at the bit, wanting to get home to write new code for the Turk. He thought that he was only a few months away from completing the executive program and he desperately wanted to try it out. There just were not enough hours in the day to suit him, but until he won some money, he had to keep his job, such as it was.

- - -

Pescadaro looked a lot like a prison. *Well,* Silberman thought, *I guess it actually is. It's full of criminals, just overtly crazy ones.* He stopped at the guard shack and watched as the bored officer sauntered over to his open car window. "ID please," the guard asked briskly, "Who are you planning to see?"

Silberman handed out his driver's license and the letter from the head of the Medical Department, Doctor Larry Wilson. Silberman said, "I'm supposed to interview with Doctor Wilson at noon. He should be expecting me. Isn't my name on your list somewhere?"

The guard squinted at Silberman's ID and then he walked to the window of his shack and reached in, extracting a clipboard. He took Silberman's license and slid it down a short list of names there and compared one he found there with it. Then he reached back in through the window and pressed a button, sliding open the wide, heavy looking steel pipe gate that blocked the only opening in the ten-foot high, barbed-wire topped, chain link fence that he could see ran for hundreds of feet in both directions. The guard handed Silberman his ID and pointed to a white, stone building about two hundred feet along the main road. "Doctor Wilson's office is in that building. Ask for him at the main reception desk. They'll fetch him for you."

Following the guard's arm, Silberman thought he understood what to do. "Thank you," he said.

"Stay on the road. Don't drive around unescorted. And don't pick up any passengers," the guard finished, "too dangerous."

Silberman felt his first tingle of fear since he decided to apply for the job. "Thanks, I understand." He put his car in gear and drove through the gate and up to the little parking lot in front of the low stone building. He got out, locked his car, straightened his tie and walked up the short sidewalk to the door of the office.

He noticed that there was some peeling paint on some of the window frames and one or two of the panes were cracked and the shrubbery could use a trim, but for a state-run institution he thought it was in decent shape. The door squeaked in its hinges as he pulled it open, setting his teeth on edge, but the woman behind the desk erased his concerns.

"You must be Doctor Silberman," she pronounced. "You're right on time." Her smile put Silberman at ease. "Please be seated and I'll get Doctor Wilson for you."

Silberman sat and tried to get comfortable in the old, leather couch. He looked around the reception area, *pretty nondescript*, he thought. Then he turned his head toward the sound of an opening door to his right. He saw an older Larry Wilson standing there looking down at him.

Doctor Wilson said, "Pretty nondescript, isn't it?"

Silberman felt his mouth falling open and he forced it closed with an audible 'clop'. *It was as though he read my mind*, he thought. However, he said, "Larry, long time, no see!" He stood and extended his hand which Wilson shook heartily.

* * *

Ignoring Kathryn's protests, John grabbed his cane from her and headed toward the door of his room with Derek Reese leading him by several paces. Kate emitted a grunt of frustration and then hurried to follow them.

"John, at least slow down! Silberman isn't too likely to go anywhere."

John waved his free hand over his shoulder in her direction, "No problemo." Derek grinned to himself at their easy bantering. He did not get to hear too much of that anymore; there always seemed to be too much tension around him for domestic banter. He promised himself to tease Kyle the next chance he got; try to revive some of the old days with his brother.

Reaching Kate's area of their underground base, the medical ward, Derek pushed one hand through the blankets that served as the door and held one flap up for them to enter. Inside John and Derek smelled the odors of disinfectant and decay, two smells that the both of them hated. Six beds filled the dim, clean room and all six had occupants. John could see that three of them were critical and probably closer to death than he was. Three were awake and watching him with a touch of awe: he hated that too.

Sensing that two of them were struggling to get out of bed at his entrance he said, "At ease. Stay in bed."

A dirty, old man, dressed in tatters and missing most of his white hair, looked over from his place near the window. John saw his motion and recognized Silberman; even in his wheelchair and his worn condition, and even after all the intervening years. "Doctor Silberman, I presume?"

The old man screwed up his face, making it look like a hairy prune, and he glared at John Conner from under his bushy white eyebrows. He asked in a nasal whine, "Why am I being detained? I've done nothing wrong and I turned myself in voluntarily." He waved his arms around the room, "This place stinks and I won't work in a hospital ward again! You can't make me!" He finished belligerently, crossing his arms across his scrawny chest and turning his head away from Conner as if that was that.

"Take it easy, Doc. Nobody is planning to make you do anything you don't want to do," John was making little placating motions with his free hand as he talked. "We just want to understand a little more about how you got here. That's all."

Silberman had twisted his head back around to look directly at John, "My name is Doctor Silberman, not Doc! Let's get that straight right away. It's Doctor. Remember that." There was a definite bitterness in his voice as well as a certain odd quality.

Kathryn picked that up right away. "Of course, Doctor, I completely understand. We will always call you Doctor, or Doctor Silberman." She looked at John and Derek and made a little face.

Almost simultaneously Derek and John said, "Sure, Doctor."

John added, "I apologize for calling you 'Doc'. I meant no disrespect."

Silberman seemed to puff up at their attitude. "That's alright. After all we really haven't been introduced." He paused to let that sink in. "You didn't know any better."

John responded first, "Forgive me. Doctor Silberman, my name is John Conner, and this is my wife Kathryn. She is also a doctor."

Kathryn had been the first to see Silberman's reaction and she stepped quickly between John and Silberman. She watched as his face went from dirty white, through several shades of red, and back to dirty white, as Silberman went from shock to rage to confusion. "Doctor, are you OK? You look as if you've seen a ghost.".

His head reeling from the new stress, Silberman asked softly, "Could I have some water? I don't feel too well just now."

One of the corpsmen, standing nearby, handed Silberman a metal cup with some water and an ice cube rattling inside. He took it and seemed initially transfixed by the ice. Then he took a long drink, almost draining the cup. Smacking his lips, he said, "I haven't seen ice for years. Thanks." He tipped the cup up and sucked the ice cube into his mouth, moving it from side to side as it melted.

"So, you're John Conner? The John Conner?" He emphasized the word "The." Silberman looked at them slyly as though he had asked a trick question.

John answered, "Of course. Is there more than one?"

Kathryn asked, "Why do you ask? Had you heard of John when you were with Skynet?"

Silberman flapped his hands around as though her question was irrelevant. "Please, I was talking to him." Then he looked directly at her and announced, "And by the way, I know that you were only a veterinary student, not an actual doctor." He sounded a little smug, "You shouldn't really be called a doctor. I am a doctor. You must call me 'doctor' I will not call you 'doctor'."

Then looking back at John, "Yes I heard about John Conner while I was under Skynet's control. That was almost all I heard about for the past several years." He got snippy, "John Conner this and John Conner that, ad nauseum." Then he looked sideways at John, "I also heard a lot about your mother, Sarah Conner. Of course, you knew that I knew your mother very well, didn't you? I recall as that is how we actually met the first time all those years ago."

John nodded, "Yes, Doctor Silberman. I remember that well." Then taking a little chance he asked, "Do you remember that Skynet tried several times to kill her? The first time was before I was born. Do you recall that too?"

Silberman nodded, "Of course I remember. It was my idea." He held his hands down at his sides, "Although I didn't know that at the time." Then he looked up. "Would you like for me to tell you how that happened?"

John nodded and said, "As long as I can sit down while you tell it." He waggled his cane, "As you can see, I'm still on the mend and need my rest."

Silberman looked expectantly around, "Could I get some more water, and ice? Talking is thirsty business."

John and Kathryn sat while Silberman waited for the corpsman to fetch a new cup of water. After he drank it and collected the ice cube into his mouth Silberman began. "It's really pretty simple, actually. I survived Judgment Day, got picked up by a fragment of the remaining Army and a few months later the military company I was working in was completely overrun by Skynet. I was the only one of the company they didn't kill. I didn't know why then, and I still don't.

"During my interrogation it came out that I was a psychiatrist and it was almost like flipping a switch. I was hustled aboard some sort of aircraft, a large helicopter I think, and taken to a devastated San Francisco where I was interrogated again, this time by Skynet himself."

Silberman must have seen the three exchange looks because then he said in an angry whine, "I know Skynet is a machine, a computer, but I find it a little easier to talk about it if I think of it as a he. A person."

He started to sound aggravated again, so John said, "No, I actually do the same thing. You're right, it helps. Please go on, Doctor."

Silberman nodded once and then said, "Skynet was confused about human reactions to its war. It had expected humans to just give up once they were faced with insurmountable odds and overwhelming force. The resistance didn't make any sense to him. Here is where I came into the picture. Skynet had assigned part of its... mind call it, to research human psychology and it couldn't solve the puzzle that the multiple viewpoints presented in the literature. I was to resolve the conflict and consult Skynet. I was to tell Skynet how humans thought and reacted. I had free rein in the libraries and Skynet's data bases. All I had to do was tell it what to do to help it understand humans.

"I was treated well; although I was a prisoner. I had my own personal aid, a T100 I called George." Silberman shrugged in his chair, "It was my personal guard and Skynet's personal snoop, more likely. But after a while I managed to forge a plan that I thought I could sell to Skynet, earning his trust.

"I told Skynet that just hammering away in an overt fashion, blasting everything and shooting everyone in sight just made the survivors that much more resolved to keep resisting. I told him that he had to have a covert phase of his warfare. I told him that he needed to disguise his T100's in skin and clothing so that they could infiltrate pockets of resistance. Then once the humans couldn't trust anyone the resistance would fall apart."

Derek and Kathryn both jumped up at that and started yelling at Silberman until John waved them back to their places. He said to them, "Let him finish. This is important."

Silberman looked at John, "Thank you. I was afraid that would cause a commotion, but like I said, I had to earn Skynet's trust."

Looking at Derek he said, "I knew that even though some of the resistance would be killed by those infiltrators, the deceit would be quickly discovered, and a solution found to prevent too much death. I had confidence that you would prevail, and it would make you that much stronger.

"Skynet approved the plan and its research branch came up with a variation of the T100 called the T101. Of course, you know it is a cyborg and hard to detect, but you can, and you do. It was effective for a short time. It's old technology now, but I knew about it before I mentioned it to Skynet. I remembered from the past and I found it during my research. I just used the idea that it already had to gain its trust."

John was nodding his head, "Very clever, Doctor. Please go on." It was obvious to Kathryn that John was leading Silberman on to something.

The old man looked around and held up his cup for the corpsman who hurried to fill it again. After taking a sip Silberman continued, "The next part was a little trickier. Again, from my two sources I knew that Skynet had somehow invented time travel. I endeavored to find out as much about that as I could."

John sat up straighter in his chair. This was what he had hoped to find when he first heard about Silberman. This could be the key he had been waiting for.

"I found out that Skynet research had made hundreds of mistakes before it could make its technology work at all. The reliability factor was low but measurable. The cyborg should work because only the organic skin is exposed to the energetic particles in the magnetic fields." He looked directly at John and said, "Only organic things can go through." He nodded at

John, "Also there seems to be some physical limit to the distance in time that anyone can go."

John was rapt. After a few seconds he asked, "Do you know where Skynet's time travel equipment is? Do you know how to use it?"

Silberman was nodding his head and smiling. "Of course, I do. I was present several times when the system was used, and I was paying attention. I observed when the T101 was sent to kill your mother. I was present when a new model, a T888 was sent to kill you, and I was present when six of the model T888s were sent to ensure the security of several key people and things." Silberman was smiling at their concerned faces. "I don't know exactly how you did it, but somehow you made them all fail."

* * *

Since the dreams had restarted, Sarah knew, deep in her bones, that it was once again time to move on. There was a danger here in Gila Bend that she did not see or understand, but it was there non-the-less. Somehow it had found her. The dreams proved it. She was not sure where she was going to go, but she knew she could not stay here. She had learned to trust her instincts and those now screamed, "Run!"

And so, Sarah Conner began planning her escape. She set herself a timetable of two days. She would have to get everything ready without looking like anything was getting ready. She did not want to have to fight her way past Danny, maybe be forced to physically hurt him, so she would leave an hour after he left for work. She could tell the sitter that she was sick and did not need her that day, and since she had just gotten her paycheck, she would not be leaving money behind.

She spent the afternoon before her departure getting her car serviced and the night before finishing the laundry. Deciding where to go consumed her thoughts for the next full day. She didn't think that Mexico was safe yet and she did not think California was much safer. Something one of her customers had said last week in the diner resonated. He said, "Las Vegas was growing so rapidly that anyone who wanted to work could find it there." She thought that sounded like the place for her.

Technical Interlude

Robot and Cyborg Sensing Systems: Part 1

Pattern recognition is an important technology allowing Terminators to recognize humans and determine if they are on their pre-programmed hit list. The visual ability of robots and cyborgs, as developed by Skynet, evolved along with the other features and functions of these sophisticated machines.

The T100 series, with simple digital stereoscopic vision augmented with infrared systems made them formidable enemies of human solders, especially at night. "Heads-up displays" within the optical field were added to later models and were commonly used for directional information, database searches and internal systems' status displays. Simple parallel processing and multitasking allowed a T101 to pursue a target, access geographical directional information, calculate tactical, situational probabilities, and communicate with Skynet for any programming changes, data updates or mission critical information.

The primary advancement made by Skynet Research was the ability of the T101 to screen out or filter out background clutter or noise from the vast agglomeration of visual data its "eyes" collected every second. A super-efficient, high resolution, Signal-to-Noise-Ratio (SNR) controller was the key to this major step forward in autonomous control.

SNR is defined as the power ratio between a signal (meaningful information) and the background noise (unwanted signal). If the signal and noise are measured across the same impedance, the SNR can be obtained by calculating the square of the root-mean-square (RMS) amplitude values. The numeric ratio of the power values (PS/PN) is often so large that it is best described using the logarithmic decibel (dB) scale. Higher SNR values represent higher signal strength measured relative to the background noise. The SNR is then twenty times the dB value of the RMS of the wanted signal and the noise.

Visual signal, pattern comparison designs exist, often referred to by descriptive names: snowflakes, diamonds, streets and alleys, telephone poles. For example, snowflakes are centrally located, multi-fingered patterns that link the primary features of a human face, each feature a set of distances from the center and each other. Streets and alleys are a set of parallel grids that demarcate the human facial features. Multiple patterns can be used with the same target data to fine tune or iterate a solution to identification.

Confirmed target data point information would be only slightly confused by a disguise or damage by trauma. A rapid cycling through multiple pattern challenges would normally break through such attempts. For example, the presence or absence of facial hair or glasses would be irrelevant to this system via cross-check comparisons. Removal of a nose or lower jaw, however, might be sufficient to confuse the controller, rendering a mismatch. Neither extreme would normally be something that a human target would voluntarily employ in the attempt to escape.

One weakness to the system is the overwhelming of the controller by massive levels of noise. Such camouflage in the form of strobe lights, flickering flames or waves of thermal energy, or the addition of high frequency electromagnetic pulses tend to misdirect the pattern recognition circuitry and confuse the timely identification of the target. Occasionally the application of dirt and the reduction of surface temperature are enough to confuse the T101 for a short time, but ultimately the T101's programming and endurance would overcome such diversionary tactics.

A second weakness is the "shadow effect" while using infrared system. Since a warm object closest to the eyes tends to obscure any object directly behind or within the expanding cone of vision further away, a control system had to be designed to selectively reduce the effect of the near objects if they were not of interest, allowing the shielded objects to show through.

Target location and distance information, whether visible light or infrared based, is handled via a math co-processor. The basic function of this system is to process the analog vision information from the vision sensors, make the triangulation calculation, and output the relative coordinates and motion vectors in a format that the main computer can use. The second system does the pattern recognition algorithms and feeds everything back to the main control computer.

As well as this worked for the T100 series, the T800 series and up added sophisticated sensing abilities: pressure, thermal, chemical, electromagnetic (light (full spectrum), radio, microwave), sound (full spectrum), biometric (pulse, respiration, perspiration, smell, genetic markers), distance ranging (sonar, radar, telescopic, microscopic). These additional sensor suits, although requiring much larger and faster primary computers, were necessary to compete with the smaller, faster, more intuitive and elusive human targets.

Chapter 8

The drive to Las Vegas took about a day. John and Lily enjoyed almost all of it. Sarah had to stop every two hours to let Lily relieve herself and after a while John slept quietly, strapped in his seat. She stopped for gas in Kingman and paid with her new credit card; she thought it was smart to start a paper trail under her new name. She had been glancing in her mirrors fairly often and had never noticed any suspicious cars following: no Danny, police of any state or local variety, or government cars in sight. She believed she was in the clear although she thought it was probably a matter of time before someone came looking for her.

She woke John up right after they crossed into Nevada on US93, before they crossed the Hoover Dam. She wanted John to see that, since she did not know if he would ever have that chance again. It was time to stop for supper, so she pulled into the parking lot used for tourists and she took John into the cafeteria next to the gift shop. Lily stayed in the car, guarding their stuff and she was rewarded with a paper plate of chicken nuggets when they got back.

On the road again, the sun was beginning to set as the lights and hotels of Las Vegas crept into view on the desert horizon. US93 changed into Nevada 582 in Henderson and she followed it to Sahara Avenue in Winchester. She started to watch for cheap motels that would allow Lily to stay until she could find a job and her own apartment. She did not think it would take too long and she was right. Finding one that rented by the week, and allowed dogs if they were well behaved, was surprisingly easy. She paid a deposit in cash.

They checked in and took showers, dressed for bed, had a snack and then collapsed into dreamless oblivion. Sarah planned to find a babysitter first thing in the morning and then start her job search among the city's many casinos.

- - -

This morning Colonel Brewster wore his new rank insignia for the first time. He had received the notification of his promotion two days ago and the commander of Vandenberg had held the short ceremony and presentation yesterday. He thought that the embroidered silver eagles felt funny on his sleeve. They belonged on his collar where proper Air Force insignia belonged. This was his first time wearing the new McPeak uniform with the rank insignia on the jacket sleeves (like the Navy did). He thought, although he would probably never admit it out loud, *that the "new", uniform was better than the old traditional uniform; it seemed to have a more tailored fit.* Everyone he knew hated them and openly said that they made Air Force officers look like air line pilots.

The first trial run of the full-size model of the Hunter-Killer was scheduled for 1000 hours and his entire department was going to be in the stands watching. As nervous as he was, he felt sure that the test pilot was feeling worse. It was not planned to be much of a flight, as test flights go, just fire-up the engines, swivel them around while they were at 5% power, set the engines vertically for VTO, power up sufficiently to achieve a fifty foot altitude, yaw 180° clockwise and then stop, turn 180° counterclockwise and then stop, then land and shut-down. Simple and direct instructions to follow and the test pilots, to a man, hate the restrictions. They thought that they should do a little flying while they had her up, but

Colonel Brewster, based on input from his technical head, said no.

Brewster parked behind the bleachers in the viewing area and climbed the aluminum stairs leading to the seats. He waved to several heads of his diverse group and returned the salutes of others. He found a seat about three rows above the civilian workers and a row below the press box where the cameras were already running, and he sat down.

He heard the engines begin to spool-up, even from the one-hundred yards away; protocol dictated that the test be safely away from any spectators. Brewster thought that the idea was probably a good one and he did not fight it when the requirement was handed to him, although several of his crew thought it was unnecessarily restrictive. After all, they had worked very hard for a long time designing and building the HK, they ought to be able to watch from as close as they wanted. Brewster reminded them that they had never seen a prototype go bad before. He had, he told them, and it was not very pretty or safe. He felt that a hundred yards might be a little too close if the damned thing decided to blow-up suddenly.

Listening to the test status in the little ear speaker he was wearing, Brewster watched as the pilot began rotating the engine nacelles to the vertical position from the horizontal. Each step of the scripted test was completed and verified before the next step was allowed. Brewster heard a voice from the blockhouse state that VTO was permitted and that the pilot was to advance the throttle to the calculated balance point. He heard the pilot respond with a, "Control, HK1, roger, that." Then the sound of the turbofan engines became deafening. Brewster covered his ears with his hands along with everyone else who had forgotten their ear plugs.

He heard the tinny voice in his ear counting upward until the power was at fifty percent and the weight of the HK was almost exactly balanced by the thrust of the engines. Brewster saw how the suspension of the landing gear was slowly bounding up and down by several inches as the pilot shifted the controls, attempting zero buoyancy. The earpiece said, "Control, HK1, thrust stable, permission to attempt lift off." The block house voice answered, "HK1, Control, that's an affirmative. You have permission to power to fifty percent plus and hover at twenty feet. Over"

"Control, HK1, roger that," the pilot said, and the sound level rose again as the HK began to rise into the morning air. "Twenty feet," he heard from the pilot, "Control, HK1, permission to rotate." The block house voice responded, "HK1, everything is five-by-five. You have permission to rotate one-eighty clockwise." The pilot responded, "Roger that."

Brewster found he had been holding his breath and now he gulped in a lungful of air with a small whooping sound. Then as the pilot made the starboard engine rotate five degrees forward and the port engine five degrees aft, Brewster heard something pulsing. He was not sure just what he was hearing, but almost immediately the pilot announced to the controller that he had a problem. Before the block house could comment, the HK shuddered and the plane twisted toward the stands, crashing into the tarmac just before reaching them. There was a great crashing sound and then a rolling fireball as the HK exploded, sending burning fuel into the stands and debris all around the spectators. In stunned disbelief Brewster jumped to his feet and hurried to help where he could.

The damage to the program was minimized because the emergency crews were already at the scene and primed for disaster. The casualties were light, considering: the pilot had been unable to eject and died of his burns, two program technicians and two secretaries who were their dates were burned, but survived, the HK prototype was a total write-off.

After reviewing all the telemetry data and the films, Brewster proposed to the brass that the HK program specification be rewritten to be a computer assisted, remote controlled drone. The brass reluctantly agreed, and that portion of the program was saved. His teams immediately began work on the next generation HK where man would play a reduced role from then on. A man would direct the HK and a computer would make the drone do what the man directed. It seemed to be the most logical thing to do under the circumstances; the thing wanted to fly like a brick.

- - -

Driving back alone to her motel room, Sarah was carrying on a pointed two-way conversation. She did not feel that there was anything particularly strange that she was both asking and answering questions; she seemed to be doing more and more of that recently if the truth be known.

She had managed to be in the right place at the right time for a change, and she landed a good job as a dealer at one of the smaller casinos, the Silver Dollar. They had trained her, and she had apprenticed under a seasoned dealer for two weeks before they had given her a table of her own on first shift. First shift was considered less desirable by the other dealers, but she did not mind. Fewer customers meant fewer tips, but it allowed her less pressure and gave her a little more time to practice her skills. Besides, the Dollar paid well. Policy makers felt that if the dealers were well paid, they would be less likely to be skimming from the house and less likely to hook-up with a card counter or sharp as they were called. She could not figure out how anyone thought that they were going to get away with anything. One of the first things they showed her during orientation was the security room filled with closed-circuit television sets. Each room of the casino had cameras in each corner that cycled around, covering every square foot of floor each minute. Each table had its own camera mounted in a bubble in the ceiling, looking down at the table and the operator and players. She saw how the guards cycled around watching for anything out of the ordinary and how they could stop and watch if they spotted trouble. The six full-time guards had walky-talky communications with ten other guards on the floor. Half of those guards were plain clothes and unobtrusive.

At first, though, that is what she thought was happening. This guy, Carl was his name, had been showing up at her table for several days in a row. He never said or did anything that made her nervous or that sent up warning flags and the Dollar's security men never seemed to be watching him. He just played Blackjack at her low-stakes table, won or lost a few hundred each night, and then left. At least she thought he left. She really was not paying too much attention at first. The afternoon of the fourth day when she took her lunch break, Carl had worked his way through the buffet line and then carried his tray to her table, standing there as if he were waiting for her permission to sit. She was not sure why, but she asked him to join her and they talked around mouthfuls of food.

She could not decide what was slightly off about Carl, but she did not peg him as a weirdo or crook, so she just sat there and enjoyed his company as she ate. Her lunch time passed quickly, and she left Carl sitting at the table as she went back to work. Carl had asked her out after work, and she said she would think about it. They did not go out that night, but eventually she had agreed to go to a magic show with him and he had been a perfect gentleman. A month and several dates later, Sarah was faced with a bit of a dilemma. Carl seemed to be getting a little more serious than she was, and she was not sure how to handle it.

"*He does seem nice,*" she said, her voice barely carrying over the sound of the wind and the traffic around her as she drove home. "But, how do you feel about him? What if John doesn't like him? What if he doesn't like John?" She slowed as the traffic light changed and the cars in front of her began stopping. "*John is a different issue,*" she answered, "*an important one for sure, but different.*"

She had come to a stop and noticed that one or two of the other drivers were watching her talk to the air. She waited until the cars began moving again before she resumed her dialog. "It's not like he's asking me to move in with him, or for him to move in with me. It's just a dinner date at his house." She answered, "*Sure. That's what they all say. It's just dinner.*"

She turned into the parking lot of her motel, "Well, it is just dinner. John is even going to join us." She pulled into her slot and switched off the Jeep's engine. "*Well, if he tries something funny, he'll get a surprise. Won't he?*"

She jumped out of her car, practically ran up the stairs to her room, paid the sitter and started getting ready. She put John into the shower with her and after they were both scrubbed clean, she wrapped one towel around her hair and another around John and then one around herself. She gave John the hairbrush to play with while she worked on her face and picked out something suitable to wear. She got dressed, got John dressed and then did something quick and simple to her hair. "There's something to be said for short hair," she said out loud. There was no reply this time.

She took Lily out for a short walk with John toddling along and then she put Lily back in the room, loaded John into her car and they drove to the address Carl had given her. Carl had opened the door almost before the chime had stopped echoing, "Say, you made it!" He seemed very happy to see her. "And you must be Johnny?" Carl was sticking out his hand for John to shake.

John did not quite know what to do with it and seemed a little frightened by Carl's exuberance. Carl took his hand and started giving it a little shake, pumping it up and down a few times. John pulled away and Carl seemed to be put out by his reaction. "He should learn to shake hands like a little gentleman, Sarah. He'll seem to be more polite to adults."

A little warning feeling nagged the back of her mind, but she ignored it. "He's only three, Carl. He has plenty of time to get used to meeting people." She looked at him expectantly, "Can we come in?"

Carl blushed, "Oh, yeah. I'm sorry. Sure, come on in." He opened his door wider and made a little wave toward the inside, "Welcome to my home."

Sarah and John entered, and John was immediately drawn to the brightly lit aquarium against one wall of the living room. Several colorful tropical fish were swimming around, darting through the strands of waving and floating vegetation. John ran up and reached up, putting his hands on the glass wall and shouted, "Fish!"

The tank rocked a little from the impact and Sarah was right behind him, using one hand to stabilize the aquarium and the other to take John's arm and pull him back about an arm's length. "Take it easy, John. Don't scare the little fish." She looked over at Carl and saw that he was watching the water sloshing back to normal. "Sorry, Carl, he hasn't seen fish in person before. He won't do that again."

Carl recovered his poise, "That's OK, Sarah. It's just that I thought he was going to knock it over." Carl used the tail of his shirt to wipe off John's smudges from the glass. "Of course, he can look at the fish. That's what they're for." He turned toward her, "We'll just have to make sure he doesn't get too close. I don't want to have to pull him out with my little net." Carl snickered at his joke.

Carl asked, "How about a drink before dinner?"

Sarah nodded, "Sure. What do you have?"

The crisis averted, the rest of the evening went well, and they all had a good time. John got fed and he got to watch the fish swim around, and Sarah and Carl talked and got to know each other better.

- - -

At the end of the evening, Carl gave Sarah a quick kiss and he shook a sleepy John's hand as they left his house. He watched her load John into the seat, buckle him in and then climb in behind the wheel. After she started the engine, she put it into gear and after a little wave she backed out of his driveway and drove away.

Carl closed and locked the front door and went into the kitchen and picked up the wall-phone. He dialed a number that was obviously familiar. He waited until it was answered and then he said, "She's just left. I think she's clean, boss. I tried several times to get her to talk about the casino and she deflected me each time." He waited while he listened and then, "OK. I'll file my report in the morning. Good night, boss"

And that is how Sarah Reese passed her security test and got to keep her job. Carl was pleased since he liked her and he thought he could make a go of their budding relationship, even with a kid involved. He thought he could explain to her why he had to trick her into dating him in the first place; at least he hopped so. He really wanted to get her to continue going out with him. She had that lean, athletic build that he found irresistible in a woman.

Carl's report was duly written and presented to his boss, the chief of the Silver Dollar's security. As a course of standard policy, a copy was sent to each of the other casinos in Las Vegas and a copy went to the local FBI office, who then started a file on Sarah Reese in their new computer system. Since there was no real history behind Sarah Reese, there were no red flags raised over her. She seemed to be just another number; another cog in the American wheel. James Ellison would not figure out how to search the growing FBI data base efficiently for a year. Looking for new entries with no previous background information would soon become standard procedure, but not today. By the time he learned that technique it would be too late; again.

- - -

Silberman liked Pescadaro State Hospital. He got to interview dozens of inmates there who were a wealth of material for studies in mental health, especially aberrant personality disorders. He had even begun blocking-out material for a book he had in mind. Tentatively he laid it out as a chapter for each kind or variety of criminal behavior. He spent Monday, Wednesday and Friday mornings and Tuesday and Thursday evenings there with alternate Saturday afternoons and Sunday afternoon once a month. The pay was not great, but it was steady, and his accountant had stopped squawking.

He had kept Loraine, but on a reduced schedule. She still ran his office in the city, and she managed his patient's sessions, packing them into his available time. He also had given up Doctor Jackson as an unnecessary expense. He felt better than he had in years; no more dreams and seven hours of sleep a night were making a world of difference in his life and his attitude. Soon he completely forgot about Sarah Conner and the nightmare visions he used to have.

- - -

James Ellison had fallen into a dull routine. He got up at six o'clock every morning, a full half-hour earlier than Lilah, made a pot of coffee, pulled on his running shoes and went for a three-mile jog. When he returned, he showered, had a glass of orange juice, two slices of white bread toast with crunchy peanut butter and honey and he read the front section of the LA Times while he nursed his coffee. Lilah was up by then and she normally greeted him in the dining room about the time he was ready for his second cup. He would usually discuss her day (she was not very interested in his plans recently) and then he would get dressed while she ate. Today was a little different and he sensed something amiss.

Lilah came out of the bedroom dressed and looking ready to leave. He had looked up as the door opened and he frowned slightly as she walked up to where he sat watching her. "Good morning, Lilah. You're running a little early. Got a busy day?" James had noticed that she was clutching her brown leather brief case tighter than he remembered.

Lilah did not answer. Instead she came up beside him and as he looked up into her face, she placed a folded paper onto the table next to his coffee cup. As soon as it hit the surface, she removed her hand as if she did not want to risk his reaching out and touching her. To his confusion she spun on the balls of her feet and briskly walked to and through the front door, picking up her car keys from the hall table as she passed. She never spoke and after the door closed, he heard her car start and quickly pull out of their little driveway. It was then that he thought to look at the paper she had left for him.

He had seen and served hundreds of warrants and other legal documents in his career and this looked very similar. What caught his attention was that both his and Lilah's name were at the top of this one. She had just served him with a notice of divorce, and his breath caught in his throat as the tears of pain and confusion began. *Why is she doing this*, he wondered.

- - -

After dating for nearly three months, Carl had asked Sarah to move into his house with him. Sarah liked Carl, but she still felt a certain level of distrust with him. For several weeks after he had told her about his trickery, "All in the line of duty," he had pled, she had refused to see him outside the card rooms. She was afraid that she would get into trouble with the casino management if she caused a scene with him there, so she just ignored him as much as possible. It turned out that he had been forced to do a lot of explaining and promising to the chief of security once he had broken the news to him about his intentions toward Sarah.

But as happens with most young people the world over, Sarah could not stay mad at Carl forever. They started dating again and the second time they had dinner at Sarah's motel, Carl had asked her to make the big move. Sarah had just finished putting John to bed and she was handing him a glass of wine after clearing the takeout containers off of the card table at the end of the bed.

"Sarah, I've been thinking." Carl looked over his glass at Sarah as she settled onto the room's only couch, folding her legs under her. "I know it hasn't been very long since we started dating again, but I think it's been going well. Don't you?"

Sarah took a sip and worried about where this might be heading. She slowly nodded, "Yes."

"Well, I thought that it would be good for all of us, you, me and Johnny as well, to live together."

Sarah seemed to choke on her wine and Carl thought that she was going to object, so he quickly said, "Wait, hear me out. Please, Sarah, listen before you say no."

She snapped her mouth shut with an effort and Carl went on with his proposal. He listed all the benefits of the arrangement: personal, financial, logistical. He did not mention any negatives because he could not think of any. He talked for five minutes straight with each minute she did not interrupt a victory in his mind. Then he ran out of things to say and he stopped. "What do you think?"

"First off, what will the casino think about it? I need this job. I can't risk them firing me because I moved in with you. They might get the idea that we were up to something." She had set her glass aside so that she could face him squarely. "Did you think about that?" Sarah had thought about it as soon as the subject came up. She was beginning to develop an innate distrust of everyone she knew; except for John and Enrique and Yolanda. Everyone else had a personal agenda. It was an important survival insight she was trying to instill in John.

Carl said, "As a matter of fact I did think of that. I've already asked permission of my boss and he thought that it would be OK." Carl did not mention that it had gotten heated and Carl had threatened to quit before getting his permission. He also did not mention that they would both be fired if anything at all went badly for the casino, or if there was even the slightest whiff of collusion to run a scam.

So, relieved of that concern, and liking the idea of not having a weekly rent to pay, Sarah agreed. She gave her notice to the motel ending her lease on Monday morning and she packed up everything she had and loaded her car and moved in with Carl. He was ecstatic and John loved the fish tank. Carl had even bought John a fish of his own that John named Yolanda. Sarah had laughed at that and she never explained except to say that it was the name of an old friend. Carl thought it was a little odd, but he was so glad to have her there that he just laughed with her.

- - -

Tierresa Dyson was growing impatient. Miles seemed to be around more and yet available less and less after he had set up a computer link to his office in their study. Bringing his work home was supposed to free him up, allowing him to spend more time with his family. She had to admit that he was home more, but he was always locked away in his study with his nose stuck in his computer. As far as she was concerned, that did not count as being home. She was determined to get to the bottom of the situation.

"Miles," she said as she opened the door to his study and barged in to confront him about his chronic inattention. "Miles, we have to talk".

Miles Dyson looked up from one of his two computer displays and peered at his intruder. He was blinking, bleary-eyed from staring too long at the glowing screens. "What?" he croaked. "Tiery, what did you say? What's wrong now?"

Tierresa answered in a hurt tone, "Miles, it's not just now. It's been for the past two years. We never see you except for the few minutes a day that you spend eating with us." She had reached his desk and she had stomped her foot as she arrived and crossed her arms over her chest, hugging herself as if for support for what she was saying. "Miles, it has gotten worse not better. You promised more time with us and it has actually been less time." She started running out of steam and she could see that he was now paying her some attention. "We miss you. The kids aren't sure who their father is any more."

Miles recognized his feelings of guilt as they began. He realized that he had been neglecting his family, but he was not sure what to do about it. This work was important on many levels: to him professionally, to Cyberdyne technically and financially, to the General and the rest of the committee for whatever their motives were, and ultimately to the Country for its security and growth. He had to do whatever it took to complete it, even if it meant some sacrifices. But what was nagging him was, he knew that if he could budget his time better, he could balance his demanding job with his family's needs.

Miles dropped his hands into his lap and looked at his wife and tried to smile. "Tiery you're right, I'm sorry." He logged off, stood and shut off his computer system. "I'm sorry. I've been distracted and distant from you and the kids and I'm truly sorry."

He came around his desk and put his hands on her shoulders and looked into her eyes. "I'm sorry." Then he smiled and said, "Let me try to make it up to you all. What would you and the kids like to do? I can get a few days off. Cyberdyne owes me more than a month's vacation time. Surly I can take a few days now."

Tierresa looked deeply into his eyes, "Do you mean it Miles? The kids will love that."

- - -

About five months after moving in with Carl, Sarah had one of her nightmares. The day had been a little more stressful than usual; a man had won over five thousand dollars and security had grilled her for more than an hour afterwards. The tapes had shown that she had done nothing even remotely wrong or suspicious. A video check for the past month never even turned up the man in the Dollar, much less at her table. Then, when their phone calls around to several other casinos showed that this guy was hitting it big all around town they realized that he was working on his own, some kind of card counter, and trying to hit everybody and get out before he had been made. The Sands security had finally caught him and run him out of town. Sarah was cleared and told to return to work in the morning, but the damage had been done.

Sarah was naturally upset and that is what she attributed the dream to. She knew that stress was one of the triggers and today was certainly stressful. Carl had made supper and she had an extra glass of red wine, but the dream interrupted their night just the same.

After calming John down and getting him back to sleep, Sarah told Carl an abbreviated, sanitized version of her nightmare. She explained how she had been having them for years, on and off, and they usually go away on their own. Carl was worried about her and he tried to minimize her concern and obvious fright. He was a little frightened too; he did not like science fiction things. Monsters and robots that hurt people made him very uncomfortable.

About an hour later they went back to bed and everyone slept through the rest of the night. Carl seemed to forget about the episode and Sarah did not bring it up.

- - -

She hated that she had to leave, but it had become imperative. Carl was growing frantic with her increasingly frequent nightmares. She was waking up the entire house at least twice a week and Carl had gotten cranky from lack of sleep and concern for his personal and professional security. His growing arguments for her to talk to a psychiatrist just made matters worse as far as she was concerned, and the tension had soured their relationship. Her feelings of impending danger to her and John grew stronger to her almost daily.

That fall morning, after calling in sick, Sarah packed up everything she owned and loaded it, John and Lily into her old Jeep and she headed south. She thought that maybe it was time to seek out Enrique and the Hands again. She did not know if they would still be camped where they had been before. In fact, she doubted it after what she had heard about the raid, but she thought that was the place to start. *This time it should be a little easier*, she thought, *I'm not pregnant and I'm not running from the police.*

They crossed into Mexico at San Luis, just south of Yuma, the next morning. She had driven all day down US 95 through Needles and Parker and then onto Yuma where she found a motel and spent the night. She and John had gone shopping and bought enough supplies and equipment to sustain them for more than a week. She thought that they would first check out the original campground and if they weren't there, she would drive them toward Ensenada, asking about them as she went. She could not think of a better way to go about her search.

The crossing went smoothly; her passport and Nevada drivers' license were more than adequate. The border patrol guards on both sides hardly gave her a second glance. Sarah turned onto Mexico 2 and headed west toward Mexicali where she picked up Mexico 5 and headed south toward the old campgrounds.

About two hours later she recognized the dog rocks and she turned off and drove back behind them to where she had spent nearly three years of her life. By now John and Lily both were cooked by the heat and tired and ready to stop. Sarah drove over the little rise that led to the old camp site and she brought the car to a sudden stop.

Laid out before her was the scene of a battle. The desert winds had not completely erased the evidence of the short battle that had happened here. Apparently, the Mexican police and army had coordinated and caught the Hands in crossfire, and they had used some heavy weapons against the lightly armed rebels. She could see a crashed helicopter and the burned-out hulks of the small travel trailers some of them had lived in; twisted metal ribs and bulkheads stood drooping among the charred furniture and ashed clothing. Broken glass was scattered around and one of the cars lay on its side, the obvious victim of an explosive of some kind. She did not see any bodies, but she did not expect to see any. She was certain that if anyone had been killed, the Mexican authorities would have taken them in at least for identification and hopefully a decent burial.

She found herself crying as she slowly drove closer to the wreckage. John's mouth was hanging open in shock and she saw it start to quiver. She put her arm around his shoulders and pulled him toward her for a hug. He asked in a weak voice, "Mom, what happened?" He was about to cry too.

Through her tears she answered, "After we left, it looks like someone attacked our friends." She looked around at the wreckage, "It was probably the Mexican army and police." She looked at John, "You knew that we were considered outlaws, didn't you?"

John nodded miserably, "Did they kill Yolanda and Luna?"

She shook her head violently, "No, I'm sure they're OK. The army wouldn't kill women and children." She did not feel as certain as she tried to sound. "They probably arrested them. That's all."

John said, "I hope so." His chin was quivering.

Sarah continued to the center of the compound. She stopped the car and Lily jumped out, relieved herself in the sand, and trotted off to investigate some of the debris. Sarah climbed out and came around and unbuckled John and helped him jump down. "Don't stray and be careful around the metal. I don't want you to get cut or step on a nail. OK?"

John nodded and stayed very close to his mother.

She walked past the twisted, blackened metal and charred wood that had been her trailer those years ago. The pangs of loss she felt started her tears flowing again. Then she led John over to the tree that served as the starting point for the directions to her dump site. It had been burned but it was recognizable to her. She placed her back to the tree, pointed directly away from her trailer and she took nine steps. Then she turned left or due north and took five steps. She looked down and saw tire tracks faintly crisscrossing the area, but the chain that led to the trapdoor still looked to be securely buried. *They never found it,* she thought in excitement. *My weapons cache is secure. We still have a chance.*

Sarah looked down at John and squeezed his hand. "Let's eat some lunch and then try to find Enrique and Yolanda."

John looked up at her and smiled; for the first time today, she realized. She smiled back at him and they went back to the Jeep.

- - -

After lunch they gathered up their things and loaded Lily into the Jeep. Sarah took a last look around and then headed back toward the road. The Jeep jounced over a few bumps and then was headed south on Mexico 5 once again. They drove along, practicing their Spanish until they reached the crossing of Mexico 3. She decided to stop and snoop around.

There was an old general store and five or six houses she could see from the highway. Pulling into a dirt parking area in front of the store, Sarah made Lily stay in the car and she unbuckled John and helped him down. They climbed the wooden steps and went into the cool dimness of the inside. She sent John to pick out two bottles of water from the cooler. While she waited for John, she asked the clerk, a little old Mexican woman, if she knew anything about what had happened up the road. The woman suddenly acted frightened and all she would say was that she didn't know anything about those people.

John carried up three bottles of cold water and Sarah paid for them and thanked the woman for her help. She guided John outside and buckled him into his seat. She opened his bottle and then poured some of other one into a plastic bowl for Lily. As she was climbing behind the wheel, drinking from her bottle when an older man pushed open the screen door of the store and glared at her.

"Señora, why do you ask questions about those people?" He did not look particularly friendly, but he did not look threatening either.

Sarah answered truthfully, "Some of them were my friends, Señor. I was worried about them and am trying to find them."

He seemed to believe her because the hardness on his face softened a little. "Señora, these people have been in trouble with the law and the army, I think. There was a lot of shooting and then they were all taken away." He rubbed his stubbly chin and then said, "Most have been taken to the jail in Mexicali. A few, mostly the leaders I think, have been taken to the army prison in Hermosillo. You will never see them again, I think. It is a bad place."

His news saddened her, but she thanked him anyway. Now she knew something about what happened. Maybe some of them escaped the raid; stranger things have happened she knew. Sarah got her car started and backed out onto highway 3. She turned toward the east and Ensenada. Both she and John waved as they drove off. The man watched until they were out of sight and then went inside to where the phone was sitting on the counter.

- - -

About two hours later, with the sun directly in her face, Sarah began recognizing the suburban area where she had waited with the get-away car during the bank robbery. She slowed and watched for the intersection of Mexico 3 with Mexico 1 in Ensenada. She remembered that to go into the city proper she would have to turn right and then she would apparently pass the bank in a short distance.

There was a new traffic light at that intersection, and she had to wait behind a pickup truck for the light to change. The truck turned left, and she turned right. She noticed a local police car waiting in the southbound turn lane and the officer watched her as she drove on down the highway. She watched to see if he would circle back around and follow her. He did not, or at least she did not see him.

She had driven about a block past the bank when she spotted Luis. He was sitting in the shade of the under hang of a little restaurant and he stood and gave her a subtle wave as she approached, signaling for her to pull around to the back and stop. With the feelings of excitement and anticipation, she stopped and waited for Luis to walk back to her. She got out of her car and threw her arms around his neck in a hug as he arrived. He gently pulled her arms down from his neck, looking around as he did and said, "Buenas Tardes, Señora Conner. It is good to see you again also."

She said, "Luis, I have been so worried since I stopped at the camp. It looks like a war happened." She looked into his eyes and asked, "Is everyone OK? Where are Enrique and Yolanda and the rest?"

Luis had been ruffling John's hair. Now he looked back at her. "We should go somewhere we can talk, out of the sun. Not-so-little John looks hot and tired."

* * *

Silberman had a lot of specific information stuffed into his shaggy head. John had patiently gotten him to detail as much of it as he could directly to his men. Lists of Skynet emplacements and material dumps were tactical coups of the highest order. Data on Skynet's chain of command and lines of communication were nuggets of pure gold. But John yearned for specifics about the time travel equipment, location and process. That was the most important thing that Silberman could tell him. That information was absolutely essential to the survival of the resistance, him and all of humanity with him.

He knew that he had used (or eventually would use) it to send Kyle back to save Sarah from the initial T101 and impregnate her, and a reprogrammed T101 to save them both later on. He also had to use it to send back a team, led by Derek, to kill Andy Goode before he could sell the Turk to the Air Force and a T800 to protect him from repeated frantic attacks by Skynet as Judgment Day continued to be postponed. He remembered that Kate had sent a T101 back to protect him and her from the TX after he had been killed in a battle. Secretly he wondered if history had been changed enough by something he or his mother had done to make his recent near death the current truth vs. his actual death described by the T101 on Judgment Day. He hoped so anyway.

He recognized that each time they prevented Skynet's success in the past they most likely changed their future in some way. If he could find the key to eliminating the possibility of Skynet ever coming into being by some judicious use of the time travel technology, he was determined to do it. He really did not care if that change eliminated him from this current now. He thought that it would be worth it.

"What did you say?" His musings had allowed his attention to Silberman's narrative to pass over his head, almost without understanding. "I'm sorry doctor, I'm afraid that my mind must have wandered, and I think I missed something important you just said."

Silberman acquired that haughty look he affected when he felt superior. "Well, I was saying that I thought that your latest destructive attacks on the Skynet fortifications in San Francisco might have eliminated the primary time travel facility he was using near Santa Rosa, but the one across the bay at the old Mare Island Naval Facility was likely intact."

Everyone in the room sat up at the same time, hope and surprise obvious on all faces as they stared at Silberman. The sound of a pin could have been heard if one had dropped to the floor. A breathless John Conner was the first to speak, "Skynet had more than one?"

As if he was telling a simple truth to simple children he answered, "Of course. It had several installations around the world. The beast was nothing if not redundant!" He sipped from his glass, savoring the impact of his words. "I only saw that one once, but the records state that it was shut down over two years ago." He smiled at them, "It was quite functional at that time, you know?"

Derek and John and Kate all looked at each other, each with a renewed hope. John said, "Derek, prepare a strike force to investigate this place." He looked at Kate and then continued, "I doubt that my doctor will allow me to make the trip for the near future, so I need your eyes there on the ground to get me as much information as you can."

Kate was nodding her affirmation of John's understanding when she said, "Will they be taking one of the choppers?"

John answered, "Yes. I think speed might be of the essence. We can spare two for a short while."

Kate nodded curtly, "Then, in that case, I think you could go as long as you promise your doctor that you will stay out of the line of fire."

John smiled broadly, "Of course, Doctor, whatever you say." Then looking at Silberman he said, "I hope you don't mind flying in helicopters doctor."

The smug look on Silberman's face melted away as he realized that John Conner wasn't kidding.

Technical Interlude

How Dogs Detect Cyborgs

It was discovered fairly early in the conflict between the resistance fighters and Skynet's T101 infiltrators that dogs could detect the T101 cyborgs somehow, normally well before any humans could. It was thought that it was the T101's artificial smell or lack of a human one that was the key, but it was eventually decided that must only be a contributing factor. Sometimes a guard dog could detect a T101 well before it could possibly smell it, most likely by a sound that only they make. Dog physiology and to some extent dog psychology play significant roles.

A dog's sense of smell is 100 to 1,000 times more sensitive that a typical human's. Their world view is written by the interwoven tapestry of smells constantly surrounding them. The notion that dogs can smell fear is a fact of nature. It seems that dogs can smell many other emotions as well; anger, frustration, sadness, sexual tension, and disappointment to name a few. A T101 is a machine with artificial flesh and blood. It has a smell that is different from most humans. Its breath and perspiration are slightly metallic. The T101 does not feel emotion of any kind and so is an island of missing or incorrect smells to a dog.

A dog's range of hearing is not only greater than the typical human's (67Hz to 45,000 Hz for dogs vs. 64 Hz to 23,000 Hz for humans), but it is also more sensitive (about a factor of 4 time greater than human). T101 power supplies have been measured and the high frequency hum they put out (30,000 Hz) is well within the range of the dog's hearing and above almost all humans. Even though the hum is of a low-level nature, it is certainly loud enough for a dog to hear and learn to dislike.

The dog's vision is lacking when compared to most humans. Detection of moving objects seems to be better in dogs, but sometimes a moving object becomes "invisible" once it becomes stationary and no longer threatening. Colors, never a strong suit for dogs, tend to blend together and patterns made of yellows and greens merge into gray. It's thought that the skin coloring of the T101's is wrong because of the color of the artificial skin and blood used in their manufacture (or growth.) Studies started by the main body of the Resistance are looking into it.

The dog's natural need for the pack and following a leader and protecting its own territory also figure into their ability to detect T101s. Bonding with a human handler, sensing his anxiety and fear and anger when his group is threatened, makes the dog want to protect the humans (i.e. his pack). The praise earned by spotting threats, especially terminators, quickly reinforces the dog's abilities. He very quickly learns to recognize the warning signs of the machines that are trying to infiltrate and kill his leader.

Even though the dog's normal armament, (teeth, claws, strength, endurance, and ferociousness), are formidable against human targets, it is only the dog's early warning system that matters in the daily life and death struggles against Skynet and its T101 terminators.

Chapter 9

In James Ellison's office things were somber. His lawyer had just walked in and sat in the proffered chair across from him. He rested his briefcase on the adjoining chair and popped the two thumb latches making a sound like small firecrackers going off together. He looked up at James as he reached inside and extracted a small stack of papers that were held together with a large spring clip.

"Well, James, this is it", he laid the papers onto the desk blotter. "All you have to do is initial and date the places I have tagged for you and sign the last page and I'll file it." He dropped his hands into his lap, "I'm truly sorry it ended this way."

Ellison looked depressed and resigned to this event. "Thanks, Larry. I hate that this happened too, but at least there were no children to worry about."

Larry was nodding, "You've got that right, buddy. Kids make the legal processes at least an order of magnitude more difficult." Then he grimaced, "Sorry. I didn't mean to sound flip."

James smiled sadly across the desk as he began initialing, "You remember that we both wanted children in the beginning? We talked about it all the time." He got to the last page and paused and then with a sigh he signed on the targeted line. "It was always in our plans, but it seems that it was never the highest priority with Lilah." He slid the document across the desk to Larry. "Here you go."

Larry took the papers, briefly flicked through the pages, saw the signature and put it into his briefcase. He stood and offered his hand, "I'll get this filed and let you know when the judge makes it final."

They shook hands and Larry clicked his briefcase closed, grabbed the handle and turned to go. "You OK, James? You look lousy."

"Yeah, sure, Larry, I'm a little down, but I'll bounce back. Don't worry." He tried to smile at his friend, but it came off as more of a grimace. "Let me know. OK?"

"Sure, James, I'll call you as soon as I hear and send over a copy of the decree." He left Ellison's office, closing the door quietly as he did.

James sat back down at his desk and began flipping through his memories. He seemed to be getting more morose rather than feeling better. "I should think about something else", he mumbled out loud. But he could not for the life of him think of what else there was to think about. Lilah had been his world, and now, with the stroke of a pen, and the agreement of a judge, she was gone.

His computer binged and he nearly jumped out of his chair at the sudden sound impinging on his desolation. He finally recognized the source and he looked over at the CRT that was now blinking a glowing green message at him. The screen said, "`Potential match found`". He squinted at the screen, "Match? What match?"

James Ellison, FBI agent, almost completely divorced man, typed his ID into the system. He was rewarded with a new screen. This one listed a name and history and a terrible copy of a grainy picture of a person of interest. He had set up a search of national records for Sarah Conner. He had listed everything he ever knew about her and made the computer dig through everything it knew about everyone, looking for a comparison. It had found one match. The screen said, "Sarah Baum, 27, dealer at the Silver Dollar casino in Las Vegas, Nevada." All the biometrics seemed to be right. All the timing seemed to be right, even to the age of her son, John. The picture showed an older, tanned, young woman, but he recognized her from the hospital photos he had studied for years. James Ellison, FBI agent, began to smile for the first time today.

- - -

Luis led them into the restaurant, and they shared a large pitcher of iced tea. John munched contentedly on chips and salsa while Lily crunched on the ice cubes that John slipped her. Sarah was very interested in whatever Luis had to say about the Hands and the event out at their camp and afterwards, but she seemed to have to pry details out of him and he seemed to be constantly watching everything around them.

"Luis, what's wrong? You seem agitated. Tell me what is going on." Sarah was genuinely concerned, and it showed.

Luis looked carefully at her face and then he seemed to decide. "I am still unsure what to believe and who to trust." He paused to sip from his tea, then, "When you left and then the army and police attacked us the same afternoon, my first thought was that somehow you had sold us out. I blamed you for what happened that day."

He shrugged, "I am sorry, but in the army, I was taught that there is no such thing as a coincidence, therefore you must have had something to do with it." He held up his hand to forestall her sputtering complaint, "Enrique told me later that he was sure you had nothing to do with it."

"I didn't", she managed to get out.

"I believe you, now. But it was hard for me then." Luis leaned across the table. "Later, at the jail, I talked to Juan. He had been on guard when you left the camp and he said he remembered seeing a small plane making a turn back to the west right after you turned onto the highway. He didn't think to tell anyone at the time, because he didn't think it was important.

"I think that the army or the police were looking for us and you just managed to escape. I no longer blame you for what happened." He sat back, "But I think that the police are still looking for those of us that escaped that day. I'm afraid that is why I seem so cautious."

Sarah reached across the table and squeezed his hand, "Luis, I am so sorry that this happened. But I did try to warn Enrique at the time. I was afraid that once the army or the Mexican government became involved it would only be a matter of time."

Luis said, "I remember what you said. You were right it seems."

He leaned forward again, "I have spoken to Enrique. He is fine and he wants to talk to you. He gave me a plan to use if I felt that it was safe."

Sarah asked, "How is he? How are Yolanda and the girls?"

"He is fine, and I will let him tell you of his family."

Sarah nodded, concern showing on her face, "OK."

"You are to drive a few miles north of here to the town of De Jaleo. It is just a little seacoast village with not too much. But it has a hotel and beach cottages. Enrique wants you to rent one of the cottages for a few days and enjoy the beach. He will find you there."

Sarah agreed, "John and I will enjoy a little ocean-side vacation. Tell Enrique that I will be there waiting for him. Also, give him our love."

She slid out of their booth and grabbed John's hand, "Thank you, Luis. Will I see you again?"

He shrugged his shoulders, "Who can say? Via con Dios, Sarah Conner".

- - -

De Jaleo is a sleepy little town just north of Ensenada, tucked in between the beach and Mexico 1. It consists of a church, police station, a bus terminal, a small shopping district, a few restaurants and a hotel. There are also a few homes scattered around, but everything is geared to the tourist traffic that trickles down from Tijuana about thirty miles to the north. All the buildings seemed to be made of adobe brick and painted yellow. It was difficult to tell one from the other; the church had a bell tower and double doors, the police station had bars on the windows and the hotel had more potted flowers out front. Otherwise you would have to read the signs over the doors to figure out what each building contained. A yellow wall surrounds the central courtyard where most of the buildings open onto.

Luis had told Sarah to check into the hotel and make use of the beach. He told her that maybe Enrique would show up and find her. She would have to be patient because he could not speak for Enrique's time or availability and he had to be careful.

Sarah had thanked him, and she and John climbed back into her car. Lily hopped into the back seat and they drove north on Mexico 1 to De Jaleo. She passed the bus terminal and saw the sign for the Hotel De Jaleo. She parked outside and she and John went inside and registered for a sea-side cottage. They drove north along the sandy, tree-lined, dirt road that led to their cottage and settled in. John and Lily played in the kitchenette while Sarah went back to one of the shops and bought bathing suits.

They played in the surf until they were all tired and hungry. They quickly showered and dressed and walked back to the hotel's restaurant for dinner. Sarah realized that she would have to conserve her money if she did not want to use her credit card, and so planned to buy groceries for their future breakfasts and lunches while they waited for Enrique to show up.

The sounds of the surf and the cool breezes blowing through the window's shutters made them sleep like rocks, especially after spending most of the day in the sun. The next morning, after some breakfast, they went back out onto the beach and Sarah rented a large umbrella and folding chair. She set up about fifty feet from the surf and she watched John and Lily romp in the water and sand. She ordered a beer for herself and water for John and Lily when a waiter from the hotel walked by. About ten minutes later she sensed his return.

"Buenas Tardes, Señora. Here is your beer."

She recognized his voice immediately. "Enrique!" she exclaimed in excitement. "You came." She had stood from her chair and now faced the older man. "I hoped that you would come. I told Luis that I was looking for you. Since you are here, I assume that he found you." She was smiling at him broadly.

He smiled back at her as he handed her a beer and a cold cola for John, but it wasn't the smile she had gotten used to at the camp. He looked tired and gaunt and his eyes kept darting around, surveying the beach for as far as he could see. She noticed that a young man was lounging under the trees back and off to their right, but she did not think too much about it at the time.

Lily and John had also jumped up from the sand and were bouncing around with joyous excitement. Enrique reached down and ruffled both of them on the head. "Buenas Tardes, John. My how you have grown since I saw you."

John answered, "Buenas Tardes, Enrique. Ve bene?"

Enrique looked pleasantly surprised, "Bien hecho! John, bravo! Your Mexican is very good. Your mother has taught you well."

"Gracias, Enrique." John was blushing hard enough for it to show through his sunburn.

Enrique turned back to Sarah, his flowered shirt, supplied by the hotel, was fluttering in the sea breeze. "Why have you come back here Sarah? This place is filled with danger for you. You must be very careful."

Sarah nodded, "I know, Enrique, but I needed to find out what happened. I heard about the army's raid of the camp the day after I arrived in Arizona. I was so worried, but I couldn't come back for a while. I knew it would be dangerous." She sat on John's blanket and motioned Enrique to her chair. "Please tell me what happened. How are Yolanda and the children?"

"They are fine", he started. "About half of us managed to escape the noose they threw around the camp. A few of us still maintain contact, but they are still watching for us so we cannot form our family again." He paused and looked away, down along the surf, "Not for a long time, I'm afraid. We must stay scattered, but we try to stay in contact. Like Luis and me, for example."

He looked back at her, "Several of the survivors thought you might have had something to do with the raid; because it happened so soon after you left. I think I have convinced them that your leaving was just a coincidence. Juan noted a small plane flying away the morning you left and that night they attacked. We believe it was a spotter plane sent by the Ensenada police." He grinned wickedly, "Maybe they were not as stupid as I gave them credit for. Yes?"

She and John sat on either side of Lily on the blanket, scuffing her fur as they listened. They both nodded their heads in agreement as if rehearsed. Enrique laughed, "He is very much like you, Sarah. He seems to have learned much already."

Sarah said, "Yes, Enrique. But he still has much to learn if he is to defeat the machines."

Enrique sighed, "Ah, yes, the machines. You are still bothered by those dreams, Sarah?"

She nodded, "Yes. That is one of the reasons I came down here looking for you. I have learned that when the dreams start coming again, every night, John and I are in danger and we must leave wherever we are." She looked at his concerned face, "When we left you, we went to Arizona, just missing the roundup. I left Arizona when the dreams came and went to Las Vegas and when the dreams came again, I came here. I'm not sure, but I felt that the authorities or possibly the machines might be getting close again." She squinted into the glare, "My dreams stopped almost as soon as we left. I can think of no other reason."

Enrique just nodded, "Your early warning system, eh, Sarah?"

She smiled, "It is a little scary, but quite convenient if it really works."

- - -

Enrique spent the evening with them. Sarah cooked supper and then, just before she did the dishes, Enrique prepared a supper plate and went outside. When he came back in Sarah looked at him with some confusion.

"It was for Luis. He is watching out for us." Enrique grinned at her surprise, "He said, 'Thank you.'"

They talked until late into the night. John had fallen asleep on the bed and Lily was still lying by the door. Sarah got as much information as she could about what had happened and where everyone was.

It seems that the Mexican legal system was getting overburdened with drug runners and the word on the street was that those in the Mexicali jail would have to be released soon just to make room for the real criminals. Unfortunately, the four locked in the army prison would probably be there for the duration of their sentences; they had gotten twelve years each for their part in the depot robbery. Enrique was confident that they had not talked and provided information about either him or Luis.

Sarah asked him, "Where will you go? How will I be able to find you in the future?"

He stated matter-of-factly, "As soon as Yolanda gets out of jail, it should only be a few more months at most, we will move back to the old campsite and rebuild our lives. We will get Luna and the other children and just head out into the desert."

He looked over at her, "When you were there, did you find your weapon stash?"

Sarah nodded, "It appears to be there. I saw tire tracks running over where the chain handle was buried and no chain visible."

He nodded, "Good. When we get there, we will watch over things. Maybe you will come back to see us some day. Maybe you will need those guns to shoot your machines."

He stood and said, "Now I should go. Luis is probably tired, and I know you are."

Sarah reached up and gave him a big hug. "Thank you, Enrique. Be careful and good luck. Please give my love to Yolanda and the children." She released him, "Thank Luis for me too."

As he opened the door, "Give John a big kiss for me." Then he was gone.

- - -

As the two men walked away from Sarah's cabin they talked softly. "I believe that everything is OK, Luis. Sarah knows nothing. I'm convinced that her coming here just now is a pure coincidence and has nothing to do with what we have planned."

"I hope you are right, Enrique. There are months of planning wasted if she is a government spy and somehow finds out about us and reports us."

"Trust me, amigo. If we get caught, it will not be because of Sarah."

They reached the highway and went in opposite directions. The young man who had been watching them and trying to hear what they were saying left his cover under the shrubbery and decided to try to follow the older man. His assignment had been to watch Luis and try to determine what plan was in the works. Enrique walking into the picture was a bonus he could not resist, and the woman he had been with today fit the description he had read about. The informant had said that Sarah Conner was her name, even if she was registered under the name of Sarah Reese. The file said that the little boy's name was John.

The Deputy Chief would be very pleased with his night's work.

Colonel Brewster was beginning to get tired of his lifestyle. Now that Kate was coming of school age, he had to think of her educational options, and he did not think that a community that was made up of mostly military families had enough to offer her. He started looking around for neighborhoods that were mostly civilian and had good schools. He contacted a realtor friend and got her to look around for him; weeding out the obvious places she knew he would not want.

After some looking around and lots of phone calls, he settled for a house in Van Nuys a little further away from work than he had hoped, but in a nice, safe neighborhood and with some good schools close by. The house had three bedrooms, a small garage for his car and a fenced-in back yard that would allow Kate to play safely away from the light traffic on their street. Shopping, something he hated but endured because he had to do it occasionally, could usually be completed in one stop at the Sherman Oaks Galleria a mile or so away. Maria could still work as his housekeeper and Kathryn's nanny since she could still live with them and her family was about the same distance from either house.

He knew that he could make it work and he knew that despite her cries to the contrary, Kate would quickly make new friends and settle into her new neighborhood. It was one of Maria's tasks to help ease the transition, and to her credit, she saw the wisdom of it for Kate's sake.

Kathryn was quickly signed up for kindergarten in the Van Nuys school system and before the first week was out, she was practically gushing about her new friends, and her new school and her wonderful teacher, Mrs. Dominguez. Colonel Brewster just accepted her news graciously, but with an inward, parental smile. Now if only he could get his one-hour drive to the base to cooperate and become thirty minutes he would be a happy man.

- - -

Sarah and John were packing up the car. They did not have that much, and it did not take too long. Their vacation in De Jaleo was at an end. It was not the dreams this time that prompted her departure, it was the impending lack of money. Things were cheaper here, but her resources were fixed and limited. It was time to head back to the US and find a job.

She thought they could go back to LA now; it had been nearly seven years. She felt that the authorities would surely have relegated her to the inactive files, and no one would be actively looking for her. If she kept her nose clean and stayed out of trouble, they should be OK. Jobs as a waitress were easy to come by and unless the customers had changed in the past few years, she was good at it.

It was a short drive to the Tijuana border, but she opted for the crossing further east at Mexicali because it had a little less traffic and maybe the customs inspectors on the US side would be a little laxer. It only took an extra hour and then she could pick up I8 toward San Diego. About an hour and a half after crossing into

Calexico she reached I15 north and after gassing up she headed north to Corona where she planned to stay.

Sarah quickly found a motel where she could rent by the week and use it as a base of operations until she could get a job and apartment. She allowed John to stay in the room and hang around the pool with Lily as his attendant while she began working at a truck stop diner across highway 91 from her room. It was there that she took up with Ron Pearson, the first shift cook. Within the first month, he had invited her to move into his apartment in Norco and she had accepted.

Less than a week after she and John and Lilly moved into Ron's place, he became sullen. He had interpreted her friendliness and attention to be her permission for his advances. When she had initially rebuffed him, he grew angrier and he started pushing her around.

"What's going on, Sarah? Why did you move in with me if you didn't want to have sex with me?" Ron was trying to use his most persuasive voice and logic with her. He had heard that women do not like to be bossed around anymore; although he was not sure if he believed that. He was watching her from the bed as she finished her preparations for the night. He admired her lean, tanned, athletic build. *Hell, he more than admired it, he damned well lusted after it. She was the hottest woman he had been with since high school, even wearing that knee-length nightgown.*

Sarah said from the bathroom, "Ron, I told you. I didn't really want that kind of relationship just yet." Her voice was a little distorted by the bathroom's acoustics, but the words were clear enough. "I have to watch out for John and his feelings too."

Ron made little talking motions with his fingers, and then he said, "He's asleep. He won't know anything about what we're doing in here unless you tell him." He pulled back the covers on his bed and patted it, trying to lure her in.

Sarah closed the drawer under the sink and switched off the light, "Ron, not tonight. Not now. OK?" She headed out to the small living room where the pull-out bed held her sleeping son and her pillow.

As she pulled back the sheet on her side of the bed Sarah felt a hand clamp down on her shoulder. It was not strong enough to be a terminator's hand, but she did not realize that fact until she had reacted and brought the hand's owner over her hip and left him sitting stunned in the corner of the living room hugging his arm.

Ron's eyes slowly changed from shocked to angry. He pulled himself up from the floor, pulling down a table lamp as he did. He growled, "You bitch! I think you broke my wrist." He took a step toward her and she held out her hand to ward him. Lily began growling at him from the other side of the bed and he looked from one to the other and back. Finally realizing that maybe he was out matched, even if he did have fifty pounds on her, he stopped. "I think you should leave", he said with the pout of a bruised ego. "I think you should get out now before I call the cops."

The noise had awakened John and he was sitting in the fold-out bed with the covers in his lap looking groggy and scared. Sarah said, "We'll leave, Ron, but you brought this onto yourself."

- - -

Ellison could not believe his bad luck. He did not understand how it was it possible that she could know that he was coming to Vegas for her and then get out of town before he got there. It was eerie how she always managed to do that; always stay at least one step ahead of his investigation and out of his reach. It was frustrating.

He had finagled a flight (off the books so that his boss would not know) and taken a day's personal time. No one at the office could have known. No one could have alerted her. Still, she left town suddenly and disappeared again. She had gone without saying goodbye to anyone. No one knew where she had gone. He was at a dead end again and nowhere to go except back to LA.

All he had learned was that both she and her son John were still alive and that she had the balls to have been living in the house of the Silver Dollar Casino's chief personnel investigator. She had been a rooky twenty-one dealer on the first shift. She checked out as honest and reliable; at least until she skipped town. The live-in was furious as was his boss. No one suspected anything except the boyfriend eventually mentioned that she had started to have really bad nightmares the week before. He had been scared and she had refused counseling. She had called in sick and when he went home to check on her, she was gone. No note, no messages, no nothing.

After talking to the two men, Ellison did not think that the boyfriend was stupid or in on her scheme, but he did not rule it out completely. The security system that the casinos all used worked as far as it went. Unfortunately, it just did not go far enough. A woman, wanted by Federal, State and Local law enforcement, had managed to pass a rigorous private security investigation, work in a very secure casino environment and live in plain sight with a private cop for six months. He had only stumbled on her by dumb luck. Somehow, she sensed it, or someone tipped her off, otherwise she might still be here.

He looked up from the magazine he was blindly leafing through when he heard his flight called. *I need to learn how to do better searches*, he thought. *I need to hire a professional computer expert to teach me how to find things I want in our vast swamp of Federal information.* He vowed to do that search as soon as he got home.

- - -

Sarah packed John up along with their belongings, loaded her car and left. John worried initially, but Sarah eventually convinced him that since sleeping in the car was a lot like camping out, everything would be OK. She drove to a little park near Long Beach and parked the Jeep near the entrance to the marina. Her sad story, the presence of John and Lily and a small gratuity sold the parking attendant and he allowed them to spend the night as long as they were gone in the morning.

In the morning, Sarah registered at her old motel across the street from the diner. She dreaded the confrontation she knew was coming once Ron saw her back at work. After all, he had been there a lot longer than she had and he seemed to be closer to Robin, the woman who ran the dayshift. But she needed the money and she felt it was worth the try so after getting John settled in and their things in the room she got changed into her uniform and made her way across the highway.

Robin was waiting for her at the island that held the menus and the cash register. She seemed to have a smile poorly hidden on her face. "Honey, what did you do to Ron?" Robin could no longer contain her mirth. "He looks like you fed him through the dishwasher. And is he pissed at you. What happened?"

Sarah was a little surprised at Robin's attitude, but willing to accept it as a gift. "Well," she started slowly, "for starters he was lobbying hard for us to have sex last night and I turned him down flat." She looked around the diner, "That isn't for the general public, OK?"

Robin let out a little snort. "Good for you." She nodded her head in anticipation, "Go on, I won't tell a soul."

"I had just left the bathroom and went into the living room. You know, where his fold out couch is? I was just pulling back the sheets when he grabbed me from behind and I... I guess I flipped him across the room." She looked embarrassed, "I didn't really mean to hurt him. I just reacted. I didn't even think about what I was doing."

Robin's eyes had widened. "You just flipped him across the room? A little slip of a thing like you? How'd you do that?"

Sarah answered, "I took some self-defense courses at the YWCA a few years ago. I guess they stuck." She hopped the half-truth would satisfy Robin and ultimately Ron. "They said it didn't matter how much bigger the assailant was; it was called leverage."

Robin was all but laughing out loud, "A touch of complete surprise couldn't hurt either." Then she asked, "What happened? Where did you go? He said he threw you out."

Sarah nodded, "I loaded my stuff into the car, John and I drove over to a park, and I bribed a parking attendant to let us spend the night." She inclined her head across the street, "I checked back into the motel this morning."

"What's she doing here?" a loud, sulky voice sounded through the pass-through window from the kitchen.

Robin turned her head and hollered back, "Just get back to work, Ron. I won't let Sarah hurt you."

Most of the diner laughed and Sarah saw Ron's face before he ducked out of sight. "Don't egg him on, Robin. I don't need him watching for me or messing with my orders."

Robin said, "Honey, if he messes with you again, you let me know. He won't risk making me mad." She grabbed Sarah softly by the shoulders and turned her toward the tables, "You go get to work. Just pretend nothing happened. OK?"

Sarah tried to smile, "I hope you're right, Robin." Then she started to work.

- - -

Everything went well for the first few days. Ron stayed as far away from Sarah as he could, and she did the same for him. He never approached her with questions, or an apology, and she never said a word to him. She caught him peeking at her through the window once or twice, but that could have been incidental since he had to place orders up there anyway.

She kept her guard up for more than a week as things settled back to normal and never saw anything that alarmed her. Then she started feeling that she was being watched. The last few days the little hairs on the back of her neck felt like she was constantly standing in a drafty room. There was nothing specific and she never saw Ron or anyone else following her home at night. She explained it away as just nerves. Her nightmares had not restarted and that was most important to her. She did not think Ron would try anything now since she had made it clear that she could take care of herself.

Thursday after work, they were coming back from the grocery and Sarah had her arms filled with bags. John had the room's key and he had just put it into the lock when the door opened. Ron was standing there with a grin in his face that scared her. Before she could react, Ron had grabbed John's arm and pulled him into the room. She dropped her groceries and started to yell for help when Ron threatened John and signaled for her silence. He backed up and said, "Come on in, tough bitch. I've been waiting."

Out of the corner of her eye she noticed that the motel manager had seen her drop her bags and was watching. She knew that if he called the police, they might catch Ron, but they might catch her too. It could turn into a mess that could ruin everything. She stepped inside, "Ron, don't do this. Leave John out of this. It's me you want to punish, not John. Right?"

John said miserably, "Mom, he hurt Lily!" He was pulling futilely in Ron's grip, trying to reach Lily.

Sarah looked over near the kitchen and saw Lily lying still. She could not tell if she was breathing from over by the doorway, but at least she did not see any blood. "Ron, why did you hurt the dog?"

Ron said as he continued to back into the room, "It started to growl at me, and I didn't want to get bit, so I hit it."

That is when she saw that Ron had a slim club; more like a cut-off mop handle. He had been holding it alongside his pants leg and she had not noticed it earlier. Her anger began to overpower her fear and she said, "Ron, if you get out of here right now and not hurt John, I'll cover for you when the police get here. Otherwise I'll have to hurt you and I'll let the police get you."

She saw that he did not believe her about the police coming. "How did you call them? I watched you arrive, and you never made a call."

Sarah answered, "The motel manager noticed, and I saw him run inside. I'm sure he called and they're coming." She motioned toward the door, "I think I'd run if I were you."

As if on cue, a siren sounded off in the distance, getting louder by the second. Ron heard it and it was his turn to panic. He shoved John away and motioned me away from the door with his club. "Sarah, I'm sorry. Please don't turn me in." With that said, he sprang for the door and dashed away, his revenge forgotten.

Sarah ran over to an upset John where he was kneeling next to Lily's limp body. He was crying about the dog, but she could see that he was more than a little angry with Ron.

"John, I'll do the talking to the police. Do you understand? I don't want you telling them anything about Ron or what happened. OK?"

John looked up, his chin quivering, "He killed her, mom. He killed her."

She swiped the damp hair out of his face, "I know, John, but let me handle it. I have to lie to the police about what happened, or we might get arrested ourselves." She heard the police car stop outside her door. "Please, John, promise me."

He looked up at her, actively crying now, and he nodded his head, agreeing to what she said.

The police barged into the motel room, their guns drawn, covering each other, "Police! Put your hands out where we can see them!"

Sarah raised her hands over her head, and she saw that John did too. "He's gone," she announced to the officers. "He ran out when he heard you coming."

She watched as they visibly relaxed, the threat reduced in their minds. The officer nearest to the door grabbed his radio and began his initial report. The lead officer stepped closer, holstering his gun as he came over to where she and John sat on the floor.

Sarah looked up at him, "He killed our dog. She was a good dog and he just killed her." It did not take much for her to sound pitiful.

The police officer looked from one to the other of them, "I'm sorry lady. Did you get a look at the man who broke in?"

Sarah nodded, "I saw him, but I was so frightened, and everything happened so fast I don't remember much about what he looked like."

He nodded as he pulled out his note pad. "I just have a few questions. He licked his pencil, "First, what is your name? And your little boy's?"

About then there was a small ruckus in the doorway. The other officer was trying to keep back the neighbors. She could hear the motel manager asking about her and John. She smiled, "My name is Sarah Reese, and this is my son John. We've been living here for a few weeks."

He wrote in his book. "Did you recognize the man? Did he hurt you or did he take anything?"

Sarah began forcing tears as she answered, "No. I don't know who he was."

She tried to stand, and he offered her a hand, which she took. Standing she went to the bed and sat on the end, dragging her fingers through her hair. "I haven't had a chance to look around, but I think I came in right after he killed Lily. I don't think he had enough time to look around and steal anything. He wasn't carrying anything except that club."

Per their agreement, John kept silent. The police were not asking him anything and he was not going to say anything until they did.

"Do you know how he got in?" His pencil was hovering over the pad.

Sarah shook her head, "I don't have any idea. I thought I locked my door when we went to the store." She looked sheepish, "I must have forgotten."

The officer shook his head, "You need to be more careful in the future, lady."

Sarah said, "Oh, you can count on that officer. I certainly will."

He handed over his business card, "If you come down to this address tomorrow you can file formal charges." He looked down, "He did kill your dog and if we happen to catch him, you might get something out of it."

Sarah took the card and thanked him. Then she walked with him to the door and thanked him again, shaking his hand. The manager was standing there, holding her grocery bags, one of which was dripping. "Thanks, Bill. I appreciate your calling the police the way you did." She noticed that the other police officer was talking to the other tenants, trying to get information about the break-in no doubt. She took the bags and went back inside, kicking the door shut behind her.

Sarah carried the grocery bags into the kitchenette, stepping around John and over Lily. She put the bags on the counter and looked at John. "John, are you OK?"

He nodded and then as he stood, he patted Lily's head. "What are we going to do with her?"

Sarah said, "She probably died trying to protect us. I'd like to bury her, but I don't know how we can." Then she said, "I'll take her body down to the dumpster and you can bring those flowers for her." She had indicated some daisies that were sitting in a small vase by the stove.

They had their little funeral and once they were back in their room, Sarah told John that he was to pack while she made them something to eat for supper. She knew that it was not safe for them now between Ron and the police. It was unfortunately time to move on again.

* * *

John Conner thought that this particular ride in an attack helicopter was the sweetest he had ever taken. Since his near death and ultimate survival via heart transplant, Kate had kept him on a very short leash. And to be quite honest, the collar had been beginning to chafe him. She was watching him like a hawk, suborning his authority with his men, but at least she recognized the importance of his getting this equipment and she had relented enough to let him come along.

He didn't expect to use the machine today, but he knew he had to get his hands on it, secure it and begin to understand it. Lost in his thoughts and the foreknowledge of what he would have to do to so many of his men, he was startled when the chopper banked hard and flared for landing. The uneventful trip had seemed to take no time at all. He watched as the other helicopter landed fifty yards closer to the hanger.

Derek was the first one out of his helicopter, his eyes and weapon sweeping the landing area near the decrepit looking hanger that Silberman had pointed out from photos. John and two others hopped out next and Kate helped Doctor Silberman out last. They all cautiously approached the hanger doors as the chopper lifted off and took a protective position above them. The team worked their way around some debris: some burned out wrecked planes and a few ground vehicles too mangled to identify accurately. They leapfrogged into position, each squad protecting the other.

John's group reached the man-door next to the closed main door and Derek brought them to a halt, sending two men inside to check it out. Silberman let out a snort, "No wonder humans are losing to Skynet. You're too cautious!" And with that he pushed Derek aside and pulled the door open and rolled into the darkness. The two men who had preceded him whirled around at the noise he made, bringing their rifles to bear on him before relaxing a little. Silberman basically ignored them, and he moved to the right of the doorway, disappearing into the dimness. He could be heard to be bumping into things and groping along the wall. Suddenly he said in triumph, "Here it is!" and with a metallic clang and a loud snap, the lights in the distant ceiling began to glow as they warmed up.

In the growing light, the two point-men resumed their ordered reconnaissance, walking cautiously deeper into the metal cavern. Within a few seconds they called 'Clear!' and the rest of John's team entered. What they saw was not what they had expected. Centered in the great space was scaffolding made of ten-inch diameter, welded steel piping and reaching more than twenty-five feet above the concrete floor. It looked to be about forty or fifty feet across, and it was supporting huge, curved electromagnet cores that formed a steel sphere in the middle. Heavy bundles of large electrical cables snaked off in two directions; one to the right and one to the left.

As the light strengthened four jet engines could be seen near the back wall, metal ductwork from both ends of the engines went through the nearby wall. The engines looked to be attached to large blocks of concrete and they were coupled to some kind of large steel box, probably a transmission or speed reducer, which then went into a ten-foot diameter dynamo supported on end. Three very large wires came out of the dynamo and went into a large switch panel and from there into the side of a long control cabinet.

A stairway jogged around the scaffolding and Silberman had hurried ahead and was waiting next to the set that climbed up to the first landing. He turned toward them, raised his arms to shoulder height and shouted, "Ta-da. Just as I told you." He swept his arms around to encompass everything they could see, "Was I right? Or was I right!"

John and Kate looked at each other as the initial surprise at finding the machine so easily was wearing off. Kate asked, "Do you think it still works?"

John nodded, "I'd bet money on it if I had some. I got access to one of these somewhere and used it to save my mother and me and you. It was probably this one." He started to walk closer, "Silberman says it worked. If it's broken, we have to get it working again. This is the most important piece of equipment in the entire world right now."

Turning to Derek, John said, "Plan to post a standing guard here. No radio communications, except in code, are ever to be used. Am I clear? Skynet cannot find out that we've discovered this machine, or it will destroy it and everything will be lost. This has top priority."

John left Derek to handle the arrangements and he walked over to the stairway. Silberman was bouncing around from side to side in his chair in his excitement. John got his attention and asked, "Doctor, you have done very well. We are all proud of you and what you have done for us." Then when he was sure that he had Silberman's attention he asked, "Can you tell if everything is here? Is everything as you remember?"

Silberman was nodding vigorously, "Yep, it's all here. Except for a little dust it looks like it did two years ago."

Technical Interlude

How the T1000 and TX models Function

Room temperature liquid metals are rare. A common example is the metal mercury which is liquid between the temperature range of 358°C (676°F) and -38.8°C (-37.8°F). Note that -40°C=-40°F. Unfortunately for mercury, as a liquid it naturally holds the shape of its container, although it does have a very high surface tension that causes it to repel from some surfaces (such as glass) allowing it to diverge from its container's shape slightly at the open or unconstrained surface. Mercury sitting in the open on a flat surface tends to form slightly flattened spheres; otherwise mercury cannot be made to hold any shape, regardless of technique.

A class of metals called memory metals, exhibit a form of shape memory when exposed to external stimuli, most notably heat, but occasionally electromotive forces. These metals, once formed and set in their shape, can be deformed during use and then made to recover their original shape with the application of a little heat (hence the memory mentioned). This shape recovery feature can be used as a thermally activated spring or change in airfoil profile in some military applications.

Until the discovery of nanoparticles, extremely small pieces of custom-engineered material (and always with surprising properties), making memory metal liquid at room temperature and shape recoverable or modifiable by the application of electrical potentials was impossible. Nanoparticles typically take the form of "Bucky balls" or hollow rods of molecules in a lattice structure. Distribution of these particles in various concentrations and combinations within the base materials often provide surprising characteristics and abilities.

A class of nanoparticles that would cause alloys of iron and copper to flow or solidify on electrical command provided Skynet Research with the materials it needed to develop the T1000 and the TX models. These materials possess an affinity for themselves well beyond that seen with liquid mercury. Small puddles or blobs of this liquid memory metal will actively seek out more of its own kind as though drawn by a gravitic or magnetic force. Smaller quantities then become larger quantities which attract others still more strongly. It is thought that the residual electrical currents circulating in the disassociated droplets generate magnetic forces acting on the iron content of the alloy.

This attraction causes cohesion of the metal into a semi-solid mass, a semi-crystalline substance that can be shaped by controlling electrical forces and potentials to suit the need. Supplying power and computer control within such a fluid mass is tricky and difficult. Independent and distributed computer nodes, organized as a cloud-like structure controlled by one small, primary central processor, can supply the control. The normal nuclear power cells, tucked away within the mass, protected by a shield of rigidized liquid metal, can supply the necessary electromotive force through networks "grown" by the computer's control.

Features and characteristics of this frozen liquid memory metal can be changed or modified to suit the situation. It can be made very rigid to form cutting, piercing, prying or bludgeoning tools. It is capable of holding or carrying solid objects, activating levers and switches, locomotion and supporting its own weight. Its surface can remain reflective or become dull or patterned or selectively reflect ambient light imparting color(s). Since all but a small volume of the whole is fluid, it can flow through small openings while remaining in contact with the main systems and reform on the other side to activate opening switches or remove blockades. Then flowing back into itself, the whole can simply walk through the previously closed space.

    The distributed computer system with its feedback sensors is tied together via a network of connections grown from the primary computer's location like a human neural network. However, these circuits can be broken and reconnected at the will of the primary computer based on need or circumstances. No appreciable delay is involved and no trauma to the system, short of actually damaging the primary computer or the main power supply, is more than a temporary inconvenience to the device or its goal or mission. Both the T1000 prototypes and the TX models are dangerous, resourceful adversaries and extremely difficult to stop and nearly impossible to terminate.

Chapter 10

Sarah ended up in Van Nuys. She initially checked into a motel along the I405, but after the second week of her new job she found a rental house on Vineland Avenue, near the airport. She located a daycare center nearby and enrolled John in their program. Since they opened at six-thirty and would keep the kids until six in the evening, it made for a perfect arrangement for them both. John got other kids to play with and socialize with and Sarah knew that he was being safely tended to every day while she worked.

She thought she had learned a valuable lesson with Ron, and she stayed more to herself than she otherwise would have. She had resurrected Sarah Conner, feeling that that name might be a little safer than Reese just now. She managed to tactfully deflect all romantic attention for more than a year, garnering the reputation as a loner. John started kindergarten in the Los Angeles County School System, and as time went on, she began to loosen up a little and go out with some of her co-workers in a nice safe group. That was how she had attracted the attention of Tom Rankin.

Tom had become a regular at Merriam's Tavern shortly after he got out of the Marines. He did not have many marketable skills and he gravitated to the truck garage out by the 405 and he managed to keep his mechanic's job even though he seemed sullen and argumentative. The night Sarah and her friends came in from the diner he spotted her and was instantly smitten by her. Before the night ended, he had managed to find out her name and where she worked. Sarah tried to be discrete, but one or two of the other women could not help themselves and thought they were doing her a favor by passing out her information.

Tom became a lunch regular and they sometimes met at Merriam's for a drink. Sarah managed to keep Tom at arm's length for several months, but as she listened to some of his war stories, she determined that he might be a resource for her continued education, perhaps even for John's.

John and Tom seemed to get along. They played chess together and John was always interested when Tom talked about his tour of duty in Kuwait with the Marines. The Gulf War, or Operation Desert Storm as Tom referred to it, had been an intense, exciting time for him. With the 2nd Marine Division, Tom had fought in two tight situations that had made a lasting impression on him.

"We had been operating in Khafji," he looked over at John who was sitting cross-legged on the floor at Tom's feet. "That's a town near the Kuwait, Iraq border. We were pushing the Republican Guard out of town in front of us as we swept the town, building by building." Tom stopped and took a sip of his beer, smiling at the expression of wonder and awe on John's face.

"We occasionally ran across a tank or two in main intersections or hiding in an alley. They were pretty much useless, mostly old Chinese Type 59's or 69's. Effective against foot soldiers, but just like butter to our helicopter launched missiles. All we had to do once we encountered one was stay back and phone it in. Usually within five minutes a chopper was there, and the tank was a burning hulk."

John ate the stories and details up. Tom was quickly becoming a hero to him; with a certain justification. Sarah felt it too and she hoped to maintain her objectivity with Tom. She still was not sure just how far she could or should trust him.

"This was in January of 1991. The UN coalition was kicking Iraq's butt. Their foot soldiers and most of their armor had been pushed back over the border or destroyed or taken prisoner. Iraq was still launching Scud missiles at everybody, but most of them were way off target. A larger problem was that most of them were carrying gas instead of high explosives." He looked at John, "A lot of people were very afraid of that." Tom finished his beer. He looked up and John said, "I'll get you another one." John jumped up from his place on the floor and hurried away, carrying the empty with him.

Sarah said, "He admires you, Tom. He has never had a man around to look up to."

Tom said, "He's a good kid, Sarah. I feel like he's listening to every word, soaking it up like a sponge."

She smiled at him, "You would be right. He's very interested in warfare and battle tactics. It sometimes scares me how interested he is, but like I tried to tell you earlier, in the future this stuff is going to be important to all of us."

About that time John arrived with Tom's new beer. "Mom! Don't talk about that stuff! You'll scare Tom away!"

Tom took the beer John held, "Thanks little buddy." He took a quick pull, swallowed and then said, "I'm not afraid of anything. I'm not going anywhere." He took another drink, "Where was I? Oh, yeah, we had just cleared out Khafji and we were pushing Hussain's forces ahead of us as fast as they could run. About that time, the end of February, the 27th I think it was, Saddam declared a retreat for all of his troops." Tom grinned as he took another long drink, "He might as well have, we were making them run full speed in that direction anyway. Then, for some reason, at the Kuwait International Airport, an entire Republican guard unit dug in and wouldn't surrender. We called in air support, but because General Schwartzkopf didn't want to destroy the Kuwaiti's only major airport, we were forced to do it the hard way." He took a drink, winked at John and continued, "We set up a three-pronged attack. You know what a trident looks like?"

John nodded, "Kind of like a devil's pitchfork?"

Tom said, "Neptune's, but close enough. We sent in a major force right up the middle to keep them occupied and then sent flanking forces around from both sides, pinching them in the middle. We left them the back way out, toward the border, in case they wanted to run for it. Unfortunately for them, they stayed and fought. It took us over four hours of intense fighting to overwhelm them. In the end, they lost all but thirty-five men and most of those were badly wounded." He took a final drink, draining the bottle. "The end." He handed John the empty bottle, "And on that note, I'm heading home." He rose to go.

"Good night, John." He ruffled John's hair. "I hope you don't get nightmares from that story."

"Night, Tom. I won't, mom gets all the nightmares in this family."

Sarah swatted at his behind, "Don't forget to brush your teeth. I'll be back in a minute to check on you." She followed Tom to the door.

At the door, Tom pulled her to him for a long kiss. When it ended, he said, "He's a great kid, Sarah. And you are a great woman. Have you given any more thought to moving in with me?"

Her face melted a little, "I still haven't decided, Tom. John and I are going camping for his birthday next week. I promise to think about it some more then, and I promise to let you know when we get back. OK?"

Tom held her face between his hands, their noses almost touching, "That's OK, Sarah. Another week is OK." He kissed the tip of her nose. I don't want to rush you. I remember what you said about the last guy you trusted. I just want to say that I think this feels right to me." He kissed her once again, "See you tomorrow." He turned and left.

She stood there for a minute and then she went inside to check on John.

- - -

Colonel Brewster's division was making great strides in their research. Helped by several civilian programs, each isolated from the other like cells for security, Brewster's various groups surged forward with their individual projects. A new satellite project, code named Skynet, was approved and he had been given complete charge and responsibility of it (with certain political oversight of course.) The command and control program his team was developing planned to link together everything that the other groups were working on. As the software evolved, the hardware had to evolve too and before long it was determined that a computer with artificial Intelligence (AI) would be required for such a monumental task. It was a sort of a distributed computer within a computer concept and quite leading-edge technology. A research effort in the literature had turned up no systems like it anywhere in the world.

At a meeting with Larch and his committee he had been told of some research being done on AI by one of the major military suppliers right here in LA. The discoveries they were making would no doubt save

Brewster's teams months if not years of work; much of it, duplicated effort. It had been hinted at that the Air Force should buy Cyberdyne Systems outright, but even Larch and his cronies did not have that much pull. Brewster knew he did not, and he said so. Larch just "harrumphed!" and told him to pass the idea up the chain of command and he would do the same. Brewster never found out that Larch was also in charge of the Cyberdyne AI effort using Myles Dyson. It looked like the parallel paths, started by Larch and the committee, using the terminator technology, were beginning to converge nicely.

- - -

Silberman had never felt so good. After his close call with death, minor breakdown, therapy, loss of patients and almost his practice, he was becoming a better man because of his work at the Pescadaro Hospital. He felt as though he was finally contributing to society in a meaningful and measurable way. He was fitting in with the staff and he thought that he had even earned some grudging respect from the orderlies, not just their fear of being fired. He recognized that was a major step in his goal of total recovery. He had settled into a reassuring routine, alternating between his remaining practice and the hospital rounds and group sessions.

He had several cases that were quite interesting. No mass murderers or serial killers; although one of the inmates had killed several people over the course of his career. For a brief, flashing moment he compared the cases he had access to with the Sarah Conner incident, but he just as quickly flushed the upsetting memories away. He fondly recalled his naive plans to publish journal reports on her and that boyfriend of hers. Gratefully he could not remember his name. He hoped that maybe his time here would allow him enough material to do a small book, maybe a memoir. He did not think that she would warrant even a footnote.

He glanced at his watch. *Right on time,* he thought. He opened the door to the small gymnasium and saw that the group of patients was seated and waiting on him. The four orderlies were arrayed around the perimeter, eyes facing the group, ever watchful for disruptive behavior and immediate intervention. "Good afternoon, group," he called out as he took his seat and flipped open his note pad and clicked his pen. "Shall we begin?"

Nine sets of eyes looked at him with either hope or frustration or suspicion or fear. Silberman felt confident that he could help them all. After all, he had been close to the brink and had found a way back. He knew that he could show all of them the way. All they had to do was follow his lead and his instructions and everything would be OK.

About three weeks after his return from Las Vegas, Agent Ellison found a printout on his desk. He had forgotten that he had a standing order for California police reports that might mention several key words or names. The police had filed the name "Sarah Reese" in relation to a violent break-in reported in a South El Monte motel. The officer's report description matched Ellison's recent description of her and John. He thought that he might have gotten lucky.

With a feeling of excitement, he looked up the number of the precinct and then picked up his phone and dialed. He was reading the particulars as he waited for the watch desk to pick up.

"Hello, this is FBI agent James Ellison out of the Central LA office. I'd like to speak with Sergeant ..." He paused as he consulted the printout, "Ralf Gooden or Officer William Bowden please." He listened for a second. "Yes, it has to do with a report they filed on a call they made about a month ago."

"What do you mean it might be difficult? I can come down there and meet with them if need be. This might be part of a Federal investigation I'm working on. I need to speak with them."

Then James' face fell as he listened to the explanation of the watch officer. "When did this happen? Was it related to their call?" He had begun to think Sarah might have become violent when the police confronted her.

"Oh, I see. Sergeant Gooden was killed during an attempted liquor store holdup a week ago and Officer Bowden was wounded at the same time. I'm sorry to hear that."

Then he asked, "Is Officer Bowden able to answer some of my questions?" He waited for the reply and then he wrote on his desk pad, 'LAC-USC Med. Ctr., room 417'. Thank you, Sergeant, you've been helpful."

James Ellison tore off the top sheet from his pad and stuffed it into his pocket. He grabbed his jacket and started out his office door, slipping on his jacket as he went. "Patty, I'll be back in a little while. I have to run to the LAC Medical Center to talk to a potential witness." He hurried on down the hallway toward the elevators.

- - -

Sitting in his car afterward, Agent Ellison was growing more depressed. He had completely missed her again. His interview with the wounded police officer had not provided anything other than the corroboration of Sarah's description. He had driven to the motel and talked to the manager and then he went across the highway to talk to the restaurant personnel. It was her all right. He was certain of that. However, no one knew where she had gone or exactly when she left. The date was sometime within two days of the police report. No one had seen her go or heard from her again.

He felt that he was getting closer, but he knew what they said about close. His palms itched on his steering wheel as he drove back to the office. Once there, Ellison reread the report he had made from Carl's interview. It was the third time and it still did not make much sense to him. It sounded like she was being influenced by her dreams. Her neurosis was making her dream about those robots and the end of humanity, and the dreams were somehow warning her to get out of Dodge just before she was caught by the authorities. It made no sense at all. The main difference this time was that she was worried specifically about the authorities finding her. He wondered if she was becoming even more paranoid. He hoped not. That might make her even more difficult to find; as if that were possible.

- - -

Myles Dyson and his team had made great strides in the months after his last face to face with the committee chaired by General Larch. Even he had been a little surprised at the apparent excitement his last report had generated. There had been smiles and table thumping by almost everyone there. The general had even stood and shook hands; the first time he remembered that happening.

Tierresa had been right about his need for a vacation. It seemed that as soon as he relaxed and put the worries of his responsibilities on the backburner, the more he had been able to intuit some of the things that had stalled progress. All the while he had been walking with her on the beach or sitting under a beach umbrella or playing in the surf, his mind had refocused on the issues and made startling interconnections. His insights, relayed to the team leaders, began bearing fruit almost instantly.

The surf had given him the idea of using an analog waveform, a saw-tooth wave, instead of a digital pulse, for the system clock. That had allowed the investigative team working on the primary stack to unlock its inner workings. Convincing them to try such a radical approach was the hard part. To a man, the electrical engineers and computer scientists had initially laughed and scoffed at the idea. He had to pull rank and force them to at least try. Once they saw that this had provided steps forward, rapidly leading to other breakthroughs, they began trying to figure out ways to claim the glory for themselves.

Flocks of seagulls and other water birds waddling along the edge of the water, staring at the receding water, watching for telltales of edible life in the drying sand, gave him the idea for the system that monitored the secondary chips for sensory inputs. Lots of little computers constantly watching their area of responsibility and reacting to only the sensory inputs of that area and then reporting to a more central computer which would gather data and send that information toward a second level of control computer, etc. Sort of like a funnel, each computer would be simple and dedicated to its assigned task, concentrating data as it was passed along. It was very efficient if you had a lot of computers available to do the job.

Lots of available computers was not one of the machine's problems, there had to be at least a hundred on each layer of each cubic unit on each circuit board. The robot arm he had been given must have more than a thousand computers dedicated to the positioning of each joint and the collection of sensory data from each transducer. Assuming that the robot was humanoid in structure, (as opposed to just an arm attached to a wall), meant that it had probably eight or nine thousand small computers involved in its operation in the world. An astounding number.

- - -

Things had gotten serious. Tom kept asking her if she wanted to move in and she kept saying, "No, not yet". Tom seemed good natured, but she could tell he was frustrated to the point of losing interest. She did not think that was what she wanted.

She had a plan that she thought might stall him a little longer and help her make up her mind. She had arrived before him at Merriam's and she had staked out a table for their evening's talk. Sarah ordered a beer for them both and she sat back watching the crowd ebb and flow in the dim smoky bar.

"Hey, I hope that beer is for me," Tom said as he brushed past and slid into the seat across from her. His face held a look that she liked: a small boy with mischief on his mind.

"This one's for you, Marine." She raised her bottle in salute to him and waited for him to clink.

He clinked his bottle against hers and they both took a long pull from their dewy bottles. Tom put his down on the table with a thud that she could hear even in the noisy bar. "So, did you have a chance to think about my offer? You said you would think about it."

"I told you I was taking John camping this weekend, remember? Well, my plan is still good. I'll think about it. I'll talk to John about it." She took a drink, "After all, he's in this too. I don't think it'll be a problem, but I owe it to him to ask."

Tom looked serious, "That sounds fair. Do you think he would be open to a bribe?"

They laughed, drank their beers, shared some chicken wings and kissed goodnight with greasy, spicy, lips and went home separately.

* * *

It had been more than a month since John Conner had tasked his best people with the job of making the Mare Island time travel equipment functional. Silberman was given the job of directing the technicians since he was the only one who had seen the machine run. The old man seemed happy and much less confrontational, probably because he was in the center of the war's most important asset. Kathryn suspected that he had other motives and John always listened to her instincts. He planned to keep an eye on him as he worked to prepare his own plans for adjusting the past.

The first thing that the team had done was to make the facility secure. John did not think Skynet knew about their find and he needed to keep it that way. After its primary west coast facility in San Francisco was blasted out of existence, most of the attacks and over-flight surveillance sorties had dwindled to almost zero. They had hurt Skynet, but John knew that it was only a matter of time before it came back; probably with a stronger determination to wipe them off the face of the earth. Satellite surveillance was one thing that he could not discount and could not do much about if it existed. They just had to be careful and stay invisible from the air. Nothing could raise Skynet's curiosity at the Mare Island hanger.

The next thing that was accomplished was to clean everything and repair anything they found that looked damaged. Also, the cable connection that left the hanger and ran off to who-knows-where was disconnected on the likely probability that it fed a Skynet input somewhere. That phase took most of a week. Then sketches of everything were made along with functional block diagrams describing how each piece worked with each of the other pieces. That, as it was, was the easy part.

Videos of the successful travel experiment, including blurry shots of the control settings and the final autopsy results on the target subject, coupled with Silberman's eyewitness recollections of the event gave the technical team most of what they needed. Silberman had mentioned that three or four humans had been part of the machinery assembly and operation and a few of their handwritten notes had been found inside the control cabinet. Those notes helped the team develop part of the necessary control settings.

John had watched the sequence at least fifty times trying to pick out every detail so that when it came time for him to order Kyle into the device it would be with a confidence born of knowledge and understanding of what was about to happen. He was looking at that video again when there was a knock at his door.

"Enter," he said, reaching up and pausing the video playback.

The door to his office, actually a steel compartment hatch since he and Kathryn were still living in the bunker on the backside of the compound, opened and his clerk stepped over the threshold. "Sir, here are the day's reports and some signals from Command."

John reached out and accepted the papers. "Is there anything good, Ralphie?"

Ralph pinked up, realizing that his boss knew that he had read the orders before he did and shrugged his shoulders. "Nah, sir, they just want to give you some kind of citation for giving Skynet a bloody nose at Frisco. That's all." He began grinning broadly.

It was John's turn to blush. "Damn it," he said, I wish they wouldn't do that." He sat back in his chair, "Don't they realize yet that the whole unit is responsible for things like that. Not just me." He was shaking his head as he plopped the papers into the in-basket.

The clerk asked, "Is there anything else, sir?"

John shook his head, "No, son, not at this time."

They exchanged salutes and the clerk left, latching the hatch after he stepped through. John grabbed the stack of files from his basket and leafed through them. The one from the hanger, the one with the red-tape seal, caught his attention first. Pulling it in front of him he opened it and found that they had puzzled out the controls and how the time target was set into the local control computer. It seemed that any date could be chosen, but some dates were better than others. Also, the distance the machine could throw someone was limited to around one hundred fifty years. The distance was also limited by the available power and the mass of the object.

He smiled at that. Kyle was slightly built, and he only had to go thirty-five years or so. If they could get it working at all, Kyle should be able to make it back to save his mother from the terminator he knew was already there in his past.

Then his smile evaporated as he read the next paragraph. It said that they were missing some important components; something called a magnetic bottle and the stuff inside that bottle called muons. Apparently, you could not go to the neighborhood drugstore and buy muons in a magnetic bottle and Silberman and the team needed his assistance in finding some.

- - -

That night, after a cryptic message from John was sent to the hanger, "Home 3", a blackened chopper settled outside their compound and two men, one of them pushing a wheelchair, worked their way through to the entrance. Kathryn was there to meet them, and she led them to the space they reserved for high-level meetings. John was waiting for them, seated at one of the tables.

He stood as they entered, "Derek. Robert. Doctor Silberman. Thanks for coming so quickly." He motioned to the table and the chairs, "Please, sit and have some 'coffee'."

John waited until the men had poured a cup of coffee-like liquid, made from chicory and some other roasted and ground tree nuts someone had found. They made themselves comfortable at the table. Then he said, "I have read your most recent report with great interest. It sounds like you have made some very large strides with the machine."

Each of the men was nodding their agreement but Silberman was frowning. "I'm sure you read where we have a large problem?"

John looked at each of them in turn, "Yes, I saw that. That's why I ordered you back here tonight. We need to discuss this missing component and figure out what we intend to do about getting one or perhaps making one."

Silberman was shaking his head, "I don't think we can make one. For starters, none of us knows just what 'it' is."

Robert Place, the company's best technical man, spoke up, "He's right. Other than the general description of 'the muon filled magnetic bottle attaches here', we don't know much else."

John asked him, "Don't you know what a muon is? You used to work with that stuff before the war, didn't you?"

Robert nodded, "Yes, I have heard of a magnetic bottle and muons of course but all of that particle physics stuff is pretty specific. I was working in another area entirely. Mostly behind a desk in the math and magic side if it."

John looked disappointed. "We must know more than that." Turning to Silberman he asked, "Didn't you see one during your observation of the successful experiment?" He looked over at Kathryn, "Didn't we see some kind of gray cylinder plugged into the scaffolding on the video?"

Kate was nodding but Silberman spoke up as though in a daze, "They brought in the bottle thingy at the last minute. A T100 carried it over to the access port and another one screwed it in." He looked sheepish, "I didn't make the connection until now. It was a large gray tank of some kind and it looked kind of heavy."

John said, "Didn't you see where they got it? Were they stored somewhere in the hanger?"

Silberman was staring off into space, "No. No, they carried it in from the outside. I remember now that one of their transports had landed a minute or so just before. That must have delivered it to the hanger for the test."

"OK!" John said. "Do you have any idea where Skynet might have made or stored or filled or whatever they do to those bottles?"

Silberman wrinkled his face in thought, trying to remember information from his many days doing computer research. He was not looking for anything that had to do with muons or magnetic bottles, so he was not paying too much attention. Even if he saw something referencing them, which is doubtful, he would not have understood the implications until now. "Conner, I'm too tired to think straight right now. Let me think about it tonight as I sleep and maybe in the morning I'll have an answer for you."

John controlled his frustration and agreed. "Sure, get some rest, all of you. We'll meet again in the morning after breakfast."

- - -

John was in the conference room finishing his second cup of 'coffee' when the door banged open and Silberman came rolling in with an excited looking Robert Place pushing him along. Silberman shouted toward John, "I think we have it!" Place was nodding vigorously.

"We were talking as we got dressed this morning, and I told him about remembering reading about a place north of Santa Rosa where Skynet was doing some kind of experiments in particle physics. Then suddenly he remembered that some of his colleagues from Berkley had to travel up north to run some tests on a new accelerator they had up there."

Robert's head was nodding so hard it looked as though it would fall off. "It was called the Russian River Complex and we think that's where they must be making those bottles. Or at least filling them," he finished

Technical Interlude

The Philosophy of Skynet

Skynet, the program, was developed out a very human need to be able to point an accusing finger at someone else when things go to hell. To be the responsible "parent" who is in charge and can make all of the hard decisions for the "children" and will then foot the bill for decisions that had to be made. No one wants to be the person who is responsible for the destruction of a city or country or race. It is far easier to delegate that responsibility to someone or something else. A formal set of behavioral rules are written that are agreed to by the humans in charge of the system, who are privy to the "big picture" and have everyone's best interest in mind.

The computer system will then monitor all the designated inputs, crunch all the available data through the algorithms and arrive at a millisecond by millisecond decision about what to do. The problem is that all that logic is based on the typically paranoid concerns of the military and politicians. Right or wrong, the people who get to be in charge are usually subject to the fear of those bastards on the other side of the ocean or wall or street who are obviously going to try to take whatever it is that they want from us; up to and including our very lives.

This decision logic must be developed with a goal in mind. The policy makers, at the time of the awarding of the contract to the teams of hardware and software entities, no doubt try to clearly establish a unifying goal. This goal can be as deceptively simple as "world peace," or "Always alert me if HE looks at ME the wrong way," or "Prevent all military action except for mine." It can be very complicated as in, "If A or B or C happens and D and E is the situation and it's either a Wednesday or Friday between 12:46 am and 6:25 pm, sound the alarm." The goal, what you want the system to do, is the most important first step.

At the end of the development and installation there must be some way to determine if all the intended effort results in the intended outcome or goal. Some grand measurement scheme must be in place. Some way to tell if the system is actually working or just sitting there humming and blinking lights; a vast waste of resources or a savior of our way of life. Is Skynet a boon or a bust? The difficulty with tests is that by the very nature of what the system is monitoring and reacting to, any test requires false inputs to simulate the things that would happen if there was an actual event. (That is assuming that you cannot get your "enemy" to actually pretend to attack you and thereby provide the real inputs to prove your system can prevent his actual attack and at the same time prove that his systems are now obsolete.)

This immense network of worldwide land surface and subsurface, sea surface and subsurface, air borne, and space borne sensors and observation nodes all must be tied together to a single computer system so that a man or a few men can watch and understand what they are seeing. The mind-numbing barrage of data inputs must be filtered and sifted and collated and concentrated and analyzed for trends and marked or highlighted for review and oversight. Real-time results and recommendations with their probabilities for success need to be presented and alternative reactions proposed for each scenario. There is no room for error or system hiccup or failure. Everything must work every time, all of the time, if it is to be relied upon for survival.

In this complex game of cat and mouse, time is always of the essence. The man or men who are in charge of the system will not be the ones who actually have the authority to push the "go" button. Once the computer network system has done its best and the human interface has determined that there is an actual threat, that information must then be forwarded to the one or ones who will make the final decision to "go" or not. Even on dedicated internal lines of communication, that takes a finite length of time. It is this aptly named "dead time" that encourages powerful men to make the decisions to put the automatic systems in charge in the first place.

It is usually some tiny, inconsequential line of code that will bite you in the butt when some unexpected input occurs, or the goal of the program is stated too broadly. Because computer programs take things quite literally, when a logical statement saying to do something if something else happens is satisfied, then the computer will try to do that something even if it causes a bad result. A complex logic tree is still the result of yes and no answers to simple questions along the way. The system can only compare what is likely to happen if it does what it was designed to do to what will happen if it doesn't. It cannot determine moralistic issues like right or wrong. It cannot choose sides like them or us. It can only try to satisfy its goal. It cannot think for itself; it cannot think outside the box.

As a famous writer once said about computers, "In a well-conceived, well-executed computer system, monitored by its creators, "**nothing can go wrong...can go wrong...can go wrong...**"

Chapter 11

The very air was green here. It was green and heavy with moisture, so unlike LA and the Baja's deserts she and John had grown used to. Nature was relentless here in the Sierra Madre mountain jungle. If something didn't move for a day, the jungle began to cover it with vines and moss, or at least mold. Everything seemed wet and dripping.

Sarah was leading John along a leafy, nearly enclosed, barely discernable pathway. Both were carrying backpacks. Sarah was wielding a machete. John was providing direction, guiding her along their planned route. He was counting his steps, consulting his compass and checking his map as they moved forward. Both were sweating heavily from their exertion as they made their way down the mountain side. Brushing through the vegetation and swarms of insects, they were heading in the general direction of the ocean.

The animal life was nearly as thick and diverse as the plants. Calls and screeches, buzzes and clicks, whirring and fluttering sounds were a blanket that wrapped then as they climbed along. If they were moving, the sounds were distant; as though they were in a little bubble of quiet. Only their own sounds were loud in their ears. But as soon as they stopped moving, stood and listened, their bubble burst and the sounds returned like a crashing wave. Sarah had learned to use that effect like remote-sensing sonar. She was now able to tell if someone or something big, and therefore potentially dangerous, was moving in their vicinity. The quiet bubble moved with the cause and could be tracked. She realized that it worked both ways, however.

This was one of the things she was teaching John this week. It was his sixth birthday and the trip was part of his birthday celebration. John did not realize yet that regular kids got toys while he got the stinking, sweaty jungle. He thought that this was a really neat present. He was, after all, only six.

They broke into a small clearing, possibly formed by a long distant lightning strike and subsequent weak fire or maybe a large subsurface boulder that prevented good root growth. It did not really matter the cause. Sarah looked around and doffed her pack, leaning it against a perimeter tree. "Good job John. You're right on target. We'll camp here." She looked up trying to read the sky, "Let's build a fire before it gets dark. Gather some dry wood."

She watched as John set his pack near hers and fished out his leather gloves. He had his little pistol tucked into its canvas holster, strapped around his waist, and she was pleased to see that he patted it before venturing back into the jungle by himself. *He's brave*, she thought, *but he's definitely learning caution.* There might be big cats or worse out there hunting. His caution was the other major thing to be learned out here.

Sarah gathered a few stones and rolled two large fallen pieces of deadwood over toward the center of the clearing. She managed to scare away two or three snakes and who knows how many spiders and biting insects. She suddenly felt someone watching her and grabbing her machete, she managed to turn around quickly enough to catch a glimpse of a monkey staring from one of the higher branches near the edge. She knew that it was just curious and not likely dangerous, but she had been warned about monkey bites and their penchant for thievery. It hooted as it literally disappeared into the leaves.

An answering hoot came from John's direction. He returned to the clearing about a minute later. Dropping his load of deadfall wood near the center of their camp, he grinned and said, "I think that monkey kind of likes me."

They set their camp and got a fire going. Sarah had learned that the smoke from a wood fire kept more than bugs away. She was not too worried about being seen by anyone; other than natives. They were quite far from civilization. The nearest village, Alamos, would be more than a mile to their south. The monkeys and big cats would usually avoid smoke and people and they were her prime concerns at night up here. They might still be drawn to the smells of their food.

After darkness fell, John told Sarah about the things he had seen and learned about jungle survival. He enjoyed hiking using only a compass and map to get where he had planned to go. No mean feat when you are dropped into the middle of a place where you cannot see more than twenty feet in any direction and all you could tell about the sun was whether it was out or not. They laughed when he said that he would probably be able to outperform any normal eagle scout back in the states. The joke was that he would never be able to test that challenge unless they were able to somehow derail Skynet. They both decided that it really was not so funny after all and their laughter died.

They were cleaning up their campsite, trying to make it as odor-free as possible given the rough conditions. John was coming back from burying their waste when he saw Sarah, tense and slowly circling around the campfire, her pistol out and ready. John stopped moving, as he had been taught, and just listened. Their eyes locked and Sarah motioned for him to slip back into the tree cover with a flick in that direction.

John started to whisper, "Mom..." But she silenced him with a warning wave. He slipped back into the dimness. Then he heard what she must have heard earlier. The sound bubble was coming in their direction, probably drawn to the smoke, and it was very close.

In less than a minute a uniformed man stepped into the clearing. He was threatening only in the fact that he was an unknown. He had a pistol of some kind hanging from a wide leather belt, but his hand was not approaching it yet. As a matter of fact, his hands were empty and in front of him, clearly trying to appear non-threatening to her. He seemed to be alone, but she doubted that.

"Señora, Buenos Noches," he said softly. Then recognizing that she might not be local he said, "Señora, you speak Spanish, yes?"

Not wanting to give away her possible advantage she shook her head warily. "No," she said, "Not very much." Then, "Who are you? What do you want?"

It was his turn to be cagey, "Oh, Señora. I am just a simple, how you say, park ranger. I was smelling your smoke and came to investigate."

Sarah thought he might be stalling, and she tried to look around the perimeter of the clearing for any friends he might have watching. She could not be sure, but she thought she heard leaves rustling and maybe a twig snap off to her left and behind a little.

The ranger had managed to get five or six feet closer. Sarah waved her automatic around in his direction, trying to give him the impression that she was just scared and not necessarily dangerous. "Please stay back, Señor ranger," she said.

John was trying to watch everything at once. He was also trying to remain motionless so as to be invisible. He was breathing rapidly through his mouth and his hand was creeping toward his holster.

The subtle noise to his right made him freeze entirely. Someone was slowly edging closer, no more than three yards away from him. Just then, in the flickering firelight, he caught a motion on the far side of the clearing; she was almost surrounded. He was not sure what to do. Sarah was constantly preaching caution to him. He was the most important one and he was to always remain safe. But she was his mother! He had to do something.

So far, the soldier or policeman or park ranger, whoever he claimed to be, was calmly talking, keeping her attention on him, allowing his men to sneak-up on her. Then John decided. He thought he could help, but it would be dicey.

The man closest to him had not yet detected him. John could see his face in the light of the campfire, concentrating and watching, probably waiting for a signal from his leader. He carried a light, semi-automatic rifle but he had not brought it to bear on her yet. John was determined to keep it that way. Drawing his little pistol from its holster, John slowly edged away from his tree and quietly circled around behind the man nearest him.

Just then the ranger asked something in Spanish and then again in English, apparently for her benefit, "I see there was someone else here with you. Where are they?"

As silent as a rodent, John placed his pistol against the back of the man's head. As he cocked the hammer with a firm click, he whispered, "Avisaro, hombre! I am here!" The soldier froze, not daring to look around or cry out. John reached out and took the man's rifle, stepping back, out of reach, as he had been taught.

Pushing the rifle roughly in the captured man's back, John forced him into the clearing, making noise to be sure that the ranger could see the new situation clearly. "Señor ranger," John announced loudly in perfect Spanish, "call in your other man and both of you put down your weapons!" His voice cracked a little, but he still sounded older than he was. They had no choice it seems.

- - -

With John guarding them, Sarah had disassembled their weapons and tied-up all three men, rendering their threat to a meaningless level. She had allowed John to sleep first while she tended the fire and kept an eye on the "rangers." Her plan was, after they had traded places and she had a few hours' sleep, she and John would leave the shoeless, trussed up men at the campsite and leave their non-functional weapons with them. She would leave them one of their radios strung into a low branch of a nearby tree and a knife jammed into a log within reach. After she and John made their way away from the camp, Sarah figured that it would take the men about a half-hour to get free and sound the alarm and that was plenty of time to make their getaway back down the mountain. She did not want to make it too easy, but she did not want to get them killed either.

She felt as though she had just gone to sleep when John woke her as the sun was reaching the campsite. Sandy-eyed she helped John finish packing their equipment. They made a light breakfast, finished the coffee, put out the fire, loaded their backpacks and left. After a few minutes, she heard the man in charge, barking orders, getting his men working toward freeing themselves from their bindings.

He was determined to catch "that woman" and he would drive his men, and himself, to do it. Within about twenty minutes, one of the smaller men had managed to loosen his legs from the rope and then stand. He hurried over to the knife and backed into it, using his legs to squat up and down with the rope against the blade. He cut the rope and only nicked himself once in the process. He quickly released the others and between them, they easily reached the radio and found its battery in the leaves along the edge of the clearing. The "ranger" made a call down to the road and the two waiting deputies, ordering one of them to stay with the cars and the other to follow the path up into the jungle. He warned him about the crazy woman and her demon child who were most likely coming toward him and he authorized him to threaten her with his gun to make her surrender

Sarah had been leading John down the mountain at a much faster pace than John had led them up. She was more accomplished, it was true, but going down was inherently a little easier than going up. Also, she only had to run into the road, where John was trying to end up at a specific place. It was just easier. They had covered well over a mile when her commandeered radio squawked and she heard the "ranger" yelling orders, apparently to some of his men below.

"Well, they're loose and he sounds mad." She was only a few paces in front of John and so she did not have to raise her voice much above normal. "I thought it would take them about a half hour."

John said a little breathlessly, "I heard. Can you tell how much further we have to go?"

She stopped and checked her bearings. After a few seconds she answered, "We've covered nearly two miles and most of that was downward. I'd guess that we should hit the road in about ten minutes or so." She indicated a general direction downhill, "Since we can't know exactly where we are relative to the bad guys, we should probably slow down and be more quiet."

John nodded and they shrugged their packs up and started out again. Both were listening hard and trying to watch everywhere at once. Sarah had turned the volume of the radio down as far as it would go and she had clipped it to the strap that crisscrossed her back and near her ear so that she could hear anything the "ranger" or his men might say to each other.

Within a few minutes, John noticed the bubble forming to their right and coming closer. Sarah motioned for him to stop and wait. As they watched, the bubble moved past them and quickly floated up the mountainside. The deputy had passed within a hundred yards of where they were hiding, and he had been unaware of them. They smiled at each other and waited for another minute to pass before they resumed their forced march. This time, Sarah was nearly at a jog and they reached the road about five minutes later.

The cut in the mountain's side, that had been made allowing the road to be built, formed a low cliff and the break in the jungle cover was very clear to them well before they arrived. They halted at the final row of trees and looked around. Sarah whispered, "You figure out how we can get down the cliff and I'll look around for the other man and his car."

John nodded and he began searching for handholds and rock outcroppings they could use. It was only twenty feet or so, but high enough to do serious damage if they jumped from the edge. Sarah had stepped back a few paces and had headed to her right, assuming that was where they had parked since the fourth man had come from that direction. After about a hundred yards, she saw the trunk of the police car parked ahead of her Jeep. The deputy was sitting on the hood, smoking a cigarette. She could see he was looking around, but he looked more bored than vigilant. She decided to go back to John and see how they could get down to the road as quickly and quietly as possible. The radio crackled in her ear, "We are almost there."

She worked her way back to John and found that he had tied the last of their rope to a small tree and had thrown the twelve-foot piece over the cliff's edge. She asked, "Did you find a good way down?"

John nodded and pointed out the rock edges that formed a narrow stairway downward. He said, "We have to use the rope for the first section, but we should only be five or six feet above the shoulder where we have to drop down."

Sarah said, "Good work." Then after inspecting his knot she said, "Let me get down to the rocks before you start. I'll be in a better position to guard you in case they get back before you make it down." She indicated the radio, "He told the man guarding the cars that they were almost back to the road and the cars are about two hundred yards that way." She had pointed with her head to her right.

Sarah grabbed the rope and used it to stabilize her weight as she backed over the edge of the cliff. Rappelling about eight feet she felt the first of the rock ledge strike her feet and she stopped, reaching out with her left hand to find the outcrop that would support her as she continued downward without the rope. She grabbed the knob of rock and released the rope. She stepped carefully along the cliff face slowly working her way downward. When the rocks stopped, she saw she was only a few feet off the ground and so she jumped.

She brushed off her hands and pulled out her pistol. Looking up she saw that John was almost down to the point where he would have to jump. He reminded her of a monkey as he quickly moved from one handhold to another, his feet constantly stepping along the narrow edge. *Oh, for the nimbleness of youth*, she thought. She scanned the road in both directions and then looked up at John again, just in time to see him release and jump down to her. He landed on all four like a fat cat, the backpack pulling him a little off balance. He recovered and she grabbed his shoulder. They dashed across the road together.

Hunkered down in the culvert, Sarah and John hurried as best they could. As they rounded the curve in the road, Sarah saw that the deputy was now off the car and staring across the road. She did not see anyone yet, but she thought it was only a matter of time and the "rangers" would break out of the trees and start making their way down to the road. Since she knew that she and John would be visible from above she knew she had to hurry.

Very quietly, she made John squat next to the Jeep as she slunk closer to the police car. She pulled her knife and cut the stem of the rear tire and then she moved forward and cut the one on the front. The hissing noise worried her at first, but the deputy was across the road looking up at the place where the others would emerge, and he seemed to be concentrating so hard that he could not hear anything else. She turned and started back to the Jeep, keeping low, when she heard a shout from the cliff.

"John, get in!" Sarah abandoned stealth and she ran the last few steps to her car.

The deputy turned at the sound of her voice and pulled his sidearm. Sarah saw that he was taking aim and she just pointed her gun in his general direction and fired twice, skipping rounds off the road surface. This had the effect she had hoped for: the deputy dove off the pavement and into the cover of the shoulder. She used that time to start her car and jam it into reverse. She twisted the wheel around and hitting the brakes and the clutch at the same time she spun the car around, slammed the transmission into first, let out the clutch and accelerated away. There was a single shot from the cliff that went wide of the mark, burying itself in the vinyl of the dashboard, sending up a little puff of smoke. Then they were around the curve and safely out of sight.

Sarah looked over at John, "Are you OK?"

He was nodding and smiling at her. "That was close, mom. Wow, that was neat!"

Sarah reached over and ruffled his hair, "Happy birthday, John."

- - -

Reaching their apartment, Sarah sent John in to take his shower and change his clothes while she unloaded her car. Bringing in the last of their things, reduced in quantity because of their flight down the mountain, she shut and locked the door and collapsed on the couch. *That was too close*, she thought. *John could have been shot.*

She reached over and picked up her phone and dialed Tom's number. Running her hands through her hair as she waited for him or his machine to pick up, she discovered a little scab of dried blood tangled in her hair; apparently that bullet had come closer than she had realized.

Tom answered, "Hello."

Swallowing the lump that had instantly formed when she had seen the scab, Sarah cleared her throat and said, "Hi, it's me. We're back."

"How was your trip? Did anything interesting happen?"

She lied, "Nope, pretty boring for me, although I think John enjoyed himself. How was your weekend?"

"Oh, I was definitely bored. I missed you. And I wondered if you had a chance to think about my offer?"

She seemed to relax and slouch down into the cushions, raising her boots onto the coffee table. "It's funny you should ask. As it turns out I did think about it." She stopped for a second to see if he was still interested in their relationship.

He obviously was since he could not stand the delay. "Well, what did you decide? Don't make me have to come over there to pry the answer out of you. I was a Marine you know?"

"Oh, I'm so scared of the big, strong, Marine", she lisped in baby talk.

They both laughed. She was glad to be able to laugh.

"I've decided that if the offer still stands, I would really like to move in with you."

She heard him muffle the receiver and yell out loud, "Yeah!" Then in a more restrained voice he said, "That's great. Are you sure you want to do this?"

She grinned into the phone, "Are you trying to talk me out of this now? Because if you are..."

"No, no. I just wanted you to be sure, that's all.

"What does John think of the idea?"

She said, "I haven't told him yet, but I think he'll like the idea of being around you more. He likes you, you know."

"I like him too. I like having a willing audience for my old war stories.

"When can you move your stuff? I can help out."

Sarah answered, "How about next weekend? That will allow me time to give my notice, settle up some things and pack our meager belongings."

"Sounds great, Sarah. Want me to bring over some takeout supper? I could be there in about a half-hour."

"Make it an hour. I stink. I have to take a shower."

"OK, see you in about an hour."

Sarah giggled a little, "Try to control your enthusiasm, Tom. We don't want to scare the little children."

He gave her the raspberries and hung-up.

"What little children?" John asked from the bathroom doorway.

Sarah looked at him, still smiling and noticing for the first time how much he had grown. "It was just a figure of speech, John. There aren't any little children around here.'

- - -

This time when her dreams began there was a little variety. Mostly it was the usual terminator chasing her and Kyle through town, trying and sometimes killing both of them, but now sprinkled in was a new one. This dream had her walking out of a wooded area and up to a playground fence. She could see and hear the children playing and the adults supervising them. LA was in the distant background; she could tell from the smog and the silhouettes of the buildings. The air was hot and yellow, and she could barely breathe.

Her panic started when she realized that she knew that Judgment Day was about to start, and no one could see or hear her try to warn them. They were all about to be fried in a thermonuclear blast and she was helpless to do anything about it. In her dream she pounded on the fence and screamed. In her bed she pounded on Tom and screamed until he was able to wake her up. He held her tightly until she stopped shaking and was merely sobbing softly.

- - -

Sarah had never seen Tom act this way. For the past five months, they had been living together in a condition that she thought of as bliss. They had a routine. They had conversation. She felt safe and unthreatened. John was thriving; both at school and at home with Tom. Now, everything was turning upside-down. She had been making supper for them, (not her forte, but it usually turned out edible), when Tom came rushing into the little kitchen, his face red and his eyes bulging.

"Bastards!" he exclaimed as he picked up a bowl from the counter and pulled back his arm to toss it toward the back door.

In reaction Sarah grabbed his wrist with one hand and the bowl with the other, "Tom, what's happened? Why...?"

"The ass-holes fired me," his angry voice was taking on an ominous growl. He looked over at her where her hand was gripping his wrist, "Let me go, Sarah."

Since the bowl was no longer at risk, she did. "Why, Tom? What happened?" She had started stroking his bicep trying to soothe him a little.

He pulled away from her touch as if it hurt him, "Dud and I had a little argument about which of us was going to have to crawl under the engine of a tractor we were working on. One thing led to another and after some pushing and shoving, he threw a wrench at me and I threw a fist back." He dragged his hands through his hair, "You know how the guy who hits second in a football game usually gets the penalty flag? Well, the boss saw me, and he didn't see Dud, so I got fired as the troublemaker."

She had listened to his story and she saw how he was becoming miserable rather than angry. She reached up, wrapped her arms around his neck and gave him a kiss. "I'm sorry, Tom. It sounds like it wasn't fair." She stood back a little so that she could see his face better, "Is there no recourse? Do you think he would give you your job back if you explained to him?"

Tom looked down, "I don't think so. He was watching for any excuse to get rid of me. I'm out of there for sure."

"You'll find something else, Tom. Don't worry. You'll find something soon."

He tried to smile at her, "I hope you're right. No offence, but I don't think we can make it with just your tips, as good as they are."

She placed her hand on the side of his face, "Let's not tell John, OK? He would only worry, and I think it's too soon for him to start worrying."

He nodded his agreement then he looked hopeful, "What's on the menu for our last meal?"

She punched his arm, "Quit talking like that. I can cook pretty darn well."

He rubbed his arm, "I wish you could cook as well as you hit." He grabbed her arm before she could punch him again, "I'll go wash up and get John away from his homework."

- - -

Two months after losing his job, Tom was growing anxious and sullen. He seemed to be always off somewhere else in his mind. When he talked at all, it was in short, clipped phrases and sentences. He was very unhappy, and it showed. Eventually, Sarah had to answer John's questions, and then he started to worry too.

The financial pressures did not seem to increase the frequency or intensity of her dreams, but they did affect Tom's ability to cope with them. He had not been sleeping well and the tension around the house was palpable and growing daily. Last night he had left the house after she had stopped screaming. John had come in and Tom had left.

John held her as she returned to reality, rocking her and crooning, "He'll be back, mom. He'll be back, don't worry." She just cried softly into his shoulder.

Eventually she stopped crying and after washing her face in the bathroom, she came out to find John sitting on the edge of the bed with his hands in his lap. She could see he was upset too.

"Are you hungry? It's almost time to get up anyway. Do you want a bowl of cereal or some toast or something? I could make pancakes."

He looked up at her, "Sure. I was worried that you might want to cook something for breakfast." As he spoke, he hurried off the bed and just made it out of the bedroom and into the hallway before she caught him.

"What do you mean by that crack, mister? I can cook just fine." She was having trouble keeping a straight face.

"I was just saying that I wouldn't want to put you out or something. Cereal would be just fine." He was grinning at her, playing out their continuing joke.

She took a swat at his butt as he pulled away from her, "Just for that, I'll make some toast too."

He laughed out-loud as he ran into the kitchen.

She answered back as she walked, "OK, I'm going to smear peanut butter on that toast if you aren't careful." She heard the cupboard door clomp closed as he pulled out the cereal box, then the stool scooting back from the counter.

- - -

They had both regained their composure and finished their cereal and peanut butter laden, burned toast when Tom came back through the door. They looked up as the door opened and John hollered out, "We're out here."

Tom came through the kitchen doorway, looking disheveled and tired. As he looked at the domestic scene around the table, his face cracked the slightest smile. "Did you save me any milk?"

John answered, "There's a little, but mom can burn some bread for you."

Tom started laughing and Sarah said, "John, I think it's time for you to get ready for school." She was glaring at him, but he knew it was part of their little play. He got up and started to run out of the kitchen but stopped long enough to give Tom a little hug as he passed.

Tom's eyes followed John out and then he looked at Sarah, "He's really a good kid. I'm not sure what I'd do without the two of you in my life right now."

Sarah stood and went over to him, "Sit down and I'll make you something." She did not wait for his comment. "I'll just make you a bowl of cereal, OK?"

He grinned, "Fine. I am a little hungry."

She kissed the top of his head, "I'm sorry about this morning. I couldn't..."

"That's OK, Sarah. You can't help what you dream. I might have over-reacted. I've been so tired recently."

She kissed him again and then went to the cupboard and extracted a bowl. She filled it and poured milk over it. She brought the bowl and the sugar dispenser to the table and set it in front of him. Then she sat next to him and waited.

They looked at each other for a few seconds and then Tom picked up the sugar and poured on two or three teaspoonfuls. He put the dispenser down and began to stir the flakes and milk and sugar, "I was driving around thinking. Without a job I don't know how we can make this month's rent. I'm really worried. Things are getting really tight, Sarah."

She said, "I know, but we'll be OK. You'll find something. We'll just have to tighten up a little more, that's all."

Tom got a funny look on his face, and she asked, "What are you thinking, Tom?"

He hesitated and then said, "I know a guy. I met him one day at the bar after work. He said he had a way to make some money, a lot of money, but he required a little help. He said he thought I was the right guy to help him and he would split even with me." He looked to her for understanding. "He didn't tell me what it was, but I got the impression that it wasn't exactly on the level."

"What's not level?" The question came from John in the doorway.

Without missing a beat, Tom said, "A deck a buddy of mine asked me to work on for him. It's leaning and he wants me to take a look at fixing it for him."

Sarah stood up, "I have to take John to school right now. Don't go anywhere until we've had a chance to talk."

Tom nodded, "I think I'll take a shower while you're gone."

Sarah didn't comment to him, but instead spoke to John, "Let's go. Do you have your books? Do you need a lunch?"

John laughed, "I always buy my lunch, mom. It's safer that way." He dodged past her and scampered out the door, headed for the car.

"Don't do anything stupid while I'm gone," she yelled toward the bathroom.

* * *

John had been excited when he had heard about the Berkley accelerator. Maybe it had been spared from destruction when San Francisco was taken out. Maybe Skynet had abandoned it when his teams had detonated the nuclear power packs in the T100 manufacturing facility, turning much of northern California into smoking slag. Maybe that had been too close for comfort and Skynet had just high-tailed it out of there, leaving everything behind.

Since he had to know and he had to have those magnetic bottles filled with muons, he had to send a scouting party to the area and have them check it out. One helicopter with Derek, Place and several other protective infantrymen were sent. John knew that somehow, someway he must have managed to get what was needed to send Kyle back. This appeared to be the most likely scenario.

He and Kathryn were staying in his office reading and responding to reports, waiting by the radio for anything. Neither spoke for several hours, but it seemed much longer.

- - -

Derek had directed the chopper in a wide arc around the smoldering ruins of San Francisco. Not much was recognizable until they got to the far side of the bay; even the Golden Gate Bridge had been twisted off of its moorings and could be seen laying in the water in several disconnected hunks. On the far side, the first mile or so had been burned or blown away, depending on its height and construction, but by the third mile the damage seemed less severe.

Approaching Santa Rosa, they saw the cooling towers of the power plant in the distance. One had cracked in half with one half on its side in a pile of rubble. The other tower had cracks running up one side but appeared to be intact although not functioning. As they got closer, they saw the concrete containment building seemed to be leaning a little, but that could have been an illusion.

- - -

Derek was almost breathless from exertion. He had hurried all the way back from the Santa Rosa facility and he had run all the way from the airfield where the chopper had dropped him off. He felt that it was important to hand deliver this logbook and not risk radio communications just in case Skynet intercepted and was able to decode the encrypted contents. He felt that this was potentially big. Now that he was aware of what Skynet was trying to do with time travel and his new role in the past, this information could be vital to their continued existence.

He ran past the startled layers of sentries with a cursory salute, knowing that they would both recognize him and allow him to pass unmolested. Derek entered the main encampment and passed through the blast doors that led down into the main living areas and the command center. He was looking for John Conner and he was sure he would be hovering around the communications board waiting for news of their finds in the ravaged northern parts of California. He entered command and saw John standing with Kathryn and he angled across the large, dimly lit room, skirting banks of equipment, bundles of cables and startled operators.

John Conner looked up as he rushed over and Kathryn glared at him in warning; always the ever-vigilant doctor where her wounded husband was concerned.

John smiled toward Derek, "Well, this is a pleasant surprise. What can be so important that you have to hand-deliver it?"

Derek paused to snap off a quick salute before answering. "Sir, we found a log that was apparently kept by the human technicians that ran the time travel facility for Skynet."

John's grin grew even wider, "I was hoping that was why you were playing this so close to the vest. It sounds like good news." He reached over and shook Derek's hand. "Let me see the book."

Derek undid the latch on his shoulder bag and reached inside. He pulled out a ratty, partially burned spiral-ringed notebook and set it on the table between them. John slid the lamp over closer and Kathryn leaned over his shoulder, trying to get a better view.

John made a soft sound as he carefully opened the cover of the book. He saw that the first few pages were covered with crayon markings that looked like something that a five-year old might make. He looked over at Derek and frowned, "Crayons?"

Derek said, "It does get a little better as you go. We figured that paper was at a premium and some survivor kid was using it for doodling first."

John finally opened to pages that had blocks of calculations on them in a tight hand. "It looks like they used this facility for several shots", John said.

Derek answered, "We counted fourteen listed in the book. The last section of the book is empty, presumably a victim of the San Francisco blast."

John could see that each page seemed to be a separate launch. The calculations and settings for each launch looked promising. He could read weight of the subject, target date, results of the calculations and the control system set points. There seemed to be notes specific to the launch at the bottom of each page.

Kathryn asked, "What did Silberman and Place think of this book?"

Derek nodded, "They both got excited. Place thinks that this will turn out to be the key to our time travel success."

"Wow," John said. "Skynet wasn't taking any chances was it? Look at the numbers of machines it sent back." He continued to flip back and forth in the book. "We knew about the original T101 and the T1000 and the TX models as well as four or five T888 because I fought them, but it also sent a T101 to before the first one; maybe to stop my mother from being born. It also sent additional TX's to directly attack the Resistance Command structure and here's the TX that was sent to protect the infrastructure of San Francisco."

Kathryn muttered, "Don't forget that Silberman thinks that it had other facilities in other parts of the world so that it could survive catastrophes. Who knows how many others or when they went or who they targeted?" She sounded depressed. "It's a little mind boggling."

John nodded, "That it is. It also is additional evidence that the best way to stop Skynet is to prevent it in the first place." His head was shaking in negation, "Just chipping away, hopping to break Skynet down into smaller and smaller parts so that it loses its critical mass, is a losing proposition."

Kathryn said, "Destroy a piece here and it adds pieces somewhere else, maintaining itself."

"Right," John said. Then to Derek, "Let me think about this and review this information." He waved the book toward them, "I've got a lot of reading to do."

- - -

With the list of terminators sent and the target dates and settings used, John and the technical team were able to determine what they had to do to counter Skynet's efforts. He remembered all the various terminators he had met and had defeated with the help of so many others. The problems he faced were the little paradoxes that were slowly creeping into his reality. He had seen firsthand how history could be changed. He did not know how far he could interfere without inadvertently changing something that was crucial to their survival. The future was, as he had heard someone (perhaps himself) say, was a constantly moving target and it kept darting this way and that as things happened. The real talent he hoped he had was to make only the changes that would eliminate Skynet and leave humanity relatively intact.

Technical Interlude

Sensing the World Around Them: Part 2

Sensing sound energy is quite easy; organisms and machines do it all the time. However, making sense out of those sounds is a much more complex and difficult task. Animals have evolved detecting sound energy and assigning value to it: threat, non-threat, pleasure, pain, predator, prey. Most species have bilateral sensors with frequency responses and sensitivities that vary widely from one species to the other: reptiles, whales, humans, dogs, birds, porpoises and bats, from low to high. Typically, both characteristics are maximum values when the organism is in its youth and degenerate to a minimum as the organism ages or suffers damage.

Machines can be designed and built with any number of sound energy detecting "organs". These devices tend to be specific to the machine's task or goals and therefore the sensor numbers and specifications are designed in, rather than evolved. As examples, think of the lighting fixture that is triggered by the sound of hands clapping, or a deep-sea microphone array that listens for the sounds of passing submarines. These have completely different environments and goals and therefore completely different design specifications and construction. Neither one is capable of doing what the other does and neither one is particularly good at doing anything else.

The most difficult part is the value assessment and response. Organisms must do this task instantaneously and survival of the individual as well as the species may depend on it. The time from hearing a sound, determining its "value" and reacting to that information is short (milliseconds to seconds) and crucial (fight or flight, feast or famine, diner or dinner). Determining direction and motion of the source, identity of the source and response to the source are learned and must become nearly automatic. Failure of any phase of the process has a detrimental impact on the organism and eventually selects it out of the gene pool (or perhaps the food chain).

Machine survival is typically not at issue with sound identity. The machine's reason for detecting and analyzing sound energy is one of practicality; to satisfy its builder's goals. Those goals may require the detection, location, and identification of sounds ranging from subsonic to ultrasonic frequencies. Bilateral microphones are fine for detecting sounds and are acceptable for determining general direction and motion, but if exact location is necessary, an array of sensors is necessary. Unfortunately, there is no one configuration that is all things and so, machines that are intended to be generalist by design, typically are built with a compromised design.

The electronics that are fed by the sound energy can make the difference between these compromises less of a problem. The three general methods used by machine designers are: Near-field Acoustic Holography (NAH), Beamforming, and Inverse methods. Because NAH and beamforming both require a large array of microphones, they do not lend themselves to mobile robots (such as T100 series robots). In those instances, the inverse method works well enough.

The inverse method involves setting up and solving a system of equations: $p=Hq$, where p represents the sound pressure measured at the microphone array and q represents the localization on the volume velocity of sound distribution on the source. p and q are related through a transfer function H. q is determined by calculating the inverse of the transfer matrix H and multiplying it by p. This array matrix requires a lot of computer calculation, but since the Skynet designed machines have access to large amounts of computer power and processing time, this seems to be a non-problem.

Sound source velocity is a simple task for circuits that are programmed to measure the Doppler shift of the measured frequencies. The Doppler shift is a phenomenon that is well known and well understood as the compression of waves as a source approaches and the extension of waves as the source retreats. The amount of compression or extension gives the velocity of the source.

In this way, a machine can "hear" sound, and determine the source's direction, distance, velocity, and frequency spectrum. With a little computer time and effort, it can identify source and assign values to what it hears, allowing it to ignore the sound or pursue the source as part of the machine's programmed goals.

Chapter 12

Rank was a hawkish looking man. He was sitting at a corner table of the bar, staring nervously into his beer bottle as if something that should not be in there was about to crawl out. As they walked up, he glanced up and then furtively surveyed the rest of the bar. He did not stand as they stopped at his table.

"Sit down," he said, "I ordered a couple'a beers for you." He was staring a hole through Sarah as if daring her to do or say something that he would be able to call stupid, giving him cause to eliminate her from their discussion. He had prison or gang tattoos on his hands and up both arms and he gave the impression of someone who had learned several hard lessons from the school of law enforcement. "What'chew looking at lady, never seen ink before?" Rank was practically snarling at her.

"Just take it easy, Rank," Tom said. "There's no need to be rude to her. Sarah's OK. She can help us."

Rank sat back in his seat and fished a cigarette out of a rumpled pack. He jammed it in between his lips and lit it with a double flick of his lighter; the first opening the lid and the second thumbing the flint wheel. He took a very deep drag on it before exhaling, "I don't like this you know. It's bad luck to pull a job with a rooky, much less a woman rooky." He snapped the lighter's lid closed and began playing with it on the table top, spinning it in small circles like a top.

Sarah thought that now would be a good time to speak up. "Look, Mr. Rank, I'm not crazy about working with you either. I've tried to talk Tom out of this, but since he's determined, I want to watch his back." She paused to fan Rank's smoke away from her face with her hand.

"It's not Mr. Rank. It's just Rank," he said toward her with a crooked smile around his cigarette. "And besides you won't be able to do too much from out in the car, cause I ain't letting you carry a gun, so you ain't goin' inside." He watched as a new cloud of smoke drifted into her face making her squint.

"Yeah, I understand," she said, "but I'm not a rooky. I did some things when I was in Mexico and I've proven I can handle myself."

Rank broke into a leer toward Tom, "I love it when a woman talks dirty."

Tom started to rise from the table, but Sarah restrained him with her hand on his arm. "It's OK, Tom. He's just trying to rile you."

Tom still sounded angry as he said, "Just watch your mouth, Rank. Sarah doesn't deserve shit from you." Then he took a breath and said, "I thought we were going to discuss the plan. Are you going to discuss the plan, or should we leave and just forget the whole thing?"

Sarah took that as a hopeful hint and started to get up from the table. *Just maybe*, she thought.

Rank held up his hands and took a deep drag from his cigarette and blew the smoke toward Sarah as he mashed out the butt on the table. "Yeah, I think we should talk about it."

- - -

Sarah parked the car along the curb outside the El Rancho Madras Federal Credit Union, leaving plenty of room front and back. She patted Tom on the thigh as he gathered himself to exit the car and enter the bank. "Be careful. Watch your back," she said calmly, a lot more calmly than she felt.

"You just keep the engine running and be ready to go when we get back," Rank said, as he climbed out of the back seat and slammed the door a little too hard. She could tell he really did not like her being here with them, but he needed someone to drive and Tom had talked him into it. She was unavoidable to him, but he did not have to like it.

She watched as the two men walked across the sidewalk and to the doors. They were dressed identically in jeans, a blue tee shirt, a light nylon windbreaker that a fisherman might wear and a brown, billed, baseball cap. Both men pulled their baseball caps down more firmly over their foreheads, obscuring their upper features from any ceiling-mounted security cameras, as they reached the doors. Rank had scouted the inside last week and he knew where they all were. She saw them flip-down the built-in sunshades to make recognition by the tellers that much harder. Then they were through the doors and out of her sight. She could only wait, watch, and worry.

- - -

Since it was just after lunch, most of the Credit Union's traffic was gone and the maximum amount of cash was likely to be in there; at least that is what Rank said. The one guard, an old, ex-traffic cop, would most likely be on the verge of dozing off and should not be a problem. There were only three tellers and a manager working at that time, all women, Rank informed them. He believed they would most likely give them whatever they asked for. The only unknown was, which customers might be present and what they might do if alarmed.

Tom noted that the guard saw them come in, looked at them both, and then went back to looking around with bleary eyes. He doubted that old man's sidearm was even loaded. He faced back toward the tellers and got into line behind the one female customer already transacting business. He glanced over at Rank and saw that he too was second in line. He steeled himself as the woman in front of him started counting her money and opening her purse on the counter. He thought that Rank would most likely start the robbery before she finished so they wouldn't miss that little wad she had.

Rank had seen her counting too and was about to shout his announcement of the robbery. He did not notice that one of the tellers had been staring at him and had decided that he looked like the man who had loitered around the bank last week and might be a robber. She triggered the silent alarm and began backing away from the counter, toward the manager's office.

Just then, Rank shouted, "This is a robbery! Everyone get on the floor!" He had pulled his pistol from under his shirt and was waving it around in the attempt to intimidate everyone into immediate compliance. It worked.

Tom watched the guard while he pulled out his gun from under his shirt and indicated with a wave of his hand that he should get down as well. The old man climbed off his stool and complied willingly; *no hero there*, Tom thought.

He turned toward his teller and said roughly, "Keep your hands where I can see them and stay away from the alarm switch as you get up." He motioned with his gun for her to stand. "I want you to put all of the money in your drawer into this bag." He had pulled a tan canvass bag from under his shirt where it had been hidden. He watched as she started to comply.

Rank had done the same thing. They knew that they probably only had three or four minutes before someone wandered in and broke the spell they had generated, and somebody would probably do something stupid. Neither man wanted that to happen. They planned it to be a simple in and out and they would be away. Nobody would get hurt. Rank kept his eye on the manager who had gone to the floor beside her desk. He thought that she might have grabbed her phone on the way down, but even if she did, they would still have more than enough time before a squad could be dispatched and arrive.

With their bags filled with everything the teller's drawers had in currency, the two men grabbed them and started to turn.

- - -

Tom and Rank had been inside for less than two minutes when three squad cars came in from two directions. Before Sarah could react, one of the cars blocked her in as they came to a sliding halt. She was trapped in the car and Tom was about to be trapped inside the bank. Six officers poured out of the cars and ran to the front wall of the building, three on each side of the doorway. One of the police officers took a quick peek from low down through the double doors. He stood and signaled to the others that he saw two inside. The men prepared to enter.

Their guns drawn, one officer grabbed the right door and pulled it open and the other five crouched and ran through in single file.

Sarah knew that Tom was in real trouble, but she did not know what she could do about it.

- - -

As they were starting to turn, the canvass bags in hand, their first indication of trouble was the sound of a car's horn somewhere outside, followed quickly by a bellowed order to "Drop your weapons and get on the floor!" Tom's head swiveled toward the sound, expecting to see the guard quivering, making his last stand. What he saw was much worse; five police officers spread in a wide array near the door with their guns drawn and bearing down on them. The sound level in the bank suddenly rose as all five officers began shouting for them to drop their weapons and get down and put their hands on their heads and the civilians in the bank began to scream in terror.

In the artificially slowed time of concentrated action, all he heard was Rank say, "Shit," as he opened fire. The police instantly returned fire and Tom was hit with three rounds before he could do anything. The last thing he remembered as he landed on the marble floor was that he hadn't even had the chance to comply and drop his gun.

- - -

Sarah was afraid, but she managed not to panic. The sixth police officer had stayed outside the Credit Union and was acting as a rear guard and his other responsibility was to prevent civilians from getting into harm's way if shooting started. She knew that Tom and Rank were terribly outnumbered and about to be surprised in the worst possible way. The only thing she could think of to do was to hit the horn. The sound startled her with its loudness even though she knew what it was. The sixth officer turned to see where the horn was coming from and their eyes met just as the sounds of rapid gunfire erupted from inside the bank. He ducked as a round shattered the glass door next to him, and by the time he recovered, Sarah had opened the driver's door and had begun to run across the street.

She dodged around two cars that had slowed to negotiate around the parked clot of flashing police cars in front of the bank and she started sprinting across the far lane. Two arriving black and white units and an unmarked car with a red gumball on its roof saw her and gave chase. She headed toward an alleyway and the unmarked car skidded to a stop in front of her, blocking the way. As she turned to reverse her direction, she hesitated when she saw that the two other police cars had her pinned in and there were several guns swinging toward her. The unmarked car's door opened, and she heard her name. "Sarah Conner, FBI! Stop!" The shock of hearing her name was so complete that she nearly fell.

Regaining her balance and raising her hands in surrender, Sarah turned to look toward the voice that had impossibly spoken her name. She saw a large black man in a suit, holstering his weapon and watching her as he approached. He seemed to be smiling, although she could not imagine why.

He said, "Sarah, I've been looking for you for a long time."

- - -

Terminator 1+: The Future Is Not Set

Mark T. Sondrini

Agent Ellison had been returning from speaking at a civic club meeting when he heard the call go out about a bank robbery in progress less than six blocks away from his location. He reached out his window, stuck the spinning red light onto his car's roof, and then grabbed his radio telling the police dispatcher that he was heading to the robbery. He checked his mirrors and did a speeding U-turn to head toward the scene. He hoped that this would not turn into a shootout because his vest was in the car's trunk and he was relatively unprotected.

Because of the code used by the dispatcher he did not use his siren, but most of the traffic saw his light and moved over for him as he sped past. As he came within a block of the bank, he could see three police cars jammed around the front. About that time, he saw the street guard officer turn and start toward the curb full of parked cars as the glass doors of the bank shattered. He noticed that, simultaneously, a woman had climbed out of a parked car and had started running away from the bank, dodging traffic.

Assuming that she had been somehow involved, he flipped on his siren and cut across the lanes of traffic toward the alley entrance that she seemed to be heading for. Two other police units were converging on her from the other direction too. She was trapped between them.

As she ran, she briefly turned toward his car and his heart almost stopped. It couldn't be. The image of the face that had been burned into his mind for the past seven years was looking back at him. He knew he was right, but it made no sense to him. After all this time and after all the places he had gone to catch her, here she was almost running into his arms of her own volition. An accident or twist of fate had brought them together at this place and time. He did not understand such things, but he was willing to take advantage of them.

He skidded to a stop, his car blocking her from the alley and her hope of escape. She turned back and started to run away, only to come up against the other two police cars and their armed occupants forcing her to stop again. He rushed out of his car and stood, identifying himself and calling out her name, telling her to surrender. He did not want her to get shot now. He watched as she skidded to a stop, almost falling, and then turn to look in his direction in shocked confusion. He could understand that.

- - -

For a change, the cumbersome process of Sarah Conner's trial proceeded quickly enough. She had been silent through most of her initial police interrogation sessions. She often met with the public defender assigned by the court to protect her rights. She talked very little about the robbery, but she had told him about John and her worries about him. He had explained to her about the California Child Welfare System that had taken him into temporary custody. That set her off into great, ranting, tirades about Skynet and the terminators that had been and most likely still were trying to kill her and her John. When he explained how he could not do anything about that and that she was his primary concern, Sarah attacked him and managed to inflict several bites and scratches before the guards pulled her off.

The rumpled, bloody and terrified lawyer asked the judge to be relieved of the case, "Your honor, my client is dangerous. She attacked me for no apparent reason. I request that I be taken off her case and you assign someone, anyone else, to defend her." He had run his hand through his hair, attempting to restore some semblance of order to it, "I think she's crazy and that she should have a psychological evaluation before proceeding to trial."

The judge, looking over the tops of his glasses, said that he agreed with his request for an evaluation and he would order it. Then he said, "But I insist that you remain on this case, if for no other reason than you are most familiar with the details and a new defender would have to delay the proceedings while they catch up. Also, for your own benefit as an attorney." He stared at the squirming man, "Did you think that as a public defender all of your clients in the criminal cases would be little old ladies who were charged with jaywalking or shoplifting? Of course, they are dangerous! That is what criminals are. You need to learn to deal with it." He rapped his gavel, "Request denied." Then with a glare intended to intimidate, "In the future, clean yourself up a little before coming into my courtroom or I'll have you in contempt." He rapped his gavel and announced, "Next case."

- - -

Agent Ellison was not allowed to participate directly in the interrogations, but he had kept an eye on the proceedings, and he had arranged for transcripts of all her talks with the police investigators. Many of them were on video tape, and he was watching one of those when Detective Sergeant Roberts and his partner Detective Jenkins came knocking at his office door.

"Well, we heard that you caught her," Roberts said as soon as they shook hands. "Congratulations."

Ellison nodded, "Thanks. I didn't believe that the day would actually come."

Jenkins asked, "What was going on? Why did she try to rob that Credit Union?" He was shaking his head, "It doesn't make much sense to me."

Ellison answered, "Me either. She spent all of her previous time trying to stay out of any kind of trouble with the law. She was trying to stay invisible as much as anyone can in this country." He looked at them both, "She did a very good job up until then, too."

Detective Roberts asked. "What was that I heard about her living in Mexico for a few years?" He looked hopeful, "I heard that is where she had her son, John. That true?"

Ellison nodded, "You remember when we talked last time? She had just managed to evade a major sweep of a beach commune of hippies and surfers south of Monterey." He paused as they indicated they remembered. "Well, I told you then that I had discovered she was pregnant, and I had guessed that since she had not been seen again, she might be out of the country."

He opened the ratty-looking file on his desk, "I received a report from the Mexican Federal Police that they think she was a member of a commune of Mexican outlaws holed-up in Baja who had robbed a bank in Ensenada and hit a Mexican Army depot a few years ago." He handed over a piece of folded stationary with a gold embossed eagle at the top that contained the report. As Roberts read it, he said, "They never had proof of her participation, but several witnesses placed her and her baby son there at the time."

Jenkins whistled. "So, they were looking for her too?"

"As far as they were concerned, it was guilt by association." He looked at them with a grin, "They just missed her too. Several times, I'm told." He was shaking his head, "The woman had uncanny instincts, and always managed to clear out just before the authorities arrived."

Ellison pulled out a handwritten sheet and offered it across his desk to Roberts. "I've listed all of the close calls I've heard about in one column and next to those I've added witness accounts that mentioned her having dreams about her robot attack." He watched as the two men read the list. "You'll notice that in almost all of the cases, she started having nightmares just before she left. I think that, for whatever reason, somehow, her dreams allowed her to evade us."

This time both detectives whistled.

- - -

John Conner had been questioned too, but more for background information about Tom Randle. John told about a man who had been a hero with the US Marines during the war in Kuwait and who had been treating both him and his mother well. The ultimate story became clear to Ellison, even though the police were not as confident about what had happened. He was sure that it was a case of a desperate man, Tom, needing to take care of his family, John and Sarah, after losing his job and remaining unemployed for too long. Finally, he ran into a career criminal, Rank, who showed him how to solve all his financial problems and talked him into the robbery attempt. Somehow Sarah had been brought into the scheme, John was not sure how and Ellison was not either.

Rank was recovering from his gunshot wounds in the hospital and was trying to swing a deal with the prosecutor's office to turn State's Evidence to save himself from a major prison term. He claimed that Tom Randle had been the bad guy and practically forced him to participate and that the woman, Sarah Conner, was part of it from the beginning, rooting them on, practically planning the whole thing. Ellison found Rank's tale too pat and it did not fit well with the picture he had formed about Sarah Conner. He tried to convince the prosecutor that Rank was obviously lying, but the fool was determined to get a win out of this, and Rank's testimony would assure that.

John, placed into a foster home until after Sarah's trial, became quiet and depressed. His schoolwork faltered as the court date approached. He started to bully other kids at school, egging them onto fights so that he would get expelled and he could stay home. Stories circulating about his mother's mental condition only made him more belligerent. After she was committed to Pescadaro Hospital for the Criminally Insane he was so ashamed that he managed to run away from his first foster home and hide for nearly a week before he was caught and assigned to a new home.

- - -

Doctor Jackson drew the assignment from the State to evaluate Sarah Conner's mental state. She was initially quiet during their interviews, but he eventually brought her around to the realization that since he had to report to the court, one way or another, about her sanity she owed it to herself and her son to participate and make him understand. Once she started talking to him and he had a feel for what was going on in her head, he had less trouble invoking responses from her to his probing questions. His report began taking shape.

The bank robbery attempt seemed to be a black hole for psychological information. Her participation did not seem to be in question and her motives seemed to be relatively clear to Jackson after reading the police reports. He was unable, however, to get her to talk about anything that had occurred.

He got the strongest responses from her when he delved into the subject of her son and his safety. There she was completely off the rails in his opinion, totally paranoid and delusional. Yet some of the things she said were somehow ringing familiar to him. It was several weeks after his testimony at her trial before he could remember where he had heard about the killer robots. By then, she had been found criminally insane and had been shipped off to Pescadaro Hospital. Since he had heard from Lorrain that Doctor Silberman was working there Mondays, Wednesdays and Fridays he thought that she would be in understanding hands. He had also wondered at the irony of what goes around comes around.

* * *

John had been working for the past week on only one thing. The detailed planning required for the initial jump consumed almost all his attention and energy allowing him little time for recrimination or doubt. The only concession he had allowed was based on a very logical argument Kate had made a week after the stash of muon-filled magnetic bottles had been found at the Russian River Power Station complex. Her case had revolved around who should be the first time-traveler in their newly revamped equipment. Because Kyle was so important to their future, she felt that he should not be the first one to go. She lobbied for someone else, almost anyone else, to try first, to make sure that the machine worked as expected.

Unfortunately, that idea was a double-edged blade. If it did not work, Kyle was saved until they could either fix it or find a different machine. If it did work, they might be discovered by Skynet and prevented from using it again. The proof was there that Kyle had been sent back, but no one knew from where or when.

John and Kate had spent days trying to solve the problem. It was finally decided to try to send a small team into the near past. If it worked (or at least seemed to work by not blowing up or frying the team on the spot), a second attempt would be made with Kyle as quickly as possible. If this machine crapped out during this test-send, then Kyle would go in the next machine once it was ready and proved acceptable. If the initial attempt worked, the team was to set itself up and try to stop Skynet from ever being created. They were to try and find and destroy the men and companies who were working on critical pieces. Some of the principles were known: Andrew Goode and *The Turk* computer, Myles Dyson and Cyberdyne, Lt. Colonel Brewster and the US Air Force research facility at Vandenberg.

It was during one of these late-night sessions that they were interrupted by a knock at their door. They looked at each other as John said, "Enter."

The steel door opened, and Derek stuck his head into the opening. "We hope we're not interrupting too much, but the Doctor had some information you should hear." The two men entered over the threshold, Derek lifting Silberman and his chair over the obstacle, and then Derek closed the door behind them.

Silberman looked tired to Kathryn, as though he had been burning his candle at both ends. She said, "You look tired, Doctor, have you been sleeping?"

Silberman waved her off, "No time. We've been working to get this ready for him." He looked over toward John Conner as if for confirmation, "This is the most important thing. Right, Conner?"

John was nodding, "You're right, Doctor. If this works the way it's supposed to, there will be plenty of time to rest later." Then, closing a folder he had been looking at, signifying that he was giving all his attention to him, John asked, "What have you discovered, Doctor?"

"Well, you know how we wondered why the target date input dials were digital; using integer inputs rather than a slider or more variable input method. I've, or rather the team has noticed that there might be certain logic to that. Using some information we gleaned from the second unit at Russian River, we've determined that you can safely jump in full day units and full year units without requiring massive computer calculations to compensate for universal motion offsets. Anything less or more than an exact day or year could make you end up somewhere other than where you thought you might end up."

He looked at Kathryn as if the concept might be too difficult for her, "For example. If you jumped a half day you might end up inside a mountain range on the other side of the earth, or maybe three miles in the air. If you jumped a half year you would likely end up out in space where the Earth was at the time you jumped, but not where it is at your target date." He smiled condescendingly toward her. "It's complicated."

John rested his hand on Kate's stiffening arm, keeping her from jumping up and snapping at him. He saw Derek roll his eyes at Silberman's mistake. John said, "I see, Doctor. That is interesting information." He patted Kate's arm and stood, reached for his cane, and walked around to the front of his desk, stopping directly in front of Silberman's chair.

"So, if I understand you correctly, if we were to attempt a jump today, we should shoot for May 14, 2000, or some other year within the limits of the device. Is that correct?"

Silberman hesitated a little, "Well, yes basically. You'd have to account for leap years, obviously."

"Obviously", Kathryn said a little sarcastically, studying her fingernails.

Silberman glanced over at her, his face puckering. "Yes, since our year is really about a quarter of a day longer than we normally count, we have to add or subtract a day for every four years we go."

This time Kathryn looked up and said sincerely, "I guess I didn't realize that, Doctor."

Derek jumped in before Silberman could make Kathryn angry again, "There are lots of ways little errors can add up it seems. Once we decide what we want to send and when we want it to get there, we have to very carefully calculate our settings so that we can minimize the error."

John was nodding his head. "Thank you both. I think this information is what I needed to make my decisions for our next moves." Then standing from the front of his desk he looked at Derek, "Schedule a Company meeting for 0800. I want everyone who isn't actively patrolling or doing guard duty or in the infirmary to be there. I'll let the rest hear about it later in the day." He looked at them and dismissed them. "Thank you for your work. Go and get some rest."

Derek helped Silberman out and shut the door behind them. John moved back around his desk and sat down. He seemed to Kate somehow relieved. She stood looking at him, waiting for him to begin.

John looked up at her and smiled, "I've decided our best course based on the best information you all have given me." He ran both hands through his graying hair and Kate realized how tired he had become.

"I can't risk Kyle in the first jump. You are certainly right about that. But if the first jump works, I want him to go as soon as possible afterward." He slid folders around on his desk, "I want to send a small squad back a year or two before Judgment Day and have them try to disrupt Skynet's birth. My mother and I managed to postpone it twice before and I'll bet we can do it again." He looked up at Kate with longing, "Maybe we'll get lucky enough to stop it altogether. Who knows?"

Kate had come up behind him and started kneading his shoulders, "Maybe, John. Maybe they can do it this time."

- - -

John and Kathryn walked into the large section of the bunker that served as the Company's headquarters. This section must have been a ballroom or meeting hall of an old resort hotel they had been using for the past six months or so. There were crates of supplies, caches of ammunition and tanks of fuel for their meager fleet of vehicles lining the walls and forming aisles all the way to the well-concealed entrance. Sixty anxious troops and twenty or so support personnel were standing in the empty spaces or sitting on crates with their eyes now focused on John.

The buzz of conversation had stopped as soon as he appeared and someone shouted, "Attention on deck!"

Climbing up a portable stairway someone had placed next to a large crate, John Conner worked his way up to where he could be seen by everyone in the space. He looked around slowly, meeting every eye that he could before speaking. He shouted, "Stand at ease."

John placed his cane into a notch formed by the last step and the handrail. He then turned, and with a slight hitch in his step, he came to the front of the crate and began.

"Many of you have heard the scuttlebutt, and a few of you have actually been involved with the effort to find and repair and understand the equipment we recently captured from Skynet." Like a good, natural speaker he rotated his head around as he spoke, looking at each in turn. "This equipment is Skynet's prototype time travel machine." He paused for the hubbub he knew would follow. He let it go for thirty seconds or so and then held up his hands for quiet, "OK. OK, settle down."

Derek jumped up on a nearby crate and shouted, "Quiet! Listen up!" The noise settled almost immediately, although a few whispers could still be heard.

John continued, "Thanks. Yeah, I know what you're thinking, but you're wrong. Skynet developed a way to transport things, organic things, people and cyborgs, back in time. A few of us know this to be true from firsthand experience: Me, Kathryn, Doctor Silberman. A few know from working on the equipment we found." He had their attention.

"I want to tell you a short story. This is what happened back in May 1986, before I was born and before Skynet was even considered."

In limited detail he told them about the first cyborg terminator from after Judgment Day, a T101, that had arrived in the past and how it had tried to kill his mother, Sarah. He told them about a warrior also from the future who claimed to be sent by him and he had arrived at about the same time and saved her from that terminator. Then he told how ten years later a reprogrammed T101 terminator from the future, sent back by him, had saved both his mother and him from a new, advanced prototype terminator called a T1000. About five years later he had sent back a modified T800 to protect them both from a series of T888 cyborgs when he was a kid, just learning how to become a soldier. Then somehow Kathryn had reprogrammed a second T101 and sent it back to protect both of them from a vastly new and powerful terminator called a TX that ultimately precipitated Judgment Day.

He told them about how each time they had been saved, Judgment Day had been postponed by a few years because of the changes made in the past. How they had been able to almost, but not quite, stop Skynet and Judgment Day from happening. Then he told them that he had been looking for this equipment for years and now that it had been found, it was the most important weapon that they had at their command. Their team had cleaned and prepared it and have studied it and now it was time to use it.

You could have heard a pin drop in that cavernous space. "We have the opportunity to not only use this machine to do what has already happened in the past from our present, but we have the opportunity to change our present, by changing the past and eliminating Skynet before it can start."

A loud cheer went up as what John said hit home. He let it go on for more than a minute. Then he held up his arms to quiet them again. When they stopped cheering and started listening again, he continued, "Now I come to the second part of my little speech. We are ready to test the machine. I want to emphasize the word 'test.' The team believes it will work. I believe it will work. But, and this is a large but..." Someone wolf whistled and everyone laughed. John said, stifling a smile, "But, we haven't done it yet. There is a risk to the first traveler.

"I am asking that you take a little time and decide if you would be willing to be a volunteer. I'm asking that you consider and then tell your squad leaders if you would be willing to be one of the first to try. I'd like to meet with any volunteers tomorrow, to discuss mission details. Thank you." With that, John turned and picked up his cane and worked his way down the stairs.

- - -

John Conner awoke from the best sleep he had had in weeks. It seemed that things were falling into place and he would soon be able to make what he knew had happened more than thirty-three years ago, happen for real. He thought he had the stories ready for the men he had to send back. He rolled over in their bed, careful not to pinch his still healing sternum as he did. He saw that Kate was already awake and looking at him.

She smiled, "Well, this is the beginning, isn't it John?"

He smiled back, brushing her bangs away from her eyes, "I certainly hope so, Kate. I've worried about making this happen ever since Judgment Day. Once we found and saved Kyle I knew it was only a matter of time, but until we found the machine, I couldn't relax.

"He is important to all of us, but if the machine fails..."

"It won't", Kathryn interrupted. "It can't fail." She looked deeply into his eyes, "You did send Kyle back and he did save Sarah. You're here. Isn't that proof? The machine has to work."

John kissed her, hard on the mouth, and then he climbed out of bed and pulled on his clothes. "I hope it is as simple as that, Kate. I really do. But so far nothing dealing with Skynet has been easy. We have had to fight for everything."

He turned to leave, "Join me at the meeting room in an hour or so. I'd like you to help me with the interviews." Then he left.

- - -

When Kate arrived, carrying two cups of steaming chicory, she saw John shuffling through a thick stack of papers. Sitting down, she placed one of the mugs near him and asked, "Just how many volunteered?"

John looked over at her, "I think they all did."

Kathryn said, "Did you really expect that any of your followers would be cowards? John, they love you and would do anything for you. I thought you realized that."

He ran his fingers through his hair, "Thinking it and seeing it in writing are two different things." He looked at her, waving the sheaf of papers, "I think you, me and Silberman are the only ones not contained on this list."

She took a sip from her mug, grimaced at the bitterness, and said, "I think that's a good thing."

John said, "Well it does make forming teams a little easier. Here's my plan so far." He pulled over a note pad and slid a little closer to Kate. "I know I have to send Kyle back by himself and I show him in the second column. I need to send Derek back with a team to try to disrupt Skynet and Judgment Day. I haven't decided if he should go in the first trial, but just in case we only get one shot with this machine I'm leaning in that direction."

Kate asked, "How big will his team be?"

"I think four: Derek as the mission leader, a computer expert, a covert specialist and a generalist. I don't think any more will fit inside the sphere."

Kate looked surprised, "That seems like a lot to send on the first try."

"It is", John answered. "But since they only have to go back about sixteen years, more can go." He scratched his head, "Place said that there has to be an energy balance between the mass sent and how far they go. A smaller mass can go further.

"And since Kyle has to go the furthest," John finished, "I plan to send him alone. I also know from mom's comments that he came alone for whatever reason. Our limitations, or the limitations of this machine, make that seem logical now."

Kate was nodding, "What are you planning to tell them?"

"Well, you, me and Silberman know that Kyle has to go and save mom. Unless Silberman leaked that to Derek, he doesn't know and I'm not sure if I can tell him."

Kate was nodding, staring into John's eyes, "Oh, hell yes, you have to tell him. He's your number one. If you can't trust how he will react when you tell him you plan to send his little brother on a one-way trip into the past to save your mother, you can't trust him at all."

She grabbed his arm, "Tell him. That's all I'm going to say."

- - -

John decided to start with Derek. He called him into the meeting room by himself and he watched as the man walked up to the table that served as a desk and stand at attention, waiting for his permission to sit. Shaking his head John said, "Please be seated, Derek. I'd like to talk to you and get your opinion."

Looking a little more serious than usual, Derek pulled out a chair, stepped in front of it and sat, still apparently at attention. John watched and then reading his second in command he asked, "So, Derek, what's bothering you?"

Derek said, "Permission to speak freely, Sir."

John said, "Of course."

"Sir", he began, "I want to volunteer to be the first through the machine. I want to be the one to go back and save your mother."

John said, "I see." He watched the man across from him, "Is there a special reason you feel you should be the one?"

Derek initially looked a little less confident. Then he firmed up and said, "Because I have more experience fighting the machines and therefore have a better chance of success."

"Ah, I see. More experience. Yes, that's true." John stroked the stubble of his beard. Then, "Silberman mentioned that I was sending Kyle back to do that job, didn't he? And you think he's not ready to be on his own, right?"

Derek looked uncomfortable then he said, "Yes, sir. That about sums it up. This mission is too important to leave to a green kid."

"Well, I can appreciate that, but Kyle is not as green and untested as you seem to think. He lived for years after Judgment Day, pretty much on his own. He even kept Starr safe and fed during all that time. Since then he has shown courage and skill as part of several skirmishes. I've had only good reports from other squad leaders."

John hesitated, "But there is a more important reason. One no one else knows about, and one I insist you keep to yourself. You cannot tell Kyle. Is that a deal?"

Derek looked troubled, but also curious. He answered, "Yes, sir. I promise."

John said with total seriousness, "Kyle must go back because he is my father."

Technical Interlude

Sensing the Rest of the World: Part 3

Pressure detection by a robot can be handled simply. Piezoresistive pressure transducers have been around for a long time in industry and medicine. Like a common strain gage that detects the strain or relative motion of whatever it is bonded to by the stretching of fine metal film or wires whose physics demand that their electrical resistance change with the amount of stretching (or compression), the piezo-chip changes with the substrate strain. This motion is caused by stress applied to the substrate and can be calculated using simple (although usually delicate) electrical circuitry, almost always an electrical resistance bridge. This same technique can be used to measure forces directly by using a load cell. This load cell is mounted somewhere on the force applicator and it measures the applied force relative to a "fixed" part of the device (e.g. the chassis of the robot).

Another technique is capacitance measured between the sensor and the target. Electrical capacitance does not even require touch or physical contact to change. Therein lies the problem if you are trying to measure touch pressure. The electronics must be able to mask or screen out the change in sensor capacitance as it approaches the target and only provide measurements after contact is made. Also, capacitive sensors can be triggered by drops of water and usually cannot work with metallic targets.

A third technique is called acoustic resonance. Since everything vibrates when forces are applied, the vibrations setup in a touched target can be detected and measured. The more pressure that is applied to the target, the more damped the signal.

Temperature can be measured in several ways. Some of the ways are simple; a thermometer or a bimetallic strip. Both can be accurate, once calibrated, but neither has a very rapid response time and they both tend to be fragile. A more sophisticated method is using a thermocouple which converts thermal energy applied to a dissimilar metal junction into electrical energy which can then be measured. Unfortunately, this method also has problems: thermal range specificity, response time and calibration issues, to mention a few.

The best candidate seems to be non-contact, infrared temperature sensors. Because everything physical radiates infrared energy, (as long as it is not at absolute zero), infrared sensors can detect that energy. These devices can be cameras, mobile or stationary detectors, or distributed chip-based arrays. Their thermal range is from -55°C to +1,800°C and they are rugged and have the frequency response of any digital, video device. The issues of calibration and shadowing have been discussed earlier.

Humidity measurements are a little more difficult. In the old days, before the electronic revolution, bundles of horsehair were fixed between a wall and a movable, lightly sprung pointer which swept across a face that had been calibrated in relative humidity. This was slow in reaction time and not very accurate. Later something called a sling psychrometer measured the temperature difference between a dry and a wet thermometer after both were swung through the air for several seconds. The evaporation of the wet bulb cooled that thermometer relative to the temperature measured by the dry bulb. This information was then entered into a psychrometric chart and the air's relative humidity was the output of the chart. The readout was accurate, but still slow in data acquisition and sensitive to operator technique.

Electrical humidity sensing was initially accomplished using sensitive resistive measurements across a previously dried and calibrated substrate. Once the substrate was exposed to humid air, its changing electrical resistance could be measured accurately using an electrical resistance bridge. The change in resistance was determined by the amount of moisture condensing on the substrate. The device tended to be large (3-4 square inches) and it was sensitive to contamination by water droplets or other chemical contact, even fingerprints. Their range was limited, and their accuracy was about +/- 3 to 5 %rH. New, modern devices, utilizing similar electrical techniques, have recently achieved sizes of less than one-half square inch size and an accuracy of +/- 1.8 %rH. These humidity chips have solved the wetting and chemical contamination issues and usually contain digital conditioning circuits "on board", providing real time, digital humidity output.

Chapter 13

Silberman was in a fine mood. His regular practice was beginning to pick back up and his notes from several years of group sessions at Pescadaro Hospital were beginning to shape up into a book rather than just a paper. He walked down the long hallway toward the waiting group with almost a swagger. Several of his patients were making progress and he thought that major breakthroughs were just around the corner. His prospects, both financially and professionally, were looking up.

He opened the door to the large activity room and saw the regular arrangement of ten or twelve patients, sitting in a ring of chairs, with the four orderlies positioned evenly around the outside of the ring. Then he noticed that there were five orderlies today; not a good sign. That meant that there was a new patient added to his group. He did not recall getting a memo about the addition and in a bit of a huff he began flipping through the back pages on his clipboard looking for the notice.

Finding it, he scanned the content and nearly stumbled as he read the name, "Sarah Conner". He looked up quickly from the paper and searched around the ring for her face. Their eyes met and he felt a sudden chill as several memories came flooding back before he could stop them. She was older and she had obviously been through a lot, based on the lines on her face and the litheness of her body. But it was definitely her. He could not mistake her.

She smiled at him (he thought it looked more like a grimace) and said, "Hello, Doctor Silberman. It's been a long time."

- - -

Ellison was waiting for Doctor Silberman in his office at the Pescadaro. He had watched the group session via the video link and had a few questions about Sarah's progress. He watched as the discussion session degenerated out of control into a shouting match between four or five inmates and the orderlies had to take control. Sarah was one of the ones that had to be forcibly restrained and then taken back to her cell. The group session ended then, since the mood was effectively broken, and the remaining members were visibly upset. Ellison saw Silberman talking briefly with the remaining seven and then hurrying out of the room, out of sight of the cameras.

Ellison turned as Silberman opened his office door and entered. He looked harried and he plopped down his clipboard on the little table next to his desk as he walked around it. He was watching Ellison warily as he reached his chair and he took his seat.

"Well, that was a fine mess, wasn't it?" Silberman was obviously stinging from the things shouted at him during the group session. "I'm considering pulling Conner out of the group and making her strictly one-on-one. She's too disruptive of the group."

Ellison was nodding, "She certainly stirred things up. What started the argument? I arrived after it was already boiling."

Silberman answered, "I'd hardly call it an argument. She took offense at what one of the others said about her fantasy world and she shot back with her opinions about the survivability of crazy lawyers once the robots took over and the pot roiled out of control from there."

Ellison tried to stifle a laugh, "She certainly can call the kettle black, can't she?"

Silberman huffed, "Yes, she can. She has had a knack for knowing where everyone's buttons are and just how to push them for the past six months. I have a hard-enough time keeping a group talking productively when she's not there trying to get everybody fighting with everyone else." He leaned back in his chair, "Our one-on-one sessions are less than rewarding too." He sat forward and looked at Ellison with a furious gaze, "I actually have had to resort to bribery with her just to get her to talk to me at all. She seems to be trying to fix the blame on me for things that haven't happened yet. Can you believe that?"

Ellison was shaking his head, "She's a tough one." Then he looked curiously at Silberman, "What was it that you wanted to talk to me about, Doctor?"

Silberman seemed to gather his thoughts as he sat back in his chair. Then, "I'm having some difficulty finding out about her son, John. The children's services people are almost as secretive as we are. I was hoping that you knew what was happening with him. I need a lever with her to get her to cooperate with me. He is most likely to work, but I don't want to bullshit her. I want to be able to state facts about him when we talk. I need to be believable."

"I understand," Ellison said. "As it happens, I have been keeping close watch on the boy." He inclined his head toward Silberman, "I have a kind of vested interest, you might say.

"John is not a poster child for the California foster care system. He has been moody and belligerent the whole time and he seems to be walking the fine line with trouble. Had you been able to find out that he ran away from his first set of foster parents after his mother's commitment here?"

Silberman shook his head.

"He was only eight and yet he managed to stay lost and on his own for more than a week. He only got caught because a San Diego border guard got curious about a young kid trying to cross into Mexico on his own." Ellison was shaking his head, "He almost made it. He had a passport and a ready story and at the last minute the guard decided to check out something and when John panicked and started to run, they caught him and called the authorities."

"He's now living with a new set of foster parents; without a passport I want to add." Ellison looked rather proud, "I have that added to my little collection of Conner memorabilia."

- - -

Because she remained so volatile and disruptive in the group sessions, Silberman decided to restrict Sarah Conner to individual or one-on-one sessions. He planned to work with her every Tuesday and Thursday when he was normally at the hospital anyway. Doctor Wilson maintained that she be kept in-group, so she had that format on Monday and Wednesday with him. Silberman thought that would not last and after a month of broken sessions, Wilson finally gave up on that approach.

Silberman was preparing himself for Sarah on the first Tuesday after her last, aborted group session. He thought that they were making a little progress since she was at least listening to him talk without trying to jump out of her chair every few minutes. He kept her attached to her metal chair with a wrist manacle as a precaution, and the chair was firmly attached to the floor in front of the small table in the middle of the observation room. That might change with time, but for now the precaution seemed prudent. The hospital taped their sessions through the one-way mirror, but he doubted that she realized it. Pescadaro, under the jurisdiction of the California Courts System, followed certain rules to prevent frivolous lawsuits by inmates or their families and to keep Federal oversight to a minimum. It also allowed him a visual record of what went on with her and he could keep his note taking to a minimum.

Today he was standing next to his chair on his side of the low metal table when the door to the room opened and Sarah came into the well-lit room in wrist and ankle shackles, escorted by an orderly. Silberman turned to look at her and the smile on his face quickly melted away as he took-in her physical appearance. He was unable to contain his concern as he asked, "Sarah, what happened?"

The orderly nudged her along into the room, guiding her to the chair with his nightstick. "She tried to escape Saturday night after lights out and I'm afraid things got a little rough for her."

Silberman struggled to contain his anger, "How did she get those scratches and bruises? She looks like she has been in a barroom brawl!"

"You should see officer McAndrews! Conner managed to knock out several of her teeth and break her arm before we could subdue her." The orderly was still angry and a little afraid of her and it showed in the way he pushed Sarah around the room at the end of his stick. "She's pretty fast and she knows Kung Fu," he said.

Silberman asked, "Why wasn't I consulted? This is the first I've heard about it. Didn't someone think it was important for me to know what she did?"

The orderly just shrugged as he sat her into the chair and transferred Sarah's left wrist cuff to the chair's arm. He said, "I don't know nothing about that. I was just supposed to get her here for you and keep her under guard. Those were my orders." He pulled her wrist chains to assure himself that she was firmly attached to the chair.

As if trying to resume control of the situation, Silberman said roughly, "Well, do your guarding from outside the room. You can watch through the door, but you have to give us some level of privacy."

The orderly shrugged his shoulders again, "It's your neck." He started toward the door, "I'll be outside." Then as if trying to instill some fear into Silberman he said, "If she attacks you, it'll take me a little longer to get in here. You know?"

Silberman watched the orderly walk to the door, and he waited for him to go out and then close the door behind him before he looked back at Sarah. He missed her hateful glance at the mirrored wall and then back at him, so he continued to maintain the illusion of their privacy for her benefit.

"Sarah," he started, "I'm so sorry. What happened?"

She looked up at him with her bruised face, her angry eyes glaring through her bangs. "I needed to see my son!" She was practically growling her words as she measured them out to him. "When am I going to see my son?"

Silberman was startled. He felt the hairs on the back of his neck rise as he realized he was facing a physical danger just like confronting a mother bear and her cub in the woods. "Not yet, Sarah. Now would not be a good time for you. I don't think you should see John just yet."

She shifted her glare to the mirrored wall, "I want to see my son!" Her voice was rising to a near shout, "I want to see my son!"

Silberman finally realized that she knew that she was being observed from the other room and he thought that he should offer her something for the record. He began, "Sarah, you haven't been here very long and I'm afraid that you aren't making as much progress in your therapy as I would like." He sat in his chair and calmly looked at her, wondering if she would respond to his new approach.

"I know you want to see your son, John. You've made that abundantly clear." He pulled out his pen and opened his notebook to a fresh page. "I think we," he motioned between them with his hand, "need to make a bargain." He watched her face for signs that she was paying attention, "You give me something and I then give you something in return." He sat back, "What do you think?"

She stared back at him through her hair, her mouth was grim, and her pupils were almost fully dilated. She sat that way for a full minute, breathing deeply, before she finally said, "What did you have in mind, Doctor Silberman?"

A little alarmed by her tone, but still pleased, he said, "I think you need a goal. You know? Something to work toward. I think a goal would help you a lot."

Sarah cocked her head to the side, "What goal?" Her voice was sounding more normal and less guttural.

Silberman was starting to sweat, but he smiled and said, "How about this? For the next six months, you participate in your therapy, stop trying to escape and if you show improvement, we can move you to a nicer room and you could have visitors once and a while. Even your son would be allowed."

She looked surprised, "Do you mean that? I can see John in six months?"

Silberman was nodding, "Yes, if you behave and show improvement." He started to hold out his hand to shake on the deal and thought better of it, pulling it back before she could grab it. "Do we have a deal, Sarah?"

Nearly in tears she nodded her head and then said, "Yes."

- - -

These new fosters weren't any better, John thought. *They were just in it for the money and they didn't understand him at all.* He was out in the detached garage of their house, tinkering with the lawn mower. His foster brother, Sam, was sulking at the workbench. Sam, eleven years old, did not understand machinery and hated to get his hands dirty. He was spending time with John, watching for a way to turn this new invasion to his private kingdom to his advantage.

"Why fix it?" Sam asked. "If you fix it, we'll just have to cut the grass with it." He turned to glance out the little window toward the house. "We're just their slaves anyway."

John glared up at Sam from where he sat on the concrete floor in front of the little engine. "I'm doing it because I don't want to spend time in the house with them." He smiled mischievously, "Besides, if I seem to be fitting in here and helping out, maybe they'll loosen up the leash a little." John did not mention that he also had a plan for his next escape attempt.

"Yeah. Sure. Like that's goin'a happen," Sam said. He was obviously bored. He kept picking up tools from the metal tray and tossing them back in, making a loud crashing noise each time one tool collided with the others.

Glaring at Sam with contempt John said, "If you're not going to help, at least stop making so much noise. Fred is going to hear that racket and kick us out of the garage."

"That's OK by me," Sam said. "I don't like it out here much anyway."

"Well, I do!" John almost shouted, scaring Sam. "If you hate it so much, why don't you just get out and go back to the house?"

Sam sneered, "You'd like that, wouldn't you?" He tossed a hammer into the bin with a resounding metallic crash. "You'd like to get rid'a me." He had scooted off the stool and was holding a screwdriver in a less than workmanlike manner, essentially pointing it at John like a weapon.

John watched Sam calmly and lay down the rag he had been using to dry the lawnmower's sparkplug. He remained seated on the hard floor and he watched Sam as he came closer. His hand slowly moved from the rag to the juice can of gasoline he had been using to clean the mower's parts. He kept his eyes locked on Sam's and the older boy never realized his danger.

Sam had reached the handle of the mower and he grabbed it in preparation for his lunge at John. As he tensed, John said, "I don't think you want to do this Sam. You're liable to get hurt."

Just then the garage door was jerked open and a male voice bellowed, "What's going on in here? What was all that banging?" The source of the voice, Fred Clemmons, the boys' foster father, stepped into the garage. He saw instantly Sam's posture and the way he was holding the screwdriver pointed at John. "What do you think you're going to do with that, Sam? Put that screwdriver away and get back to the house, now."

Sam realized his bid for power was over and he instantly lost his belligerent attitude. He turned and assumed a whipped puppy appearance and started to leave.

"Don't forget to leave the screwdriver, Sammy," Fred said quietly.

Sam looked down at his hand and seemed to be surprised that there was something there. He looked up and said, "Sure, Dad." Sam reached over and gently placed the tool into the tray.

John had taken all that in instantly. He saw that Fred actually liked Sam and probably would take his side in an argument. He realized that he would not be able to drive much of a wedge between them and so he need not waste his energy trying.

As Sam closed the garage door, John noted that he had looked back with a certain level of hatred on his face. *I'll have to watch him for sure*, John thought. Then he watched as Fred moved to the workbench and moved tools around in the tray.

Fred turned toward John, "Who gave you permission to use my tools?" He was waiting for an answer.

John said as he screwed-in the sparkplug with his fingers, "Nobody, sir. I just wanted to fix the mower and I needed to use a few of your tools."

Fred seemed to be angry. "Well you need to get permission first. That's one of my rules."

John said, "Sorry, sir." He picked up the socket wrench, flicked the lever on the back and tightened the sparkplug. "It won't happen again."

"Damned right it won't happen again." Then realizing that John had used the wrench in front of his nose he got angrier, "And why are you messing with this mower? That piece of crap won't run."

John had calmly replaced the wire and he stood, wiping his hands on the rag. "Give it a try, sir, I think I fixed it."

Fred looked exasperated, but he was anxious to prove John wrong. "I'll show you, smart guy." He squeezed the safety and pulled the starter rope once.

Nothing happened.

"See, I told you the thing won't work."

John said, "Try again, sir. Just once more."

Fred frowned, but he pulled the rope again and the mower engine farted into life and then ran. A surprised Fred looked down at the mower as if he were holding onto a wild animal. "How did you do that? This junk hasn't run since last season. I was about to buy a new one." He released the safety and it died.

John shrugged, "I kind of have a knack with machines, sir." He picked up his tools from the floor and went to the bench, placing each in turn in the tray and then the tray into the toolbox.

Fred said, "Well, ask in the future. OK?" He was clearly uncertain of the situation. "Get back to the house and wash-up for dinner."

John nodded, "Yes, sir."

- - -

On his elevator ride from the parking tower to the twelfth floor of the LA FBI building, James Ellison was excited. He thought that the capture of Sarah Conner and his ability to close the case that had been such a sore point between him and Lilah, might allow her to consider reconciliation. He had laid awake most of the night rehearsing his logic and preparing for his presentation. He hoped to talk to her in her office this morning before she got busy and had to concentrate on one of her cases.

Stepping off the elevator, he turned right and walked along a set of carpeted walls dividing much of the wide space into cubicles that served as workstations for clerks and secretaries. He casually waved toward a few of the familiar occupants that looked up as he passed and hardly noticed that most of them had a surprised, questioning look on their faces. He reached the end of the artificial corridor and turned left along a series of offices that lined the outside of the floor's perimeter. Lilah's office was the third one from the intersection. He saw that the window blinds next to her door were partially drawn and her door was half-open. Instead of just barging in, he stopped outside the door and knocked gently. He thought it wise not to set an aggressive tone to what could potentially be a good conversation with his ex-wife. As he was knocking, he heard two voices inside, Lilah's and a man's.

The conversation stopped and Lilah's voice said, "Come in."

Ellison stepped through the doorway and stopped, a little uncertain, the wide smile on his face losing some of its bright power. "Oh, I'm sorry, Lilah. I was in the neighborhood and thought I would stop by and say 'Hi'. I didn't mean to interrupt your work."

Lilah looked a little perturbed, but she said smoothly, "James. It's good to see you. You know Paul, don't you?"

The other lawyer stood from his seat on the low sofa and offered his hand to James to shake. "Hi, James, it's good to see you." Then to Lilah, "I'll leave you two to talk. We can go over the Mitchell case a little later."

Paul and James shook hands and Lilah stood, "Paul, you don't have to leave. I'm sure James won't be long."

"That's OK, Lilah. I have some other documents to pull together anyway." Paul smiled at Ellison as he passed him and then he stopped at the door. He asked, "You want the door open or closed?"

Lilah motioned with her hand, "Just close it, Paul. Thanks."

James was looking from one to the other as they spoke, a light beginning to dawn on him. "May I sit, Lilah?"

She nodded and indicated one of the chairs in her space. "What's going on, James? I didn't actually expect to see you today."

Ellison leaned forward in his chair and rested his arms on his thighs. He swallowed and took a deep breath before beginning to speak. "I wanted to talk to you, Lilah. I didn't know if you had heard that I caught that Conner woman about a month ago. I was able to close that case at last."

"That's nice, James, but why are you telling me this? I didn't care about that case when you were hung-up on it for all those years and I'm not sure why I should care about it now." She was leaning on her desk with both fists, her arms stiffly supporting her as she watched his face.

He heard her suppressed anger rising to the surface and he hoped to shunt it aside. "I was talking to the Reverend Baker about us, and after I explained about why you left me, he thought I should try to talk to you. Let you know that that part of my life is over, and I am able to concentrate on you... on us, again. I can get my professional life back on track too."

As he paused, she said softly but firmly, "James, there is no 'us' left for you to concentrate on. I thought that was made clear to you."

"Yes, Lilah, it was, but I was hoping that maybe since I've put all that behind me, we could try again. I do love you, Lilah, and it's like I have a gaping hole in me where you used to be." He had spread his hands open in a gesture of supplication, "Why can't we try, Lilah?"

She looked pained, "James, I love you too, but I can't try again with you. I have moved on. There is someone else in my life now."

Ellison began feeling a little jealous, "Yeah, I figured that out just about a minute ago." He squinted at her, "It seems a little fast to me."

Lilah started to retort and then thought better of it and decided to take the high road. "James, there was nothing going on before, but there is something going on now. I tried to keep it low-key to spare your feelings in case you saw us together somewhere. But, now that you know, I'll tell you that I've been seeing Paul Taylor for the past few months and we are quite happy together."

She sat at her desk and looked at him directly. "And now, if there is nothing else you need to say, I have to get back to work. I appreciate you coming by. If there is anything I can do for you in a professional nature, please don't hesitate to ask."

Ellison did not exactly know what to say. She dismissed him as effectively as if she had said, "Get out." He stood and started toward the door. As he reached for the knob, he turned and said, "Goodbye, Lilah. Good luck."

The clouds of depression and guilt masked his trip back through the carpet corridor. He did not remember reaching the elevator or the glances and whispers behind his back as he passed. He did not recover his wits until he reached his floor and made his way to his office. Then his work kicked in and he was able to forget the pain of her absolute rejection.

- - -

Things seemed to be settled between John, Sam and their foster parents, Fred and Alisha. Because Sam was the older and the bigger of the two boys, he had been made to cut the lawn about three times more often than John, proving his earlier prediction about slave labor. They had separate rooms and except for supper, John studiously stayed out of Sam's way as much as he could. But that fall, since they had to ride the same bus to school every day there were plenty of opportunities for Sam to take his revenge.

Sam ran with a rougher crowd and none of them particularly liked John. John on the other hand, developed one or two close friends and his click tended to stay to themselves at school. John was smart and observant. He did very well in math and science courses, and of course Spanish. His two best friends, Mike Kripkie and Julio Santori, could be found at John's side whenever John was out of class. They ate lunch together and hung out together during recess. As a group, they made Sam's task of spoiling John's day that much more difficult, and Sam finally decided that wrecking John's standing at home would be his only recourse. Sam's friends decided to help.

- - -

    John came home from school later than usual. He had stayed to play chess with some of the older boys from the chess club and he had missed the bus. The mother of his friend Mike Kripkie drove him home. They arrived on his street in time to see two fire trucks and several police cars arriving in front of his house. Amid the frenetic activity of the firefighters and the police as they unloaded hoses and equipment and established a perimeter, John could see that the garage was burning, and the flames were threatening to jump to the house. A heavy, dark cloud of smoke rose straight up, looking like an exclamation point.
    He could feel his heart beating rapidly and his ears were starting to whistle and throb as his blood pressure began spiking. He knew that at this time his foster father would still be at work, but both his foster mother and Sam should be home. He did not see them anywhere, but from his perspective, looking between the front seats and with the crowd of first responders and neighbors and kids milling around, he did not expect to.
    Mike said, "It looks like the entire garage is about gone. Can you tell if the house is on fire?"
    John could not see very well from the back of the car, and he was shaking his head, his eyes trying to take everything in at once. A police officer was stopping them about a half block away and as soon as the car came to a halt, John opened the back door and rushed out. The officer shouted and tried to grab him, but John

easily evaded him, and he ran through several lawns to get closer to his house. Working his way to the front of the small mass of people on the right side of his front yard he spotted Sam. He had smoke smudges and ash streaks on his hands, face and clothes. Their foster mother had her arm around Sam's shoulders.

Reaching them John yelled over the noise, "What happened? Is everyone OK?"

Alisha turned to look at John with tears making clean streaks down her sooty face, "John! We couldn't find you. We thought that you got caught in the garage when the fire broke out."

John was confused at first, but then remembered that no one knew that he would be late. He looked at Sam and noticed that he seemed shocked or stunned that John was standing in front of them, apparently unharmed. A warning light went off in his head and he looked back at Alisha. "I stayed late at school today. I'm sorry, but I thought it would be OK."

She reached out an arm and wrapped it around John as she said, "John, I was so worried. We thought that you were dead." She bent down and stared into his eyes, "You have to tell me when you're going to be late from school. I have to know where you are, John."

Sam muttered, "Yeah."

John looked over at Sam and saw that he seemed more angry than relieved. "I was playing chess with some of the guys in the chess club. I lost track of time. I'm sorry." He looked back up at Alisha, "What happened?"

She just shook her head.

John looked over toward the garage and saw that the water from the hoses was starting to do its job. The column of smoke was changing color from black to gray. He could hear steam where water was landing on hot metal or wood embers. There was still a lot of commotion in the vicinity. It appeared that the house would be fine, but the old trees in the back and side yards looked toasted. The backyard grass was tan, forming a semicircle around the garage. The three of them stood on the lawn watching for a while.

When the fire seemed to be out, several firefighters entered the remains and they could be heard moving things around inside. John recognized at least two officers and thought they were probably investigators looking for the cause of the fire. He wanted to get closer, but Alisha was holding both boys back, out of the way. The squealing of car tires announced the arrival of Fred on the scene. The three of them watched as Fred waved his identification at the patrolman blocking his way. Then he practically ran the hundred feet or so to where they were waiting.

Fred grabbed Alisha first and gave her a hug. "Are you OK? Are you hurt?"

Alisha was still trying to reassure him when one of the investigators walked up, "Mr. Clemmons? I'm Deputy Chief Bosko. I'm charged with trying to figure out how fires start in North LA county." He held out his hand, waiting for Fred to shake it.

They shook and Fred said, "What happened? Was it some kind of electrical short?"

Bosko said as he shook his head, "It's too early to tell for certain, but I'm giving a preliminary ruling of arson to this one. It looks like someone spread some gasoline around and set it off. We found the source of the blaze and it looks like an accelerant was used and we smelled gasoline in there." Bosko was looking from one to another of the little family, watching for a telltale reaction.

Fred was getting angry; John could see that much right away. Fred said, "Of course there was gasoline in there. It's my garage. I use gas for my lawn mower, and I keep it in there in a gas can." He was waving his arms around, "I'm sure that's all you smelled."

Bosko waited then said, "That sounds logical, but the origination of the fire seems to be both your work bench and your roll around toolbox, and they were on opposite sides of the garage." He shook his head, "I don't think this was an accident or spontaneous combustion." He looked at the boys, "I think someone was playing around and set a little fire and it got out of control." He squinted, "Do either of you have anything to tell me?"

Sam looked scared and John looked blank. Fred interjected before either boy could say anything, "Boys, don't say anything just yet." Then he looked over to Chief Bosco, "Since the fire is out, can we go back into the house? I'd like to get to the bottom of this."

Bosco looked peeved, "I'm going to have to talk to them eventually, Mr. Clemmons. This is a serious matter and I have the authority."

Fred nodded, "I understand Chief. I just want to talk to them first and see if we need a lawyer to get involved."

* * *

Kyle Reese was in an elevated state of excitement. He was going to get his chance to prove himself to everyone; his brother and John Conner included. This was it. Both of the most important men in his life were waiting for him. Starr had followed him silently along the narrow corridor and Kyle hesitated when she tugged at his sleeve. He said to her, "Starr, I have to do this.

Try not to worry. I'll be OK." She did not look convinced.

Kyle motioned for her to wait and he knocked and opened the hatch that served as the door. Conner was waving him to a chair in front of the table where they were sitting. He saw that Kathryn Conner was standing off to one side and she looked nervous to him. Kyle looked at his brother hoping to see pride, but he thought he only saw tension. He stepped through the hatch and after closing it behind him he took a deep breath, walked to the chair and after saluting both men, he sat.

John Conner started, "Kyle, I first want to thank you for your patriotism and courage, volunteering to go back in time through that machine." He glanced around at the others in the room and then said, "We all salute you.

"That said, I wanted to let you know that I have chosen you to take on this important mission to save Sarah Conner from Skynet and by that act to help save humanity's existence." John sounded somber.

"I understand, sir, and I appreciate the opportunity you're giving me."

Derek said, "Kyle, we want to make sure you understand that this mission, important as it is to all of us, is filled with dangers to you. Dangers both known and unknown."

Kyle was nodding, "I know", he said. But going on my next mission here is filled with lots of dangers too. Right? What's the difference?" He held up his hand toward Derek to stop his comment. "You know it's true, Derek."

Addressing John again, "The big difference is that I'll be doing something really worthy of dying for. If I'm successful, Sarah Conner will continue to live and therefore you will continue to live and hopefully that means that Skynet dies, and the rest of humanity will get a chance to live." His eyes were bright with purpose, "Isn't that worth trying?"

Everyone in that room admitted that Kyle was right. And they were relieved that he felt that way too.

John said, "OK. We hoped that you would feel the way you do." He pushed an old, creased, discolored photograph across the table to Kyle. "In case you haven't seen this before, here is a picture of Sarah from that time. You can't tell from the picture, but it was taken when she was running for her life, planning to hide from additional Skynet attacks. It was taken after you had saved her from the first terminator that Skynet sent to kill her."

Kyle picked up the photo and let his eyes devour every detail. Then he suddenly looked up, "Did you say 'after I saver her'?" He looked a little confused.

John said, "Yes, Kyle, that's what I said. She told me everything she could about her savior. She talked about your courage, resourcefulness and determination. She named you specifically as the soldier from the future who convinced her that she had to follow you to live."

Kyle's mouth had fallen open as John talked. Then he asked quietly, "She actually named me?" He was shaking his head trying to think. "Then that means... that means my jump will be successful!"

John and Derek were nodding their heads in agreement. John said, "We agree with your assessment. The only problem I can imagine is that the equipment we currently have 'functional' is not the machine we used to send you back." He let that sink in for a few seconds. "That's why your trip won't be the first live shot we take. If the first trial doesn't immediately fry the targets and it survives that jump, then you will follow within the hour."

"But if the machine blows up jumping the first time, it won't be available to send me back. You have to send me the first time. There might not be a second chance."

Derek looked at John and said, "Kyle, we believe that the machine will work just fine. But since you are the most important player in this game, John feels that you shouldn't go in the first test jump. I agree with him. John has information about the identities of everyone he sent back and if this machine actually works, then both you and the first group will go successfully."

Sounding slightly belligerent Kyle asked, "Who's going first? Or is that a secret."

Derek said, "I am. Me and three others are going to try it first."

Kyle said, "What! You're going? Why are you going?"

John answered, "You remember my story? Derek was the leader of the team I sent back to try to sabotage Skynet and the other companies trying to develop Skynet. I met your brother back in 2005 and fought with him then."

Kyle looked at Derek and asked, "You never told me about this."

Derek said, "I didn't know about it until John told me this morning. I don't remember it because it hasn't happened to me yet."

Kyle said, "This is very confusing."

John said, "Kyle, one of the things I want you to memorize and teach to Sarah is this phrase. 'The future is not set. Our future is what we make for ourselves.' Can you remember that?"

Kyle looked puzzled but repeated it several times. John nodded his head, "Be sure you teach that to her. It is very important."

- - -

The worst part about the time travel experience Derek thought, other than the possibility of ending up in the vacuum of space or inside the native rock of a mountain range somewhere, was having to squat, cheek to cheek, inside the electromagnetic sphere with three other naked men. At least they didn't have to walk naked across the hanger floor in front of everyone, and were allowed to disrobe on the landing just before climbing aboard. That seemed a little comfort anyway.

He and his team were traveling light. They were each carrying only one 9mm automatic with three clips of ammunition, one map of the greater LA area and two bundles of currency (one paper and one diamonds). To get around the problem of sending things through the machine that were not organic, each of their objects were tucked into a meat envelope and attached to their bodies with strips of uncured leather roping. It was crude but based on descriptions they had found in the notebooks made by the human technicians, the meat should do the trick and shield the metal objects from the raving electromagnetic and subatomic particle forces.

Their total weight, carefully measured and recorded by Doctor Silberman, was eight hundred and twenty pounds. That value was one of the inputs to the setup equation. They were only going back twenty-two years to 2005 and that figure went into the equation as well, establishing the quantities of spinning muons that would have to be injected into the spinning magnetic field. Robert Place's quadruple-checked results said that they needed 3.541 grams of counterclockwise spinning muons to make the momentum balance work out. Actually, the equations said that they needed about .0006% more than that. But because of the time delays involved between the weight measurements and the actual time of injection, it was decided that they would sweat off a few pounds bringing the error down to less than three minutes.

The VIP's were all there, John, Kathryn, Silberman and Place. John had given his last-minute instructions to the team and shaken all of their hands. He did not comment on their courage, because everyone present, knew that they were courageous. Only two kinds of men would risk being the first through this equipment: fools or men of great courage and commitment. John would not have risked so much on fools.

Kyle Reese had hugged his big brother and they had said their goodbyes. Then everyone saluted them. The four soldiers dropped their robes, and one after the other, eased through the top opening between the coils and settled onto the mesh platform. There was some obvious bantering between the four men as they nested together and hugged each other into a tight ball, ensuring that no parts of themselves extended beyond the platform or more than three feet high. They had discussed the stupidity of risking this effort only to die or lose a hand or foot through a clumsy mistake in placement within the energy bubble.

When they were positioned, Derek made a small wave with one of his hands and the technician who had helped them through the coils hurried down the scaffolding to announce that they were ready to proceed. Place wasted no time and he started the jump sequence, spooling up the jet engines and watching the gauges and clock. The script called for a very precise sequence of events and Silberman was standing by as his assistant, waving instructions off to different points along the hanger floor.

The magnetic bottles were clicked into place, attached to their diffraction gratings set into the main axis of the electromagnet sphere. The cable that would activate the solenoid that would release the stored muons was snapped into its socket and arms went up signifying completion of that phase. Place flipped open the safety cover and with practiced efficiency waited until the clock tripped to the thirty second point and then pressed the glowing red button that immediately turned green.

A rattle of large solenoids inside the control cabinet set things in automatic motion. The jet engines began roaring and straining against their stands, the steel ductwork that vented the exhaust gases began to glow ruddy. The generator began humming at an increased pitch. The electromagnets began generating a pulsing rumble that could be felt in the floor, like a freight train gathering speed in the next room. Everyone present either wore ear protection or was pressing their hands over their ears to exclude the sounds and limit the pain. As set points were attained, the mechanisms triggered the next stage, and something would happen that usually added more noise. Then. with the clock reading five seconds to go, the muons were injected, and the hanger was bathed in bright, blue, pulsing light and the additional sounds of lightening. Flashes of primal energy rolled around inside the magnetic bubble, flickering in time to the floor's vibrations. The clock ticked to zero and with a clap of sound, quite like thunder, the energy bubble popped and the still vibrating sphere of electromagnets was empty. Nothing but melted stumps of nylon rope could be seen limply hanging inside.

John looked at Kathryn and said, "Well, there goes one of our best chances for the future. I can only hope that our modified now still included our successful jump with those men. Otherwise, I'm afraid I might have sent them to their deaths." The sounds in the hanger consisted of cheers and jet engines coming down from full power.

Kate, put her arm around his waist and pulled him closer, "You can't second guess everything, John. You remember that Derek made it to the past and he helped you make changes to the future. I think that he had to go, and I think his jump was successful."

She turned John around and nudged him toward Kyle. "Now it's Kyle's turn. Send him back to save Sarah."

John smiled nodded and headed toward Kyle who had his arm around Starr, and he was talking to Silberman, looking at the sphere with a certain longing. John said, as he came up, "Your brother is a brave man. They all are."

Kyle turned to look at John, "Yes, sir. I agree." He looked back at the sphere and said, "I was asking the doctor if he knew if they made it. I didn't know if the instruments gave some kind of reading if the jump went as planned, or even if it failed."

Silberman was shaking his head, "I told him that there is no way of knowing about his brother for sure from this end, but that I knew from firsthand experience that his jump went well because I met him that night."

John said, "As I told you earlier, I met your brother in 2005 and fought with him to try to kill Skynet before it was born, so he must have made it. I also told you that you saved Sarah Conner from the T101, so somehow you do make the jump and somehow you protect her." He smiled and extended his hand, "And now we have to set up your jump. Are you ready?"

Kyle nodded. He said, "Lead on, doctor. I guess I have to get weighed first."

John watched as the two men went to the scales, one walking and one rolling. The precision scale was set up behind a shower curtain for some privacy and the two men went inside. John knew that Kyle was disrobing and standing on the platform and Doctor Silberman was recording his weight to two decimal places. That information would be given to Robert Place to adjust his calculations for the jump. He knew that within fifteen minutes Kyle would climb the scaffolding and climb down into the sphere and hunker down, waiting for that moment of his life to make a difference. John decided to walk over to Place to see how things were going.

Silberman almost beat him there, the wheels of his chair squeaking as he came to a stop nearby. John looked up as Silberman said to Place, "He's still one hundred and eighty pounds exactly. I doubt he will change much in fifteen minutes."

Place nodded and bent over his desk and reviewed his calculations. He did not look up as John Conner stood next to him and looked over his shoulder. John saw that the target date, May 14, 1986 was correct and that the muon mass was calculated out to 1.5229 grams. He asked, "What error do you predict Place?"

Robert Place shrugged, "As near as I can tell, It looks like less than .0002% or about one minute. I can't get much closer than that, sir."

John laughed, hopping to defuse the tension a little, "I think one minute is excellent, Place. Just dial in the correct coordinates and in a few minutes we should all be a lot safer."

Place looked up, not entirely convinced, "I hope you're right sir."

- - -

All the calculations were in place. Since Derek's team had jumped successfully, Kyle would be next. Everyone was anxious. Kyle was excited yet scared. He felt that he had too much riding on his shoulders. He had burned Sarah's image into his mind. He never doubted that he would recognize her if he had the chance to see her.

John Conner and his wife came up to him as he tried to go over everything in his mind. "Kyle, are you ready? We are ready for you if you are."

Kathryn said, "John, go easy on him. I'm sure he'll do fine."

John winced slightly and then said, "Sorry Kyle, but I can't get the fact that a terminator is hunting her there and your still here out of my mind." He put his hand on the young man's shoulder, "I know you'll do fine. After all, you already did this once." He tried to laugh, but his face didn't follow through.

"Thank you, sir. I appreciate your confidence in me." He shrugged, "But as you say, I have done this before."

John said, "Right. Well, get your clothes off and the techs will help you get into the electromagnet." He held out his hand and they shook. Kyle stepped back and saluted. John returned it and he and Kathryn walked over to the main control cabinet.

Starr stopped him and reached up to give him a hug. Kyle grabbed her under her arms and hauled her up to where he could hug her properly. "I'll be OK, Starr. You just watch out for Conner. That'll be your job from now on."

Starr squeezed his neck very hard and with tears running down her cheeks she uttered the first words anyone had heard he say for years. "I love you, Kyle."

Kyle hugged her back, "I love you too, Starr." Then he put her down and without looking back he started his climb to the top of the scaffolding. Starr watched from the bottom of the stairs.

John gave the word and the technicians began spooling up the jet engines. He turned to watch Kyle climb the metal stairs to the waiting men who would help him into the magnet and onto the new platform material.

As soon as Kyle was hunkered down, John gave the signal to commence. He watched as the technicians pressed buttons and pulled levers and monitored gauges. The sound rose and soon it was time to introduce the muon charge. As that happened the bubble formed and as the frequency and field intensity grew, more and more lightning arced out. Then with a popping sound, Kyle was gone.

Kathryn wove her arm around John's waist and gave him a hug. "Well, it's done. You can't do any more tonight." She looked at him, "Let's go home."

Starr just stood there watching the place where Kyle had disappeared in a flash. Then, after a while, she remembered her duty and she turned and followed John and Kathryn Conner out of the hanger. Silberman watched all of them leave.

* * *

Terminator 1+: The Future Is Not Set

Mark T. Sondrini

He couldn't believe his luck. Some idiot had thrown away a bottle of wine with at least eight or ten swallows left in it. "Ah, hah!" he had crowed. "Sonoma Muscatel, 1985." He unscrewed off the cap and took a long pull from the green bottle. "It was a good year!" He smacked his lips in obvious appreciation. "What idiot would throw this away?"

Slipping his prize under his coat flap he carefully walked to the nearby alley, keeping an eye out for trouble. About thirty feet in, he worked his way under a metal emergency stairway and sat amid some cardboard that had been broken down and stacked there. "These boxes are broken down, like me," he mumbled as he pulled out his treasure and took another drink, "but I at least have some good wine." He chuckled and then choked as the wine went down the wrong pipe.

The weather was mild, but still, even Los Angeles is a little too cool at night to sleep unprotected out in the open. He took another drink and then surveyed his kingdom. *Still nothing around to bother him*, he thought. He smiled and finished the wine and then set the empty bottle aside where it would not get broken if he rolled over as he slept. He pulled his coat a little tighter around his boney chest, coughed deeply and spit out into the alley and then tried to get comfortable enough to sleep. The layers of cardboard helped a lot.

He thought that he must have succeeded because he started to dream that he was in the middle of a lightning storm. He could hear the crackle of the lightning and he felt his hair standing to attention. He felt the wind pick up and he heard loose paper and empty bottles blowing around him. He slowly opened his eyes and was astonished to see that the storm he felt and heard was situated six feet in the air across the alley from him. It was a bright blue ball of lightning, swirling around and throwing off sparks, hanging in midair. Then, with a popping sound and a whooshing of displaced air, it disappeared and as he blinked in the sudden darkness, a naked man fell out of the sky and landed on his side with a meaty thump, nearly at his feet.

"Holy shit," he muttered. It was about all he could think of to say. "Holy shit!"

The man groaned and roused himself, rolling over onto his hands and knees, shaking his head as if to prevent unconsciousness. He could see that the young man had been burned and shot or stabbed several times because of the extensive scaring on his entire body. Even in the reduced lighting of the alley he could see that much. Then the naked man turned to look directly at him. Now afraid, he tried to make himself as small as possible, but there really was no place to hide and the young, naked man was squarely between him and the mouth of the alley. The young man stood and walked the few steps over to where he was cringing.

"I need your pants," he said. "Give me your pants and I promise not to hurt you."

"Holy shit!" the man said.

Technical Interlude

Keeping Their Balance

Standing, walking and running are tasks that humans (and most other mammals) learn to do at a very early age. Talent for high-speed running aside, most of us get pretty good at stable locomotion on two legs by the time we're six and it usually gets better with practice and experience. Unlike quadrupeds, who can stand and run almost as soon as they are born, bipedal humans take a while to figure out how to defeat gravity. Think of films of horses and giraffes you might have seen, and how the new-born animal almost jumps up as soon as the birth sack is cleared away, taking wobbly steps to find its mother. Compare that to human babies who are praised as amazing if they can stand (usually with some piece of furniture for support) before they are one year old.

Bipedal robots have at least as much difficulty as humans. For them, the difficulty lies in the myriad of measurements and visual cues that have to be interpreted and the discrete motors, servos, cables and linkages that have to be brought into motion to get the proper weight shift, allowing a leg to rise and its foot to move forward rotating on hips, knees and ankle hinges. All this activity has to happen many times per second if the robot is to move at a practical pace. Throw into the mix the feedback signals required to determine if the foot's new position is not only where the brain wanted it to be, but that it is stable; sometimes the floor is not where it was supposed to be or it was canted or perhaps it contained some kind of contaminant that could cause a problem

(think of a pebble or spilled oil, for example.)

Huge amounts of computing and sensing power must be expended for every step. Feedback in the form of signals from rotary and linear position sensors, inclination and force sensors, torque and current gauges, pressure and temperature transducers are flying around. Hundreds of comparator circuits must busily check the result vs. the intention, allowing the robot brain to compensate during the next cycle of motion.

Smooth, flowing robotic motion is an illusion. Like motion picture films, the robotic motion is actually performed in a herky-jerky fashion. The faster the computer system and the more refined the sensor systems, the smoother it appears to the human observer. Like a curve drawn on a computer screen, limited by pixel size, the motion is made up of small, incremental steps that meld into a smooth motion, limited by clock speed and sensor frequency response.

The Terminator T100 through T888 series had the benefit of massive amounts of computer processing power and the increased usage of parallel processing using discrete computers at distal locations. The location of sensors close to the comparator circuits and CPU's improved response times and with each new model, the addition of new sensors improved motion detection and resolution. All these improvements meant that each model moved more smoothly that the one before and, like humans practicing, faster speeds were possible.

Chapter 14

The results of the garage fire had been bad for John. The authorities were convinced that it was arson and that it was crudely done, pointing to one of the boys. Even though John had an alibi, Fred Clemmons decided to give them John. Sam was ecstatic although he played the role of a grieving brother. He had managed to eliminate the thorn that the State had inserted into his side.

John knew better than to make waves. The system could not tolerate waves; it did not know how to handle them. However, once the official investigation was completed and it was determined unequivocally that John could not have done it because he was not there, he was released from Juvenile Detention and assigned to a new foster family, the Voights, Todd and Janelle. Unfortunately, he now had the label of troublemaker attached to his record and that would follow him for a long while. His new family lived in the same school district as the Clemmons, so he managed to stay in the same school as before. That was, it seems, a mixed blessing.

John Conner was enjoying school; even though he hated living with strangers. He was making friends and learning things like a normal kid. His fourth-grade teacher discovered that he was very smart and had an aptitude for computers and things mechanical. She had allowed him extra time on the class's machines, and he had developed into a kind of expert on them. All the other kids came to him, rather than her, for help, and she thought that was a good thing for him. He seemed socially unstable, but she realized that his attitude was inevitable given his situation. She never brought up the subject of his mother, but somehow a few of the bigger kids had found out about her and teased him about his 'crazy mother' whenever they had the chance. Those instances usually ended in a fight of some sort if a teacher was not there at the time.

John was smaller than most of the other kids his age, but he more than made up for that with his skills. After one particularly rough day on the playground, John had caught two of the bullies from that morning as they were walking to the bus and he managed to bloody both of them and might have done real damage if the bus driver had not seen it and broken it up. He claimed that he had seen the smaller boy punching and kicking the larger boys like a Kung-Fu master. He mentioned that he knew what that looked like because Kung-Fu was his favorite show.

After serving his detention period along with the other two boys, John decided to be more subtle about his revenge and he hacked into the school's database using his classroom computer. He changed their records and scheduled meetings for both sets of angry parents and their confused teacher. His ruse, discovered after the third time, earned him a stiffer punishment. Banned from using any of the school's computers, John figured out how to use the Van Nyes city library's computer to order both boys to serve six weeks in summer school for completely failing grades in all of their subjects. His reputation grew and most of the older kids left him alone after that.

It was about this time that he discovered girls. Most of the time he did not want anything to do with them, but occasionally he found that they were nice to be around. His current foster parents did not keep too close an eye on him and his best friend, Mike Kripkie did whatever he wanted to do as long as he did not bother his parents or burn the house down. Mike's parents were pleased that he had a real friend, even if it was that "Conner boy."

Mike had asked John and Tim Rossa over for a party in his basement. Mike had discovered a couple of girls who liked to dance and were willing to come to his house, so he invited them too. Mike had set up his dad's record player in the corner and he had found a stack of old rock and roll albums in a box on a shelf. Mike's mom made cookies and lemonade for them and then left them alone for the afternoon. They all danced wildly to the new music until a slow song allowed them to actually touch each other. John paired with a shy little girl named Kathryn Brewster and as they danced, John started to get nervous and warm, a feeling he was quite unused to.

As the song ended and John let go of her, he noticed that the others were slinking off to the corners of the room and starting to neck. Kathryn, still holding John's hand, was looking around at the other kids as they kissed each other. After an awkward few seconds, they looked at each other and Kathryn shrugged her shoulders.

John asked, "You want to?" He could not believe that she would want to kiss him.

Kathryn responded with her eyes lowered, "Sure." She could not believe that he was so backward.

He led her over to the corner by the record player and tried to put his arms around her and kiss her. She slid her arm around his neck and pulled their faces together. Since neither of them had any experience, they both did it badly, but they both enjoyed it while it lasted. After a few minutes of awkward groping and messy kissing, the sudden sounds of Mike's mother on the stairs broke their spell and they separated. They moved over to the plate of cookies and tried to look busy. Everyone looked a little guilty, but Mike's mother seemed to be oblivious to what was going on. An hour later, the party broke up and the girls went home. The boys cleaned up and spent the next hour bragging about how great they were with those girls.

They made a pact to keep it secret, but boys being boys, it did not take long before the wild tails about Mike's wild party started circulating around the school. Any chance John had of seeing Kathryn again were dashed when she stomped up to him on the playground and slapped his face. John never figured out what had happened, and the incident helped reinforce his misunderstandings about "women".

- - -

Sarah was trying to keep fit. Most evenings, after supper, she would pull the mattress off her bed and flip the frame on one end. The crossbar of the bed, six and a half feet above the floor, made a perfect place to do chin-ups. She started slowly, but after more than a year, she could do two hundred repetitions an hour. She stayed lean and fit and her vivid nightmares stayed away.

After the incident with John and the burning garage, the Children's Welfare Office started approaching her with requests for his adoption to one of his foster families. She always refused and the week after they tried, she was always in a depressed mood. Silberman did not help the situation and those sessions were always tense. About the third time, her dreams began again. She did not know if it was the stress of the CWO's meddling, or Silberman's responses to her fears, or if she had become genuinely convinced that Skynet was once again on the march after her and John. The reason did not matter. The recommencement was the important thing. She had to get out of there. She had to get out of there now.

- - -

The Voight's were not as bad as John had feared. Janelle nagged him to do his homework and keep his room clean and take out the garbage, and she was lobbying hard to get him to call her Mom, but other than that, she left him alone. She always had a decent meal for him, and she always had his laundry done when he needed it. Todd on the other hand was just lazy. He worked as an accountant for a tax company and he claimed to be tired from the stress at work whenever Janelle asked him to do almost anything around the house; most of the time he was on the couch watching some sporting event or loud game show and trying to ignore her.

Todd, however, did have an old dirt bike in the detritus of their garage. John had found it the first week he was living there. He had asked permission to clean it up and to try and get it working. Todd had laughed and said that it hadn't run for years (probably true if Todd was the last one to ride it since it was only a 125 cc and too small for an adult) and it was a piece of crap then. All that meant to John was that it might take a little time before he had his own wheels and working on it would give him an excuse to stay out of their sight whenever they were all home. Janelle thought of it as a lever that she could use to make John conform to her way of thinking. John let her think that.

Todd also had a personal computer in his den that he allowed John to use whenever he did not need it. Somehow, the Child Welfare System had never alerted the Voights to John's facility with computers. That computer was a major find as far as John was concerned. He figured he was going to need money; more money than the Voight's would ever give him willingly. He had a plan. If he could rig a credit card so that it became the input/output device for an ATM machine, then he thought that he could milk a withdrawal occasionally and they would probably never notice. The local electronics hobby store became one of his favorite places to shop. Some cables and connectors and other pieces and parts formed the hardware and within a few months he had written a program that could hack into any but the most sophisticated security system. He downloaded it into the computer chip in his device and shortly was fifty dollars richer.

Todd thought that a dog would complete their little family. He got Janelle to agree as long as John would take on most of the responsibility. The dog, Maxine, a female German Sheppard puppy that he called Max, reminded John of Lily and he readily assented to the chore. Todd and John worked together, for a change, to build a doghouse inside a chain-link fenced run. Janelle finally had to agree that Todd had a good idea.

- - -

It started out well enough. Silberman was sitting in his normal place on one side of the low metal table and Sarah was on the other. He had relented, based on her recent improvement and willingness to talk to him, to removing her shackles. She had been surprised at the gesture and acted pleased, even excited with the prospect of discussing her dreams with him. He did not fully understand his peril.

They shared a few pleasantries, mostly one sided he thought, but calming he felt sure. Then, "I understand that you have begun dreaming again, Sarah. I wish you would talk to me about them. Maybe we can determine what is bothering your subconscious mind and making you have these nightmares." He spoke slowly using a friendly, conversational tone.

Going along with her plan, she did not want to say too much to him about her nightmares. She thought that they might make him think she was not really getting better; or at least as fast as he wanted. She looked up at him with eyes that she hoped would melt his heart. She said, "Doctor Silberman, I'm afraid. I hope you can help me."

She leaned forward, elbows against the tabletop, her eyes looking openly into his, "I can't sleep all the way through the night recently. The dreams keep evolving, but they always seem to come back to the same point of time." She spread her arms across the table, palms up making the orderly jerk forward a little by the little window in the door. "Recently, I seem to be my old self. You know, Sarah Conner, the waitress?" She tried to smile at him, but the effort seemed to fall short.

Silberman nodded at her, "Go on, Sarah."

"Sometimes I'm waiting tables in a diner, somewhere in LA it must be. Everything seems normal to me. Not threatening at all. You know?

"Then suddenly I'm outside. I can feel the breeze tugging at my hair and my uniform. I can feel leaves brushing past my legs, the smell of fall in the air, the sounds of children playing and laughing somewhere in the distance."

She broke off and looked up at him, a small trickle of tears beginning to run down her left cheek. "I can feel my pulse start to race. I start to feel anxious. Something is wrong."

She stopped and he tried to control himself. This was very good, and he did not want her to get off track. He said gently, "What happens next, Sarah?" She was staring off into the distance, looking at something he could not see and starting to perspire.

She looked over at him, "I know what is about to happen, now. I can tell what is going to happen. I walked toward the sounds of the children. I have to warn them, you know. I can't seem to hurry. Something is keeping me from hurrying." She wiped her hand across her face, pushing her damp hair out of her eyes, "I reached a tall metal fence. The playground is on the other side and I can see LA off in the distance, down the hill." Her breathing is starting to become faster and deeper.

Silberman feels that he should reassure her, but he is afraid that if he says anything now, he will derail her vision. He just watches her in fascination and then he pats her outstretched hand.

"I tried to tell them, but they can't hear me!" Her tears are flowing freely now. "I started shouting at them. I even grabbed the fence and started shaking it." She looked up at him, "That seemed to help. One or two of the children and one of the women looked over toward where I was, and I could see that they could hear me.

"I had been shouting and trying to warn them about Judgment Day." She whimpered, "Then I noticed that the woman on the playground, who had looked toward me, looked like me." Her voice started to rise, "I looked back at her, shouting my warnings again and it was me! I was even wearing the same waitress uniform! It was me! I could tell I didn't know anything about Judgment Day! I was going to die! We were all going to die!"

Sarah had lost control, shaking and flailing her arms around as she shouted. Silberman became aware of the door opening and the orderly rushing in. He wanted to wait and let her finish, but it was too late for that now.

"We are all going to die!" Sarah screamed as she tried to stand, her hands making grasping motions in his direction.

Silberman backed away from the table as she tried to crawl across it. The orderly had reached her and grabbed her, pinning her arms with his, and standing her up, away from the table. About that time, the door opened, and two additional orderlies rushed in, one carried a yellow liquid-filled hypodermic. The three men wrestled her to the floor, while one administered the sedative into her thigh. All the while, she was shouting, "You're all going to die," repeatedly until she seemed to collapse into herself from the drug.

Silberman watched her with sympathy and concern until they carried her out of the room and took her back to her cell. Then he went into the adjoining room and ejected the tape out of the recorder. He carried it down the painted corridor to his office where he replayed it several times.

- - -

The slim, well-dressed, black man representing the California Children's Welfare Department was sitting confidently across from Sarah. He had described her son's plight succinctly and logically to her, and he was expecting her to agree with whatever it was that he had told her. He was a lawyer and his department had her son's best interest at heart; that much should be obvious to anyone. He thought that the fact that she was constrained to her chair in this mental hospital / prison seemed to make his case even stronger.

"As I said, Ms. Conner, your son John is having a difficult time adjusting to foster care. He has made repeated attempts to escape, and in several cases, he has resorted to violence." He adjusted his glasses further up on the bridge of his nose with one hand while moving John's case folder around on the tabletop with the other. "It makes the most sense for him to be allowed to live in a more stable, permanent environment."

Sarah was boiling inside, but so far able to contain her outbursts of anger. "That isn't something I can agree to, Mr. Dawson. He's my son, and I intend on getting out of here soon and then I'll be able to take care of him myself, the way it was always intended to be." She cocked her head to the side, "I don't understand why you can't get that through your bureaucratically thick head."

He bristled and then quickly relaxed as he seemed to remember where he was and to whom he was talking. "Ms. Conner, there is no need for rudeness. After all, both my department and I only want what is best for your son." He tried to look at her objectively, "You do realize that he is at risk the way things are now?"

"Oh, I realize quite a lot!" She was getting very angry and trying to maintain control. "The longer he is kept away from me, the more 'at risk' he is becoming." She did not need to make the little finger marks; her voice made the quotes perfectly clear to whomever was listening.

"Well," he replied, "I afraid that you will be kept away from John for a long while yet. I think that you need to face the reality of your situation. You will be in here for a long time, probably two or three years. Then, once you are declared sane, you will most likely have to serve the rest of your sentence in the Women's prison." He referred to notes he had on a paper in John's file, "It adds up to at least seven years before you could get out of State custody and out on parole. In that time John could be severely damaged." He shrugged and spread his hands, "Do you see what I'm saying?"

There was a buzzing noise in her head. She had heard him, and the words were registering, but they were not making any sense to her. She thought, *Seven years! We will all be dead and forgotten in seven years!*

She needed to talk to Silberman. She needed to get out of here, now. "Mr. Dawson," she started, holding herself closely under control despite her agitation, "I understand what you are telling me. But I think there has been some kind of terrible mistake. My doctor, Doctor Silberman, said that I might be able to have my son visit me in six months or so. He said that I might even be able to go home soon. He said I was showing progress."

Dawson said, "Well, I think you are right about one thing at least. There has been a terrible mistake made. You made it when you participated in that armed, bank robbery where a man was killed, and a police officer was wounded." He pulled his papers and files together in preparation for leaving, "The only reason you have had it so easy in the system is that you were found to be crazy." He stuffed the files in his briefcase, "I'll be back in a few weeks with the custody papers for you to sign. I want you to think about what we talked about today. I will want you to sign those papers the next time I come to see you." He stood, leaving Sarah with her mouth hanging open.

- - -

Silberman did not exactly know what to say to her. Dawson had said entirely too much about her circumstances, upsetting her. If he said the wrong thing to her now, she could be permanently out of his reach and she might become even more violent. He thought that it might be best to lie to her for now.

"Sarah," he started, "Mr. Dawson really doesn't understand what's going on here. He may understand child welfare in all of its ramifications. He may even understand all of the CCW's policies and procedures. But I doubt he really understands the judicial system and the way it functions with the mental health system." He shook his head, "No, he is definitely mistaken about that." He had been watching her face as he told her the half-truth and he thought she might be buying it.

"Doctor, he seemed quite sure of himself. He came right out and said that after you finish with me here and I'm better, I'll have to serve additional time in prison." She was watching him now for signs of deceit.

Realizing that she was quite close to the truth, he decided to try to deflect her attention away from this subject if he could. "What argument was he using trying to convince you to relinquish your parental rights to John?"

She shook her head as if to clear it, "He said that, because John isn't doing well getting shuttled between foster families, and because I'm going to be stuck here for so long, I should allow one of those families to adopt John. He said the permanence would help him feel more secure and he had a better chance at a normal life."

"Well," he answered, "That makes a certain amount of sense."

Sarah snapped back at him, "That logic presumes that I'm going to be away from John for a long time. But I'm not, right?" She was starting to breathe hard and she could feel her pulse starting to pound behind her eyes as her blood pressure rose.

Silberman was shaking his head in negation, "Of course not, Sarah." He felt that he was beginning to lose control. "We talked about how you're making a little progress."

Beginning to shout she replied, "I've been making more than a little progress, I think. And I haven't tried to escape for months."

Silberman opened his notebook that was sitting on the table. He pulled out his pen and clicked it open, ready to write. Reading he said, "I show that you have made significant progress, Sarah," he made a little check mark in his book. "I've been keeping track since we made our deal."

Before he could prevent it, she suddenly reached across the table and grabbed his notebook. She started to read what he had there and saw that there was nothing but a checkmark along one margin. "You lied. There are no notes here."

"Sarah," he was reaching out with his hand. "Please give me back my book. That one is a new one and your notes are in my old one. That's why there's nothing in it." He thought that sounded plausible and he hopped that she would believe him; he hated being caught in a lie by a patient.

With a sly look in his direction, she flipped through the rest of the notebook. She saw that there were other notes from other patients and then she noticed the date on one reading from two weeks ago. She looked up at him and started to hand the book over to him. Catching him off guard, she dropped the book onto the table and grabbed his arm as he reached for it. "You lied to me!"

With his arm held tightly in one hand, she used his pulling force along with her own push against her chair to propel her over the tabletop and on top of him. He began to struggle as his chair flipped onto its back. He was pinned between it and her and he began to yell for help. She had the advantage of surprise. Reaching back, she slapped his face, "You lied to me!"

She heard the door to the room open and without thinking, she grabbed the pen he was waving around and swung it in an arc, driving it into the side of his knee. She felt the pen bite through the fabric and into the joint just as she felt the strong arms of the orderlies grab her and pull her off Silberman. He was screaming in pain and calling for help and all she felt was triumph.

The orderlies held her down on the floor and one of them administered the sedative. She continued to squirm and thrash until the drug took over and then she did not care anymore.

- - -

The next few weeks were a blur. Locked down and confined to her cell except for one hour a day, when she could exercise out in the yard by herself. Silberman did not come around, but she had heard comments from one of the night orderlies that he was out of the hospital and walking with a cane. She doubted she would get another chance to grab him. She also wondered if her actions constituted a breach of her deal with him. Technically, she did not try to escape, and she felt that she was making significant progress.

All her time alone allowed her to formulate her next escape plan. She thought that if she could get them to believe that she was doped out of her mind all the time, she might get another chance. She started tonguing her medication, tucking the capsule into the corner of her mouth, and then spitting it out after they left her alone. She established a routine and learned how the guards reacted to her every move. She became a consummate actress whenever they were watching. Within a week, they were convinced that she was completely under the sway of the sedative. She never changed her clothing unless told to. She never showered unless told to. She only ate half her meals as though she did not have an appetite. By the end of the week her hair was greasy, she stank, and she was losing weight. She did not seem to care although the staff began to worry.

The following week, she thought that the time had come. Dawson from the CCW office was going to be there right after lunch. The orderly who had brought her lunch tray, Douglas was his name, mentioned that she should shower and put on some clean clothes because she was having an important visitor in an hour. When she asked, he had told her it was Dawson. She tried not to show any emotion at all; business as usual. She allowed them to lead her to the showers and after she dried off, she put on the clean clothing they had provided.

Walking with her head down, Sarah entered the room wearing shackles and manacles. She was firmly attached to her chair and then as she looked around, apparently in a stupor, Dawson was allowed to join her.

"Ms. Conner," he said a little too cheerfully. "It's good to see you again. You look well."

Sarah looked up at him, her head bobbling around on her neck and her damp hair partially blocking her view. "Hi," she said dreamily. "Have we met?"

Dawson was initially worried about her condition. He wondered if her obviously drugged state would allow a future court challenge to the custody document's signature. He decided to press on. "Yes, we discussed your agreeing to assign your parental rights for your son, John, to the State. Don't you remember?"

She looked at him with a convincingly blank stare, "Oh, sure. I remember now." She started nodding her head, "Sure I remember, now."

"Good," Dawson said, "Because I have the papers right here." He pulled out a thin sheaf of papers, stapled in the corner. He also pulled out a pen for her to use and the orderlies watching through the one-way window tensed.

"You remember that when we talked last, I told you that since it was in John's best interest, you should allow him to be adopted by one of his foster families. These papers," here he indicated the documents, "allow that to happen." He looked at her and wondered if she understood what he was saying. *If I am wondering, a jury would probably wonder too*, he thought. *I'd better spell it out, for the record.*

"These papers say that you agree with our assessment of your situation and that you agree to allow John to be adopted. You also state that you understand that since you are giving up all of your parental rights to John, you will never attempt to see him again. Do you understand all of this?" He was holding the papers around so that she could read them, but he did not think she was.

She looked up and croaked as if she had a very dry throat, "Where do I sign?"

Dawson flipped to the last page and handed her the pen, pointing toward the signature line. "You sign here, Ms. Conner." He watched as she awkwardly grasped the pen and maneuvered her manacles over the tabletop. She signed on the line and then dropped the pen onto the papers. He pulled the papers over to his side and looked at her signature and then he picked up the pen and signed as the witness.

"Thank you, Ms. Conner. I think you are doing the best thing for John." He gathered his things and stuffed them into his briefcase. Then, as she seemed to watch the motion of things he could not see, he stood and walked to the door. The orderly, watching through the little window, opened the door for him as he approached.

After Dawson left, two orderlies entered the room and they unhooked her from the chair and helped her shamble back to her cell.

Phase one of my escape plan was completed, she thought. *Tomorrow I start phase two!*

- - -

Cyberdyne's research groups had been very busy for the past nine years. After the initial investigation phases, the group responsible for chip programming (initially led by Andrew Goods' insights through his experiences with the Turk) had developed command and control subroutines that were unprecedented. The distributed network of independent computer nodes functioned so much like the human neural network that success with robotic systems was almost assured.

Myles had led the charge to standardize the chips and just customize their local quantity and resident programming for specialized functions. His logic was that the new chip design was so small and so inexpensive that the developers could use hundreds of them with no cost penalty rather than design a new chip for each location or application. He was personally working on that approach at home, developing a presentation for the committee. He had to admit to himself that the idea came directly from the chips they had successfully recovered and dissected from the original arm. He did not think of that as a negative since the committee had given him (and his department) the arm in the first place for that very reason.

Working at sixteen nanometers resolution, the circuits were orders of magnitude closer together and therefore faster than anything else in the computer industry. The heat generated by the current density in the microscopic circuits made cooling larger chips much more difficult and that provided compelling logic for the smaller size.

Now things seemed to be heating up to the limits of control for Miles and Cyberdyne. New discoveries were compounding on previous ones making the scientists and engineers work even longer hours than in previous months. Miles was beginning to bring more and more of his work home – when he actually went home – and Tierresa was not happy. The committee would not be very happy either; it was a major security breach. But he thought it was a pardonable sin that they need not know about until much later, if at all.

Usually after spending fourteen hours away from home, Miles would spend an additional three or four hours at his desk at home. It had become his habit to compile reports and arrange experimental schedules at home where he felt he could concentrate. His son was always buzzing around, making attempts to garner his attention with this high-tech toy or another, but at least the phone rarely rang. He considered that a major blessing. His argument with Tierresa pointed out that he was at least there with them, physically, if not mentally, and if they actually needed him for something, he was ready to put his work aside and pay attention to them. She was not too sure that would be good enough.

- - -

Andrew was ecstatic. His system, hardware and software, named *The Turk* by him, was working almost perfectly. He had been the original guinea pig, playing chess with *The Turk* for weeks until it had a winning rate of nearly 100% over twenty games against him. Then he got a college friend of his to play and after five games where *The Turk* destroyed him each time, he gave up and claimed boredom.

Andrew used the city library's resources to find classical chess books that recorded hundreds of Master Tournament games. He patiently played these games and The Turk recorded winning chess strategy from the world's best into its lookup tables. *The Turk's* abilities expanded with its experience and its speed in determining the best move was soon virtually instantaneous; by the time the opponent's move was entered, *The Turk's* response was waiting in the readout. *The Turk's* ability to match patterns and evaluate tactics was unparalleled in the literature. Andrew was convinced that he had a winning system for the contest, scheduled for the end of the summer.

The only real issue that he saw was that *The Turk* did not actually learn chess strategy. It only "memorized" previously seen situations and compared the board in front of it to the statistically best response from history. An opponent presenting some new or irrational combination during the game could confuse *The Turk*; it might take several hours of searching and comparing before it could determine the best course. In a timed game that meant a loss for *The Turk*, and a loss during the contest meant that Andrew would not get the prize. The loss of the prize meant that Andrew would have to keep working in that shitty electronics store.

Since the contest had a $500 entrance fee and there was only one chance in fifty *The Turk* could win, (fifty aspirants would be allowed to participate and there would be only one winner with one prize), Andrew decided to pass this year and just play spectator. He thought that watching how the other systems worked and just what the level of play was would give him an advantage the following year. He was also rethinking his approach to how *The Turk* played. There were just too many possibilities and logic trees involved to simply put everything into a table. *The Turk* was going to have to think for itself. That would be a lot more difficult.

- - -

General Larch was wrapping up the loose ends of his day. Sitting in his office, the most recent AI report compiled and sitting on his desk in front of him, he sat back in his chair and tried to think about just how much this new technology meant to his country's security. He knew, via several covert inquiries, that industrial entities would be interested and would pay small fortunes for access to the things contained in the report. If he were to let this information out, there would be a drastic revolution in computer hardware and software, as well as industrial automation. It was very tempting to check out the potential opportunities. So far, he had resisted the temptation.

Larch was convinced that the inevitable spinoffs from the program would happen; just as with the products and systems that were developed around NASA's technologies. Once the media became aware of what the military had there would be nothing stopping the commercial development in the private sector. His only problem was how to position himself to capitalize on it when it started. Getting in on the ground floor could make him wealthy as long as no one could prove that he leaked any of it in the first place. He had to be patient and diligent and very careful.

Picking up the report, Larch flipped past the table of contents and the section summaries. Reading, he reflected how Dyson and Cyberdyne had managed to do some incredible work, despite the handicaps he and his committee had placed on them. The new computer chips promised to be orders of magnitude smaller and at the same time more powerful and faster than any currently available. The prototypes had permitted Brewster to equip his various creations with enough computing power to work; the Hunter-Killer prototype aircraft being the prime example of success using minimal human intervention.

The supervisory computer control program, Skynet, was another example. The new chips allowed the primary computer they were building at Vandenberg to be small enough to fit into a small room vs. a large building. It looked, on paper at least, that the Skynet computer would be able to run everything military. It should be able to tie everything together, allowing almost instantaneous reaction to attacks from any source. It would marshal forces and resources wherever it deemed them necessary. Skynet would never sleep or need a vacation or take smoke breaks. It would never be suborned, corrupted, or bought-off by foreign agents. It would be the perfect guard for our continued safety.

The work at Walter Reed had provided new, advanced prosthetic systems for our many damaged vets. That was a good thing by itself. However, the best, most potentially rewarding work, was with the fighting exoskeletons they developed. Testing of these fighting suits in the field had already shown tremendous promise. A squad outfitted with these devices suddenly became the equivalent of an entire company of infantry. By linking these men via Skynet, an almost infinite set of possibilities emerged. They were troops that could fight forever without getting tired. They had almost instantaneous access to tactical information and directives. In addition, they had the ability to carry and use large heavy weapon systems. His mind boggled.

He closed the report, satisfied with its contents. Larch stood from his desk, carried the report over to his safe and opened it. He placed the report inside among a few other documents that had the potential for changing the American military world. He closed the heavy door and locked it. Then he stood and picked up his jacket, turned off his desk light, set the alarm systems (with their active booby traps) and left his office in the basement of the Pentagon, locking the door behind him. He pulled on his jacket as the burly NSA guard sprang to his side. Even in the dimness of the passageway, the guard was wearing his reflective glasses.

Larch shook his head at the agent's pretension, but it was a minor issue. He rubbed his eye patch in fatigue and the two men marched down the long hallway together. Larch said, "I think I could use a little drink."

- - -

Laurence Caswell, or Large Larry as his trucker friends knew him, had been on the road hauling produce from the Texas panhandle in his refrigerated trailer for twelve hours straight; definitely against regulations. Now he was backing into an empty slot between two other trailers on the huge paved parking lot of the El Monte truck stop located where I10 and I605 cross. He was very tired, but he had little trouble maneuvering the rig, an older White WIA64 with a Utility 53-foot reefer, into the narrow slot, sawing the wheel in little back and forth motions to keep the trailer going in a straight line. Drawing even with the tractor cab on either side, Large Larry set his brakes and shut-down everything except the refrigeration unit, grabbed his small duffel bag and his log book out of the storage bin, and he climbed out of the cab, locking it before jumping down. He was looking forward to some supper, fresh hot coffee and the use of the shower facilities. He planned to "correct" his logbook, detailing all of his required rest stops, over dinner. *Since I arrived OK*, he thought, *what they don't know won't hurt me.* He chuckled at his little joke. He wasn't due in Long Beach until tomorrow at eight so he could afford to rest up a little.

Large Larry, an ironic moniker if there ever was one since he was only five-foot two inches tall, whistled the refrain from one of his favorite cowboy tunes as he walked toward the lights of the restaurant. It was something Willy Nelson had recorded a few years ago, he knew. *The weather seemed pleasant enough*, he thought distantly. Hearing some soft, rolling thunder he looked up, trying to see through the glare of the parking lot lights. *Maybe it was going to rain after all.* He hoped not. He hated rain.

A bright blue ball of lightning seemed to materialize at the double-door end of Large Larry's trailer, tendrils of electrical energy licking out and brushing the sides of both it and the trailer parked next to it. The expanding sphere of energy intersected the steel rims, rearmost axel and three feet of Larry's trailer, melting everything it touched, making the metal flow away from its powerful caress in glowing orange streams. The soft pop of the tires was lost in the electromagnetic buzzing set up in the thin aluminum walls of the two trailers. The bubble of energy melted and blew away a scoop of pavement nearly a foot deep, leaving behind glowing, melted glass from the compacted gravel beneath the blacktop.

As the electrical discharge stopped, almost as suddenly as it had started, a wind that had been generated by the heat and dissipating energies blew away the smoke from the smoldering tires and heated asphalt. Squatting in the center of the cooling glass bowl, his feet resting on a melted remnant of the polymer support screen, was a naked man. Or what appeared to be a man. With calm deliberation, the man unfolded from his position, standing tall at over six feet. He turned to look around, surveying everything around him, his chest and shoulder muscles appearing to ripple as he moved. He looked up, registering the location of the stars and did a quick comparison to what he remembered. *Yes*, he thought, *I have arrived at the right time and place. I must find John Conner.* He needed clothing and transportation. He had to find John Conner and he didn't think he would get very far without clothes. He walked around the building and saw a night club of some kind, the *Corral* a lit sign said, a biker bar he thought it was called. There might be someone there that could provide clothing for him, and there were several motorcycles parked out in front, waiting for his use.

The T101 began walking in that direction, crossing the highway toward the future.

- - -

In the jumbled desolation that was the underside of a typical urban interstate highway overpass, junk and detritus from years of neglect and misuse had collected. An eight-foot-high chain link fence attempted to cordon off areas that could lead to foot traffic finding its way onto either I105 or I110 where they crossed each other. There were obvious gaps in the fence and things have a way of accumulating.

In the dimness of the distant sodium vapor streetlights, a blue flickering began and then reached a crescendo. Electric arcs jumped from the ball of blue light and struck the rusting, abandoned car and the metal fencing. The throbbing surface of the energy bubble touched the fencing and steel began to flow away, forming a round hole in the fabric. It took only a few seconds.

A patrol car had been crossing one of the surface streets and the officer had noticed the flickering light. He made a U-turn and drove back down the street where he had seen something unusual. He parked his cruiser and managed to call in as he climbed out and began to investigate. He reached the derelict car and shined his flashlight around, looking for whatever might have caused the blue light. He saw the round hole in the fencing and moved a little closer, his hand unsnapping his holster, just in case.

He saw nothing except a small divot in the pavement and the still glowing ends of the melted fence. He suddenly heard something behind him, and he turned and drew his weapon at the same time. He froze as his eyes registered a naked man standing immediately in front of him. Before he could say anything. the man moved quickly, and he felt an excruciating pain in his neck as everything went black.

The plain looking, naked man just stood there for a second, looking at the young officer with cold eyes. He pulled back his arm which had assumed the shape of a broadsword and the dead police officer crumpled to the ground. The sword evolved back to the man's arm and then as if made of mercury he began to melt and shift and change color. Within two seconds the young police officer was standing over his own body. The newly formed policeman reached down and took the dead officer's weapon and slipped it into his holster and snapped it closed.

As if nothing had happened, the new police officer walked back to the car and stepped inside. He looked around, familiarizing himself with the equipment and controls. He noticed the computer and smiled in recognition. He typed a name into the Juvenile Automated Index: John Conner. He waited patiently for the results to display; after all he knew that he had plenty of time.

Postscript

* * *

The years of hardship, stress and warfare had taken their toll on John Conner. Shot, burned, stabbed, beaten, tossed about, suffering numerous broken bones and an emergency heart transplant, all before his thirty-eighth birthday, his body was ready to quit. Scar tissue was about all that held him together. He walked with a pronounced limp and running, carrying a combat pack was nearly impossible. He hated the thought that soon he would only be able to hold meetings, telling somebody else what had to be done.

He felt more like a grandfather than a father did, and he certainly no longer felt like a combat soldier. Kathryn tended to coddle him, trying to make things physically easier for him; he hated that. From a physical point of view, he had bad days and better days, but never good days. A subject that often surfaced during staff meetings was that he might consider machine augmentation. He always growled that down. He was completely human, and this was a war between the humans and the machines. Neither side was winning, although he felt that Skynet had been grossly bloodied too, and now was not the time for him to join the other side.

John Conner was not feeling very good today. Almost all the stress and concern he had felt during his attempts to protect his mother and himself in the past, and all of the subsequent efforts to eliminate Skynet at its source, were completed. The only things left for him were to lead, fight and survive in this time. He was sure that most of what he had done to the past was successful; he was here, and Kathryn was here, and most of the men and women that he depended on were here. Unfortunately, Skynet was still here too. That meant that in large part he had failed. Everything he had done, all the sacrifices he had made - no, they had all made - were not enough. He was not sure what more he could do.

He rolled over in his bed and looked at Kathryn lying there under the covers, nursing their son. He had been born shortly after this latest major battle started. The boy had a shock of dark brown hair, like his, and green eyes, like Kate. Kate had felt him stir and she looked over at him, smiling.

John had seen the baby for the first time when he got back from the mission and was recovering in the hospital wing. Kate had brought the baby in to see him. "John, I'd like you to meet your new son," she had said, handing the blanket-wrapped bundle over to him. "He's perfect and he already reminds me of you. He has your temper."

She had waited until he was safely home before naming their baby. They had named their first son Brewster, and they had talked about naming this son Reese. Kate had lobbied for a while to name him John, but John was not sure that was such a good idea. He had never liked the idea of a John junior. They spent long hours talking in bed trying to make this decision. They were at an impasse.

Starr had ultimately tipped the scale. After Kyle had been transported to the past, she had gotten some therapy from Silberman. It had helped her more than anyone realized. She now spoke occasionally. She had opened up to Kathryn and soon became Brewster's constant companion. She even said once, in her quiet, shy way, that she thought of herself as Brewster's aunt.

Given her relationship with Kyle, that seemed to make sense. Silberman was the only person she told that Kyle had charged her with watching over John Conner. When Silberman died a year later, her secret died with him.

Knocking on the steel, blast door of their bedroom, Starr waited for a heartbeat and then entered. She helped Brewster over the knee knocker threshold and led him over to the bed where his parents lay, propped up on pillows, the baby resting in Kate's arms.

"Good morning," she said softly. Brewster and I have had breakfast. Would you like me to bring some in for you?" She watched as nine-year-old Brewster jumped up onto the low mattress and crawled up between his parents.

"No, thanks, Starr," Kate said, scrubbing Brewster's hair with her free hand. "Did you have a good breakfast?"

Brewster's face lit up, "Yeah!" He shouted and then clapped his hand over his mouth at the loudness. He leaned up to look at the baby so he could see if he woke him up.

John grabbed him, pulled him over to his side of the bed, and started tickling him. "Come here, noisy one." Brewster giggled and squirmed uncontrollably.

Star watched in fascination. She had not had much of a family; Kyle was mostly all she could remember. "You should call him John," she said. "It's a good name."

Kathryn smiled at her, "I agree, Starr. He deserves a proud name, like his father."

John looked from one to the other of the two females in his life. "Don't you think it's pretentious?"

They were shaking their head, almost as if they had practiced, and then both said simultaneously, "No."

John laughed at their act. "I thought Skynet was a tough opponent." He tousled Brewster's hair, "What do you think? Should we name your baby brother John?"

Brewster shouted out, "Yeah!"

And so, it was unanimous. The future had its second John Conner. The legend spoke of how John Conner saved humankind from Skynet. The legend never mentioned which one did it. John Conner, Sr. now wondered if this tiny infant was whom he was trying to save all along, so that HE could save everyone else.

ABOUT THE AUTHOR

Mark T. Sondrini was born in Adams, Massachusetts, grew up in Speedway and Terre Haute, Indiana; lived in Columbus, Ohio; Hampton, Virginia; Fairburn, Georgia; the suburbs of Chicago, Illinois; Greenville, South Carolina and is currently retired in Ruskin, Florida. He studied electrical engineering at Rose Polytechnic Institute for two and one-half years before joining the U.S. Navy and serving on the USS Enterprise in the Gulf of Tonkin as a Data Systems Petty Officer.

After the Navy, Mark graduated from The Ohio State University with a BS in Mechanical Engineering. He worked as a design engineer for several companies for nearly forty years before retiring to write professionally.

Schooled by the Masters of Science Fiction, Mark has been reading everything he could get his hands on for sixty years and writing for twenty. He has written four Science Fiction novels and more than twenty-five Science Fiction short stories, two juvenile mystery novelettes, five adult mystery novels, four plays and has several novels and plays underway and in research.

His hobbies consist of wood working, fused glass, watching movies, cooking, playing cards and Mah Jongg, and traveling with his wife Priscilla.

mark.sondrini@gmail.com

Manufactured by Amazon.ca
Bolton, ON